Pauline

Charlotte

&

Arthur

Merdog Books
The Exchange, Castle Avenue, Buncrana, Co. Donegal, Ireland
Web: merdogbooks.com
Email: info@merdogbooks.com

First published 2021

2 4 6 8 10 9 7 5 3 1

ISBN 978-1-9165016-7-6

Cover art by Rois Davis and Merdog Books

Typeset in Ireland by Merdog Books
Printed and bound in Great Britain by Clays Ltd, Elcograf S.p.A

For Dave, Leah and Katie, for always believing.

Chapter One

The smell of boiling ham wafting its way under the door nauseated Charlotte. Despite a rather debilitating head cold, she could still get it, that unmistakable whiff of cooking flesh. The wedding breakfast would take place immediately following the nuptials. A small party had been invited. Charlotte did not want a fuss and Mr Nicholls had honoured her wishes. As she sat on the edge of her bed, she imagined that the salty, fleshy smell of the pig was working its way through the keyhole, across the room, and weaving its fatty odour into the fabric of her dress, draped like a deflated ghost over her easy chair. Her bonnet, a lavish affair of rippled fabrics and fake flowers, rested on her dressing table. It was far grander than any she had designed for her fictional brides. Her packed travelling chest lay open on the floor. On the top she could see copies of her novels, it had been her idea to bring them as presents for the hostesses of the houses they would be staying in on the honeymoon. *Jane Eyre* was on top. Charlotte scoffed at the sight of it. '"Reader, I married him." Indeed', she offered to the cold bedroom air. She thought of Jane and Rochester's dark secret and a thought occurred to her; what if Mr Nicholls had such a secret? What if her novel's plot had been a premonition? A foreshadowing of her real life. The thought amused her. The likelihood of Mr Nicholls, her future husband having a dark, secretive past involving a passionate affair was as slim a possibility as was that of her friend Ellen Nussey ever being proposed to. Charlotte smirked at the idea of her prettier friend remaining a spinster – what an ironic twist of fate – but then she smacked the back of her hand for harbouring such an unkind thought. Why couldn't she be nice and saintly like her dearly departed Anne? Poor Anne. Poor Emily. Poor Branwell. Poor Maria. Poor Elizabeth. Poor Aunt Branwell. Poor Mother. What a household of ghosts. Perhaps it was a good thing after all to be marrying and getting away from the parsonage for a while. Charlotte rose from the bed, she bent her knees and grabbing her nightdress on two sides she rose her arms up and over her head, threw the garment to the floor and stood naked, defiantly facing the door. It was not a daring gesture; Papa would never enter unannounced or uninvited.

He was supposed to give her away: Papa. All he had to do was walk the short distance from the parsonage through the graveyard to the church, deliver her safely to the waiting groom and then take his place on the altar for the proceedings. This was important to Charlotte. It spoke of his approval for the marriage. The preamble to this wedding had been a messy affair. Papa had been outraged at Mr Nicholls' first proposal. The sheer brazenness – his word – of this young curate with nothing to offer, thinking that he could have the hand of the most famous authoress in the land was an affront to his expectations. Charlotte went along with his wishes on that occasion and rejected the offer. Nicholls, a broken, rejected man, left the parish only to be replaced by a curate, a Mr Renzi, who was not to the Revd Brontë's tastes, a fact that may have influenced his reactions when next approached on the matter.

Charlotte and Mr Nicholls continued to correspond by letter, feelings grew stronger and Mr Nicholls proposed for a second time. This time when Charlotte approached her father seeking permission, and perhaps worn down by the incompetency of the new curate he gave in, citing the Irish expression of the 'the divil you know…' as his axiom for accepting Arthur Bell Nicholls. And so, Charlotte had understood that the marriage was going ahead with her Papa's approval. Until the previous evening and what she had called his little strop – an expression she had picked up from him. He said he was not feeling well and would not be attending the ceremony. Charlotte was silently furious and left his study under the pretence that she needed to ask Martha, the servant, to make up one of her concoctions for him, after all she had said, his health was more important to her than anything else in the world. When she got outside, she shook her fist at the door and bared her teeth like a madwoman. It was later decided that the job of giving her away and being witness to the event would fall to her old schoolteacher from Roe Head, Miss Wooler. The shame. She liked Miss Wooler, which was why she was one of the few wedding guests, but Charlotte felt there was a certain ignominy in having a woman, and an old maid at that, walk you down the aisle.

Her slightly off-white undergarments, folded on top of her packed travelling chest, were chilled from the bedroom air. She had not invested in any new ones. The expense, indeed, the extravagance of the dress and bonnet was quite enough as far as Charlotte was concerned. Her money was hard earned. Some people thought that all a writer had to do was sit down and write. How ridiculous; they knew nothing of the stubborn rock from which stories were chiselled. And why she had let Ellen convince her to have the garment made continued to baffle Charlotte. She was not romantic about such things and yet there it was, the dress that cost a small fortune only to be worn once. As she tied her stays there was a comfort in the familiarity of the well-worn fabric against her skin that acted as a balm to her troubled mind. She tried to resist thoughts of later and the circumstances under which she, or God forbid, he, might remove these same garments. Imagine if a lascivious wolf lay beneath the sheepish collar of Revd Arthur Bell Nichols? Charlotte felt faint at the thought of it and would have sat down were it not for the tapping on her door.

'Yes, who is it?' she said.

'Ellen. Charlotte, I thought I should come and help you dress.'

Charlotte, making no effort to cover up her state of half dress jerked open the door.

'And how, my dearest Ellen, do you suppose I have managed to drape myself in suitable, presentable attire, every other day of my life since early childhood?' she said, standing back as an indication that Ellen should enter the room.

'But, Charlotte, this is no "every day". This is your wedding day and surely it is the first duty of the maid of honour, such as I am, to be just that, your maid, and therefore the person who dresses you,' Ellen said, as she crossed the threshold. Charlotte closed the door, not because she wanted Ellen to stay, she just did not want Miss Wooler to come along and assume an open door was an invitation to enter. Miss Wooler and Ellen had arrived the previous day and stayed the night in Charlotte's room; having a view of the moors it was considered a more appropriate guest room than one that overlooked a graveyard.

'Oh, Ellen, if I could swap this day for the yesterdays of hope, when I dreamed of a different today and a different tomorrow.' Charlotte made a sound, a small sound not unlike the tiny whimper that Keeper, the dog, used to make following Emily's untimely death.

'Charlotte, you mustn't think like this,' Ellen said and turning her back on Charlotte as she spoke, she lifted the wedding dress and turning back she thrust her arms towards Charlotte as if she were holding the figure of Jesus in Michelangelo's

Pieta, 'This, my dear, is the hope for your future.'

'Ellen, sweet, sweet Ellen, how can you ask me to think of the future when I can only recall the past. I woke so early and all I have been thinking on are narrow, cloistered, cold beds. Where is my Anne, my Emily, my Mama, even Aunt Branwell? The noise these ladies would make this day, the clamours of joy that would reverberate and burst forth to our beloved moors. Listen, Ellen. What can you hear? Alas, only the sound of the clock on the stairs lurking like King Hamlet's ghost, ticking out his plaintive words, "remember me, remember me".' She raised her arms in straight lines as she finished and Ellen, understanding the gesture, approached with the dress, and lowered it over her diminutive frame.

Charlotte surrendered in silence to Ellen's fussing as she buttoned up the dress, puffed out the sleeves, removed invisible particles of fluff from the shoulders, walked around her, stood back, and studied her with narrowed, scrutinising eyes, blinked away tears, and finished by cupping Charlotte's face, bringing it forward and kissing her forehead.

'I am the luckiest woman to be part of this day, to be able to say for all years to come that it was I who dressed the most famous authoress in all of England on the morning of her wedding. You look beautiful, Charlotte, I will leave you to arrange your bonnet, such a splendid thing it is, and I will see to it that Miss Wooler's nerves have calmed. This last-minute business has quite unsteadied them.'

'Last minute business indeed.' This was addressed to the back of the door as she closed it after Ellen.

What good was being bedecked in the finest lace in Yorkshire, wearing your best bonnet, embarking on a honeymoon to Ireland to rival that of the great queen herself if all you could associate with the day was the failure of your father to attend? Your only living, flesh relative feigning sickness to avoid witnessing the spectacle. Charlotte felt that it could not augur well for future happiness and no amount of plámás from Ellen or Miss Wooler or indeed, Mr Nicholls, lord bless his good intentions, was going to change that fact. Besides, one Brontë wedding in that small church could not obliterate the bitter memories of the funerals, of the bones lying beneath their feet and those in a cliff top graveyard in Scarborough. What joy was to be had on this day?

Chapter Two

As Charlotte approached the door of the study, she knew her father was in there. It was his morning ritual to read and pray there before breakfast. And what would he pray for on this auspicious day? Stasis? His adversity to change, especially change in his domestic affairs was no secret; when he had railed against Mr Nicholls' first proposal, his chief concern was for himself, how was he to survive when she moved out, and why did she need to be married at all, wasn't their domestic arrangement a marriage of sorts, what more did she expect from life? And if his last remaining child were ever to marry, his least hope was that it would be a financially rewarding affair: he was only too aware of the spectre of impecuniosity that haunted the religious life; Nicholls, as his curate, even as his successor, had nothing to bring to the marital table. Eventually, Charlotte's persuasive powers convinced that as they intended remaining on in the parsonage, the only alteration to her papa's life would be the added assistance of Nicholls when it came to all parish matters.

Charlotte paused and thought of knocking but then to what purpose? Papa would remain stubbornly steadfast to his refusal to attend. In a moment of lapsed awareness, she blessed herself, perhaps it was the proximity of the holy water font on the opposite wall that prompted the gesture. This made Ellen giggle, which made Charlotte smile, which made Miss Wooler revert to a time when she was school mistress to both, as she tutted impatiently, and ushered them out the door. As the proxy father-of-the-bride, Miss Wooler, hooped her arm through Charlotte's and they led the wedding procession down the stone path that divided the front garden, proceeding through the graveyard to the church beyond. Ellen, who had recovered from her nervous, giggling fit, followed, and taking up the rear was Martha, who would much rather have remained in the kitchen tending to the fare for the wedding breakfast; she worried that the ham had been lifted too soon from the boiling pot. The older servant, Tabby, hobbling beside her, tilted her head, keeping her eyes forward facing.

'Thank God for this day, it gladdens my heart when that old fogey doesn't get his way,' she said to Martha. The old fogey she referred to being the Revd Brontë.

'Tabby, I hope you're right, but you didn't see that flaysome look our Mr Nicholls gave Miss Charlotte when Bishop were here a year gone.'

Martha was referring to a moment she had witnessed from the kitchen door, where she often kept watch when Mr Nicholls was in the house. Bishop Longley and the local parsons, Grant from Oxenhope, Smith from Oakworth and Nicholls, had been invited to tea. This was the February after the failed proposal and Nicholls still wore his dejection like a tragedian's mask. As the party left the dining room to retire to the parlour, Martha noticed the bishop put his arm around Nicholls' shoulder and briefly give him a sideways embrace, one that seems to say, 'I understand'. Nicholls allowed all the party to go before him into the room, all except Charlotte, whom he stood in front of, blocking her way. No words were exchanged, there was no time, for without hesitation, Charlotte stepped around him and fled towards the stairs. Before scurrying into the kitchen, Martha saw Nicholls clasp his hands to his ears as if he were about to lift his head clean off, a look of rage distorting his features. Later, when she told Charlotte about the expression, she was bitterly disappointed to find that her mistress had no appetite to converse on the matter.

'When you've lived as long as I have, and encountered as many folk, you'll believe more in a body's ability to change. That look were then Martha, he'll have no cause for sorrow or rage from this day. Mark my words,' Tabby said.

'I hope and pray so, but I've a funny feeling, somethin's not right, not proper.'

'Mayhaps your funny feeling is from the sliver of ham you tested earlier,' Tabby coughed away a titter after she spoke.

'You're a wicked crone, Tabitha Ackroyd.' Martha slowed her pace so that she did not have to walk beside Tabby.

Because of the early hour, the late June sun had not yet made its mark on the earth, and while it was not a cold morning, the glare of Charlotte's dress leading the way lent a funereal air to the procession making its way by the headstones.

Charlotte knew that Mr Nicholls and his friend, the Clergyman, Sutcliffe Sowden, who was to perform the ceremony, were already in the church, as a young messenger boy had been dispatched by John Brown to inform her earlier. John, Martha's father, was the parish Sexton and Nicholl's landlord. She expected that he and the parish clerk, Joseph Redman, would also be in attendance, but there would be no one else present at the ceremony. Charlotte had also insisted that no word be relayed to villagers and so was surprised to see a few shawled women peeping from the shadows. She hated spectacle of any kind, but especially when she was the centre of it. Charlotte felt a tighter squeeze on the arm being linked.

'They mean well, my dear,' Miss Wooler said.

'You know how I loathe exhibition,' Charlotte said. 'And how utterly embarrassing that you and not Papa escorts me.'

'God bless you, Miss Charlotte, you look just like a beautiful snowdrop.' It was roared out by one of the half-hidden onlookers, and despite herself, Charlotte smiled; never had anyone compared her to a flower.

Mr Nicholls was standing tall and proud in the doorway ready to escort his bride into the church, and yet he was not a proud man, it was his very humility that had eventually won Charlotte over: that and a sense of pity for him. The pity began that fated night in December, a night that she would rather forget; that they both would rather forget.

It was a Monday, not long before Christmas, and as usual, Mr Nicholls was around for tea. He was not himself, there was an agitation about him, and Charlotte felt that his looks suggested that something was playing on his mind, something that involved her. After tea, she withdrew to the dining room, as was usual, to work some more on the *Villette* proofs. It was Mr Nicholls' habit to stay conversing with the Revd Brontë until nine. Charlotte heard the parlour door close and instead of the front door clashing to a close, the next thing she heard was a tapping. A sixth sense informed her what was to come. Mr Nicholls entered the dining room and stood before her, looking pale and shaking; actually, physically trembling.

'Charlotte, I think you will have noticed that I sometimes have a queer feeling with regard to you, especially when you are near me as now,' Mr Nicholls said in a low, yet vehement voice. There was something in the intonation that sounded rehearsed, and to Charlotte's ear, familiar. He did not look like himself.

'Mr Nicholls, I won't pretend that this "queer feeling", as you call it, has entirely gone unnoticed, but what of it, why trouble me with your ailments, what possible cure can I offer for your queer feelings?' As she spoke, a part of her brain stayed focused on his words, they niggled, as if she had heard them before. She could see beads of perspiration form on his brow. Oh, how she loathed any dramatic manifestations of emotion.

'It is as if I had a string somewhere under my left ribs, tightly and inextricably knotted to a similar string situated in the corresponding quarter of your little frame.' He circled his upturned right hand as if the movement magicked the words from thin air. Again, the tone sounded rehearsed and the words familiar, and as the clock on the stairs struck nine, Charlotte, suddenly realising what she was hearing, rose defiantly, her eyes widened with astonishment.

'You use my words. The words I gave to Rochester when he declared his love for Jane. You are quoting from *Jane Eyre*. Mr Nicholls, what is wrong with you, what indeed is wrong with me that provokes you to make sport of me in this way? This is a wickedness I would not have thought you capable of. Next you will be asking me to hear the nightingale, and then you will be offering me your hand, your heart and all your possessions.' Charlotte made a sound that could have been a scoff or the nervous laugh of one anticipating an offer of hand and heart and all possessions. Mr Nicholls made as if to move closer to where she stood, but she stopped him with her outstretched arm.

'Charlotte, I am a fool, and I know that you deserve a man of intelligence, and charm and words; words that were not available to me growing up in the bog lands of Ireland. The only part of me that emulates your romantic hero is the deep regard I have for you, indeed the ...' Mr Nicholls looked to the door, took a handkerchief from his coat and wiped his brow; he was clearly in some distress. Charlotte closed her eyes and breathed deeply, her patience for melodrama was so limited. Mr Nicholls cleared his throat, making a noise that unfortunately sounded rather pathetic.

'Ever since I first set foot in Haworth, ever since we have

become acquainted, I have regarded you as … I have admired you and marvelled at how you have held up in the face of great adversities … your dedication to the Reverend is a model for daughters of clergymen the world over … your talent, your remarkable talent, displayed in your many volumes have moved me; you know already how much I enjoyed and laughed heartedly at your portrayal of us curates in *Shirley*, your—'

'Mr Nicholls, it is my turn to borrow the words of another: "more matter with less art", or I fear I will never see the back of you this night.'

'I believe you to be a very capable woman, Charlotte, but like all of your sex, I believe you to be in need of protection against the vagaries of life such as a male companion can bring, I believe I could be that fortress, that fortification, that f—'

'Oh please, Mr Nicholls, spare me the alliteration. Is this a marriage proposal?'

'Dear, Charlotte, with hope and boldness, and deep affection that I believe to be the foundations of a great love, will you—'

'Have you asked Papa?'

'… I have tried but I—'

'So, no, you haven't. Mr Nicholls, I am not a free agent in these matters, my will is not my own, everything I do must be predicated on how it brings alteration to the life of the parsonage. I will ask Papa on your behalf and bring you my answer on the morrow. Now for decency sake, you must leave, the hour is too advanced for this private intercourse.' As she spoke, she had moved to Mr Nicholls and with a hand to his back she was ushering him out of the dining room, towards the front door. She did not give him an opportunity to utter another syllable. She had heard enough. As she leaned with her back to the door, bracing herself for her father's study, she had no name for the emotion that rose in her gorge.

The Revd Brontë's reaction was stormy as he worked himself into a feverish temper, such was his outrage at Nicholls' audacity. Charlotte remembered how the veins on his temples started up like whipcords and his eyes became blood shot, and more from fear for his health that any deep conviction against the proposal, she assured him that she would refuse Nicholls the following day: which she did. But a seed had been sown, and in the months that followed, grappling with her emotions regarding the Revd Arthur Bell Nicholls, Charlotte knew, despite the pity she felt for him, a part of her had fallen a little in 'like' of this Irishman: a proposal of marriage will do that, and besides how could she not like someone who harboured such feelings for her.

The church was cold and dark after the bright morning light, and the sound of her echoey footsteps made her wish she had arranged music. Mr Nicholls turned to her and as their eyes met, he winked. Despite the stiff exterior of this conservative clergyman, there was a rather impish, Irish rogue beneath, one that Charlotte had grown rather fond of. As they took their place at the altar rail, she breathed in the mustiness of religion, but instead of feeling the weight of commitment, she felt an approaching freedom and her own words floated before her eyes, above her head in the air of the chancel: 'no net ensnares me'.

Chapter Three

'Charlotte, hurry, hurry, your conveyance is here.' Miss Wooler was flushed and breathless as she called up the stairs having rushed in from the garden on seeing the gig arrive in the lane. It was to take Charlotte and Mr Nicholls to Keighley to catch a train to Wales.

Charlotte had changed into clothes more convenient for travelling. It pained her to take off her wedding dress and lay it on the chair, it had such a short expensive life. She would make alterations to it when they returned from Ireland, it could rise again as a good wear dress. Her going away outfit was a dress of grey-mauve shot silk, a grey cashmere shawl and a grey bonnet with pink roses, and despite her reluctance to doff the muslin wedding attire, the heftier feel of the shot silk warmed against the chill she was feeling from a persistent head cold.

'I am almost ready, he can wait,' Charlotte called down. If there was one thing fame, and the constant travelling it required, had taught her, it was how to interact with transport services. There was a time when she mistakenly believed that the traveller was the servile partner between driver and passenger; a time when perhaps her purse was as light or lighter than the drivers of public conveyances, but now, with her purse fattened from the proceeds of her pen, she understood who it was who cracked the whip.

Some of the wedding guests remained in the dining

room, chatting over cups of tea and glasses of port wine. Charlotte could see that Papa and Mr Nicholls had taken their conversation to the garden. When she left to change, they had been discussing the alterations that had been made to the old peat house at the back of the dining room to accommodate a study for Mr Nicholls. To see her papa engage in this mature way with a person he had hitherto referred to as 'an unmanly driveller', was very encouraging, although it had irked Charlotte that he was talking as if he had made all the reconstruction decisions and supervised the rebuild. Her sole responsibility for it had been an added pressure in the weeks leading up to the wedding.

On seeing Charlotte arrive on the steps, Mr Nicholls bent towards the Revd Brontë, a gesture of apologetic leave-taking, and rushed to her side.

'Oh, thank God, you're here, I have been in a state of apoplexy since the gig arrived trying not to visit my nervousness on the Reverend, you know it seems to take so little effort on my behalf to find myself once more out of favour with him.' As he spoke, instead of looking at his wife, he constantly swayed from side to side, looking over her shoulders; he would have had a clearer view of whatever it was he sought had she not been standing two steps above him.

'Are you looking to see who is bringing the luggage out?' Charlotte said, correctly guessing the reason for his agitation.

'Where is Sowden? I have already instructed him to have it down and ready to be loaded on to the gig.' Seeing him lean against the jamb of the dining room door conversing with an invisible Ellen who stood inside the room, Mr Nicholls stepped up and around Charlotte. 'Sowden, I give you one job and find you wanting. The luggage, man, now. The lady's carriage awaits.'

'Relax, Arthur, oh you of little faith, I have already brought out both trunks and a carpet bag. And just for the record, I had three jobs today; get you to the church on time, preside over the ceremony, and be your luggage handler. I think I have acquitted myself remarkably well, thank you very much.' Sutcliffe Sowden, the curate from Hebden Bridge, was Mr Nicholls' closest acquaintance, theirs was an easy friendship based on common interests, and not just of clerical matters, they had often enjoyed long walks together across the Yorkshire moors. Joseph Grant, the curate from Oxenhope, who had also been in attendance that morning, and whose parents had joined the wedding party for the breakfast, was a close second friend. Charlotte approved of this trinity of friendship and secretly hoped that it continued after the marriage; the intensity of Mr Nicholls' affections for her and his desire to be constantly by her side had the potential to smother.

Having relayed last minute instructions to Tabby and Martha, mostly concerning the care of the Revd Brontë, Charlotte, helped by John Brown the sexton, took her place in the carriage. John was a loyal family friend over the years who held the welfare of the Brontë children as close to his heart as if they were his own. Even though he knew Mr Nicholls well, having been his landlord for years, Charlotte wondered about his approval of the match. Eighteen months earlier, after the infamous bungled marriage proposal, John Brown declared that he wanted to shoot Mr Nicholls, such was his fury at the upset he caused in the parsonage, and in his house: John's wife was upset because Mr Nicholls was refusing to eat and, as his Landlady, she felt that his dwindling health would reflect badly on her and the way she kept her house.

'You take care to mind that head cold, Miss Charlotte, you'll need your strength for what's ahead.' John Brown reddened as he spoke and in a faltering manner added, 'I mean, what I were trying to say, strength, you know, for the journey, I weren't …'

Charlotte, placing her gloved hand on his shoulder, squeezed it reassuringly. 'I know what you meant, John, it is indeed a long journey we face, but let's hope the length is only measured in miles.'

'You did the right thing, Miss Charlotte, if there's one thing I know about our Mr Nicholls, it's the kindness in his heart and his regard for you. That'll take a marriage down many's a rough road.'

'So, you must be glad you didn't shoot him?'

'Oh, but you're wicked yet, Miss Charlotte, c'mon, where's this lucky lad, 'til you be getting on road. You'll miss that train.' Charlotte watched John Brown go through the parsonage gate, his arm rotating in a beckoning gesture to Mr Nicholls. She was grateful for all the Brown family and their loyalty, but especially John and his fatherly ways with her. She admired his uncomplicated philosophy of life's fulfilment being founded on acts of kindness. Papa was escorting Mr Nicholls to the carriage, still pontificating about something or other.

On the way to Keighley nothing would do Mr Nicholls but to recount everything from the morning as if Charlotte had not been there. She could tell that he was in a heightened state of animation and could only hope that it would wear off before the train journey, she was used to travelling alone, where she could read or take in the views or observe the fellow travellers. She had a headache and could not be sure if it were a symptom of her chill or his incessant chatter.

'Did you note how affable the Reverend was behaving, he was in top form, joking with me even. I think it is all going to work out, Mrs Nicholls, I do indeed.' He nodded and slowed his speech as he pronounced 'Mrs Nicholls', his delight at the pronouncement glistened in his eyes. Fearful that he was about to take liberties and kiss her, she turned and faced the moors. Mrs Nicholls. How quickly he had appropriated her identity.

She did not feel anything like a Mrs Nicholls, a Mrs anybody for that matter. She wanted to find comfort in the adage, 'a rose by any other name ...', but it was not just the name change that bothered her, it was the changed status it suggested. Was her whole identity to be swallowed up by another?

As Mr Nicholls continued to regale her with the stories Papa had told him about the pet geese, Adelaide and Victoria, who were once housed in the peat house, laughing in amusement at how the Reverend had said that Mr Nicholls would be the first gander to occupy the space, Charlotte couldn't help but wonder if indeed she had married some unintelligent St John Rivers character. His wit was no match for her Papa's; although not witness to the remark she could hear the sardonic tone in which the quip was most likely delivered by her father, a tone that obviously fell on ears deaf to its mocking jibe. This marriage was a risk, to marry a man she knew to be her intellectual and emotional inferior, she worried that his dullness in matters that were important to her: literary matters, political matters, matters regarding her status as a celebrated, independent authoress, would be as a wedge driven between them.

The late June sun shawled her shoulders and the warmth she felt made her grateful that Mr Nicholls had the presence of mind to order a phaeton as opposed to a closed carriage, giving them the option of an open top ride if the weather permitted. The undulating hills of the Worth valley were at their most splendid, their most verdant, at this time of year, and looking out over the roofs of the houses to the pastoral landscape beyond, perhaps for the first time in quite some time, Charlotte's mind was not cast back to former walks enjoyed with her sisters, instead she imagined a future with Mr Nicholls reaching out to help her over a stile, while Flossy barked impatiently for them to keep up. Would there not always be other men and women to stimulate her intellect, to share her literary world, to debate on the political and theological issues of the day, but to be the first object with a man's affections as she was with Mr Nicholls was a very great thing. Charlotte knew her reasons for marrying this man beside her, she could trace the slow unfolding of them to the previous May.

Following that botched late December proposal of marriage and the subsequent refusal, Mr Nicholls' demeanour in the parish had changed. Whenever he was out and about, when duty necessitated, his manner with people was frozen and his countenance constantly overcast. He refused to speak to the Revd Brontë, who in turn made little effort to speak to him, and so what happened on the occasion of the tea-drinking at Whitsuntide somewhat surprised Charlotte.

The Whitsun celebrations was a great day in the parish of Haworth, one that Charlotte loved, when the high and low born of the neighbourhood descended on the transformed schoolroom to eat cake, drink tea and in general make merry for a couple of hours before retiring to the church for services. As Charlotte attended to the guests she watched her papa, with somewhat constrained civility it must be noted, approach Mr Nicholls just as the latter was about to lift a teacup to his lips.

'Another splendid turn-out, is it not, Mr Nicholls?' he said.

At first it appeared that Nicholls was about to walk away without responding, but he turned only to place the cup and saucer on the table.

'If you'll excuse me, Revd Brontë, I believe I see Joseph Redman has just come in and there are some matters I need to discuss with him.' And with that he left the Reverend, whose thunderous expression said more than words bellowed from the rafters could have sounded. Charlotte, knowing that she would get the brunt of his vexation, rushed to the far end of the room to help Martha pour tea and plate cake. She smiled in admiration at what she deemed to be Mr Nicholls' small triumph.

Later in the evening, Mr Nicholls conducted the church service, since it was likely to be his last in Haworth; having secured a curacy in Kirk Smeaton, over forty miles away, he was due to leave within the week. Revd Brontë, following the snub at the tea-drinking, refused to be in attendance, so Charlotte, even though she did not want to be there, decided that it was the prudent thing to do; a show of support for the departing curate.

The church was packed to capacity, much of the congregation being made up of womenfolk, all looking summery, their bonnets bedecked with splashes of colours from seasonal flowers, as was the custom, but alas, this gay spectacle of Whitsuntide, along with the scent of late May that hung in the air could not dispel an anxious, almost tangible, aura of gloom that one can expect on valedictory occasions. Even before the service began Charlotte was sure she could detect sobbing sounds from some of the women in her pew and out of the corner of her eye she noted much handkerchief eye-dabbing. She had been too attentive to the gossiping of Martha Brown who had said that the parish hated Nicholls, couldn't wait to see the back of him, especially the womenfolk. In fact, Martha words were, 'Sad state of affairs, Miss, when only female who will suffer him has four legs, is wha' I say.' The female she was referring to was Flossy, Anne's dog, who, following Anne's demise, had continued the habit of following Nicholls on his daily walks on the moors.

When the service began, Charlotte was surprised that the usually booming voice of Nicholls sounded so low, and even more surprised when it became lower and lower until only a whisper could be heard. He looked so pale, there were beads of sweat on his brow, and even though he gripped the pulpit with both hands she could tell that he was shaking. At one point, the parish clerk, Joseph Redman, had to have some private words with him. All this time the sobbing sounds from the females rose cacophonously, and Charlotte herself, moved by Nicholls' distress, felt a prickling in her eyes. The only solace she could gain from the entire experience was her profound gratitude that her father was not present to witness this lack of composure, this obvious breakdown of poor Mr Nicholls.

Patrick Brontë found out: either Redman, although he was not a prating type of man, or John Brown, the sexton, relayed the whole episode in all its shameful detail to him. Witnessing his increased ire against Nicholls, as he paced the parlour declaring the latter to be an 'unmanly driveller', caused something to shift deep in the core of Charlotte. The pity she had felt for Nicholls was morphing into a different feeling, like that rebellious feeling of desire for the very thing your parent forbids you to have. Her father's anger and lack of compassion gave pause for thought in Charlotte and she could not help but wonder who she would rather be shackled to for life; an aging despot whose constant demands she could never fully realise, or a man, who despite a tendency towards moroseness, was a man incapable of hiding his true affection for her, even if it meant publicly putting his reputation on the block.

This shift in Charlotte's regard for Mr Nicholls unfolded some more on his final evening in Haworth. Much to Charlotte's surprise and delight, and her father's disgust, there was a collection made among the parishioners, and at a service in the school room, the Board of the national school, on behalf of the teachers, scholars, and the congregation of St Michael's Church, presented Nicholls with a gold watch on a fob chain to thank him for the services he had provided to the parish, especially the manner in which he had run the national school. Following the presentation, Mr Nicholls made his way up to the parsonage to hand over the deeds of the school to Revd Brontë. Charlotte seeing him from her position at the parlour window, watched as he came through the garden gate, and guessing the purpose of his visit decided that she did not want to speak to him in the presence of her father. Normally she would retreat to the dining room but as it was being cleaned at that time, by local lads employed for the purpose, she quickly excused herself to her father and retired to the kitchen. She knew this visit was goodbye and she was wrestling with her conscience as to whether it was fair to meet him, shake his hand and wish him well on his way, or ignore him and allow him to continue to hate her, which he must now do, or would do in the future when he reflected on this dreadful period in his life.

The sound of muffled voices from the parlour was some- what comforting, at least they were being civil as the deeds were exchanged. She heard the parlour door close and then the following exchange in the hall.

'Excuse me, young lad, is Miss Charlotte about?'

'She were here earlier, but that were just to give us instructions.'

'Thank you.'

His voice was low and the despondency in it was enough for Charlotte to resolve that it was only right that she say goodbye in person. When she reached the front door, she watched him pause at the garden gate and waited, expecting him to turn and notice her but he did not, he just shook his head and slumped through the gate, turning into the lane, his gait like that of a man about to face the gallows. Charlotte hurried down the path determined to catch him before he reached his lodgings at the Sexton's house. She did not get far, as she turned the corner, there he was leaning into the garden door, in what she would later describe to her friend Ellen as, 'paroxysm of an- guish, sobbing as women never sob.'

'Mr Nicholls, I am sorry I missed you just now, I've come to wish you well in—' Charlotte was interrupted, but because of the sobbing she could not make out what he said.

'Mr Nicholls, you know it is my father's will that has determined my—' Again, Nicholls placing a hand on Charlotte's arm stopped her from continuing.

'Please, Charlotte … I just … sorry … I can't help my …' Mr Nicholls buried his head in the arm he had leaning against the garden door, clearly too embarrassed to even look at Charlotte.

There were so many things that Charlotte wanted to say, things she had rehearsed saying, but in the heat of this moment she did what seemed to be the only human thing to do, she embraced him and as her arms encircled his torso, she squeezed them ever so faintly and decided that if Providence ever brought them together again, she would see it as a sign from above and despite what her father might say, she would one day be Mrs Bell Nicholls.

And here they were, Mr and Mrs Bell Nicholls, riding in a carriage which was about to go through the pillared portico of Keighley station, from where they would board the train and begin their honeymoon.

Chapter Four

Travelling by train, especially a journey from Yorkshire to North Wales, that involved three changes along the way was something to test the stamina of much hardier passengers than Charlotte. But Nicholls, who had planned the entire trip, had anticipated a certain amount of hardship and had taken steps to alleviate as much unnecessary trauma as possible. He had booked them into a four seat, first class, closed coach, where at least the seats were cushioned, and the windows curtained: he said he was thinking of how Charlotte was prone to headaches, so with the willingness of the other occupants of the coach, it would be good to be able to block out the light which intensified her pain. That was how he justified the extravagance to her. Charlotte had not seen it as overly extravagant, she always booked a closed coach, but she allowed Mr Nicholls to have his moment, he had not had the numerous occasions to avail of public transport that she had had. When the porter was taking their luggage to place it on top of the coach, Charlotte was surprised to see Mr Nicholls hold on to a rather bulky looking carpet bag.

'Mr Nicholls, I don't believe that bag will fit under our seat, and what a nuisance for you to hold it on your lap for the journey,' she said.

'Don't you worry, my dear, if I have to place it on my lap for the first stage, it will most probably fit under the seat after that,' he said, smiling as he placed his arm across her shoulder and drew her into his side. It was not the first time he had embraced her in this way, but now it felt different to Charlotte, she felt protected in a way that she had no memory of feeling before.

'Well, aren't you the man of mystery, what does it contain that can be dispensed of so readily, hardly a small, orphan child. Are you smuggling a child Heathcliff on board to be deposited on the streets of Leeds or Manchester, in a some-what reversal of fictional fortune?' she said, tilting her head to address him, a gesture her neck was going to have to become accustomed to as the difference in height between them was quite substantial.

Mr Nicholls laughed his hearty, Irish laugh. 'And that, Charlotte, is what I first admired most about you, that wicked wit. No, you will be glad to know that I have no live cargo here, but thanks to Martha we have the contents of at least three picnics comprising bread and cheese, some wine and the wedding's baked meat.'

'Thrift, thrift, Horatio! The wedding baked meats,' Charlotte said.

Mr Nicholls furrowed his brow, and rubbed his beard, a habit of his when he was confused.

'Never mind, Mr Nicholls, I am being facetious in paraphrasing Shakespeare's Hamlet,' she said.

'Ah, that wicked wit, again. One of few of the bard's works I am not familiar with,' he said, frowning as if to suggest it was one of life's great regrets.

Charlotte doubted the use of 'few', and while she could tolerate a husband less literary than she would have liked, pretention and false representation of the self could be problematic for her. But for now, he was making amends for his shortcomings as, for the first time in all her travels, she did not have to worry about bookings, or tickets, or numbers on luggage, all she had to do was to sit into her coach and endeavour to stay warm so as not to escalate the cold that had been troubling her for a fortnight. There was a charming authoritativeness in the way Mr Nicholls conducted the business of boarding, conversing with the station employees in a friendly, yet not obsequious manner, Charlotte could see that he was proud to be in control of all the arrangements, she admired those who knew how to organise and manage affairs such as these.

When the whistle shrilled its way down the platform to indicate that the train would soon be chugging out of the station, the other two seats in the coach remained unoccupied. It was unlikely that someone would come along now; first-class riders always got priority boarding, and so, Mr Nicholls, transferred his carpet bag from his lap to the vacant seats: Charlotte had been correct earlier, it did not fit under the seat.

'Are you going to claim this was also your doing, that you've booked out the entire coach to have me to yourself?' Even as she said it, Charlotte regretted the flirtatious suggestiveness in the question. The truth was she would have preferred other travelling companions, it was one of her favourite pastimes when traveling, to study faces and observe the behaviour of fellow passengers, and on occasion, if the mood took her, to engage with them. And she was in that mood, how pleasant it would be to share with others the fact that it was her wedding day, that they were not just another, ordinary couple travelling by rail.

'I wish I had thought of that so that we could be guaranteed to remain undisturbed until we reach Conway, but experience informs me that the trains will become busier after Manchester and Chester,' he said.

'Don't be silly, Mr Nicholls, I am glad I have not married a reckless spendthrift, how ridiculous it would be to book tickets for a carpet bag,' she said.

'Thrift, thrift, Horatio! The wedding baked meats.' Mr Nicholls said, and laughed.

Charlotte smiled indulgently even though the reference made no sense in the context, when they knew each other better she would educate him in moments such as these, for now she was grateful that she was the only witness to the senseless quip.

The journey from Keighley to Leeds, one that Charlotte had made many times before, was one of her favourites, perhaps it was because of the familiarity of the Yorkshire landscape where a pastoral, brownstone farmhouse scene, with the blink of an eye or the rotation of the wheels on the track became an industrial sprawl of gargantuan mills and towering chimney stacks belching their black vapours to the cosmos beyond. Unlike some of the more romantic writers of her day, Charlotte found accommodation in her heart for both settings; while the natural landscape was a visual delight and a balm for the soul, she understood and accepted man's need to progress, otherwise what faced humanity other than the prospect of remaining as cave dwellers. Besides, there was a certain majesty to the mills, she saw them as the amphitheatres and pyramids of the time.

Musing on the morning events, the scenes in her head changing as constantly as the world outside, Charlotte was glad that Mr Nicholls had the copy of Bradshaw's Railway Guide from the parsonage to keep him amused; perhaps it was because he too was anxious and nervous about the road they were setting out on, but his garrulous nature of conversation since the church had been something Charlotte had not noticed before and something she knew would be intolerable if it were to become a constant feature of their shared life. Through the carriage's window, Charlotte observed the dominant yellows, whites and deep pinks of the summer landscape and it was the deep pink of the betony plant that brought her back to the previous summer.

After that brief embrace by the garden gate on Mr Nicholls' last evening in Haworth, when Charlotte decided to leave their future in the hands of Providence, life became bleak and hopeless at the parsonage, loneliness stooped in, bringing her spirits low, stretching her nerves and causing a depression which she knew would end, as it did, as it always did, in physical illness. Despite the growing light and warmth of those June days, a time when she should have been walking the moors with friends, friends like Mrs Gaskell or Ellen, Charlotte was confined to her bed with influenza, followed by a very debilitating attack of tic douloureux, a painful face condition she often suffered from. When she recovered and was finally able to walk again on the moors, imagine her surprise when one sunny July day, coming from the direction of Oxenhope, she saw a figure striding towards her, a figure very much like that of Mr Nicholls. At first, because of her recent confinement and the medicines she had been taking, Charlotte was convinced that she was hallucinating, that the figure on the hill above her was a figment of a yearning that had smouldered beneath the performance of domestic and filial duties, but as he drew nearer her heart beat a little bit faster as she realised that this was no figment. What was he doing back on these hills? One thing she was certain of, it was not by design that he came along as she had not been in any regular routine of walking for some time and there was no way he would have known that she was to resume her habit on this occasion. Rather than continue the climb, she waited and let him come to her.

'Mr Nicholls, I think it is fair to say you are the last person on earth I expected to see here today, I feel I should touch you to convince myself that you are not some spectre, but the gesture may be too bold or misconstrued,' Charlotte said.

'Miss Brontë ... Charlotte, I heard you were ill, and therefore this is such a pleasant surprise to see you abroad. I am visiting with Mr Donne in Oxenhope,' he said. The reference to Mr Donne made Charlotte laugh, it was of course Mr Nicholls' friend, the Revd Joseph Grant, the source of inspiration for Charlotte's fictional curate, Mr Donne, in her novel *Shirley*.

'Please tell me that you do not address him by that name to his face?' she said.

'But of course, I do, we all refer to each other as the characters you portrayed us as, it is the cause of much amusement between us, and for the record, I'm happy to be referred to as Mr Macarthey, delighted to be cast as ... how did it go? "Decent, dignified, and conscientious,"' he said.

'Decorous,' Charlotte said.

'Decorous?'

'You said "dignified" but the word I used was "decorous".' Charlotte explained.

'And I'll take that too,' he said, 'and any other flattering labels you'd like to attribute to me, but enough about that, how are you, Charlotte? Joseph tells me you have been unwell.'

'I am much recovered, thank you, hence this walk today, the first in quite some time,' she said.

'And the Revd Brontë, he keeps well?' Mr Nicholls asked.

It pleased Charlotte that she detected no rancour in Mr Nicholls' tone as he asked about her father, the question sounded sincere and therefore she replied with sincerity.

'Mr Nicholls, Papa has been far from well but thank God he does seem to be on the mend,' she said.

'Despite what you may think, Charlotte, it grieves me to hear that,' he said.

'One night, this was during my own illness, I heard him

pause on the staircase in coming up to bed, I listened carefully, he seemed to be paused for the longest time, then I heard my name being called. Arthur, I hastily went to him, and found him stood there with his candle in his hand, strangely arrested. His sight had become extinct, he was in total darkness—'

'Oh, goodness, you poor thing, what a fright you must have taken, Charlotte,' Mr Nicholls said.

'We had an anxious fourteen hours or more, medical aid was sought, and it was believed that the seizure might herald the end of his seeing days but miraculously his sight returned the next day. He said it was as if a thick curtain was gradually drawn up, and since then, although his vision is still somewhat impaired, his ability to read a little has returned,' she said.

Perhaps emboldened by the fact that Charlotte had referred to him by his Christian name and shared this private episode, Mr Nicholls asked if he could correspond with her so as to keep abreast of happenings at the parsonage; he added that he would like to think that he could still be of service if needed in the future.

Standing together, two lone figures, with clusters of betony swaying on either side of them in all its magenta magnificence, Charlotte felt the July sun's rays on her shoulders like the fingers of destiny tapping to say this could be your tide in the affairs of men, take it now at its flood.

'I would like that very much,' she had said at the time.

As the belching stacks of Leeds darkened the sky and the water of the Aire seemed murkier, Charlotte, knowing that they were approaching Wellington Station, donned her gloves. Even though it was summer, she hated to have her hands exposed when travelling, touching things with bare hands, that others, whom she knew not, had been in contact with repulsed her, and to her ever-practical mind, increased the risk of catching something infectious. Also, they had at least a half an hour to wait on the connection to Manchester, and waiting rooms, even on the sunniest of days, were inhospitable, draughty apartments. Mr Nicholls had shifted his position and sat on the edge of the seat as one ready to bolt as soon as the train came to a stop.

'I fully intend to supervise the transfer of luggage every step of the way, it would be a fiasco if it went astray. Just imagine!' he said.

'I don't have to imagine, it has happened to me before, I'm surprised I haven't told you already. Remind me to recount the woeful tale when we are settled on the next leg and our luggage is secured above us. To tell it now would be sure to invoke invisible, mischievous sprites to re-enact the occurrence,' she said.

Wellington station was a bustling, noisy place and Charlotte was glad to be back in a closed coach, this time bound for Manchester. Their luggage was once more safely stowed on top, Mr Nicholls had engaged the services of a porter and as they parted company, judging by the grin on his face when he viewed the coins in his cupped hand, Mr Nicholls had paid the same porter handsomely for his trouble. While they waited for the train to depart, Charlotte told the story of how her luggage box had been lost while changing trains when she was holidaying the previous year with Mr and Mrs Joe Taylor. Joe was the brother of her other school friend from the Roe Head days, Mary Taylor.

'If I am honest, I was glad of the loss as it meant I had to bring the holiday to an abrupt end,' she said.

'You were glad? Why so? Were you sick?' he asked.

'Sick of the fuss they were making over their child. We had already left "Bonnie Scotland" early because the pygmy despot had diarrhoea, and even though Ilkley, where we were, was beautiful, I could not bear to see two grown adults indulge a senseless child as they did. They even ate separately, so there was always one on nurse-guard. Ridiculous.'

'You would think that they would have brought a nurse with them,' Mr Nicholls said.

'They did! Poor creature was just an anxious, waiting sinecure, as the child did not take to her.'

'I will bring you back to Ilkley, Charlotte, we will holiday there yet, and who knows, we might have—' he said.

'Don't finish that sentence if it involves having a tiny tyrant of our own. Having witnessed first-hand how the world of parents seem to revolve around their children, I'm not sure it is something I wish for.' Seeing how Mr Nicholls' expression darkened, she quickly added, 'At least, not yet, let us enjoy our time, and leave the next generation in the hands of the divine.'

'Indeed, the responsibilities of parents have nothing to do with honeymoons. And now, I wish this train would move as it looks like we, once more, have the coach to ourselves. Come here.' Mr Nicholls drew his wife closer, and as she lay her head against his chest, Charlotte thought of her father and how in many ways, she and Mr Nicholls had a child to mind when the honeymoon was over.

Her head pillowed on Mr Nicholls' chest, despite the rattling of the locomotive, Charlotte drifted to sleep, and woke in an agitated state, momentarily unaware of where she was, just as the train was coming to a stop at Sowerby Bridge station. Straightening, she leaned towards the window to see where they were and as she caught sight of the name, she sighed.

'There's a sigh.' Mr Nicholls said.

'Branwell worked here as station clerk, and he did such a fine job they promoted him to "Clerk in Charge" at Luddenden foot. He was not always the Branwell of his Black Bull days,' she said. There was so much about her family that Mr Nicholls did not know and perhaps there were things he would be better off never knowing, but as the latter, shameful part of her brother's life was well known, she wondered if it was his spirit who had woken her at this very junction so that she could share with Mr Nicholls some of his better days.

The reference to the inn, the Black Bull, just down the lane from the parsonage in Haworth, was to allude to Branwell's drinking habit, a habit that no doubt led to his premature death. What Charlotte did not share with Mr Nicholls was how her brother had come to be a clerk in Sowerby Bridge after being dismissed in disgrace as a tutor with the Postlethwaites in Broughton. The dismissal followed an alleged affair with the mother of the boys he tutored. Not that she would ever admit it, a part of her was in awe of her brother's alleged affair, to her he was the fiery, romantic hero of their shared childhood tales in Angria, their make-believe land. Branwell had obviously fallen in love, and in Charlotte's philosophy, that mischievous imp, Cupid, knew nothing of manmade, marital rules, the target of his quarrel's trajectory being the human heart, not the head. Mr Nicholls would not understand this, his conservatism would not have had room for such errant behaviour, this she knew; her husband might be inclined towards romance, but only that of the licenced kind. Already, only hours into their marriage, she sensed a greater liberty in his embraces, a liberty he dared not have taken before, even when they met incandescently on the moors. Such liberties she would welcome for now, so long as they hailed from a heart of longing and not a mindset of entitlement. His arms enfolding her should feel as an extra shawl feels on a winter evening; to be pressed against his torso should be as to lean against the great oak seeking shelter from the wind and rain, but if that hold were ever to feel too rigid, too restrictive, and this was something Charlotte had already warned, Mr Nicholls would be reminded of Jane Eyre's words to Rochester as she struggled to free herself from the enclosure of his arms: 'I am no bird; and no net ensnares me: I am a free human being with an independent will; which I now exert to leave you.'

The rest of the journey to Manchester was as uneventful as any railway trip, the newlyweds passed the time by reading, occasionally dozing, or gazing out at the passing world. The wait in Manchester for the train to Chester was a long one. Charlotte wished she had arranged to meet Elizabeth Gaskell, who lived in the area. As if reading her thoughts, Mr Nicholls asked:

'Can I let you in on a secret, Charlotte?'

'Oh, no, please don't tell me there's a Bertha Mason lurking in an attic space in Banagher!'

Mr Nicholls laughed, while his literary knowledge was not expansive, there was one area where he was well versed: Charlotte's novels.

'Silly girl, no, it concerns your friend, Mrs Gaskell and what, I'm afraid to say, I deem to be her interfering ways,' he said.

'Really, you must explain, Mr Nicholls, I have never known her to be anything other than kind-hearted, friendly, and helpful,' Charlotte said.

'You have heard of the Member of Parliament for Pontefract, Richard Monckton Milnes, I presume?' Mr Nicholls asked.

'Well, yes, but I probably know him more as a poet, or at least one who writes what he terms poetry, he tries too hard to make them rhyme, they all sound terribly childish to my ear. Are you acquainted with him?' Charlotte said.

'He called on me when I was in Kirk Smeaton, quite unexpectedly, as I had no prior business with him and no need for his intervention in my business. He said he was acting on behalf of the Vicar of Leeds and had come to offer me a church position in either Lancashire or Scotland, both of which would give me a greater annual income than I currently enjoyed,' Mr Nicholls said.

'And why was the Vicar of Leeds so interested in your financial status?' Charlotte asked.

'Exactly! I don't believe he was, but, following the visit, I enquired further about our Monckton Milnes and how he might know anything of me, and the only connection I could make between us was you and he had a mutual friend in Mrs Gaskell. Do you think she sent him, in the hope that I would take up one of those positions and thus lose you forever, as either one would have brought me so far away from Haworth?' Mr Nicholls' searching stare which could be somewhat hard featured, as of now, disconcerted Charlotte, it was one of the few times she felt cowered in his company.

'You think Elizabeth set it up to get you far away from me? Why would she do such a thing?' As she spoke, an answer to her own questions was forming. Charlotte had shared enough with her friend to indicate a growing fondness for Mr Nicholls coupled with her increased desire to avoid a life of spinster-hood. If indeed, Elizabeth was behind the visit and the offer, Charlotte was sure it was not designed to remove Mr Nicholls from Haworth, it was to get her away from the parsonage and Papa. When Elizabeth had visited them, although the Reverend was open and affable, Charlotte could read in their visitor's narrowed eyes a disapproval of the domestic situation. Charlotte was aware of the acquiescent role she played, the way in which Papa was made to feel masterly—the king of his castle—it was what worked and made life easier.

'Other than what you tell me, I don't know the woman, but I sense something, something interfering, something unkindly in her interest in you,' Mr Nicholls said.

'Her interest in me? Don't you mean our friendship?' This suggestion of Mr Nicholls' rankled Charlotte, it touched on

one of her concerns regarding the motivation of her new,
literary friends, a self-awareness that knew it wasn't her vivacious charisma that attracted them. 'Really, Mr Nicholls, lest
we have our first marital disagreement, so soon after our vows,
perhaps we should leave your conjectures and the Monckton
Milnes of this world in the place they belong; Pandora's tightly clasped casket,' Charlotte said, adding, 'And to think I was
regretting not organising a meeting with the same Mrs Gaskell
here at the station, if of course, it had suited her busy lifestyle. Perhaps I need to keep my friends at a remove from you.
Interfering? Unkindly? Quite absurd.'

Mr Nicholls' eyebrows were knitted into an expression of
quizzical confusion, he opened his mouth as if to say something,
but closed it again. They sat in silence. Charlotte looked away
from him, giving her attention to the station wall clock as one
does to the pendulous swing of the hypnotist's timepiece. She
pondered the actual possibility of her friend being the agent
behind the visit, and the offers, and she thought what a lovely
thing it was to no longer be the subject of a charitable, albeit
misguided, interloper in her affairs. There was something quite
untouchable about a married woman, untouchable that is to
anyone other than her husband.

Chapter Five

It was well after eight o' clock when the couple arrived in Conway. The distance from the train station to the Castle Hotel, where they were staying, was a short enough walk, but the rather inclement weather for late June made it an arduous one for Charlotte, that, and the contributary nature of a head cold, a day's journey, and an anxious excitement for what lay beyond the hotel entrance. A porter wheeled their luggage up the cobbled street as he and Mr Nicholls discussed the engineering merits of Robert Stephenson's tubular bridge that the train had come through before entering the station. Charlotte was too tired to care, although she did harbour a small delight in Mr Nicholls' knowledge of engineering, this was something of him she had not known, and it thrilled her to think of all the novelties and surprises that possibly lay ahead.

The hotel was pleasantly warm and floral scented from the urns of flowers guarding the entrance. While not a splendid affair, it was more elegant than Charlotte had anticipated; she was expecting something more akin to a traveller's inn. The lobby had the air of a gentile drawing room. A log fire danced in a rather cavernous grate, the furniture, a mixture of upright ladies easy chairs with low arms and deeper chairs for male occupants were arranged around the space, all angled towards this heat. It pleased Charlotte to note that the predominant colour of hard and soft furnishings was crimson, which reminded her of the recent décor adjustments she had made to the parsonage, but this hotel lobby was much grander than the confined spaces of home and she welcomed the difference. As Mr Nicholls finished his business with the porter, a lady bustled from behind what appeared to be a writing desk, Charlotte understood it to be the reception area, and as she approached with outstretched arms and the expression of one about to greet an old, dear friend, every sinew, muscle, nerve in Charlotte's slight frame contracted in anticipation of the unwelcome contact.

'You poor, dear child, what an unfortunate turn in the weather to greet you, you must come and sit by the fire and let me bring you something warm to drink. Tea? A hot port?' She said, as she looped her arm through Charlotte's and guided her towards the hearth. Charlotte was too stunned to protest.

'Tea would be lovely, thank you, and you must be?' Charlotte said.

'You, my dear, must call me Cordelia, Mrs Owen sounds far too officious. And you, I believe, are none other than the great authoress, Miss Currer Bell. Don't look so surprised, I am no clairvoyant, your good husband, for so I believe him to now be, told me as much when he wrote to confirm the booking. And can I say that only an establishment good enough for our Queen is good enough for you.' As she spoke, she eased Charlotte into one of the aforementioned velvet chairs, and bringing her mouth close to Charlotte's ear, she whispered, 'I know that Currer Bell is not your real name, Miss, Brontë—', and here, she broke away, laughed and announced, as if the discovery was hers alone, 'Why, you are not even she anymore, I must call you Mrs Nicholls, am I the first to do so, please say I am?' she said.

Mr Nicholls was a frequent guest at the Castle Hotel whenever he journeyed back to Ireland ever since his first

stay when he arrived fresh from his studies in Trinity College,
Dublin almost ten years previously. He knew Cordelia and her
husband, Samuel, from these visits, and because of Cordelia's
loquaciousness he knew more about them than anyone ever
needed to know about the landlady or landlord of an inn. Mr
Nicholls had recounted all he knew to Charlotte to prepare
her for the overpowering, yet kind-hearted nature of Cordelia
Owen. Charlotte was beginning to understand what he meant
and regretted not asking for a port instead of the tea. She did
not answer Cordelia, there had not been time, for as soon as
she had finished talking, the hostess spun around and rushed
to greet Mr Nicholls who was just finishing with the porter.
Charlotte found herself sinking deeper into the chair, the glow
and warmth from the fire were soporific aids to her already
exhausted state, she wanted to tell Mr Nicholls that she had no
appetite for the evening meal he and Mrs Cordelia Owen were
arranging, but her head felt too heavy to do anything but rest
against the wing of the chair.

'Here we are, a port for the gentleman and a nice cup of
tea for the lady. The dining room is busy, so I have brought
them myself. Don't get me wrong, my girls are very efficient
at their tasks, but set in their ways. Once the dining room is
opened for the evening meals, they cannot think to do anything that does not involve a knife and fork.' She laughed at
what she obviously thought was amusing, a laugh that sounded
to Charlotte like it might easily morph into something more
ghoulish and menacing. How she longed to be shown to their
room. As if reading her mind, Mr Nicholls spoke up.

'Could I trouble you, Cordelia, to bring these refreshments
to our suite, it's been a long day, and comfortable as this fire is,
I suspect that there is as warm a welcome awaiting us upstairs.'

To Charlotte's horror, she whipped the tea back and with
a theatrical wink to Mr Nicholls, addressed Charlotte, 'Oohh,

he's an eager one, is he not.' Mr Nicholls made as if to protest, but Charlotte stopped him with a raised palm. She knew what he had meant, and she was happy to let the hyena think of them what she liked if it meant they could be where no intercourse from her was possible.

Just as Mr Nicholls suspected there was a fire lighting in their bed chamber. Not that Charlotte had ever seen one, the room put her in mind of a courtesan's boudoir. A wooden, rosewood, four poster bed engraved with medieval figures dominated the space. Armchairs almost identical to what had been in the lobby, covered in a garish, bright purple velvet, squatted either side of the window. A chaise longue with a floral design lay at an angle in the centre of the room, a writing desk in walnut leaned against the wall under an enormous, gilded mirror, footstools, at least four, were scattered about, and, at an initial glance, Charlotte counted no less than five mahogany tables holding pewter candelabras with lit candles. The drapes matched the material of the chaise longue but clashed dreadfully with everything else in the room. The only item in the room that held her immediate interest was the writing desk as she had promised Ellen that she would write to inform of their safe arrival.

Using persuasive powers beyond her energy levels she eventually convinced Mr Nicholls that it would not appear strange for him to dine alone. As far as she was concerned the only person to know they were a honeymoon couple was Mrs Cordelia Owen, and Charlotte would take pleasure in knowing that the sight of a lone Mr Nicholls would put all lewd thoughts out of the hostess' silly head. Besides, she knew that Mr Nicholls was hungry and had been looking forward to beef and gravy since Chester, while she had no desire to smell food, never mind try to consume it. She said that she would content herself by writing some notes, she did not say to whom these notes would be written. Ever since she and Mr Nicholls had become correspondents by letter, she had sensed a growing jealousy on his part if the recipient of her epistles was anyone but he, and she had noticed that his little pique seemed all the greater if the recipient was Ellen. Although he had never said it in so many words, she knew that he was wary of Ellen, perhaps he viewed her as a rival, which was something Charlotte knew she would have to deal with in time, should this become an issue between them. There were many things Charlotte was prepared to sacrifice to the marriage contract but her correspondence with friends was something that she had no intentions of ever forsaking. Resignedly, Mr Nicholls gulped the last of the port, assuring that while he would not invite later indigestion by bolting his food, he would not stay any longer than needed. He promised that he would not return empty handed, that while she might not feel like food, a little wine after the day's travelling would surely be welcome. Charlotte agreed, any aid to dismantling the wall of her virginal reserve that imbibing could afford would be very welcome that night.

Left alone in the room, noting again the bed and the red cover that draped it, Charlotte felt cold despite the glow from the grate. The looming presence of that wooden, four poster, giant tabernacle threatened like the one in the centre of the fictional Red Room in *Jane Eyre*. Jane was locked in the room as a form of punishment and petrified with shock and fear at being alone in her dead uncle's room, she imagined that the light thrown from a lantern outside was a preternatural force, perhaps her uncle's ghost. It was too much for the young orphan who screamed and screeched like a threatened bird until she lost consciousness. Charlotte ran her hand over the ruffle of the bedspread, smoothing it, taming it. The wine Mr Nicholls promised was a good idea, she wished she had some now to sip on while she waited, and then, as if her wish had somehow magicked it into being, her eye fell on a decanter of red wine and two crystal glasses on a table, tucked into the corner beside the door that led into the bathroom. A note beside it welcomed Mr and Mrs A.B. Nicholls to the Castle Hotel, Mrs Cordelia Owen might redeem herself yet in Charlotte's estimation.

It was more difficult than she would have thought to write to Ellen. She did not want to sound triumphant or too smug, after all this was a new venture that poor Ellen was unlikely to ever experience, despite it being something Charlotte knew she desired as much as any woman. Besides, the intimacy of previous correspondence would not be appropriate, Charlotte had to learn a new writing code that could accommodate verisimilitude and discretion, she had entered a more sacred bond than that of friendship and she must be loyal and respect the privacy of her husband. She would be brief and insinuate that the brevity resulted from exhaustion rendered from the day's journeying, which was not entirely an untruth.

> *(Conway), Thursday Evening*
>
> *Dear Ellen,*
> *I scribble one hasty line just to say that after a pleasant enough journey, we have got safely to Conway and are; the evening is wet and wild, though the day was fair chiefly with some gleams of sunshine. However we are sheltered in a comfortable inn. My cold is not worse. If you get this scrawl tomorrow and write the next day 'by return', direct to me at the post-office. Bangor and I may get it on (Saturday) Monday. Say how you and Miss Wooler got home. Give my kindest & most grateful love to Miss Wooler whenever you write. On Monday I think we cross the channel, no more at present*
> *Yours faithfully and lovingly*
> *C.B.N*

There, that would do for now, she had kept her promise to write, leaving enough time to get ready for bed, have a glass of wine, and hopefully still be awake when Mr Nicholls returned from dinner.

Chapter Six

The coastal train to Bangor was an evening one, leaving the couple a full day to explore the medieval town of Conway. Mr. Nicholls had drawn up an itinerary, which Charlotte dismissed.

'Why, Arthur, do you think I am interested in architectural wonders, and a fishing industry, even if it is a pearl one?' she had said at breakfast, calling him Arthur for perhaps only the third time in their acquaintance despite his many remonstrances at the formality of Mr Nicholls.

'But the castle, Charlotte, is said to be the finest in the world, and I thought that it would appeal to your romantic nature,' Arthur protested, albeit in a whisper, as the tables were quite close and the dining room, unlike his experience the previous evening, was full. All the guests were tourists of one kind or another, all with the same intent on breakfasting early in order to make the most of the day.

'On one condition, Arthur. I refuse to engage in steep climbs to the top turrets, even if it means that the most spectacular views are beyond my sights. I hate to complain, but this cold is not getting any better, and my energy is quite sapped.' As she spoke, she could feel her cheeks burn as she remembered certain activities of the previous night that may have added to her depleted energy reserve. It was a rather embarrassing thought, not that they had done anything shameful, the consummation of their marital vows was as she had imagined it would be; a little awkward at first but once their bodily functions took over, they were no longer Charlotte and Arthur, they were any man and woman in a darkened room finding each other. After an initial stabbing pain, his gentle rocking movements thrilled her, and having no previous experience she could not be certain, but she wanted to believe that she reached as much satisfaction as the female body was capable of. He most certainly had, his audible sighing and the physical evidence were proof of that. Rather than allow Arthur to see the memory glow in her face, she gave all her attention to cutting the bacon on her plate. The moment had not escaped his notice.

'We are going to be very happy, Charlotte,' he said, reaching across the table and cupping her hand.

Without looking up she nodded, and while she may not have used the superlative, she did feel that the dull days she had worried about, with a man whom she knew to be her intellectual inferior, might not materialise and this bond could bring satisfaction after all.

'Why don't we forget about plans and just see where the day takes us,' he said.

They visited the castle and Charlotte found the energy to climb the stone spiral staircase and was rewarded with what she described as a royal view, such as the Medieval kings and queens must have enjoyed. Arthur reminded her that the guide had said that it was hardly ever occupied by Edward I, who built it, or by subsequent kings, and that maybe a queen never saw it, except when it was under construction.

'Don't be tiresome, Arthur, facts should never get in the way of romance. Besides, can you not hear the babble of voices on the wind, perhaps it is the spirit of Glendower or his daughter, Lady Mortimer, speaking in their native tongue, no longer silenced by The Bard,' she said, placing winged hands against either ear in a pantomime of listening.

'Charlotte, you confound me, I have no idea what it is you allude to? What Bard? Who is this Glendower and his daughter?' Arthur asked.

'Shakespeare's *Henry IV, Part 1*?' Charlotte looked to Arthur for some acknowledgement, some opinion, and seeing a blankness, she was about to ask if this play, along with Hamlet was one of the 'few' plays he claimed to be unfamiliar with but an innate instinct to never be intentionally cruel stopped her.

'Ah, I see,' Arthur said, and left it at that.

They spent the rest of the morning, into the afternoon, walking the streets of Conway. Arthur was like a child observing the boats coming and going down by the harbour, he said it reminded him of Banagher, and that he still had to pinch himself to think that within a week he would be showing Charlotte all his childhood haunts. There was something unreal about it to her as well, throughout the day, whenever she caught the attention of a passer-by or a shop assistant, she wondered if they could tell that she was no longer a virgin, she felt different and could not fully comprehend what was different, how anything had changed, and yet, since the previous morning everything had changed. Haworth was so much more than three train journeys away.

In the late afternoon, mindful of the train timetable, they returned to the Castle Hotel for afternoon tea. It would once more be a late enough check in when they arrived in Bangor, and considering Charlotte's lack of appetite the previous evening, Arthur was determined that she eat something substantial before the journey. Charlotte called him Tabby Nicholls, after the servant who had minded and fussed over all the Brontë siblings down through the years, which made him laugh heartedly, a little too heartedly for Charlotte, she did not want to think she had married an imbecile.

Mrs Cordelia Owen was once again full of bustle and prattle, questioning what they had seen and scolding their failure to visit her 'must sees'. She was aghast that they had missed the tablet in St Mary's church dedicated to one, Nicolas Hookes who was the forty-first child of William and Alice Hookes, and who himself was the father of twenty-seven children.

'Can you imagine, Mrs Nicholls, forty one children, why it is unseemly to even think about, immoral is what it is, if you ask me, or then again maybe not to them what's on their honeymoon.' She gave that laugh of hers again and winked at Charlotte. The woman was a horror in Charlotte's estimation, and she really wished that Arthur did not feel the need to indulge her with silly smiles. To counterbalance the lewdness of her innuendo, Charlotte spoke of some of the things they had noted in the ancient church and the graveyard, all the time addressing what she had to say to Arthur.

'We were delighted to visit the grave that inspired Wordsworth's poem, "We are Seven", weren't we, Arthur,' she said.

'Delighted,' Arthur said, addressing their hostess.

'And the castle was every bit as splendid as in Turner's painting of it. The one that hangs in Grosvenor Gallery in London?' Charlotte had seen Turner's painting, along with many others by the famous Renaissance masters, when aristocratic friends, the Kay-Shuttleworths had arranged a visit to the private gallery.

'Not my cup of tea, hah, cup of tea, speaking of which, I best leave you to it.' That laugh again as she turned and toddled out of the dining room.

'You can always rely on cultural references, Arthur, to banish philistines,' Charlotte said, daintily lifting her cup to her lips, and cocking her little finger out in an exaggerated fashion.

'You are wicked, Charlotte Brontë,' he said, smiling in a manner that indicated a love for that wickedness. She liked that he had addressed her by her maiden name.

It was a cloudy evening for their coastal railway journey from Conway to Bangor but the weather in no way diminished the spectacular scenery they passed. Going through Penmaenmawr, the railway track was practically on the beach. The sea had a mesmerising effect on Charlotte, whenever her mind brought her to lapping sea water, she saw dear Anne paddling in it at Scarborough, her dress hitched up above her ankles, forever looking towards the horizon, freed from life's valley of tears.

'Our lives are so meaningless really, aren't they Arthur, when you behold the majesty of the natural world.' She hadn't meant to think out loud, to stray from anything other than ordinary discourse, or what she deemed to be usual, honeymoon patter, now was not the time to vex her husband with her tendency towards a morose disposition. Arthur did not need to know the inner workings of her mind, her philosophies, she feared that allowing him in would expose the mismatch that they were and perhaps reveal how unsuitable she was for any life other than the semi-solitary one she had been living in the parsonage.

'But without our human senses to give meaning to this world and all its glories, without our emotions to take pleasure in nature, without our spirituality to give praise to the divine creator, what is it all but rock and water and air,' Arthur said.

How handsome he looked to her at that moment. She had not expected such philosophy, if he could always surprise her in this manner, saying unexpected things, unveiling a mind, that might not be a literary one, but had the potential to match hers in depth and understanding of the human condition. A sensation coursed through her, she felt an eddy from her heart redden her cheeks and had she been more expert in these matters, she might have recognised it as the thrill of physical desire.

As the train neared Bangor, a castle on top of a hill could be seen. It had a fairy tale quality to it, with its turrets and towers, and put Charlotte in mind of her stories from Angria. Once again, Arthur had organised everything in advance. The horse and carriage waiting for them was a grander affair than Charlotte was used to, it had the name of the hotel it belonged to painted in gold lettering on the door, 'The Penrhyn Arms Hotel', and when it turned from the road into a long avenue, the hotel rising up out of a landscaped, pastoral scene, made it seem to Charlotte that they were being driven into a painting hanging in the National Gallery. The confines of the parsonage, the mundane, daily rituals of its occupants, the rugged moors that even in summer glory could not be defined as picturesque in the manner of a landscape painting seemed so removed from Charlotte as she observed the evening sun wash across her husband's kindly face. She wanted to say something to him, something personal, but what if this was just one of those fleeting moments that balmy, summer evenings trick us into believing are glimpses of eternal happiness.

Because the hotel was a much more commercial affair than the Castle Hotel in Conway, the receptionist was perfunctory in his dealings with the Bell Nicholls. In a rehearsed manner he gave them the opening hours of the dining room, the time that it would be necessary to vacate the room each day to allow for household to perform their duties, and, handing over the key – a rather elaborate, iron affair attached to a wooden plaque that bore the number 39, and put Charlotte, rather unfortunately considering their circumstances, in mind of Bluebeard's castle – he gestured towards a large, affable looking fellow perched behind a lectern style desk. This fellow was the concierge, who would look after any other needs they might have during their stay. Charlotte considered the fellow, whose smile and nod indicated that he knew he was being referred to. She returned the awareness with a slight tilt of her head, she was unused to engaging with concierges but thought their presence in any establishment to be a capital idea, and, liking the look of this one, she would be asking his opinion about that castle they saw back along the way and the possibility of finding a spot from where she might sketch it.

A boy dressed in a blue and red uniform looking like a miniature soldier, led them to room 39, Charlotte cursed her poor eyesight as she fumbled in her purse for some coins to give him. Arthur attempted a mimed protest when he realised what she was doing, but it was too late, the bellboy was already pocketing the cash as he headed back down the corridor.

'Well, that was rather embarrassing,' Arthur said, as he closed the door and leaned against it.

'What was?' Charlotte said, although she knew exactly what it was Arthur referred to.

'You being the one to acknowledge the boy's services. Please, Charlotte, leave all the financial matters to me when we are in public. Why would you want to unman me in such a way?' Arthur said, and there was a familiar hurt settling into his features, an expression that Charlotte remembered from before their betrothal, one that she had hoped to have seen the last of, as it spoke of a petulant disposition, a trait she could not abide.

'Don't be absurd, Arthur, how could such an ordinary gesture unman you? Now, I am tired, and I need to rest if I am to dine with you later.' As she spoke, Charlotte removed her outdoor clothes and taking three chairs from various spots around the room she arranged them to form a couch, as a quick scan had informed her that the place did not boast one; then taking a velveted cushion from the bed, she arranged it as a pillow and stretched out across the chairs.

'I will leave you to rest so, besides, I feel the need to walk and say some prayers and the grounds looked so inviting.' Arthur left without waiting for a reply. Charlotte lifted her head to gaze at the closing door, she knew his pride was shaken but the walk would do him good and she was confident that the Arthur who knew better than to hinder her independence in any way would return in time for dinner.

Charlotte realised how exhausted she was as her bones sank into the makeshift couch, apart from the traveling and the sightseeing, she knew it was the perpetual presence of another that tired her, being accustomed to a semi-hermetic existence, matrimony was going to take getting used to. She was relieved to have some time now to herself but would not want the achievement of it to always be the result of a disagreement with Arthur, perhaps it was something they should discuss; how to effect occasions for personal space and quiet, surely no marriage could survive on constant companionship. Apart from her need for time alone, there was another casualty of continual togetherness that was a greater source of regret to Charlotte, and that was the lack of any need to write to Arthur; what greater torment for a prodigious epistolarian than to lose a correspondent. The thrill of receiving Arthur's letters, of finding an appropriate sanctuary of solitude to read and relish them, in that interval between meeting him inadvertently on the moors, and his triumphant return to Haworth as her betrothed, had played a major role in the drama of their courtship, and in some ways had been the reason she concluded there was nothing else for it but to marry him.

She had been slow at first to reply to his letters, slow enough to have received six before she sent one. There was no reason for this silence other than the sense that she felt it was a sin against her father, it certainly was not because of any untoward content. Arthur wrote conservatively about his days in Kirk Smeaton, how he continued to walk for at least an hour every day, but missed the moors, the heathers and the pee-wit sounds of the lapwings, he wrote about how the children in the local school were not nearly as clever as those in Haworth, and perhaps because they were still getting used to him, how loath they were to ever raise their eyes to look at him, so that he could tell who was who by the arrangement of the hair on the top of their heads. Charlotte laughed when she read that. She longed to hear the latest about his new parishioners, even though that news often weighed heavily on her mind for days after; families struggling to keep food on their table; the poor woman who had eight children under ten and a drunk for a husband to contend with; the factory owner and his ostenta-tious, philanthropy; the local vagabond who liked to hang out in the graveyard attached to the church and who had taken a shine to Arthur; Charlotte admired the time Arthur gave to the unfortunate soul, it spoke of a nature she could respect.

In every letter he asked about Revd Brontë, Tabby, Martha, the Browns, John Redmond, and Flossy, the dog. And of course, he always ended the letter enquiring about her welfare, how her health was, how the writing was going, if there were any visits being planned, to her friends or to her publishers in London, and how, if she could find the time to write to him, how that would make him the happiest man in all of Christendom. When she eventually responded, and one letter led to the next and the next and the next, she made certain to include something personal in each one, benign words in terms of declarations of affection or desire, yet words wherein he might read secrets of her heart, such as, '…how we all miss you here in Haworth and at the parsonage, like all prophets in his own land, I fear we took for granted the nature and strength of your qualities when you walked among us.'

As her mind slowed and she drifted into that sweet, stolen slumber that can only be experienced during daylight hours, she wondered if Arthur had kept the letters she sent him, she must ask. Because of the clandestine nature of his, she should have destroyed them, had her papa ever found them, God only knew what fit of distemper they could have induced: but she did not destroy them. They were wrapped in a handkerchief that had belonged to Emily, tied with a plait she had made from her own hair and placed in a small box she had decorated with shells collected from the beach at Scarborough, collected following the occasion of poor Anne's burial in the graveyard looking down on the same beach. This box was not in the parsonage, it was secreted under a mound of stones at the waterfall on the moors where the three sisters had carved their names into a rock many moons previously. It was their favourite place where they had whiled away many hours sharing their plans for future happiness.

As she slept – what turned out to be a fitful sleep – she dreamt of her papa striding across the moors, his gait was that of a much younger man full of purpose. She knew where he was going and what it was he sought. When he reached the waterfall, she saw him kick at small stones and larger ones until he found her mound and as it exploded with the force of his boot, he reached down to collect his prize, and for the benefit of an invisible audience, he held aloft the sea-shell casket as if he had magicked it into existence. His features were a pantomime of triumph as he strode across the moors, now a gargantuan colossus of black and white. She could see her diminutive form curled in foetal fashion on her bed in the parsonage, there was a loud knocking on the door, it must be her papa come to thrust her forbidden treasure at her feet, he was calling her name, 'Charlotte, Charlotte, open the door, open the door …' She could see her form writhe, her head whipping from side to side, she was unsure if the form was struggling to stay asleep or wake up. What was she to do, if he knew of this correspondence, he would never permit the marriage to go ahead, but in her sleep a voice was telling her that it was too late, the marriage had happened, she should wake. As the knocking continued, getting louder and louder, that inner voice was telling her it was Arthur. She sat up, hardly awake, but aware that she was not in the parsonage, it was not Papa knocking at the door, and her letters were still secreted under a mound of stones.

Chapter Seven

'Happy July, Mrs Nicholls.' Arthur was already up, dressed, and to Charlotte's naked, myopic eyes appeared as a transfiguration in the morning sunlight streaming in their east facing window. Arthur had initially been disappointed that the room was not at the rear of the hotel, facing west, where the windows commanded spectacular views of the town of Bangor, Beaumaris Bay beyond, the shores of Anglesea, and the castle Charlotte wished to sketch, Penrhyn castle. Charlotte's preference had been for where they were, perfectly located to greet the rising sun, to awake as newlyweds, subjects of an aubade that she might one day compose. This romantic notion was not one she shared with Arthur, rather she had won his acceptance for room 39 by suggesting that the lack of the splendid vista from their window would encourage them to seek it outdoors in the pleasure gardens, also at the rear of the hotel, and thus, rather than be caged birds peering longingly through a glass divide, they would walk freely, at one with nature. Arthur, who loved the outdoors, was easily coaxed.

'What time is it? Once again, you are up and dressed before me, not two days married, Arthur, and already you see you have a spoiled sluggard for a wife.' Charlotte sat up, and immediately set to arranging her hair into a chignon, securing it with clips gathered from the nightstand beside the bed. She would rather have Arthur see her half clothed in the glare of day than think he had married Medusa.

'Nothing could be further from my thoughts, Charlotte. It delights me to see you so rested as it is how you will shake off that head cold. Our kindly waitress was correct in her prescription.' Arthur was referring to a hot drink Charlotte had after their dinner, on the recommendation of the young girl serving them. At the start of the evening they had exchanged silent, optical messages of annoyance at her garrulous nature as she attended the table, especially as her thick Welsh accent made for dubious interpretation, but by the end of the meal they had warmed to her friendly banter, their ear becoming attuned to her sing-song speech, and Charlotte, who would normally be mortified at anyone commenting on her health, did not even think to be embarrassed when, alluding to her constant sniffling and the overuse of her handkerchief, the waitress said, 'Best con-coction to clear that up, missus, is a good sup of brandy and port, hot as you can bear to swallow.' Not only had the 'con-coction' cleared, Charlotte's blocked sinuses, but the sedative effect of the mixture, on top of the wine imbibed over the course of the meal, afforded her a sound night's sleep, which she was grateful for after the day's exertions, even if it meant no conjugal activities were to be enjoyed. It pleased Charlotte that Arthur put her wellbeing before any of his personal de-sires, as he had been the one to insist that she retire first, in the hope that she would be fast asleep before his snoring dis-turbed her. He knew about his propensity to this habit from his landlady Mrs Brown, back in Haworth. Many mornings she had greeted him at breakfast with the same words, 'Nowt but yon self, Mister Nicholls, got ere a wink last night, I'll not be surprised if Reverend above in parsonage heard your rum-bles.' He had light-heartedly told Charlotte as much after she had agreed to marry him, and she had joked that his lack of disclosure beforehand might someday be grounds on which she could leave him.

After breakfast, and a brief stroll around the grounds, the honeymooners consulted the concierge regarding the typical pursuits for holidaymakers within a reasonable radius of the hotel, and consequently found themselves at eleven o' clock sharing a rather splendid Clarence carriage with two fellow travellers on the way to Beaumaris. The concierge, whose name was, not surprisingly, Mr Jones, knowing that Charlotte was the celebrated author, Currer Bell, had said they would be doing him a favour by agreeing to be part of the excursion, as the guest who had ordered the coach and horses had requested the company of fellow day-trippers to Beaumaris. In Mister Jones' opinion, the Bell Nicholls would be the ideal travelling companions. He added that they would be sharing the experience with incredibly important tourists and were being asked to respect their privacy should the latter reveal their identity. As a thank you from the hotel, Charlotte and Arthur would be incurring no cost for the excursion. Intrigued, yet a little apprehensive, they had agreed, Charlotte, perhaps, more readily than Arthur. Because she was an avid reader of newspapers, mostly to keep abreast of the war in Europe, she was aware that the young king of Portugal, Pedro V, and his brother, the Duc D'Oporto, were on a state visit and were currently touring the provinces. As they sat in the carriage awaiting the arrival of the mystery travellers, she shared this knowledge with Arthur and they amused themselves quipping about how one addressed royalty in Portuguese, so, you can imagine the surprise our newlyweds got when two young foreign boys, dressed in the style of English country squires, boarded the carriage and greeted them in English but with a strong accent of Mediterranean origin. The older of the two, by perhaps a year, certainly no more, addressed Charlotte.

'It is my honour to meet you, Miss Bell, I have heard of

your works from my Uncle Albert, who encourages me to read, not just in my native tongue, but in English. I regret that I cannot say I am familiar with those same works.'

Because of the mechanical rhythm and elongated vowel sounds, Arthur wore the expression, a sort of pained smile, of one who had no idea what had just been said. At the mention of Uncle Albert, Charlotte was in no doubt that the two young men were the royal Portuguese guests of the nation, the uncle referred to being none other than Queen Victoria's Albert. Charlotte, not one to be overly impressed by those of rank, or subdued in the presence of celebrity, smiled at the young Pedro V, barely seventeen years old, and excused him for his lack of knowledge of her novels, adding that she was sure he would make amends some day for his ignorance. As the carriage made its way through Bangor and down towards the Menai Bridge, a silence that could have been the ruination of the tour, was broken by Arthur, looking, it must be said, rather flushed.

'Can either of you two young men tell me the name of the famous architect behind the construction we are about to cross?'

The younger of the two burst forth.

'Yes, yes, of course, it was Tomas Tellyford.'

Arthur and Charlotte smiled at the mispronunciation, as Arthur congratulated him on his knowledge. And for the remainder of the journey, the four exchanged, intermittently, comments on the scenery, the weather – which had taken a nasty turn as the rain pelted the carriage windows – and rather surprisingly the works of William Shakespeare. The younger one, who introduced himself as Luís was, what he himself termed, a scholar of The Bard, stating that his greatest ambition was to translate the plays into Portuguese so that his countrymen could also enjoy them.

'My favourite one is Amleth,' he said.

'Yes, indeed, the Prince of Denmark,' Charlotte said, privately hoping that Arthur would not add to the conversation in an effort to appear knowledgeable. She asked him some questions about the works of Shakespeare; his favourite characters, favourite scenes, who he would most like to play on stage, what ending would he change, falling readily into the role of schoolteacher, perhaps because his accent put her in mind of the students she taught during her time in Brussels.

'And why would you like to play Shylock, surely, a young man like you would prefer Lorenzo, or Romeo, or even the aforementioned Hamlet?' Charlotte asked.

The Duke began to recite some of Shylock's famous quotes, intoning in a curious, sing-song manner, much to the amusement of his brother and Arthur, the latter still looking like he had no idea what he was laughing at. Charlotte regretted what she had started.

The journey to Beaumaris was short, and while normally there was enough to see and do in the seaside town to fill an entire day, the inclement weather meant that the tour party had to confine their stay to a drive around the bay, and views of the great fortress from the carriage. Arthur expressed his disappointment when they arrived back in the hotel shortly after two o' clock. Charlotte was glad that the weather had truncated the trip, she found the youths, despite their regal status, to be rather tedious after a while and their phlegmy accents, perhaps because of her own ailment, nauseated her. She contented herself for the remainder of the day in front of the unseasonal open fire in the hotel lobby, listening to the melodic, Welsh strains from the resident harpist, while reading about all she had not seen in Beaumaris from Leigh's *Guide to Wales and Monmouthshire*. Arthur, undeterred by the rain, went on a walking tour of the town and again went to the Menai Bridge so that he could marvel in private at the achievement.

Charlotte was happy to have a reason to let him go unaccompanied, matrimony was already becoming an educational institution for her and one early lesson she had learned in terms of mutual interests, was what little interest she had in traipsing around castles and suspension bridges.

The weather worsened on the Sunday, but it did not deter the Nicholls from their plan to visit Llanberis and Beddgelert. Charlotte knew that her friends, the Kay-Shuttleworths, had connections with the Goat Inn in the latter village and she was determined to introduce herself to them. They had intended it to be a day excursion but because dark clouds were shrouding the whole of North Wales, obscuring the very views of vales and dells and lofty mountains that attracted the many tourists who visited, they hoped that an extra day might see the same blanket of grey lift to reveal the verdure of the valleys they had come for – and their hope was not in vain.

During the summer season all manner of public conveyances carried passengers on daily tours of the Valleys of North Wales, unfortunately though, for Charlotte and Arthur, Sundays were an exception, so at a cost greater than the one shilling fare of the typical omnibuses, they were obliged to hire a private cab to bring them to Beddgelert through the Llanberis Pass: for the return trip the following day, it being a Monday, public transport would be available to them.

As the carriage made its way through Llanberis Pass, the constant rain, while doing its utmost, failed to detract from the majestic landscape they witnessed through the window that formed the front projection of the coach. Arthur's constant expression of awe as he took it all in, an expression that enlarged his eyes and gave him a childlike appearance put Charlotte in mind of Branwell, her Brannii, and how he had looked in the days leading up to his death: watchful and startled. It also rained heavily on the day he took his last, laboured breath.

Although unaware at the time that darker days were to follow, the period immediately after her brother's death saw Charlotte walk through the valley of the shadow of death. Apart from the suddenness of his demise – only two days previously he had been walking in the village – it was the loss of hope for a more fulfilled life, coupled with a powerful pity that he had wasted his talents and ruined all promise of where his gifts could have taken him, that caused her to write to her publisher, W.S. Williams, that his death was, '… the untimely, dreary extinction of what might have been a burning and shining light … '. In the same letter, sent a week after the death, Charlotte expressed a new hope that time would allay her feelings of pity for him: and she did right to trust in old Father Time, with his scythe and hourglass, as the intervening years had assuaged her pity for him and had abated the heartache he caused, particularly in those final months, replacing those feelings with memories of their more animated days when they co-authored the stories of Glasstown; wrote letters to their literary heroes; and dreamed of being famous writers. And when she recalled this pursuit of their literary ambitions, another balm to her heavy heart was his lack of knowledge that his three sisters were already published authors by that September, in 1848. Although he had been living at the parsonage when proofs for *Jane Eyre*, *Agnes Grey* and *Wuthering Heights* were arriving from their respective publishers, his lifestyle of addiction – one that caused so much grief to the family and left him for the most part in a stupefied state – created for Branwell an oblivion for anything that did not present itself in a drinking glass or a phial.

Despite the pain this episode caused Charlotte, she never questioned or doubted God's will. Had Branwell survived the 'Chronic bronchitis – Maramus', that his death certificate stated as the cause of his death, Charlotte believed that the reformed spirit they witnessed on the death bed, the former atheistic soul that said 'Amen' in response to his despairing papa's prayers, would no sooner have regained his health but he would likewise have resumed his pitiful life of self-destruction. Branwell could never have thrived on earth, which she believed, was why God called him home as soon as he had attained a state of grace. And why her only brother, whom she believed had more talent than she and her sisters combined; more opportunity for preferment being male; more ambition than anyone she was acquainted with; why he allowed his life to spiral downwards when it could so easily – much more easily than the efforts her advancement necessitated – have tended towards an upward course, was a question that remained for her, unanswered. How could one seed give rise to a misshapen tree that bore no fruit, no blossom, when planted in the same fertile soil and tended to with the same degrees of love and nurture? Her greatest consolation regarding her brother's premature demise was the relief that he did not have to experience what surely would have been a further torment for him of seeing her star rise while his plunged into the Slough of Despond.

As the horses drawing the carriage negotiated a tight bend on the mountain pass, the coach listed towards the precipice and the dark clouds of lakes in the valley below opened like a dreadful abyss. For a terrifying moment, Charlotte thought she had conjured up the blacker spirit of her brother, come now to reclaim her from the clutches of a rival. Arthur's instinctive reactions were swift and reassuring as he reached and drew her closer, his exhilarated whoop, in unison with that heard from the cab driver, indicating that what was an instant terror to Charlotte was a thrill to her male travel companions.

'Have you ever seen the likes,' Arthur said, now leaning across Charlotte, as the more spectacular view was on her side. Charlotte agreed that it was the most dramatic landscape imaginable but that she would be glad when back nearer sea level, adding that perhaps there was a less vertiginous route they could take for their return journey to Bangor on the morrow. Arthur, smiling, assured her, that her comfort and safety were his foremost concerns, not just for their honeymoon, but for their shared life to come. Charlotte wanted to touch him as a gesture of gratitude but as they were still at a great height, she preferred to remain completely still, a rather petrified stillness that she hoped could influence the balance of the carriage.

The rain was easing as they arrived in Beddgelert, so that alighting from the carriage outside the hotel, the couple, rather than have to make a hasty dash for shelter were able to pause and drink in the Eden they had entered. Lofty mountains encircled the village, and beyond them could be seen the cloud-capped loftiest one of all: Mount Snowdon. The verdant meadows bloomed with nature's most vibrantly coloured palette from thousands and thousands of wild flowers, and closing her eyes lest she swoon from the excess of visual delight, Charlotte hearing the murmurings of the brooks and smelling the musty incense of the after rain air, as one in a state of religious meditation, quietly ejaculated a prayer towards heaven that He, who had made all of this possible and available to them, would always provide such beauty when the clouds of life lifted.

Because they had not booked in advance, they were alarmed to find the hotel so packed with tourists, but the landlord explained that they were mostly pedestrian tourists, 'confined to barracks' because of the recent heavy rains, so there was still availability for the honeymooners. Charlotte thought to ask him about his knowledge of the Kay-Shuttleworths, but the noise from the travellers, already drowning out the efforts of a harpist, was competition beyond her amplification abilities, and she was not one to raise her voice. She would enquire at a later stage.

Their accommodation was typical of any travellers' inn, but after the grandeur of the Penhyrn Arms, the sparsity of furniture, save for the bed, one table holding an oil lamp and two kitchen style chairs, gave it a rather decrepit atmosphere.

'Aha, now the reference to barracks makes sense,' Arthur said, placing their one piece of luggage on the bed, 'it is a good thing the rain has passed, at least we can avail of a temporary release and be pedestrian tourists in the vicinity of the village. What do you say?'

And that was precisely what the Bell Nicholls did for the afternoon in the company of a local guide and four fellow guests of The Goat. For such a small village, Charlotte was bewildered at the volume of tales, anecdotes and legends the local tour guide, a rustic native from the nearby area of Moel Hebog, regaled them with; from the legend of the faithful hound who gave his name to the village, to meadows called after nuns, Roman shields found in fields, harpists – the greatest to be found in all of Wales according to the loquacious cicerone – the benefits of a locally distilled whisky, the tragedies that had befallen reckless, over-adventurous travellers, and on and on, and perhaps, if she had not had to try so hard to understand him, she may have retained her patience. It left her as the small party were being led out of the village confines, up a steep path, to discover some rock of great import. Taking Arthur aside she encouraged him to continue with the tour.

'Besides, Arthur, I daresay you are missing your daily walks on the moors, the absence of my current, retarding torpidity will afford you the opportunity to embrace these mountains akin to the creature whose portrait swings above the door to our lodgings.'

Arthur protested, concerned for her safety as a lone traveller returning to the hotel.

'Arthur, having successfully navigated my way as a solitary

figure through the streets of London and Brussels, through the often-lonely retreats of lesser populated but no less potentially menacing regional metropolises, I think I can safely make my way through Beddgelert's thoroughfare.' She left before Arthur had a chance to further protest, and had she looked back, his dumbfounded expression would have amused her. There was another reason for her desire to return to the hotel alone, and that was to inquire after the relative of her friends, the Kay-Shuttleworths.

The Kay-Shuttleworths were possibly Charlotte's most fashionable associates. Sir James, formerly James Kay, the son of a wealthy, woollen manufacture, became Kay-Shuttleworth when he married the wealthy heiress, Lady Janet Shuttleworth, of Gawthorp Hall in Lancashire. Sir James had taken a great interest in literature and literary society when he retired from a hectic civil service career that almost broke him, and on discovering that the celebrated author of *Jane Eyre* lived just over his county boundary in Yorkshire, he and Lady Janet went about making themselves known to her by calling to Haworth. Charlotte was not readily interested in pursuing a friendship with them, mostly because she did not like being in the company of a class to which she did not belong, but also because she found Sir James rather hard going and was always only half at ease in his company. Nevertheless, after lots of pestering from Sir James, she had visited them at Gawthorp Hall and their London residence, and vacationed at their Lake Windemere retreat, the latter being where she first met Elizabeth Gaskell. She remembered on one of those occasions Sir James speaking of his brother and his association with Beddgelert and the local inn, and even though a future meeting with Sir James was not something she longed for, his past persistence suggested that it would happen, and rather than having to be bored by his pretensions towards artistry, she could talk about meeting his brother. It would also be a conversation topic for Arthur when meeting them for the first time.

The hotel continued to be a bustling concern of predominantly male customers, causing Charlotte to think that she would prefer to slip away to her room unseen, but that would not serve her purpose of inquiring about Thomas Kay, for that was the name of Sir James' brother. This was not an establishment that could boast of anything so grand as a concierge or even the constancy of a receptionist, the land-lord they previously met was nowhere to be seen, and thus, to play the amateur sleuth, Charlotte would have to address her questions to the rather gruff looking specimen behind the bar.

'Well, isn't it you is the sight for sore mountain eyes, what can I get the little lady this good day of our Lord?' he said, leaning a crooked elbow on the counter, and twitching his eyes, which Charlotte presumed was supposed to effect a flirtatious wink of sorts. So much of what he said and how he looked, with awful, wiry hairs sprouting from his ears, offended her, but the greatest offence was addressing her as a 'little lady'. How she hated any reference to her stature, which always diminished her.

'Nothing, thank you, I will wait for my husband to arrange any refreshments we require,' Charlotte said, glad to be able to establish her status. It was not something she had ever been troubled by in the past – liberal advances from the opposite sex – and while irritated by the rustic's lame efforts, the ironic timing of it amused her. There was a thrill in being forbidden fruit.

Completely nonplussed, it would appear, by what she said, the same rustic bartender, adding a second crooked elbow to the counter to facilitate the cupping of his head, giving him the appearance of a child looking longingly through the win-dow at some unattainable pleasure, asked again if he could be of assistance, this time adding some choices, 'I can get you a nice cup of tea served with some cake, or maybe something stronger, what do you say?'

'I do require something. Information. I am going to assume you are not the owner of this establishment and therefore ask if you could direct me to him.'

'Aye, you'd be right there. As my name is Davydd Evans, and the name on the deeds of this fine inn be Pritchard, the little lady is correct.'

Charlotte turned, about to walk away, her temperament was not suited to indirection and there was that 'little' again.

'Wait, wait, I see I've insulted you. Let me give you a straight answer. Robert, for that be the man you are seeking, is not here just now. He is away for a few days. But p'haps I have the information you seek; I know all that happens in this place. Ask me anything,' he said, straightening up and assuming a more officious stance.

Turning around to witness the altered poise, Charlotte ventured to test his claim, 'Can you tell me if one, Thomas Kay, is married to Mister Pritchard's daughter?'

'I can tell you, and what I can tell you is that he be married to his daughters, one, God rest her soul, as dead as the hound of Gelert under a lump of rock, and the other, still breathing and breeding from what I hear, in some fancy house in London,' and again, adopting the manner of the child gazing through the window, and lowering his voice, he added, 'they were twins, Mary and Alice, he married Mary first and when she died, after waiting a decent enough length, over a year if memory serves me right, he takes the sister to the altar.'

Sir James had never mentioned this to Charlotte, perhaps for the same reason that caused her informant to speak as if revealing a great secret. She was unsure what to say, should she be offering condolences on the death of Mary or congratulations on the nuptials of her sister. Besides, surely it was illegal to marry your sister-in-law: she had always assumed that was the reason her Papa and Aunt Branwell had never wed.

'It's a hard one to figure right enough, locals jokingly called him Solomon, you know the Bible fella with all his wives. That annoyed our landlord so much we're now forbidden to talk about it, so if I were you, Miss, I'd be leaving well enough alone.'

'I see,' was all Charlotte could think to say before walking away. Apart from the illegality of it, this practice disturbed her: although she was claimant to just four days experience of matrimony, it was enough for her to find solace in having no sisters to inherit her incumbency in Arthur's bed should she predecease him.

Once back in the bedroom, she had intended to work a little on her latest story, especially as it had been some time since she had had the leisure to do so, what with the preparations for the wedding and planning for her long absence from the parson-age, alas, the lack of a suitable writing desk, and exhaustion from the early rise – they had attended a morning service at 7.30 am in Bangor before setting out – saw her instead curl up on the bed and sleep soundly until Arthur returned.

After dinner – a homely concoction of fish from the mountain lakes and buttery potatoes – the couple went for a walk, just as far as the bridge, to take in the night air and to aid digestion; Charlotte, unlike Arthur who had been reared on a diet of fish from the Shannon, was unused to the fare. There had been little intercourse between them since Charlotte had related the case of Thomas Kay and his two wives. She was taken aback that Arthur did not share her misgivings about the event. He seemed to think that Kay had done the honourable thing and made a great deal out of how natural it was that he would be equally attracted to a twin sister, and that sisters would share the same taste in men, being sisters. There were far too many 'sisters' in his surmising for Charlotte's liking, and it put her to thinking of something she once suspected but had long since buried in that subconscious house of doubts and fears. Perhaps it was the sad murmurings of the brook complete with an owl shrieking from somewhere far up in the hills, or the faint shadows of rock materialising when the clouds cleared, or the moon illuminating the scene with its ghostly rays, that evoked a melancholic mood. Charlotte's thoughts darkened, a door to that house of doubts and fears opened, and she decided it was time to address the matter of her sister Anne, and Arthur.

'Arthur, did you love Anne?' she asked, glad that the veil of night prevented any scrutiny of her expression.

'Of course, I loved Anne, poor gentle soul, it was hard to have any other feelings for her.'

'And had she been the one to survive, and I were the one looking down from above, would she be standing here with you?'

A sigh and the silence that followed was felt by Charlotte as a sharp dart in her chest, in that place where the heart sits.

'Too long a pause,' she said, consciously echoing Portia from *The Merchant of Venice*. The owl screeched once more.

'Oh, Charlotte, it's just that it seems nothing I have said or done has been enough to convince you of my feelings. I loved Anne in the same way that I loved Emily and Branwell. My biggest regret where Anne is concerned is that I did not follow my heart and accompany you and she to Scarborough, when I knew she was dying. I would have liked to officiate at her funeral, just like I had done for Branwell and Emily. And to have been there for you.'

Charlotte would always regret Anne's burial in Scarborough,

the seaside town where they went that May in 1849, less than six months since Emily's death, nine since Branwell's. Instead of the sea air restoring Anne's health, three days after their arrival the Angel of Death came and took her away. Not wanting to put her papa through the pain of having to open the family vault for the third time in less than a year, Charlotte organised the interment to take place in Scarborough. Arthur's reference to the funeral felt like a reprimand.

'I did what I thought best at the time.'

'Of course you did, and it was the right thing to do, besides Anne is not lying there far from home, she is here, and here,' he said, placing one hand on Charlotte's chest, the other on his own.

Later, back in the bedroom, as he gently tugged on the clips that held her hair in its tidy bun, he whispered in her ear, 'there will always be enough room in my heart to accommodate those I love, but you, Charlotte, hold that heart in your hands. Without your support it would sink into my boots.'

Charlotte, with slight movements of her head, let her hair tumble over her shoulders as she took the hand he offered.

Chapter Eight

The journey back to Bangor was for the most part uneventful. The omnibus was full with fellow tourists, all six of whom were part of the same group, a walking club from Switzerland, which delighted Charlotte as she could refresh her French by closing her eyes and endeavouring to translate what they were saying. After a while she tuned out, it seemed the all-male group were just interested in complaining about the cuisine in Wales and how unfavourably it compared with the continent. Arthur had no knowledge of their language but whenever he was caught staring, he smiled and nodded knowingly, and Charlotte, rather than be irritated by this affectation, was beginning to warm to his affable, outgoing nature, or at least his more beneficent disposition compared to hers. How different this Arthur was when he was not discussing the school or parish concerns or the washerwomen who were still annoyed at him for campaigning against them drying their clothes on the headstones. Confident that the foreign gentlemen probably had a limited grasp of the English language, and hence would not be privy to their intercourse, Charlotte, realising that she had never discussed the 'clothes drying' matter with him, brought it up now as the carriage trundled through Llanberis Pass: contrary to what Charlotte had hoped there was no alternative route back to Bangor.

'Arthur, I am curious, why were you so vexed by the

washerwomen's habit of drying their clothes on the tombstones?' she said, raising her voice beyond its natural pitch as she competed with the Swiss chorus.

Before answering, Arthur gave a startled look towards the said fellow occupants, 'Charlotte, maybe we should discuss this at a more opportune time,' he whispered, leaning sideways towards her but keeping his gaze and his smile, now looking rather pained, on the others.

'Don't be silly, can't you tell, they neither understand nor care about what subject we decide to converse about,' she said, and added, 'besides, why should we allow them to silence us, did they pay extra to monopolise omnibus discourse?'

Arthur smiled more effusively at the men, lines of apology creasing the corners of his mouth, and that, dear Reader, did irritate Charlotte, her patience never extended to anything approaching obsequious behaviour.

'Arthur, I asked you a question!'

Still in a whispering voice, Arthur answered, 'It was so unsightly to see clothes strewn over headstones, and undignified. I mean, sanctified ground, Charlotte.'

Arthur had not been in Haworth that long when he kicked up a fuss about this habit of the local women, and, it must be said, also the habit of the Brontë women. It was a long-established custom and the women resented Nicholls' interference and his long campaign until he got his way, forcing them to find alternative means of drying their washing. The Revd Brontë watched the battle from the side lines, and the level of his amusement at the affair was evident in a poem he wrote at the time.

'You do know that there were women who wanted you dead because of that whole debacle? When you went home to Ireland for a holiday it was their greatest hope that you would not return,' Charlotte said, smiling and shaking her head, the tiny tremors indicating an amused disbelief.

'Well, who had the last laugh? Hmm?' Arthur said, straightening his pose.

'Apparently, Papa. He wrote a poem about it all. It's very entertaining,' Charlotte said.

'He never!'

'He did, let me see if I can recall the most risible section,' Charlotte closed her eyes and tilted her head backwards, then bringing it back and opening her eyes she continued,

'"His curate who follows, with all due regard ... something, something, something, has reform'd the Churchyard.

The females all routed have fled with their clothes, to stack-yards and backyards, and where no one knows,

And loudly have sworn by the suds that they swim in,

They'll wring off his head, for his warring with women."' Oh, I wish I could remember more of it,' Charlotte turned to better gauge Arthur's reaction.

'I should like to see all of that composition; it sounds very amusing. The Reverend is a man of many talents, it seems,' Arthur said, not sounding in the least amused or impressed at Revd Brontë's poetic ingenuity, as he rolled his shoulders and tightly folded his arms; the poise of the sullen, crest-fallen little boy.

'Oh really, Arthur, you should be flattered. To be the subject of a poem is a fine thing,' Charlotte said, placing her hand on his forearm.

'I suppose you are correct. You would think I would be used to his Ulster wit by now,' Arthur said, patting her hand.

'*Je pense que le poème semble très drôle.*' It was one of the Swiss gentlemen.

Arthur whipped his head around and looked to Charlotte, 'what did he say?'

'He thinks the poem sounds funny,' Charlotte said, and

smiling at the gentlemen replied, '*Très bien, moi aussi.*'

'What did you say?' Arthur asked.

'I told him I think the same,' Charlotte said.

Arthur did not speak for the rest of the journey, and as his head was lowered and his eyes closed, Charlotte presumed he slept. She hated to think that he was hurt and emanating from an urge to protect him she wanted to stamp on the foot of the Swiss who spoke, enraged now as she was at the affrontery of him to conceal his knowledge of English. Instead, she spent the remainder of the journey staring at each of them in turn, her eyes narrowed and piercing, and as she disembarked in Bangor, her parting words were, '*Ayant passé beaucoup de temps à Bruxelles, permettez-moi de vous dire que la nourriture y est horrible. Au revoir.*'

'What did you say, now,' Arthur asked again.

'I just thanked them for sharing the journey with us.'

Back in the hotel, as the rain was pouring down, Charlotte decided she would spend some time writing, while Arthur, undeterred once more by the weather, went for his daily walk. He said he intended to cross the Menai bridge and maybe go as far as Beaumaris. Charlotte had known of his custom of walking long distances each day, but until now she had not understood how pressing the need was for him; she too liked to walk, but only if the conditions were pleasant, which was probably why she was not a common sight on the moors.

Sitting at the dressing table, for there was no writing desk in the room, Charlotte considered writing to her Papa, but a reticence, never before experienced when it came to their correspondences, prevented her; in the past her letters to him were always detailed accounts of what she had experienced, who she had met, and how she felt about it all, but to write in that manner now would feel like an act of treason against Arthur, perhaps there were particulars he would not wish her to disclose, and in an epiphanous moment, she realised that from now on she would have to be more censorial of her effusions, lest they, however unintentional, visit a hurt on her husband.

Opening her journal, she carefully unfolded loose pages she had tucked inside, pages that contained fragments of what she hoped would be the beginning of her next novel. The writing was in pencil, which was how she liked to commit these early imaginings to the page. The piece was something she had begun the previous November and she wanted to believe that the hiatus in its progress resulted from temporal commitments to wedding plans, and the supervision of domestic alterations to the parsonage.

There were more worrying possibilities for the silence of her muses that she dared not entertain.

Writing her last novel, *Villette*, had at first been a lonely, depressing exercise in discipline, it was not the same without her sisters; she longed for the times when they discussed each other's latest outpourings while walking around the dining room table. Writing then had never felt like a chore, but without Anne's constant encouragement and Emily's wildly expressed enthusiasms, a cloud hovered over each page and the ensuing dark mood it shrouded her in had manifested itself in the mental anguishes and breakdown of *Villette's* heroine, Lucy Snowe. But she persisted and over time began to notice that despite the heavy heart Charlotte Brontë brought to her writing desk, when Currer Bell picked up the pen, the spirits of Acton and Ellis came winging about her chair and whispered in her ear, and so she continued to have belief in her creativity; faith in her God-given gift; confidence that a pen and paper and some quiet time was all that were needed to conjure up this ethereal scene and bring Emma into being: Emma was the title she had given to this latest work, although as yet, Charlotte had no idea who or what this Emma was.

Because of the length of time which had passed since she had written the fragments, Charlotte needed to reread them to remind herself of the story. She knew these characters! There were the Wilcox sisters, running a school for young ladies and struggling to secure pupils, a school just like the one she, Emily and Anne had hoped to open back before they had ever dreamt that one day, they would be published authors. Charlotte remembered their establishment's title, boldly stated on the cards she had printed to advertise their business venture, and she remembered, not the anxiety of those days when no pupils were forthcoming, but the giddy, shared hope of the three of them that this was a means to a livelihood that kept them together in the parsonage. She could hear the clanking sound of a press as words ghosted onto the blank page before her, letter by letter, and there it was in its entirety:

> *THE MISSES BRONTE'S ESTABLISHMENT*
> *FOR*
> *THE BOARD AND EDUCATION*
> *OF A LIMITED NUMBER OF*
> *YOUNG LADIES,*
> *THE PARSONAGE, HAWORTH,*
> *NEAR BRADFORD.*

But before Charlotte could bring her eyes close enough to bring it into focus the black markings faded to white and, once more, all that she saw was the stark, blank page.

As well as the Wilcox sisters, there was much about a Mr William Ellin in the fragment, with his taking of tea and muffins at the Misses Wilcox's establishment and his fondness for walking through fields and lanes, and how he was a great shot at angling; and it struck Charlotte, although she had been unaware at the time of writing that these were practices and characteristics that might easily be attributed to one, Arthur Bell Nicholls. She now sat, the pen redundantly poised over her notebook, in a state of utter perplexity; it had hardly been her intention to include him in her next novel? Besides, she knew she was not one to write in an intentional fashion, when she sat down, all conscious thought was abandoned as she allowed the inspiration to course unsolicited like life-giving-breath through her veins and arteries until the momentum stirred her pen into action. Autobiographical and biographical manifestations were incidental, and those who thought they had recognised themselves between the pages of her novels, were victims of their own vanity. She blamed the cooling relations with her publisher, George Smith, on such presumptions. She had failed to convince him that any resemblance between he and his mother to Doctor John Graham Bretton and his mother, Mrs Bretton, in *Villette*, was merely coincidental, and she attributed the dwindling correspondence between them to that failure.

But now what was she to do with Mr William Ellin? What if further characteristics of Arthur appeared unbidden on the page? It was one thing to allow her father's curate to be an unconscious source of inspiration, as was the case with Mr Macarthey in *Shirley*, but to, however inadvertently, expose her husband in her writing was another matter entirely. That could be misconstrued as an act of treachery, an exploitation of their intimate relations. She would not, for the sake of her art, expose their marriage to the glare of a judgemental literati.

But these were not the only reflections that stilled her pen as she gazed out on tumbling grey clouds in the North Wales sky. Her thoughts were of Arthur and the hope that he had been able to secure an umbrella from the concierge as the last thing she wanted was for him to be caught in a downpour that might bring on a chill. She wished he would return, she was in no mood to write, she would rather discuss their plans for the next day and their journey to Holyhead from where they were to catch the paddle steamer to Ireland. She refolded the pages and placed them back in the journal, returning it to her trunk. Seeing her Bible and a copy of Dr John Forbes' *Memorandums Made in Ireland in the Autumn of 1852*, tucked in beside her rolled shawls, she ignored the Bible and took out the latter; being married to a curate, she reasoned, was duty enough, for now, to her religion.

Charlotte was acquainted with Dr Forbes through George Smith. He had given medical advice during Anne's final illness, and despite his high profile and busy life, had even offered to come to Haworth to attend on her. Charlotte refused the offer, anxious not to upset the Leeds surgeon already treating Anne. When she eventually met Dr Forbes, Charlotte was thrilled to discover he was the gentleman she had imagined him to be, and even more delighted to discover that he, like her Papa, had married a woman from Penzance. Bonding over this and a shared interest in the Arts, the two became fast friends. His pamphlets on the medical benefits of the Arts were often part of the book bundles Charlotte received on a regular basis from her publishers, the travel book she held had also been sent in such a bundle. It had been a great favourite in the parsonage, the Reverend delighted in reading about his home country, and so Charlotte thought it would give equal joy to Arthur and perhaps encourage him to include some of Dr Forbes' itinerary in their plans.

Arthur returned, cold and wet, he had not taken an umbrella, but seemed to brighten on seeing his wife laughing out loud. She offered the book she was reading to him.

'Arthur, you must read this, apart from providing ideas about our excursions in Ireland, it is so entertaining about your fellow countrymen. Read here,' she said, her fingers tapping at a certain passage, 'about a hotel in Dublin and its many short-comings. Let us hope we are not due to stay there.'

Arthur frowned, 'I have read it, Charlotte, on the good recommendation of the Reverend, and have accordingly planned to visit some of the places Dr John writes about, but now you've ruined my surprise.'

'How have I?' Charlotte said, flicking the pages back to the contents section, 'Look at the list of places he has visited, we could not possibly cover that ground, so what little we can do will still remain your secret until we arrive at the selected destination.'

'I suppose,' Arthur said, his tone still indicating a deflated humour.

'And now, you must change out of those wet things and tell me all about the marvels of construction you've witnessed at the bridge,' Charlotte said, placing the book on the table and moving to help Arthur out of his overcoat.

Chapter Nine

There was a festive air in Bangor railway station despite the early hour. Charlotte had not slept well, she never did when she knew she had to be up early, but also, she had developed a rather irritating cough – always a cause for concern, considering her siblings' medical history – and yet, despite these indispositions, her spirits were high; perhaps it was Arthur's enthusiasm; or perhaps it was something buried deep in her psyche, a ghostly trace of a heritage she had always denied, and what she felt was excited anticipation for her first trip to Ireland; the land of her father and forefathers.

The train left the station at exactly 4.48am, as scheduled. The passengers in the carriage with the Bell-Nicholls were also, it was established, bound for the 6.00am steam packet from Holyhead to Kingstown in Ireland. These passengers, a couple returning to their home in Wicklow, and two ladies on tour, made their introductions and promptly closed their eyes, to catch some more sleep, no doubt. Arthur, undeterred by their veiled lids, struck up a conversation with the only other male occupant, just as the train was approaching Britannia Bridge.

'Is this your first time?' Arthur asked, nudging the gentleman's knee to rouse him, as the carriage was plunged into darkness, the train having entered the tubular structure of the bridge.

Charlotte looked out at the blackness to disassociate herself from the question but was surprised at how quickly the gentleman answered: clearly, he had not been asleep.

'Indeed, it is not, I have been across it now many times, but that never detracts from my marvelling once more at its inventiveness and magnificence. This Stephenson is a capital fellow, just like his father,' he said, 'and you, is this your maiden crossing?'

'No, similarly, I have travelled it before, and now I am happy to be accompanying my wife on her first, as you say, maiden crossing,' Arthur said, and then, as if forgetting that anyone else shared the carriage the two men continued swapping their knowledge of how the bridge came into being, with much talk of metal girders and hydraulics and ground-breaking engineering. Charlotte was relieved that the journey was only thirty minutes duration, she had heard enough of hard facts, it was like listening to one of Mr Dickens' latest characters, Mr Gradgrind, trying to outdo a more knowledgeable version of the same Mr Gradgrind.

After a short journey in a horse drawn omnibus from Holyhead railway station, and a mercifully shorter wait in the cold, open air of Admiralty Pier, the couple boarded the boat and were on their way to Ireland. The boat, much to their mutual amusement was called the *Prince Arthur*. They stayed on deck as the packet clanged and groaned away from the wall and sailed through the morning mist that shrouded the shoreline, before emerging into the light and stilly, blue calm of the Irish Sea. Charlotte moved close to Arthur, and not just because of the chill in the air, she had an urge to say what she was thinking; 'we're going home', but even in this moment of giddy intimacy that she was feeling, her reason did not allow for absurdity.

Charlotte would have liked to stay on deck longer, there was an energy in the bracing sea air instilling in her a sense of wellbeing and vitality, but precedential experience at what exposure to even the slightest wind could precipitate, especially when she was already compromised with a chill, saw the couple go below deck to the dining saloon, where breakfast was being served. Charlotte's only other experience of sea journeys were her two trips to Belgium. The motion of the boat, while still but a gentle undulation, threatened the security of the plates on the table, causing Arthur to continuously reset them after each slight slide. The movement put Charlotte in mind of those other two occasions when she was at sea.

The first journey was one Charlotte would always remember with great fondness, when she and Emily went to attain a foreign education that would equip them with the skills necessary to establish a school for young ladies, a scheme very much the brainchild of Charlotte, as a means of avoiding a lifetime spent working for others. Charlotte, unhappy in her position at the time as governess to a family in Rawdon and influenced by accounts of life in Brussels from her school friends, Mary and Martha Taylor, convinced her Aunt Branwell – who had the means to fund the venture – that in order to hope to attract pupils, in an already competitive market, they would need superior talents such as could only be achieved by way of a continental education. Papa had accompanied them on that occasion, and their friends, Mary Taylor and her brother Joe, seasoned travellers on the same route, completed the merry party. Her second journey, as a single traveller, was a different episode; apart from the loneliness occasioned from missing the lively company of the Taylors and the reassuring, organisational ways of Papa, Charlotte concluded that individual travel was not the business of young women: a conclusion reached following incidents with various officials which, while not physically intimidating, left her feeling vulnerable and fearful.

'I am so relieved to have a travelling companion for this, my maiden voyage to Ireland,' she said.

'A travelling companion? Not necessarily this travelling companion?' Arthur said, indicating himself.

'Oh, you men, always in need of reassurance, how tiresome,' Charlotte said. 'Instead of seeking to be further flattered why not amuse me by telling me all about these relatives of yours I am to be subjected to for the next month.'

Before Arthur got a chance to reply, Charlotte added, 'No, before that, I want to know about your real home in Ulster, seeing as I won't get to visit there.'

'Hmmm, well firstly, Charlotte, Cuba House in Banagher is my home, I am the fortunate son of two real homes,' Arthur said, and leaning his elbows on the table, forming a bridge-like structure with his forearms and joined hands, on which he rested his chin, he proceeded to recount how he, and his brother Allen, came to leave their family home in Antrim and travel south to live with their cousins in King's County.

'How old were you, Arthur?' Charlotte asked.

'I had turned seven that January, this was July when we left with my Uncle and travelled South to Banagher, my brother, Allen, you'll be meeting him in Dublin, he was nine,' Arthur said.

'And that was the last time you ever saw them?' Charlotte asked.

'Yes, the last time I saw my father; my mother; my brothers, other than Allen; and my sisters. They are both dead now, father and mother; mother in 1830, she was just forty-four years old. I am not sure of the cause, maybe it was having the ten of us. I cannot remember her, Charlotte. Is that a terrible thing?' Arthur, folding his arms on the table – the breakfast dishes having had been removed – looked down as if the answer to his question was to be found in the grains of wood.

'Do you remember how she looked when you last saw her?

Perhaps what she said to you?' Charlotte, as she spoke, was thinking of her own mother. She had so few memories to draw on being just five when she died. One, which might have been some fanciful imagining was of a young woman, a prettier version of Aunt, playing with Branwell in the parsonage parlour. The light streaming in, unimpeded by curtains – there were never any curtains due to her Papa's paranoia regarding fire – haloed both heads, as this woman, her mother, sang to the delighted child, who nodded and clapped in rhythm with her melody.

'She wasn't there, Charlotte, and perhaps because of my excitement for the adventure I was embarking on with my big brother, I didn't think to seek her out,' Arthur said.

Lost in her own memory, Charlotte was momentarily confused, 'Who, Arthur, who wasn't there?' she asked.

'My mother. How was I to know it was the last time I would see her. I did not even glance back, Charlotte, as I sat proudly, my first time in a gig. I have suffered since for that failure, that heedless selfishness.'

As Arthur continued his account of the day he left, Charlotte saw another scene she had fancifully composed based on what their servant at the time, Sarah Garrs had told her. It was of six children gathered at the foot of a bed, the eldest, Maria, who was seven held the baby, Anne. Emily and Elizabeth stood side by side, the same height despite the difference in age, with their hands curled around the bed rails, and she, Charlotte, had a firm grip on her brother's chubby hand. Papa sat at the top, his elbows resting on the edge of the mattress, his head bowed on his joined hands, and Aunt Branwell sat opposite him. The only sounds in the room were the faint suspirations of her mother, mingling with the pureness of Anne's baby notes of innocent joy. In recent years, when she conjured up this deathbed composition it was not her mother who lay in the bed, it was Anne as she had lain on the couch at their lodgings in Scarborough, and it was Anne's voice that spoke, repeating her final words, 'Take courage, Charlotte, take courage'.

'My punishment, Charlotte, is an image that haunts me. It is of my mother sitting at a kitchen table, her fingers pressed to her eyes, her mouth a grimace of pain.' Arthur said, and as they both looked at each other, Charlotte felt a connection, like an invisible thread, pull her heart that bit closer to his.

'It was Aunt Harriette who told me of her death.'

'This is the same Aunt Harriette in Banagher with whom we will stay?' Charlotte said.

'Yes, I think you will like her, Charlotte, she is the dearest, kindest soul. She tried to comfort my twelve-year-old self that day, but I brushed away her arms, poised to enfold me, and ran to the door, out around to the back of the house and across the north facing fields, and I kept running, unsure if I was running away from the news or towards it. I cannot remember what halted my flight, but when I returned to the house, Aunt was still there, her comforting arms still reaching towards me and as she held me tight against her chest, I felt, not the absence, but the presence of a mother. Aunt Harriette and Uncle Alan had extended a great kindness to my parents by bringing us south to be reared and educated, thus lessening the hardships on my original family's already, straitened existence.'

'We have both been very privileged to have women such as Aunt Harriette and Aunt Branwell in our lives, Arthur,' Charlotte said, and as the movement of the boat increased, causing them both to sway from side to side, she wondered if it was the spirits of their mothers conjuring up the winds to rock their children one more time.

'I see I have depressed your spirits with my sad remembrances, why don't we go up and take a turn about the deck?' Arthur said, standing and offering his crooked arm as an aid.

The breeze proved to be too bracing for Charlotte, as the combination of her continuing chill and want of sleep made her shiver, so the remainder of the journey was spent in the commodious comfort of one of the many saloons on board, where she slept, her head resting against the shoulder of her husband, who kept awake by reading from the Book of Isaiah.

Chapter Ten

As soon as she alighted onto the pier, Charlotte sensed a familiarity with her surroundings; she heard it in the Irish accents dancing like a chaotic jig on the fishy, seaweed air and although not one to pander to superstition, or déjà vu, or any philosophical theory that was not bedded in Christianity, she had a sense that she had been here before.

'Arthur, if you had brought me from Haworth blindfolded, and landed me on this very spot, I declare I would know I was in Ireland. Isn't that the strangest thing ever?' she said, straightening the creases of travel from her dress with downward ironing movements.

'Not in the slightest strange, my dear, it is your Celtic soul welcoming you. How could it be otherwise with a mother from Cornwall and a father from Ulster.'

Charlotte welcomed the reminder with both a smile, and a knitted brow, the latter an attempt to understand herself; an English woman experiencing a strange sense of belonging, a sense of standing on home ground.

Kingstown was nothing like Charlotte had imagined, the entrance to the harbour was dotted with boats bobbing on the waves, some looked to be pleasure sailing boats, while the majority were fishing vessels of varying sizes, and working tugs: to their right it appeared as if another pier was under construction. The East Pier they had disembarked onto and the marina beyond was a heaving mass of people; tourists, fishermen, dockers, carters, and labourers, and then there were the waiting cars and coaches, the horses looking as splendid as any in England; the drivers, perhaps a little less splendid in Charlotte's estimation, nevertheless, the entire scene could easily have been the wharf in London from where she was rowed out to board the ship to Belgium. What had she been thinking? She felt rather ashamed that she had expected something more primitive, more savage, when in fact this was a port that could have easily competed with the most advanced in Europe. And as for the approach from the water – she and Arthur had gone up on deck to take it all in – it was exactly as her Queen had described it when she first visited a few years previously, likening the sweep of Killiney Bay to the Bay of Naples. Charlotte had never been to the Bay of Naples, but she had seen and scrutinised many depictions on canvas, of Naples, Venice, Genoa, and the French Riviera, and as she and Arthur stood beside their luggage, waiting for a driver to approach, Charlotte knew what it must feel like to be that tourist on their 'Grand Tour'.

She noted a specimen walk towards them in a black suit – that had seen better days, probably on a different body, of higher social rank – doff his hat while at the same time spit something that could have been straw out of the corner of his mouth, from where it had been hanging.

'Leave this to me, there is a skill in dealing with this lot,' Arthur whispered to Charlotte, and for once it was not irritation that she felt but rather gratitude that she had an Arthur to deal with such affairs: interacting with public transport officials required a bolder, more assertive Charlotte and she was currently too travel weary to rise to that self. A boy porter masquerading as a toy soldier was one thing but the men belonging to the public transport system had a way about them that easily intimidated her.

'Good day t' you, Sir, and th' good woman too, if it plaises you, where might I be taking you t'day,' the suited, cud chewing individual said, as he made a movement much like a genuflection in front of Charlotte, who had to clasp her mouth for fear of laughing and pretend that a coughing fit had overtaken her.

'Good day to you too, and a fine day it is, thank the Lord. It would most definitely please us if you could carry us into Dublin city, but you will need an assistant to help with the luggage, and I don't see such a fellow,' Arthur said, looking around as if to seek such a person.

'Ah now, Sir, you see youse ar' lettin' me butty appearance fool youse into thinkin' I'm one of them babbies as couldn't lift a female shift, if they had a notion itself,' he said, extending his hands and turning them over as if for inspection, 'them paws have th' strength to lift th' boat youse came in on clear out a' th' sea,' he said.

'Oh, dear God, it's worse than usual,' Arthur muttered as if to himself, but Charlotte had heard. He held up his arm, a beckoning gesture, made to no one but with the obvious indication that he sought another potential driver.

'I'm not offended, if that is what you're thinking, Arthur, I like this fellow,' Charlotte quietly said, pivoting her head as if she addressed someone standing behind them, in the hope that the driver would not hear.

Arthur sighed.

'The cost? And please do not start suggesting you would do it for nothing but would welcome a donation. I prefer these transactions to be business-like,' Arthur said, and although he sounded impatient, Charlotte suspected that he was enjoying the interlude as much as she was.

'A man afther me own heart, keep everthin' cut 'n dry, that's me motto, never was one for the palaver meself. Youse tell me where exactly in th' city beyond youse want me to carry you, and I'll name me price,' he said.

Charlotte did not know where they were staying, Arthur had said it was a surprise, so she too was eager to hear his reply.

'Ah, now you know, and I know that one place is as near or far as the other, so let's have a price first to take myself and my wife, and the luggage that apparently is going to be of no consequence to your mythical strength, to the city,' Arthur said. Charlotte assumed that his lack of disclosure was to extend the surprise for her sake, but later Arthur would explain that had he mentioned where they were staying, the reputation of the hotel and the financial status of the clientele who usually frequent it would have had the crafty driver increase his price accordingly.

The drive into the city took them through some of the quaintest seaside villages Charlotte had ever seen, and while the carriage also passed what looked to be the poorer neighbourhoods judging by the dishevelled state of the housing there and the bare-footed raggedness of the children playing on the street, it all had a charm for her. Arthur played the role of guide, directing her attention at times to specific buildings and monuments, regaling her with their history.

'And if you look to your right, Charlotte, I think you might just be able to see one of the Martello towers. You know about the Martello towers?' Arthur asked, not in an interrogative way but rather assuming a knowledge on her behalf. Arthur himself was very aware of these fortifications because of the one in Banagher.

'Arthur, I thought I knew everything about the Napoleonic wars, including the construction of Martello Towers as a defence against attack, but you know until this moment I had not considered that Ireland would be a place of interest to the

Frenchies. Is not that the silliest thing. I forget that Ireland and England are one country in political affairs. I know it is a different matter when it comes to culture,' she said.

'Comes to culture. Meaning what?' Arthur said and his expression was of one who has been slighted.

'Oh, Arthur, your face, I am not suggesting that this Ireland of yours has no culture, I am merely alluding to it having a separate culture. You know, music, art, literature. I expect fiddles and storytellers and the like, but I am not expecting to run into a Dickens or a Turner at any given corner, or be brought to the Opera,' Charlotte said, as she patted Arthur's knee.

'Charlotte, I think that is the most condescending I have ever known you to be, but not one to suffer affront, especially when the cause of affront is such a ridiculous conclusion, I will prove to you, before we are done with this fair isle, that Ireland is not only as highbrow when it comes to culture as your England, it is superior ...' Charlotte made as if to interrupt but he placed his finger on her lips and continued, '...and furthermore I vouchsafe that one day Ireland will have writers and artists to rival any of your Turners or Dickens. In fact, perhaps it could already claim half of an accomplished author that I happen to be intimately acquainted with,' Arthur, as he spoke had removed his finger from her lips, and now that his cultural gauntlet had been thrown to the floor of the carriage, he leaned and placed his lips where that finger had been.

Charlotte, at first, welcomed the kiss with a slight opening of her mouth but as Arthur's advance seemed to become a little more enthusiastic, a little more eager, she took his head in her hands and moving it away from hers entreated him to begin her Irish cultural awakening.

'Besides, Arthur, you must start by informing your ignorant wife about that Martello tower we passed,' she said, sitting back and assuming with raised head and widened eyes, the rather exaggerated pose of the attentive pupil.

As the journey continued Arthur pointed out the location of other Towers that were not in their eyeline, he spoke of the wisdom of King George III in raising the towers to defend the Irish coastline, he spoke of pivoted mounted canons and walls with slits for musket fire, he mentioned Napoleon quite a number of times, he alluded to how the towers got their name, and such was his spirited delivery that Charlotte wondered if it had all been rehearsed for her benefit. Politics and history were not areas of interest she associated with him.

'Are you doing this to impress me, Arthur?' she asked.

'Doing what?'

'All this talk of the Napoleonic wars, I was unaware of your great interest and knowledge. It is fascinating but rather uncharacteristic of you to be so animated about such things,' Charlotte said.

'I cannot claim to have your degree of interest or indeed your breadth of knowledge, but it is for these very reasons I have done my homework so that, if not exactly entertaining, I can present myself as less dull and a little more amusing to you,' Arthur said, and with a coy smile added, 'have I in any way succeeded?'

'Admirably, but for one omission in your history lesson, not once have I heard you mention the Duke of Wellington. Perhaps your research has not yet reached the Battle of Waterloo?' Charlotte said.

'Oh, you of little faith, don't you know I was deliberately avoiding his name lest I give away a surprise I have in store for you. Do you think I am unaware that my greatest rival for your affections was the same Arthur Wellesley? It is why I waited until after his death before I proposed,' he said, pursing his lips and nodding as if to indicate that it was a very judicious decision.

'Don't be absurd, Arthur, the man was eighty-three years old when he died, besides, I had no romantic interest in the Duke, my obsession is rooted in an admiration for his military pursuits, his political endeavours, and of course a certain toy soldier I named after him,' Charlotte said, as she turned away from Arthur and looked out on the terraced houses of Blackrock.

'You must tell me more sometime about those toy soldiers. I seem to remember Anne telling me something about them. Were they Branwell's and you each took one and gave it a name and made-up games or something?' Arthur asked.

'Yes, something like that, we were incredibly young. It seems such a long time ago now, I have almost forgotten myself,' Charlotte said, turning back to Arthur, 'but, I have not forgotten you mentioning a surprise. Would the historian extraordinaire of all things Napoleonic care to elaborate?'

'Ah, I am afraid the hero worshiper extraordinaire will have to be patient. Now, let me see where we are on the road,' Arthur said as he leaned out the open window.

As the carriage got nearer to the city centre the streets widened and the Georgian buildings were as grand as any Charlotte had seen in London, and as they turned onto Merrion Street such was the width of the road, it was practically a plaza. There were many single horse cabs like the one they travelled in but also quite magnificent four horse drawn carriages moving through the area, elegantly dressed couples could be seen strolling arm in arm, business like, top-hatted gentlemen in dark suits were conversing in earnest fashion in groups of three and four, and of course the females whom Charlotte was particularly drawn to were those pushing perambulators or firmly holding the hands of children dressed in more elegant attire. Charlotte knew these females to be the nannies and the governesses. Even from the distance of her carriage window she could sense in their exaggerated animated smiles and gestures, their loneliness and longing for a more fulfilling existence. How different her life could have been, had not her creative gifts freed her from what was to her a life of slavery to families who, regardless of how included in their domestic life they endeavoured to make you feel, they were always quick, especially when visitors called, to remind you of your lower station and your servile position. Quite unconsciously she leaned and placed the side of her head on Arthur's shoulder, but he hardly noticed as he stuck his head out the window and instructed the driver to stop.

'Indulge me some minutes, and do not think this means you can add to the fare. I think your one shilling and six pence is enough extortion,' Arthur said, and stepping from the carriage, taking Charlotte's hand to help her down, he continued, 'and so my dear, your cultural education begins. I know it is not looking as complete as it did this time last year but behold our Irish Crystal Palace.' As he spoke, he stepped to the side to reveal an edifice, that although appearing to be either halfway up or halfway down, did have a remarkable resemblance to the building that housed the Great Exhibition she had visited on numerous occasions when in London a few years previously.

'You are looking at the home of the Great Irish Industrial Exhibition, organised by, and this will no doubt amaze you, Charlotte, but organised by the Royal Dublin Society, founded for the purpose of preserving and promoting cultural life in Ireland. See, your eyes are widening, you are amazed,' Arthur said, clasping his hands in triumph.

'Of course, I have heard of this society, I have been following their campaign for the establishment of a National Gallery. Actually, Arthur, I am not sure what I was thinking, perhaps I have been listening too much to Papa's boyhood stories from the last century, or reading accounts of the famine in the newspapers, so that when I thought about Ireland the images I conjured were either of fireside gatherings in pleasant, white-washed cottages or of a peasant's cabin and a starving people, such as the barefoot children we passed along the way.'

'When I visited here last year, Charlotte, I remember staring at paintings in the fine arts gallery and all I could see in each one was your face. You will recall I had left Haworth for what I thought was the last time and come home to, pardon the expression, lick my wounds. It was my brother who persuaded me to visit the exhibition to take my mind elsewhere. Afterwards, as we walked back up the street he stopped outside a certain house, telling me who had been born there, and I know you will think I am fabricating, but there and then I swore to God that one day I would bring you here as my wife. And here we are.'

'Well hopefully you did your swearing in *voce magna*, so that I can verify the facts with your brother when we meet?' Charlotte said and went to laugh but the breaths mutated into a paroxysm of coughing.

The driver, who all this time, was leaning against the flank of the horse, again chewing what was surely the horse's food, interjected as soon as Charlotte's fit passed.

'Jaysus, but that's a right dose you have, missus. You know wha' youse need now, youse need a bottle from one of the quacks over in Gardiner Street. I can arrange it for you, if you plaise,' he said.

'What you can arrange, my good fellow, is to take care of your own business, if you don't mind, and leave my wife's healthcare to me,' Arthur said, taking Charlotte by the arm and guiding her away from the driver towards a row of neat townhouses. He stopped outside one that had an iron number 6 nailed to the wall left of the front door.

'And this is the house my brother indicated, and my first

Dublin surprise,' Arthur gestured towards the house in such a lavish style that any onlooker might easily assume that the house itself was a gift he was bestowing on his wife, 'here stands the very house where your Duke of Wellington was born.'

Charlotte, continuing to experience the weakening effects of her earlier coughing outburst, barely managed a smile as she said, 'How thrilling. Perhaps we could come back later to savour the fact.'

'Of course, forgive me, Charlotte, how selfish of me. Here you are, unwell, exhausted from the journey, trying to find your bearings in a foreign country, while I disport myself like some self-professed expert on the culture of Dublin. Let me get you back to the carriage, we are close to our hotel,' he said, as they both returned to the waiting driver, looking, it must be said cheerful and pleased to see them, clearly not in the least peeved by Arthur's previous reproach.

'First surprise?' Charlotte said as the horse turned from Merrion Street onto Merrion Row.

'Pardon?' Arthur looked confused.

'You said the birthplace of Arthur Wellesley was your first surprise. Am I to expect to be showered with surprises like one of those silly, empty-headed wives who require constant amusement? Have you forgotten me already, Arthur?' Charlotte said, her tone laden with accusation.

'You are tired, Charlotte, we both are, let's get settled into our accommodation, and later when our good humours have returned, we should draw up, together, an itinerary for our city vacation,' Arthur said, making no reference to the wrapped book he had in his pocket.

The carriage stopped outside the Shelbourne Hotel, which was connected to Arthur's second surprise – the book secreted away in his pocket – but again he remained mute on the matter. There was no doubt as to what hotel it was as the name was blazoned across the top of what appeared more as three red brick houses than a single edifice. The reception desk was an ornate, marble topped table, tucked under a staircase, behind which stood a portly gentleman in an ill-fitting tailed jacket. He introduced himself as the hotel manager. An enormous urn of red and white roses resting on the table perfumed the air with the aroma of fruits and teas, a scent that would normally be a pleasant olfactory experience for Charlotte, but on this occasion it made her nauseous, and that sensation, combined with the dread of having to climb the steep staircase that spiralled upwards before her proved too much, she swooned and swayed, but thankfully the assiduous celerity of the manager, despite his bulk, prevented a more unfortunate outcome as he caught her before she hit the floor.

She woke many hours later to find Arthur kneeling beside the bed, his head in his hands either praying or crying, and rather than feel any great guilt for the concern her faint must have caused him, she could not help but feel that it served him right for underestimating the severity of her illness.

'I am alive,' she said, sitting up in the bed, 'there will be no obsequies required on this occasion.'

Chapter Eleven

The dining room was a noisy cacophony of voices, rattling china and the clang of silver with waiters gliding around tables, starched, folded white napkins swinging from their forearms. Charlotte continued to feel tired and worried that she was developing a fever. The food was perhaps the finest ever placed before her, but she could only manage to nibble at it. Arthur made up for her reduced appetite by finishing his and her mussels and entrée of roast lamb. When she felt like this, as was unfortunately far too often, her preferred company was her own and her preferred space was her bedchamber back in the parsonage. Arthur meant well, she knew his intentions were good as he planned out their days with a heightened degree of animation in his tone and physiognomy, but he was exhausting the already diminished reserve of her strength.

'And at some point, tomorrow, Allen will meet us, perhaps when we visit the Botanic Gardens, oh, and I believe my cousin, Mary Anna might come along, she is so excited to meet you, Charlotte. It is the reason she has come to Dublin, as it seemed too long to her to wait in Banagher for us to go there. And when we are with them, we can make arrangements for moving over to Allen's house, where we should probably stay until Sunday or Monday, and in the meantime——' Charlotte interrupted.

'Please stop talking about plans and meeting people and

excursions and further travel, and, and, and. Arthur, I am so terribly tired and anxious that this cough is going deeper into my chest. You know how any ailment related to breathing is as an alarum for me,' she said, and even as she spoke her breath laboured and taking the white napkin, she used it to stifle a cough, 'I thought the rest had done me enough good to dine. I am sorry, Arthur, I was wrong. I need to return to the room.'

While she was still talking, Arthur had beckoned to their waiter.

'Sir, is everthin' alrigh', was there somethin' up wit' th' mate? Yer missus doesn't look well,' the waiter said, and turning to Charlotte, 'yous look fierce white, mam, did somethin' not agree wit' ya?'

'If you could be so good as to arrange to have tea brought to our room, that would be most helpful. Oh, and perhaps some sherry. The food has been excellent, please pass on our compliments to the kitchen,' Arthur said, linking Charlotte and heading towards the door.

'Sorry, Sir, wha' room are yous in, and will ya be wantin' cake wit' yer tay?' the waiter asked.

Arthur looked to Charlotte who shook her head, and so he declined the cake and told the waiter the room number. On hearing which room they were in, the waiter threw his head back and rolled his eyes towards heaven.

'Ah, shure, no wondher she's lookin' shuck. Maybe I should axe for a double sherry for ya?' the waiter said.

Arthur, looking somewhat perplexed declined the double, but asked that he could be prompt about bringing the tea.

'Arthur, please reassure me that I can expect a more comprehensible brogue from your relatives. If not, I am afraid you will have to become my translator, and I will be misjudged and abhorred for my deficient ear,' Charlotte said.

'Be reassured, I am probably the most Irish sounding of

them all. The lot of the emigrant who works extra hard to hold on to his native sound,' Arthur, as he spoke, had such a firm hold around Charlotte's waist as they mounted the grand stairs, she felt as if her feet were barely touching the ground.

Charlotte was attired for the night and reclining on the bed against a mound of pillows and cushions when the waiter arrived. Arthur was obliged to take the tray from him at the door as he said that he was not allowed to enter the room after a certain time. It was Arthur who informed Charlotte of this, as once again, the exchange at the door was an incoherent muddle to her ear, not helped by the hushed tones.

'And why the conspiratorial whisperings?' she asked of Arthur.

Arthur threw his hand back from the wrist in dismissal of what was said having set the tray on a round, walnut breakfast table at the foot of the bed. When he had served the tea, he took up the position of watchful nurse in a chair he had pulled over to the bedside.

'It is probably too late now, Charlotte, but tomorrow we will seek out an apothecary and see if we can get something for that cough. I know you have medicines with you, but they don't seem to be making a difference.'

'We will do no such thing, Arthur. Ever since my affair with Ruddock and his blue pills, I am inclined towards caution in terms of who prescribes what for me. Besides, I know what I need to do, rest and some remedies that Mr Teale recommended, and on that note, perhaps you would be so kind as to pass me the bottle of Friar's Balsam from my bag.' The Ruddock affair, Charlotte referred to had happened a few years previously, when William Ruddock, a doctor from Keighley, had prescribed a pill containing mercury to treat what he considered to be a liver complaint, as well as her ongoing depression. Charlotte had a severe reaction to the medicine and suffered a bout of mercury poisoning, which had caused her tongue to swell and become ulcerated. Ruddock had been horrified at the distress caused but Charlotte had reassured him that he was not to blame, allowing him to continue treating Papa as a way of demonstrating a surviving faith in his practice. However, with regards to her own health, since then she had deferred to Teale, the doctor from Leeds who had treated Anne.

'Charlotte, do you honestly think Friar's Balsam is all you need? Perhaps something a little stronger, especially if you feel feverish. I have a bottle of Paregoric Elixir and a packet of Dr James' Fever Powder. It might help you sleep more soundly,' Arthur said, taking a spoon from the tray as he brought her the bottle of Friar's Balsam.

'Well of course you have stronger drugs, you are, after all, so prone to premature death when your desires are checked,' Charlotte said, and laughed, the laugh once more ending in a coughing fit.

'Well, that was how I felt at the time,' Arthur said, his smile indicating a requited amusement.

The couple settled into a mood of still reverie as they consumed their respective nightcaps. Charlotte watched Arthur as he sipped on his sherry, the glass a mere thimble in his hand. She remembered the episode they referred to and how it had aroused in her feelings other than just respect and fondness towards him, a playful tenderness animated their togetherness following the episode. It was towards the end of May and Charlotte had heard from a third party that Arthur had become very thin, almost emaciated, and that they suspected it was his usual complaint of rheumatoid affliction, so then when he wrote to announce his intentions to visit, she expected something spectral to show up. The visit was not convenient as she had so much still to finish before the wedding – at the time she was stitching night and day to finish curtains for what was going to be Arthur's study – but such was her anxiety caused by the report she wished to see the deterioration for herself. The Arthur who arrived at the parsonage was indeed wasted and rather strange looking, his whole manner being nervous, but after gentle inquiry Charlotte concluded that nothing other than impatience for the upcoming nuptials was the cause of his affliction. No touch of rheumatism troubled him, and a consultation with Dr Teale in Leeds had informed him that nothing other than an over-excited mind was the source of his nameless ailment. And yet, at the time, Arthur had protested.

'Charlotte, look at me, I am wasting, I am in danger of disappearing completely, dying you might say for the want of holding you close as my wife. Why is July still so many weeks and weeks away? I cannot last.'

'The dying, Arthur, do not travel fifty miles to announce their imminent departure. You are not about to meet your maker, but you are about to enter a realm where such infantile exaggerations will be duly checked. Expect admonishment for such senseless fretting and wilful nonsense when I am your wife and master. A child of eight, a female one at that, would have more wit. Dying indeed!'

And because they were alone in the parlour, Arthur had swept Charlotte into his arms, holding her tight, so tight that she worried for her ribs, and then he had kissed her deeply and passionately. This childlike longing of his, and the delicious abandon in his lovemaking all combined to create in Charlotte a yearning, and while not perhaps as debilitating as Arthur's clearly was, it was nonetheless an increased enthusiasm for the marriage. Over the remainder of that visit a jovial intimacy energised their courtship as Arthur, whenever he got the opportunity, groaned over the prospects of a few more weeks of bachelorship as if it were a term of imprisonment, while

Charlotte, in reference to the larger portions of dinner she placed before him, joked that she was the witch feeding Hansel so perhaps he should curb his enthusiasm for the release.

And now how robust he was filling the chair he sat in, how manly he looked, how masterfully he had managed everything since the wedding day, and how ironic, Charlotte thought, that it was she who was in need of care.

'I will be better tomorrow, Arthur. Sleep is all I need, that and to finally meet your family. You know how introductions are always a cause of stress for me,' Charlotte said, holding out the empty cup and saucer to him.

Arthur, like the dutiful nurse, helped her get settled under the bedclothes before resuming his watch, assuring her that he would wait until she was sound asleep before he retired for the night.

The room was cold as winter when Charlotte woke some hours later. Arthur slept soundly, so rather than move closer for warmth and risk waking him she rose to get a shawl from her trunk. A light from the street below attracted her attention to the window. The gaslights at intervals around the black mass that was Stephen's Green dotted the darkness in fairy fashion. As her eyes grew accustomed to the night, the buildings, the tree shapes, and even the still water of the lake in the park, came into focus and were further revealed when the clouds parted allowing moonlight to flood the cityscape. Faint clip clopping broke through the silence, the sound rising to a crescendo as the horse and carriage materialised beneath the window and then faded again to quiet as it made its way up the street into nothingness. Apart from the flicker of the lights the scene was corpse still. Charlotte disliked being a lone observer of the night, not because of any fear or suggestion that things were anything other than what they were during light hours, but because her grief, like a leviathan lying beneath the waters of her unquiet soul, fed on her loneliness, grew strong, rose up and broke through the surface. And as this monster of grief opened its jaws, there they were, huddled inside, all her siblings and her mother, the adult faces, ghastly pale and stretched into tortured grimaces, and little Maria and Elizabeth, who still wore the expressions of innocent youth, had they not looked so sad could have been deemed to be angels; but surely angels always smiled.

Charlotte shivered, drew her shawl in closer and was making her way back to the bed when movement from where the washstand was caught her attention. She might have dismissed it for a moth attracted to the reflection of moonlight in the mirror if it had not been for the sound of water being poured into a receptacle. She leaned towards the burble and the gaping empty circle in the stand where the pitcher and basin should have sat. The room became even colder, she could see in the mirror the clouds closing across the moon, and there, there, quick as lightening, there was that movement again, a streak of white that flashed through the darkness. Charlotte wanted to make haste to the bed but found that she was unable to move and in that state of petrification as she gazed at her shady figure in the mirror, she saw it behind her, standing beside the walnut breakfast table, the pitcher in one hand, the other resting on the basin, and the only thing that kept Charlotte from passing out was the resemblance of the child, for child it was, to her little sister, Maria. It spoke.

'Have you seen my sisther, Lady?' it said.

'What's her name?' Charlotte answered, expecting to hear her say, Elizabeth. The child poured water from the pitcher. She rolled up the sleeves of what to Charlotte looked like the dress Maria was wearing when Papa came and took her home from Cowan Bridge; the last time Charlotte saw her older sister. Instead of answering, the little thing began to hum as she washed her hands.

'What is your name?' Charlotte asked, her curiosity and keenness to determine if this was Maria's spirit displacing any horror such an apparition should normally conjure up in the haunted.

'Mary,' the child said, momentarily interrupting her humming.

'Don't you mean, Maria?' Charlotte said, continuing to address the mirror.

'Mary,' the child repeated.

'Maria,' Charlotte said.

'Mary.'

'Maria.'

'Mary.'

'Maria.'

'Charlotte, Charlotte, come back to bed.' It was Arthur. He gently guided her back to the bed, took the shawl from her shoulders and settled her under the covers, and before he had reached his side of the bed, she was once more asleep.

Chapter Twelve

The waiter from the previous evening served their table in the coffee-room the next morning.

'And how ar' we t'day?' he asked.

'Okay, so I think it is going to have to be the broiled herrings for me,' Arthur said, handing him the menu.

'And I will have some eggs and bacon,' Charlotte said, also ignoring the waiter's question.

'Feelin' betther, missus?' the waiter persisted.

Charlotte looked to Arthur for assistance.

'He wonders if you are feeling better,' Arthur explained.

'Yes, actually I am, thank you for asking,' Charlotte said.

'Tha's good so, no sign' of th' lickle one?' he asked.

Even Arthur looked baffled this time.

'Th' ghosth, lickle Mary Masthers lookin' for her sisther?' he said, and without bothering to wait for an answer, he went to the table next to them, asking of the couple there, the same question, 'and how ar' we t'day?'

Despite the dubious articulation of 'ghost', Charlotte understood what he had said, and even though they had not discussed anything about the previous night or what she had witnessed, she knew by Arthur's reaction that he had an awareness of the nocturnal happenings.

'Did you see her, Arthur. The Ghosth?' Charlotte asked, shaking out her napkin and placing it on her knee, as if it was no great consequence whether he did or did not.

'I have been reluctant to make reference to last night, Charlotte, for fear you had no memory of it. When I woke you were standing at the end of the bed, you had moved the pitcher and basin from the washstand and you were shouting out two names, Mary and Maria. It was the shouting that woke me. I think you were sleep walking,' Arthur said.

'But you saw nothing. Thank God. Clearly, I was dreaming, and the fact that my dream presented a 'lickle wan' is sheer coincidence,' Charlotte said, unconvinced by her own logic. Where had the name, Mary, come from? And a ghost? She must have read something about it, perhaps in Forbes. She continued, 'such coincidences, Arthur, give credence to the existence of preternatural occurrences in simple, excitable minds.'

'Neither of which will ever be attributable to you,' Arthur said, and added, 'simple or excitable.'

The waiter returned with a pot of tea and triangles of toasted bread arranged in a silver rack. He made a great production of pouring the tea, during which time he performed a dumb show of raised eyebrows and knowing nods to Charlotte, as much as to say, your secret is safe with me. She returned these looks with a questioning frown of indignation.

'You must tell me more about this dream. And sleep walking. I didn't know I was marrying a somnambulist!' Arthur said.

'Neither did I, although I do recall an incident when I was in Roe Head school where I was told that I had been sleep walking, but I am sure there was only ever that occasion,' Charlotte said, 'I saw my sister, Maria, in my dream and she asked me if I had seen her sister. Our Elizabeth.'

'The sisters I never got to meet. Indeed. How old were they when ...?' Arthur asked.

'Maria was eleven, Elizabeth was ten. Papa had come to

the school that February to take Maria home. That was the last I saw of her. In my dream she was wearing the same dress she wore that day,' Charlotte, as she spoke brought the napkin to her eyes and pressed it there.

'You loved her dearly,' Arthur said, reaching across the table.

'So much, Arthur, she was more than my big sister, since Mama had died, she was my mother, and a kindlier, more protective angel tread not this ground. From the moment she was born, it is my belief that God was just biding his time before he could bring her home. Imagine, Arthur, it only took her eleven years to sanctify her soul in preparedness to meet her maker. Some cannot manage that in eighty or ninety years of terrestrial existence. Her life was one of pure goodness,' Charlotte smiled at Arthur, 'pure goodness.'

'And Elizabeth?' Arthur asked.

'Sweet Elizabeth, so obedient, always behind one of us, our little follower. She too was taken home from the school because of illness, but this time Papa, seeing the similarity to Maria, brought us all home. Two weeks later she died. It was only then, seeing her white smallness in the coffin, that I realised I would never see Maria again. I miss them yet, Arthur,' Charlotte said and reaching across to touch Arthur's hand continued, 'and seeing as how I have managed to deflate your mood, I should stop this sentimental indulgence before you decide to put me and my misery back on the next packet to Holyhead.'

'Quite the opposite, Charlotte, this is exactly what our honeymoon is for, affording us the luxury of having nothing else to do but indulge our every mood so that we can grow to know and understand each other. Although it saddens me to see you sad, I love to hear about your life before my time in Haworth, especially your childhood,' Arthur said, as he leaned back to allow the waiter to place the breakfast before them.

'There ya are now, eggs and rashers for you, and fish for

yerself,' he said, 'can I brang ya more tay?'

'No, thank you, everything looks great,' Arthur said.

'Before you go, can I inquire as to how old this ghost of yours is?' Charlotte asked, troubled by how much younger than Maria or Elizabeth the girl she saw was.

'Roundabou' six, so the' say, poor thing, use' t' live round here. The cholera kilt her, so the' say. That's why she always washes her hands. Cape herself clane, so the' say,' he said, gave a quick bow of his head and was gone.

'Still convinced you were dreaming?' Arthur asked, and winking added, 'or maybe it was the little girl who haunts the hotel, or so the' say.'

His mimicking made Charlotte laugh, and served to lift both their moods, as he smiled and shook his head, indicating an incredulity. Charlotte was content for now to allow Maria and Elizabeth and even Mary Masters return to their realms while she and Arthur got on with their corporeal reality.

'And what have you in store for me today?' she asked.

'Firstly, let's take stock of how you are feeling,' Arthur said, as he spread butter on a triangle of toast.

'Yes, I am feeling rested, and as you may have noticed I have not coughed since we came down. Perhaps if we limit the amount of walking we do, I will survive another day. You are going to have to become accustomed to my short legs and the extra efforts needed to match your stride.'

'Okay, does that mean we can give Sweny's a miss?' Arthur asked.

'Sweny's?'

'Yes, it is an apothecary over near Trinity, and seeing as we are, more or less, going in that direction, I thought it would be convenient,' Arthur said.

Charlotte waited until she had swallowed before saying that she had no need for an apothecary, and in keeping with what she had said the previous night, she would prefer not to have to consult foreign doctors. Before their breakfast was finished, they had decided that they would take a walk in Stephen's Green, get a cab to visit the Botanic Gardens, and at 3pm make their way back to Sackville Street where Arthur had made arrangements to meet his brother by Nelson's Pillar.

Before leaving the hotel, Arthur presented Charlotte with the surprise he had been hoarding in his coat pocket. It was a copy of William Makepeace Thackery's *The Irish Sketchbook, 1842*.

'You probably have read it before, but I thought it would be nice to refer to it as we go along, and of course, I know how much you admire the author. In fact, between him and Wellington, I have Titan shoes to fill if I hope to ever make it to the wall in the parsonage,' Arthur said, referring to the portraits of Wellington and Thackeray that hung in the dining room, alongside Charlotte's own portrait. They had been gifted to her by George Smith, her publisher.

'How thoughtful, Arthur, however Forbes is my preferred reference, Thackeray's wit is so laden with bitter sarcasm, and his opinions so vociferously expressed I fear they may instil his judgements and prejudices in the reader. I would rather be guided by Forbes unbiased narrative,' Charlotte said, retrieving his book from her trunk, 'remember, this one, I told you about it in Bangor.'

'Choosing another over your great hero, Thackeray! There is hope for me yet of making that gallery, it seems the mighty are slipping,' Arthur said, as he buttoned his coat in readiness for their walk.

'Please don't tease me, Arthur.'

Arthur's open mouth stare suggested confusion. He was about to speak but Charlotte interrupted.

'I admire him for his intelligence, he is a writer such as I can never be but having met him on several occasions, I have concluded that he is one to be admired from a distance. I always feel rather stupid in his presence, he is a great one for jesting and I suspect, although I am never quite sure, I suspect that I am often the target of his sarcastic humour,' Charlotte was tying her bonnet as she spoke.

Arthur's expression darkened, 'How dare he make fun of you, give me back that book so that I can fling it from Carlisle Bridge into the Liffey.'

'Stop it, Arthur, now you jest with me, as if you would ever do such a thing, and now that you have changed my humour, I feel I am too tired to walk in the park,' Charlotte said taking off her bonnet, and sitting on the edge of the bed.

Arthur, looking totally confused, knelt before her, his hands on her knees and asked in an imploring tone, 'Charlotte, what is the matter, this is most unlike you, and I am sorry, it was a silly thing to say, it was the idea of him ridiculing you that … I was ignorant of any relationship you might have with Thackeray other than that of admirer,' Arthur asked.

'I admire him greatly, Arthur, but whenever we met, while I wanted to discuss our writing and things literary, I got the impression that his preference was to play to the gallery of the societal sycophants he is constantly surrounded by. These are mostly women, tiresome Duchesses and Marchionesses, affecting an interest in things they have no natural inclination towards, and yet I was the one left feeling small and insignificant.'

'Well, the lesson for me, my dear, is to do my homework more thoroughly when planning surprises. I suppose between the pride of place given to his portrait and the fact that you dedicated the second edition of *Jane Eyre* to him, I assumed. Wrongly,' Arthur said, getting up from his knees, 'come now, put your bonnet on and we will skip the walk and go to the

Botanic gardens,' he said as he helped her off the bed.

A little later as their cab made its way over Carlisle Bridge, they looked knowingly at each other and laughed, restoring the jovial mood from breakfast. Charlotte shared her embarrassment regarding the preface she dedicated to Thackeray. Unbeknownst to her at the time, events of *Jane Eyre* mirrored tragedies in Thackeray's personal life, like Rochester, he too had an insane wife, who, for her own safety he had placed in a secure home. Apparently, the gossip around London at the time was that Jane Eyre was an autobiography and Currer Bell was Thackeray's governess and mistress. Thackeray had had a rough time of it disabusing the tittle tattlers of their conclusions.

'So, you see, even though he said at the time that it was a great honour to have the preface dedicated to him, I believe I had inadvertently sowed the seeds of rancour in his opinion of me,' Charlotte said, and leaning to look out on the expanse of Sackville Street, added, 'and that, Arthur, is enough of time given to vanity affairs. Pun intended. Look at what I am missing. These Dublin streets are finer than any I saw in London; I had no idea that they would be so wide.'

The cab stopped before Nelson's Pillar as Charlotte had instructed the driver, who was the same one who had brought them from Kingstown the previous day. He was dropping off a customer earlier at the hotel as she and Arthur were engaged with the doorman, getting advice on how best to arrange their day's itinerary. Charlotte recognised him, even before he spoke, and she was glad to see him. There was a comical sort of honesty about the fellow that reminded her of John Brown back home.

'Ah, will you look a' who it is, how's th' bark t'day, Missus,' he said, addressing Charlotte, while at the same time pocketing money he had received from the previous customer with one hand and saluting the said customer, in military fashion, with the other hand, 'Hav' a good day, Sir Barth, shure, I'll be seein' you lather on,' he said, addressing him, and then turning back to Charlotte and Arthur added, 'Sir Malby Crofton, soundest gent yous'll ever meet.'

'Indeed,' Arthur said turning back to address the doorman, when Charlotte asked of him, 'de bark?'

'The cough, jaysus, but youse were in a' awful state yestherday, I says to m'self afther I dropped youse off, tha' poor woman needs t' see a docther, but, if you don't mind me sayin', yer lookin' betthar. Nothin' like a good kip ta sort you ou', Shure ther' isn'th?'

Charlotte understood most of what he said, but his words were not important, it was the concern expressed in his voice and in his eyes; the fact that he remembered her, and he took the time to ask after her health; that and his likeness to John Brown, which endeared her to this rather forward, loquacious hackney man. Before Arthur had time to protest, Charlotte had made arrangements with Barney, for that was his name, to be their driver for the day. Arthur had remained silent, perhaps cautioned by the Thackeray matter and the capriciousness of Charlotte's humour.

Sackville Street was as busy as Merrion Street had been the day before, and again to Charlotte's observations, it seemed to be mostly pedestrianised with persons from the ranks of fashionable society. The air here was fresh, there was little of the smoke and smog that was such a feature of London, and the fetid smell of horse droppings that assailed you there was a bare whiff in the Dublin air. Arthur explained that it was one of the few advantages of the lack of industrial progress.

Charlotte had hoped to climb Nelson's Column but its Babelian form decided her against what Arthur had already deemed to be injudicious given her compromised state of health. Instead, they contented themselves to read the engraving on the plinth and admire instead the architecture of the buildings that lined the street, especially the one nearest to them, the General Post Office. Much to both their surprise, Barney, was an encyclopaedia of knowledge on, well, apparently, everything to do with Dublin. Charlotte's increasing fondness for his lack of social etiquette or awareness of boundaries was matched by her increasing amusement at Arthur's impatience, evidenced in the clipped manner of his speech when he addressed him.

'So, as I was sayin' the same fella who built th' pillar, built th' post office, in fact, if ya axe me, he built all th' monstrosithies dotthed abou' the city,' Barney said, twirling his hand as if he was some Prospero conjuring up the buildings.

'Francis Johnson, you say?' Charlotte asked.

'Th' very man, ah now, dont ge' me wrong, clever fella, you know, jus' no' my cuppa tay, made a' awful daub of th' area over by Grangegorman. Nuts n' bolts squire is wha' we call i',' he said, 'Ican go tha' way to th' botanicals if youse like, if youse wanna see wha' I mane.'

Charlotte, whose ear was becoming accustomed to Barney's Dublin brogue but not always his understanding, asked, 'Nuts and bolts squire?'

Before Barney got a chance to respond Arthur interjected, 'I am presuming you are referring to the square with the penitentiaries, workhouses and lunatic asylums?'

'Tha's them,' Barney said.

Arthur explained to Charlotte that it would take them out of their way and besides, it would also take them through some of the more squalid and dangerous parts of the city.

'And what makes you think that it is only the shining city I have eyes for, Arthur? There is more danger lurking behind the smug smiles of snobbishness than there is behind the weary grimace of poverty,' she said.

'So?' Barney asked.

'You can take us the longer way,' Arthur said, and perhaps to reclaim some mastery over the situation added, 'but there will be no stopping.'

On their way, Arthur revealed his familiarity with the area. He recounted how his Aunt Harriette's Uncle, the Revd Arthur Smyth Adamson, was attached to St Paul's parish in the same area and was the chaplain to the house of industry.

'When I was in my student days in Trinity, I often visited with him and I became interested in his chaplaincy work, especially the visitations to the various institutions in the area, including the female penitentiary,' Arthur said.

'And does he remain in the area?' Charlotte asked, 'perhaps we should call on him.'

'No. Unfortunately he died before I had finished my studies,' Arthur said.

'Of course, if he was Aunt Harriette's uncle, he must have been a fine age,' Charlotte said, 'such a shame, I should have liked to ask him all about his dealings with the downtrodden.'

'I would have liked you to meet him, you would have enjoyed his feisty, opinionated manner,' Arthur said, dropping his chin towards his chest, closing the discussion. But Charlotte's curiosity had been tweaked.

'Tell me about your experiences in the female penitentiary. How did their misery affect you; did you see their plight as hopeless?' There was an ebullience in her voice, which was not indicative of a ghoulish disposition but rather her interest in female suffering and struggle, however that struggle manifested itself.

Arthur explained how he came to be allowed to accompany the Reverend on visits to the penitentiary.

'There was a lot of talk going about then about moral

reform and the rehabilitating benefit of instructing the inmates on religious matters. From what I saw and heard, Charlotte, it was not Bible study these poor women needed, it was a means of making money,' Arthur said.

'Oh, Arthur, that has always been my contention, whenever I hear of a woman committing a crime, be it larceny or worse, I am in no doubt that there is a gaping mouth or mouths waiting for her to return home with food,' Charlotte said.

'It broke my heart to hear their stories, and yes, "want" was the root of their crime, want of an education that could free them from impoverishment,' Arthur said, and turning towards Charlotte continued in a more effusive manner, 'but, you know, incarceration was not always such an ordeal for them, they were fed and sheltered, and I believe that the head matron there, a Mrs Rawlins was a positive influence.'

'Tell me about the saddest case you encountered,' Charlotte said.

'Charlotte, do I detect a ghoul in you, we are on our honeymoon, on our way to the most splendid gardens in the entire world, and perhaps, all this talk of destitution is matter for another day.'

'Don't be absurd, Arthur, female survival is an appropriate topic of conversation regardless of circumstance, in fact, one might argue that a honeymoon is the most opportune occasion for such debate,' Charlotte said, and turning away from Arthur, she could see that they were passing the very penitentiary that they spoke of.

It was an impressive grey stone building, with a rather majestic looking clock tower rising from its centre, and yet to Charlotte's eyes it was the heavy iron doors and barred windows that dominated the façade. It reminded her of when she visited Newgate Prison the previous year with George Smith. She approached one of the inmates, a young, tall girl, who reminded her of Emily and taking her by both hands asked how she came to be there. The girl said she thought maybe it was because she had eaten too much food for her stomach had grown so big of late. Charlotte recalled how her face, a protrusion of bone beneath tautly stretched skin betrayed her alibi, she wanted to hear more about her life, but the warder had interrupted her saying that visitors were not allowed to speak to the prisoners. Later George had told her that the girl's crime was infanticide.

'Arthur, be proud that you took the time to come and speak to the poor wretches, I am sure that regardless of what you said, your kind face was succour to their troubled minds,' Charlotte said, taking his hand and bringing the back of it to her cheek, then kissing it before placing it back on his lap. There was a sense of mutual understanding in the easy silence that marked the remainder of the journey up the Phibsborough Road to the Botanic Gardens.

Chapter Thirteen

Barney, having tied the horse to the railing, turned to face the Bell Nicholls, his fists embedded in his sides, his chest pigeoned forward, the poise of one about to launch into an authoritative delivery. He got as far as, 'Well, now, here yous ar' ...', when Arthur interrupted.

'So, Barney, my good man, I am going to suggest that you be back in approximately two hours, as that should give us ample time to view the gardens and perhaps avail of some refreshments. We have arranged to meet some others at three o'clock back at Nelson's Pillar, so let me see, does that leave enough time for the return journey,' Arthur said as he took his gold watch from his pocket and examined it.

Charlotte smiled. It was the one presented to him on the occasion of his leaving Haworth over a year previously. She was glad that he was using it. Papa, had resented the presentation, considering it a reward for petulance, which was how he viewed Arthur's resignation. And when he learned of their wedding plans, he jibed about how he should take the gold fob watch back and keep it safe until Arthur made his next bolt for freedom. Charlotte, vexed at his childish response, and the implied doubt as to the success of the marriage, had scolded him, reminding him that he ought, firstly, to be grateful that Arthur, the best curate the parish ever had, was returning, and secondly, that he should place more faith in her ability to choose wisely in marital matters.

'Plenthy a' time,' Barney said, also consulting a timepiece he had taken from his trousers pocket, his exaggerated display of it with his extended arm indicating either a difficulty with his vision, or an attempt not to be outdone by Arthur.

'Splendid,' Arthur said, and Charlotte added, 'Enjoy your afternoon, Barney.'

Having signed the visitors' book and read the rules of entry the couple made their way along a gravelled path, lined with the most remarkable trees Charlotte had ever seen. Arthur bought a guide book, and as they walked towards a range of curvilinear glass buildings which reminded Charlotte of Crystal Palace, he was reading aloud from it the history of the place. He read how the site had been the demesne of the poet Tickell.

'Tickell?' Charlotte asked.

Arthur shrugged and continued to read.

Charlotte was not listening; her mind was still clouded with thoughts for the women back in the penitentiary and of that woman she had encountered in Newgate. It did not feel entirely just that one female should walk freely amidst the exotic plants imported from all corners of the empire, while another awaited transportation to those same corners. Her head hurt as she endeavoured to find a neat answer to the conundrum.

'And so here we are at what is called the Octagon house, oh, I see we must wait our turn,' Arthur said, as he and Charlotte stepped aside for a group of students, judging by the notebooks and pencils they carried. A tall, distinguished looking gentlemen who appeared to oversee the troop, thanked the Nicholls, explaining that they were indeed medical students taking a break from the theory of the lecture hall to witness the reality of nature.

Charlotte, enviously watched the all-male throng enter,

chattering noisily amongst themselves, and reminded of the prohibition of women from universities she no longer felt as removed from the plight of the female convicts. Entering the building, she was immediately struck by the overpowering heat and the gargantuan height of some of the trees and plants. Arthur too noted the change in temperature, judging by the fanning actions he made with the guidebook. At first, Arthur continued to read the notes as they both enthusiastically bent towards the specimens, read the labels, admired the colours and the textures, marvelled at the foreign origins of much of the species, and careful not to touch as much as a leaf, as instructed in the rules, breathed in deeply, filling their lungs with the perfumed air. However, it did not take long for the wonder of it all to exhaust Charlotte.

'Arthur, do you think, instead of following this handbook of yours in exact fashion, we should perhaps choose the areas we are particularly interested in viewing. I am quite amazed at the vastness of the place, I expected something on a smaller scale,' Charlotte said, as she took the book Arthur had extended to her before she had finished speaking.

'I agree entirely, you choose, although, I do think we ought to make it our business to see this Amazonian water-lily which is making the headlines,' Arthur said.

'And as it so happens that is next on the list here in the Aquarium house,' Charlotte said, placing her finger under the heading for Arthur's perusal.

The Aquarium comprised of a large rectangular pond of water in the centre and then some smaller tanks in the corners. In the centre tank green lily pads of fantastical proportions, hovered on the surface of the water. Charlotte felt threatened by the enormity of them and was about to tell Arthur that she had to leave, when a gentleman, not unlike how Charlotte remembered Mr Dickens, on that single occasion of their meeting in London, approached the couple, suggesting that it must be a huge disappointment that they could not witness Victoria Regis in bloom. Charlotte, who had not even been aware of the giant lily's name, and never one to dissemble, answered him saying that on the contrary, as she had no prior knowledge that such a plant existed, she had harboured no expectations. He said that due to the late finishing of the house in May they had not been able to get it in on time. Arthur remained listening to the gentleman as he continued to speak knowledgeably about recent additions to the aquarium and how the Society was so indebted to donations from a certain gentleman in Jamaica. Charlotte tuned out as soon as she heard Jamaica, her thoughts wandering to Bertha Mason and her brother, her fictional creations in *Jane Eyre*. She was still lost in her fantasy world when she noticed a small boy staring into a tank in the corner. There was nothing of particular note about him other than the fact that he seemed to be unaccompanied by any adult, a breach of a rule they had read on admission. Curiosity brought her towards him. On closer examination she remarked how sickly he looked; the pallor of his skin suggested a young life lived out of the sunlight. Without looking at her, but perhaps sensing her presence he spoke.

'You will have to come back tonight if you wish to see the flowers,' he said.

'I beg your pardon,' Charlotte said, as a very peculiar feeling washed over her; it was as if she knew this child, his voice sounded so familiar. Was it that he sounded like Emily when she was young?

'Nymphaea Blanda and Nymphaea Nocturna, the flowers only come out at night. Is not that a rather distinctive thing?' the child said, pointing to water lilies that shivered, almost imperceptibly, on the water.

'Indeed,' Charlotte said, struggling to think of something

else to say to keep this strange child engaged; later, she regretted that all she could think to say was to enquire as to the whereabouts of his parents, she knew it sounded somewhat admonishing. The boy turned and stared at her, his eyes dull and red-rimmed, his brow creasing into an adultlike expression of disdain, he made as if to walk away from her but stumbled and was caught by a rather burly looking gentleman. An elegantly dressed lady rushed forward, thanking the gentleman for his attentiveness, and addressing the child, said, 'Bram, you know you must not attempt to walk unaided, to do so is folly, come along now, I think we've seen enough for today.'

'Charlotte, that was no other than Mr Moore, the Curator of the gardens,' it was Arthur who had re-joined her.

'Don't be silly, Arthur, he's but a boy,' Charlotte said.

'No, dear, the man we were speaking with, such an interesting fellow, he tells me that most of the plants here, like those Pitcher plants you see there,' he said, pointing to another tank of lilies, 'have come from Africa and Australia, and that he in turn sends out plants to them. He is concerned that the emigrant vessels used for the transportations are not ideal as they are so overcrowded, and the plants and seeds need special care on the long sea voyages, preferably under the care of a sur-geon. Isn't that fascinating? This man speaks of them as if they were important people,' Arthur said, and taking the handbook back from Charlotte, he flicked some pages and continued, 'ah, here we are, Mr Moore tells me that the top attraction this summer has been the new Museum of Economic Botany, and he strongly advises that we include it in our itinerary.'

Charlotte looked at Arthur rather as if she was looking into him, searching his soul, and after some moments she said, 'Sometimes, Arthur, I have no words.'

'Hmmm?' was all Arthur said in reply.

'The plants on an emigrant ship need a surgeon? I have

never heard anything so preposterous, so odious, so, language fails me, so lacking in morality. I wonder if those in positions of influence have as much concern for the humans who travel the seas, most often against their will or better judgements. I have read about your coffin ships. And those poor souls back in the penitentiary, who deliberates on their potential need for surgeons? Yes, Nature ought to be revered after a pantheistic fashion, but perhaps humanity should leave natural habitats alone, perhaps, just perhaps, we can admire the beauty as it is depicted in books, why must we always feel the need to up-root things, transplant them, and expect them to thrive just the same.' Charlotte's tirade, for that is what it was, brought on a fit of coughing, but it did not deter her from continuing, 'I care nothing for these labels, with their unpronounceable, scientific classifications, and I cannot think of anything more tedious than a museum of the same.'

'Gosh,' Arthur replied, 'I am a little lost for words myself as to how to respond.'

Charlotte looked up at him, and seeing the bewilderment worry its way into the creases of his cheeks, she sighed audibly.

'I am sorry, Arthur, it's this heat in here, and maybe the mention of pitcher reminding me of my strange dreams last night, and that stranger child I have just been speaking to, I believe I just need to get some air,' she said, and taking the still perplexed looking Arthur by the hand she led him back out the door they had entered through.

Having sat for some time on one of the many benches that lined the pathway, they leafed through the handbook and decided that the only house worth a visit was that housing the ferns and orchids, Charlotte agreeing with the author of the handbook, none other than the same Mr Moore of earlier, that the beauty captured in tropical flowers was the most manifest representation of Godly design in nature. Once again, they encountered a group of students, this time they were from the Government School of Art, who circled in front of various flowers, their heads rising as they gazed at the displays and then lowering to their sketch pads where they made slow, meticulous strokes with their pencils. Charlotte wished she had some materials so that she could join in the activity.

'I have been known to sketch and paint flowers,' she said, 'but, nothing so exotic as tropical orchids.'

'We must get you some supplies, Charlotte, there will be far more exotic, indigenous flowers to capture in the fields and laneways of Ireland,' Arthur said.

'I do have some pencils with me, but, yes, I would very much like that, Arthur. Do not expect anything spectacular, my skills amount to rude portrayals of wild roses and pansies,' Charlotte said, as a self-effacing smile played about her eyes.

'Sounds delightful, just like you,' Arthur said.

Barney was standing where they had left him when they returned, and again he greeted them as one would do a dear, old acquaintance. Charlotte enquired as to his favourite part of the garden and was surprised to discover that he had never been.

'You see, when it doesn't ope' on Sathurdays or Sundhays, I'm never not workin' t' be able t' go,' he said.

'I wouldn't worry too much, Barney, if I were you, I am sure there are other important activities that occupy your leisure. These gardens are quite overrated, in my opinion,' Charlotte said, as she climbed into the carriage.

'A woman afther me own heart, a rose be any other name, an' all tha' as th' great man himself writ',' Barney said, closing the carriage door.

Charlotte whispered to Arthur, 'Shakespeare no less.'

'Indeed, there you go, and you thought we were an uncultured lot,' Arthur said, and winked.

The journey back to the city centre was faster as they followed a more direct route by the North Circular road and Dorset Street before turning down Frederick Street, past the Rotunda lying-in hospital, and back on to Sackville Street. Charlotte had so many questions that she would like to have asked about the relatives she was about to meet, but instead, exhausted from the morning's exertions, she drifted to sleep, waking to the sound of Barney's voice announcing that they were at the Pillar.

A young woman, her wide smile animating her entire face ran and to Charlotte's observations seemed to leap into Arthur's arm, and as he spun her around it appeared that were she to let go of the grasp she had around his neck, she was likely to go flying up towards Nelson. The men who accompanied her looked on in bemused delight. The younger of the two stepped towards Charlotte and extended his hand.

'Hello, Charlotte, I am Joseph, and that circus animal is my sister, Mary Anna,' he said, stepping aside to allow the other gentleman to introduce himself.

'Allen, Arthur's brother, it is such a delight to finally meet you, how has your journey so far been?' he said.

In the meantime, Arthur had brought Mary Anna back to earth, and she, taking him by the hand approached Charlotte.

'And now it is my turn, Arthur you must do the introductions,' she said, beaming at Charlotte, who thought her to possess the most pleasant face she had ever seen.

'Charlotte, this giddy goat is my little cousin, Mary Anna, whom I'm afraid sometimes forgets that she is no longer the child I donkeyed around on my back. Miss Bell, allow me to introduce Mrs Bell Nicholls,' he said.

'Pleased to meet you, Miss Bell, but I am sure we will both be more comfortable with Charlotte and Mary Anna,' Charlotte said, holding out her hand.

'Yes, of course, Arthur is a goose, Charlotte. You look so pretty, your dress is beautiful and very fitting for the trip you have just had to the Botanic gardens. Such delicate flowers,' she said, trailing a finger over Charlotte's sleeve, 'Did you enjoy it there? I have never been, nor have I been to the zoological gardens. I am not overly fond of seeing things in cages and glasshouses. I prefer the bog lanes. I will bring you on these walks when we get home. Oh, I am talking too much. It is so good to meet you. I have read all your books—' Allen, Arthur's brother interrupted, 'Mary Anna, Charlotte and Arthur are going to be with us for many days, you do not need to assuage the entirety of your curiosities in one fell swoop.'

Charlotte had to stop herself from saying, Macbeth, in reference to the expression, 'fell swoop', which she thought was rather an unfortunate usage of the phrase as in the play it was how Macduff responded to the news that his entire family had been slaughtered, '… all my pretty chickens, and their dam, at one fell swoop', but she had enough propriety to understand from this briefest of introductions, that the choice of expression was of no import, there was a spontaneity about the group gathered around her that suggested the Bell family did not interact with each other in a formal, measured way, and already she was liking their easy, relaxed style.

'Thank you,' Charlotte said to Mary Anna, pointing to her sleeve by way of indicating that the gratitude was for the complimentary comment on her dress.

Mary Anna linked Charlotte and led her away from the men, 'Come along, Charlotte, we can chatter as we walk to lunch and these men can follow as our servants, I'm sure their conversations will be too tedious and meaningless for our ears,' she said and laughed gaily at the three males, whose shaking heads and smiles of endearment expressed a great love for their relative. As they walked, Charlotte noted from the rhythmical tug on her elbow that Mary Anna walked with a limp.

As the small gathering crossed Carlisle Bridge, Allen insisted that everyone stop and slowly turn a full circle to take in what he deemed to be the most spectacular view of the city. As they looked east where the Liffey made its way out to sea, Allen pointed out the Custom House, and probably because of his shipping background seemed to delight in asking them to note how little water could be seen around that area because of the ships and other vessels that teemed the river. Although the vessels were of considerable size, the enormity of the Custom House reduced them to mere leisure boats. Charlotte could see that there were four statues on top of the building but could not make them out from where they stood.

'Which four deities guard the scene?' she asked in general, adding, 'I am presuming they are of Classical origin, judging by the architecture.' Arthur smiled a proud approval and looked to Allen for an answer.

'Indeed, they are, and quite fittingly too; Neptune, Plenty, Industry and Mercury, and if you care to look back down Sackville Street, you can see that Mercury, with his purse, also stands guard on top of the Post Office, along with Hibernia and Fidelity. Is it any wonder that commerce flourishes in the city?' Allen said.

At the mention of Mercury, Charlotte and Arthur exchanged knowing looks, and they both simultaneously looked to the ground to hide their shared amusement. However, the moment did not escape Mary Anna's constant regard of Charlotte.

'I see there is a private understanding between our newlyweds, perhaps an association with one of our stony gods?' Mary Anna asked.

Arthur looked to Charlotte, his raised eyebrows seeking a permission of sorts, and as the slight tilt of her head and coy smile suggested accord, he said, 'Charlotte has a tale to tell regarding mercury which I am sure she will be happy to share with you some other time,' and addressing Charlotte, said, 'perhaps, a cautionary tale that Aunt Harriette might also be interested in hearing.'

'Oh, now you tease me as I shall have to wait until we are home,' Mary Anna said.

'If I may continue with my guided tour from the bridge?' Allen asked, and without waiting for an answer directed their gaze south of the bridge towards Westmoreland Street, the direction they would shortly be headed.

Charlotte's attention stayed on the façade of Trinity College even though Allen had moved on to discuss the east portico of the Bank of Ireland. They were due to visit it the following day and she was aware of Arthur's impatient anticipation to introduce her to his Alma Mater, and the great pride he harboured in being one of its alumni. She had not expected so impressive a building and rather than fill her heart with admiration for her husband, she remembered the group of male students in the Botanic Gardens as her female heart sank in envy. But it was difficult to dwell for any length on sombre matters when there was a Mary Anna to gently pull you closer to the balustrade in order to better see the Wellington Testimonial that rose above the trees of the Phoenix Park on the western limits of the view.

'Arthur has told me of your great allegiance to our Duke of Wellington,' Mary Anna said, 'isn't that right, Arthur, I myself am indifferent to most military but—', here she interrupted her sentence with a weary sigh, 'in these unromantic times, even a dead hero is still a hero.'

'You are incorrigible, Mary Anna, I pity the poor man who is unfortunate enough to take you as a wife.' It was her brother, Joseph who spoke, and the playful slap Mary Anna gave his arm indicated to Charlotte their endearing fondness for each other.

'Charlotte, I would suggest a closer inspection of the memorial, for such it now is, but I fear you would be rather disappointed, it not being a very elegant affair, and besides the proposed equestrian statue of the Duke has yet to be added, so really all that is to be seen is a towering lump of granite,' Allen said, and Joseph added, 'Methinks, dear cousin, it is a statue of Mercury that is needed in order to raise the funds.'

'Clever quip,' Arthur said as they all laughed.

Taking one more glance down towards the Four Courts, allowing her gaze to pan the skyline of spires and domes and the elegant bridges that decoratively spanned the river, Charlotte understood why it was considered to be the most majestic cityscape in all of Europe. The Classical architecture that columned the quays and the streets, winging the Liffey, gave her a sense that she could be in any great city of the ancient or modern world.

The walk down Westmoreland Street to the Tavern on College Green where they were headed was, for Charlotte, much longer and more arduous than Allen's description of it as a short stroll from the bridge. Although Mary Anna's gay spirits were infectious, Charlotte's energy was sagging and had she been given a preference she would have preferred to return by cab to their hotel.

Anderson's Royal Arcade Hotel, for so it was called according to the menu, was a crowded spot, the majority of the clientele were clustered groups of young men, all versions of Joseph. Arthur explained that its proximity to the college made it a popular place for students. Charlotte was pleased that everyone ordered mutton broth and breads from the Lunch menu, allowing her lack of appetite to go unnoticed, she had feared that the advanced stage of the afternoon would be deemed to be dinner time.

As the men chatted about current affairs from the papers and Joseph brought Arthur up to date on college matters, Charlotte found it impossible to concentrate on Mary Anna's chatter as her ear tuned in to recognisable content. When Joseph asked if Arthur had read the latest edition of the University Magazine, her interest peaked, and she found it impossible to refrain from commentary.

'It was Arthur who introduced the parsonage to that publication, and ever since it has become a favourite whenever we can get hold of a copy. We are not subscribers, neither is our local Mechanics Institute, so regrettably our access is unfortunately rather sporadic,' Charlotte said, as she placed a hand on Mary Anna's arm which could have been interpreted as an apology for interrupting her account of when her mama was presented to Queen Charlotte, or a more cynical eye might have viewed it as an indication that this Charlotte had heard enough about the royal introduction.

Undeterred by the touch, Mary Anna took up the new subject, and assured Charlotte that their house was 'falling down' with back copies of the Dublin University Magazine as every male in the family had attended, or was currently attending Trinity College, so she could have a gay time reading them over the course of her stay. Arthur told them about how Charlotte had two of her publications reviewed in the magazine and Charlotte added how pleased she had been on both occasions at the generosity of the reviewers who favoured her work, and that of her sisters.

'Have you read the stories of Sheridan Le Fanu, Charlotte?' Mary Anna asked, 'he is my absolute favourite, he writes ghost stories, that these brave fellows here pretend to scorn but secretly they believe every horrific detail. Don't say it is otherwise, especially you, Arthur, I have heard you talk about one of them to Mama.'

'The story Mary Anna alludes to was in the magazine a few years ago if memory serves me correctly, it was part of a collection called, *Ghost Stories of Chapelizod*, and the only reason I brought it to Aunt Harriette's attention was because in one story, Le Fanu uses the expression, "that bangs Banagher", and we had great sport debating the possible origins of the phrase and how it became the more common idiom of "that beats Banagher and Banagher beats the divil".'

'Ghost stories no less,' was all Charlotte said. Joseph, the youngest present, but the most serious, perhaps intuiting a note of disdain in her tone, said that he would bring the latest edition the next day for Charlotte as he thought its content would be more pleasing to her.

'The poetry section, Midsummer with the Muses, has some delightful stuff,' he said.

Charlotte nodded and returned his smile, she liked this young cousin with his grave expression. She imagined that this was how Arthur may have looked when a younger man.

Before the group dispersed plans were made to meet the following day at the gates of Trinity. Allen listed the many places they ought to visit and suggested that he could also organise a cruise of Dublin Bay as part of the itinerary, as his position as Manager of the Grand Canal meant he had many influential connections amidst the waterways fraternity.

Charlotte and Arthur walked back to the Shelbourne, on Charlotte's insistence, even though she was feeling weak, and again, as was the case the previous evening, she suspected the onset of a fever, but she believed that the walk was needed to clear her head. Arthur began to suggest ideas for their night's entertainment, naming theatres and societies and parks as if reciting a litany from a prayer book. Charlotte could only think of how little more of Dublin she wished to see at that point and how much she needed to lie down and sleep, and a niggling concern that twitched at the base of her neck was how she was going to cope in Banagher if all of Arthur's relatives proved to be as lively and talkative as his brother, Allen, and his cousin, Mary Anna. Lovely people though they were, theirs was an animation she could never match.

Chapter Fourteen

Although there were no more spectral visitations, howsoever imaginary or not, Charlotte did not have a good night, her cough preventing her from sleep of more than twenty- or thirty-minutes duration. Arthur was a vigilant nurse, who spent the night in a chair, dozing when she slept but becoming alert again when the first notes of what was now a hacking sound fractured the silence. The window-framed dappled skyline that heralded the morn, despite how she physically felt, gave Charlotte a sense of strange delight, not because of any macabre doubts against surviving the night, but because, they had agreed that they would bring the Dublin stay to a premature end, which meant this would be their last full day there. Although apprehensive of the unknown that awaited her in Banagher, this city was for Charlotte as considerable a metropolis as what she termed the great Babylon that was London, and thus was equally, utterly exhausting. Yes, she liked to see the architectural wonders and have that sense of being physically present, but depictions in sketches and paintings afforded her the same pleasure, and besides, the memory of a place held a greater gratification than the actuality of being there, the Wordsworthian emotions recollected in tranquillity justifying the efforts; alas, the efforts of the previous days seemed to be beyond her physical abilities, so rather than mar the entire honeymoon, mutual accord had been reached.

'Good morning, my Dear, I am wondering if even the sightseeing decided on for today is a good idea. I can go now and make arrangements for travelling today and pass on our apologies to Allen?' Arthur said, as he leaned over and stroked her hand, before taking it to his lips. The previous evening, following their decision to go to Banagher on Friday as opposed to the original plan of Monday, Arthur had left Charlotte in the hotel and walked across the city to Allen's house to discuss alternative arrangements. The original plan had been that Charlotte and Arthur would stay with Allen and the cousins for the weekend and then, as organised by Allen, in his role as Manager of the Grand Canal Company they would travel by boat to Banagher. Charlotte had been looking forward to that trip as the thoughts of tugging along at near walking pace on inland waterways was so much more comforting that the rattle of metal that reverberated through every bone and sinew, and considering how she was feeling, even the thoughts of that jolting sensation was a cause of anguish and pain. But Arthur had pointed out that the relatively short journey by train was the preferred option, as his priority now was to get Charlotte home where he knew Aunt Harriette's skills in the sick room far surpassed his. To attenuate Charlotte's disappointment, Allen had sent notice that he would make sure to organise a boat trip on the Shannon before they left Banagher.

'No, no, once I have had some breakfast, I have no doubt that I will rally, and this bleached, broken thing you now look upon will be replaced by your wife; ruddy faced and eager to, "Once more unto the breach, Dear friends ...",' Charlotte said, raising a clenched fist into the air before bringing the same fist to her mouth to catch a cough.

'Hmm?' Arthur looked confused.

'*Henry V*? Shakespeare? Never mind, what say you to asking for breakfast to be brought to the room, what is it with you Irish and the loquacity of mealtime, I have never known dining rooms to be quite so noisy, it is a wonder how any food is ever consumed,' Charlotte said, pointing to her shawl on the end of the bed, which Arthur duly reached for and wrapping it around her shoulders, he used their proximity to gently hold her against his chest.

'Your knowledge astounds me, Charlotte, and yes, of course, room service is a capital idea,' Arthur said, placing a kiss on her brow.

As the walk from the Shelbourne to the gates of Trinity College was not that long, Charlotte insisted that there was no need to hire a cab, an insistence she later regretted, as it surely contributed to her sagging energy. Arthur's relatives were waiting at the allocated spot, and it cheered Charlotte to see Mary Anna waving vigorously as soon as they came into her sights; there was an infectious quality to her youthful zest that had lifted Charlotte's spirit the previous day, despite her exhaustion from the tour of the Botanic gardens. Joseph and Allen bowed a greeting, their demure gesture contrasting with Mary Anna's immediate possession of Charlotte, looping her arm as they went through the gates.

'Dear Charlotte, you will not believe this, but at some point yesterday I must have snagged my hem on the cobbles, and I fear if I do not catch it in time the entire thing will be trailing the dust before long. After this visit we must go to Cannock and White to buy some thread,' Mary Anna said.

Charlotte bent her head slightly to examine the dress.

'Oh, no, it is not this one, I dare not risk it unravelling before the repairs,' Mary Anna said, 'I believe the men have some business of their own to attend, travel arrangements or religious matters, I presume, so we will have the wonderful luxury of time to ourselves in the store. Do you too love to touch all the wonderful fabrics from around the world, it is often the highlight of my excursions here, Mama has accused me of deliberately tearing my dresses in order to occasion my trips to the haberdashery. Silly Mama.' Mary Anna giggled and squeezed Charlotte's arm.

Charlotte was reminded of her trip to the dressmakers in Halifax earlier in the year and the ordeal it was trying to decide on the materials, including her wedding dress. When the finished garments arrived at the parsonage, they remained in the package they had come in for days, as the very thought of pulling the cord off the box, never mind unwrapping them and trying them on, was of complete disinterest to her. As she had bought four dresses on that occasion for her trousseau, she had hoped to have seen the last of draperies for some time. She was about to share this with Mary Anna when Joseph interrupted.

'Seeing as I am the most contemporary in this trinity of Trinity students before you, we have decided that I should be your tour guide. Correct?' Joseph said, addressing the question to Arthur and Allen, who smiled indulgently at him.

'I think you will find, ladies, that our cousin, despite his youth, and tendency to overstate, is the most eloquent among us, and seeing as his knowledge is fresh, he has been unanimously selected by the aforementioned triumvirate,' Arthur said, deliberately affecting the voice of the master of ceremonies. Everyone laughed, including Charlotte, who was genuinely amused by the charade.

The party entered the college grounds through an octagon vestibule. The Corinthian aspect of the front entrance gave Charlotte the sense of entering a Roman Forum or Greek Agora, and, had the plethora of students who roamed the expansive square worn togas as opposed to what looked to be a uniform black suit, the picture would have been complete. It pleased her that Arthur and his relatives were part of this space, and a thrill of pride stirred her heart as she thought of how her Papa had also once been part of an equally, auspicious, academic setting. Their first visit was to the chapel, as Joseph, who, Charlotte had previously noted, did have a rather pious intonation to his speech, suggested that some moments for private prayer would be an appropriate, official, commencement to their itinerary.

The exterior of the chapel presented as a rigid block of stony perpetuity and to Charlotte seemed more parliament than church-like in design. The vastness of the interior, the air heavy with the aroma of polished oaks, the windows of the chancel reaching to the heavens was dizzying, and Arthur, ever watchful and gaining in expertise at interpreting every slight change in Charlotte's physiognomy, perhaps reading there her sense of being overwhelmed, took the opportunity to reclaim her from Mary Anna, and led her to a pew where they sat side by side in silence. Charlotte was in no mood for prayer, there was a masculine whiff to the place that felt oppressive, so unlike the chapel at home with its vases of flowers and soft cushions.

'Arthur, Mary Anna wishes to bring me shopping for thread later. How am I to refuse?' she whispered to Arthur, keeping her head bowed as if in prayer.

'Would you like to go? Perhaps it would be more pleasant than waiting in the hotel alone while Allen and I arrange rail tickets, but if you would rather not I can object on your behalf, my concern for your health will be my reasoning,' Arthur said, also whispering and feigning prayer.

'Thank you,' Charlotte murmured, laying her hand briefly against his thigh, causing Arthur to stir a little in his seat, a movement that did not go unnoticed and occasioned a contented smile to flit about her lips.

Before they left the chapel, Joseph, in hushed tones had delivered the history of the place, with much pointing to the ceiling, the organ, the semi-circular windows, with expansive talk of organ case designs, architects, and stuccodores. His encyclopaedic knowledge and the litany of names and dates that wove through his narrative impressed Charlotte, but as she stared at the ceiling to admire the plasterwork, her head titled at an awkward angle, she began to feel dizzy, and without giving any warning to the group she rushed to the door for air. Once it was established that her health was not in any grave danger, Arthur joked that perhaps it was the Roman Catholic persuasion of the stuccodore, Michael Stapleton, decorating a Church of Ireland ceiling that prompted the near faint. The implication of bigotry annoyed Charlotte, however, as she was not yet fully at ease with the company, she confined her annoyance to a pained grimace surreptitiously directed at Arthur.

As they crossed the quadrangle towards the library, the bell rang out from the campanile, and Joseph stopped their progress so that he could give an account of its provenance.

'And so you see, even though it was only positioned here last year, superstitions have already abounded that the unfortunate Fellow, Pensioner, Sizar, whoever, caught underneath it as it rings is doomed to fail his exams,' Joseph said, once more leading the way across the square.

'Pity it wasn't there in your time, Allen, it would have been the perfect excuse,' Arthur said, as he playfully patted Allen on the back.

'My inconsiderate brother, ladies, is referring to the fact that I did not graduate from the college, because I wished to pursue business matters that did not require any degree in any faculty,' Allen said, and continued in the same jovial tone, 'which is why I will one day be a rich man and these two religious fanatics will be as poor as the mice in the churches they work in.'

Charlotte was bewildered at the absence of any sense of slight in Allen's demeanour at what she considered to be

Arthur's betrayal regarding his failure at college, surely that was a cause of shame for him and the family.

'Touché, Mr Nicholls, touché,' Arthur said with a feigned sigh, 'but who needs gold coins when there are greater treasures to be found in those same churches.'

'Charlotte, pay no heed to these men, I am afraid you will have to get used to their cruel jibing ways, which they refer to as brotherly banter,' Mary Anna said.

'You misread my expression, I am bewildered as to these treasures Arthur has found, very much hoping that I am not considered to be one of them,' Charlotte said, deliberately dissembling as she realised that to state her thoughts would be to reveal her judgement on Allen's incomplete education.

Joseph stopped once more as they reached the doors to the library continuing 'in medias res' fashion having been clearly oblivious to the good-humoured exchanges taking place behind his back.

'... and that is why it is called Parliament Square. So, here we are, in Library Square where the pièce de résistance is about to be unfolded. Follow me,' Joseph said.

'Do what the man says, look lively,' Arthur said as they entered, and it was very clear to Charlotte that Joseph's youthful enthusiasm and conspicuous pride in his college was endearingly indulged by his older cousins, and sister, an opinion confirmed by Mary Anna leaning towards Charlotte and whispering, 'such a dear boy.'

They entered the library through double doors, and there it was in all its oak-partitioned, balustraded, Corinthian pillared glory, the many thousands of tomes nestling on closely placed shelves, guarded by the white, marble busts of great philosophers, historians and poets watching from their pedestaled perches at the end of each partition. Joseph was again a fountain of knowledge, as he spoke eloquently about the collections, the most valuable being the bequest of Archbishop Usher. As they walked the length of the Long Room, so called for obvious reasons, he went into detail about a collection known as the Fagel collection which had been brought from the Netherlands by the family to prevent it being destroyed during the Napoleonic wars. Charlotte, whose attention had been waning as she wished to sit down, perked up slightly at the mention of Napoleon, but as Joseph went on to recount how the college acquired the collection for the sum of £8,000, she found her mind wandering once more to her state of unease. She loved books; she came from a family of book lovers. In the Parsonage, books never got a chance to linger on dusty shelves, they were read, discussed, reimagined, annotated, read again, consulted, translated from, sketched from, in short, they had a utilitarian purpose. She wondered how long it had been since a human hand had reached for the leather-bound ones coffined around the room, what use could it be to them to be merely admired. She imagined she could hear the characters from down through the ages, plaintively calling from the yellowed pages, begging to be released into a human psyche, for how else could they breathe again.

'Ah, and this one will be of interest to our author, for this is our great writer, Jonathan Swift,' Joseph said, referring to the bust of Swift.

'Indeed, perpetually overseeing a Brobdingnagian library,' Charlotte said, 'perhaps someday the college authorities will see fit to raise a female bust on their wooden plinths.'

'Hear, hear, my sentiments exactly, Charlotte,' Mary Anna said as she applauded.

'Shh, you have to be quiet, Mary Anna,' Joseph said.

'Why, there are no stuffy students here pouring over their stuffy books?' she asked.

'Well, that is because term time and the examinations have

finished, but it is still a place of silence,' Arthur added, and no doubt sensing a weariness in Charlotte's demeanour he suggested that they move on to see the Book of Kells.

Charlotte smiled affectionately at him and he returned the acknowledgement with a slow wink.

Mary Anna observing the exchange, tutted and said, 'You two.'

Joseph surpassed himself in relation to the Book of Kells. As they allowed Charlotte to step forward and peer closely at the opened page, she being the only one among them who had not seen it before, he took them through over one thousand years of history. Charlotte listened attentively while simultaneously scrutinising the illustration of the Virgin and Child on the left side of the opened tome.

'... so even though it was begun in Iona, it is called the book of Kells because that is where it was brought when the Vikings invaded. Is it not a miracle that this delicate manuscript survived that perilous sea journey?' Joseph recounted, 'and if that was not sufficient a test for the miraculous nature of this precious artefact, it was stolen in 1006 AD and found two months and twenty days later buried in the ground. Alas, the cover was lost, one can imagine the magnificent, probably bejewelled, Celtic artifact that must have been.'

'I should have liked to have seen that,' Mary Anna said.

'And when did the college acquire it?' Charlotte asked, without lifting her gaze from the manuscript.

'Gosh, such an obvious fact that one should know and yet it escapes me. Arthur?'

'1661, I believe,' Arthur said.

Undeterred by the gap in his knowledge, Joseph continued as he made reference to the artists, including goldsmiths, portrait painters, and perhaps young children believed to have drawn the miniature figures. He spoke of the four scribes, the ink made of oak apple and iron, the colours made from berries and insects, the vellum parchment and the herd of twelve hundred calves needed to produce enough folios, the detailed intricacies of the illustrated pages, the perfection of the calligraphy, the exactness of the lines and circles, the Celtic spirals and whirls within whirls, the sacred text of the four gospels, the playful aspect of some of the depictions, and on and on and on he waxed, concluding that despite all the obvious human input into the artistic masterpiece, he was inclined to believe that it was indeed the work of angels. All this time, Allen had taken himself to the table in the centre of the room where he remained seated for the duration of Joseph's history lesson, clearly less interested than the others.

Charlotte was mesmerised by the detailed illustrations on the Virgin and Child page. The closer and longer she gazed the more was revealed, such as the transparency of the Virgin's clothes, possibly to suggest that they were made from fine silk, however what fascinated Charlotte was not the luxurious material but the outline of her lactating breasts clearly visible beneath the cloth and the child Jesus's hand placed on one of those breasts. It seemed such a daring, sensual representation of the mother of Christ; these early Christian monks were making no effort to hide the feminine, instead they were celebrating it, placing Mary, like some great empress, on a jewel encrusted throne, dressing her in purple, the colour of royalty, and surrounding her with four male guards in the form of angels, which Charlotte believed to be Gabriel, Michael, Raphael and Uriel, the archangels of her religion. Charlotte was about to comment on the Columban monk's celebration of the female when Joseph remarked on the page being the only one in the entire book that featured a woman. She remained mute.

Having concluded his background to the book, Joseph had as much to say about the opened pages. This time Charlotte paid no heed to his narrative as her gaze was drawn to a box in the corner of the page containing the profile heads of four men, all looking to the right to bring the reader's attention to the recto side of the next folio which contained a summary of Mathew's gospel. What concentrated Charlotte's inspection was a familiarity she detected in the rather crude, childishly drawn faces. Then it dawned on her, these medieval drawings, lacking the perspective that only became a feature of artwork from the Renaissance period, reminded her of the way she and her siblings used to sketch as children. In particular, she was reminded of a self-portrait she had included in a letter to Ellen when she was in Brussels. In her drawing she is standing on a shore waving goodbye across a channel of water to a glamourous depiction of her friend and a gentleman, whom Charlotte labels as Ellen's beau.

Allen re-joined them and wondered if he could be excused from the rest of the day's touring as he had work to attend to. Mary Anna reminded Charlotte of their intended trip to Cannock and White's.

'Perhaps we should find an eatery beforehand, as I know the benefits of my breakfast have quite deserted me,' Joseph said.

'I have a suggestion, Ladies, why don't we retire to the Shelbourne and avail of the splendid afternoon tea service they are famed for,' Arthur said, 'and rather than have to canter across the city again, allow Joseph or myself to get whatever it is you require from Cannock and White's.'

And so, it was decided.

Later that evening, back in their hotel bed chamber, both agreed that while the company of others was pleasant, especially when that company was so entertaining, so well-informed regarding the city, so courteous, so delightful, especially Mary Anna, with what Charlotte described as her 'ladylike, gentle English manners', there was a much greater comfort to be enjoyed when it was just the two of them. Charlotte admitted to feeling utterly fatigued and somewhat in dread of the journey the following day, but Arthur assured her that it would not be anything like their journey from Haworth to Wales and added that before she knew it, Aunt Harriette would be fussing over her and brewing all sorts of concoctions to restore her to full health.

'Do you think she will like me, Arthur?'

'My dear, my only fear is that you will usurp my position in Aunt's affections.'

'You are kind to say thus. I very much look forward to being mothered by this lady I already hold dear in my heart.'

Chapter Fifteen

Barney held the carriage door open for Charlotte. When Arthur went to make travel arrangements the previous evening, Charlotte had asked him to seek out Barney as she would like to say goodbye to him before leaving the capital.

'And so when I says t' me missus, th' husband told me she writes under th' name of Currer Bell, well, jaysus, I'm no' jokin' you, her eyes lit up, shure, she's read all yer books, and yer sisthers' too,' Barney said, continuing to speak in through the window, 'I know wha' you're thinkin', how did I find an edjamacated wife, well, wait 'til I tell you, she grew up in a big house in Kildare, her mother was th' cook and her father was th' groundsman so t' say, and shure as a child she hung around wit' the chislers belongin' to th' house, and when the' were doin' ther' lessons wit' th' governess, well, Kate, tha' is me wife's name, well she listened in an' learnt. Now, wha' do ya thin' of tha'?' Barney leaned on the ledge, a pose suggesting that he was settling in for a conversation.

'I think that is wonderful, Barney, but I also think we should be looking smart, or that train will leave the terminus without us,' Arthur said.

'Did Kate become a servant in that house?' Charlotte asked.

Arthur looked at her, a look of questioning confusion.

'She did indeed, you're a sharp one, ya know the dhrill. Eventually took over from her mother, and tha' is how we met.

144

She mad' me a cup a tay, whilst I was waitin' to bring th' Lord of th' house and th' fella I had brough' from here, to th' races on th' Curragh. It was luv a' first sigh', and th' rest as the' say is history,' Barney said, and this time made to move to the driver's seat.

Charlotte leaned out the window and said, 'When you go home you must call her Nelly Dean; she will understand my meaning.' As she sat back into her seat there was a smugness in her raised chin, the look of a person extremely pleased with oneself.

'Really, Charlotte, you mustn't encourage him, the man would talk all day given half a chance,' Arthur said, taking his watch from his pocket and checking the time. Their train left at nine o' clock. Mary Anna had said that they were expected home in time for lunch. 'Besides, Charlotte, Aunt Harriette, if I know anything, will have a feast prepared for us, which will be utterly spoiled if we have to wait until the afternoon train.'

'And if we miss the train, we will just have to hire Barney to take us all the way to Banagher,' Charlotte said, and laughed at the look of horror elongating Arthur's face.

'I think I would rather walk; God only knows what liberties he would take after such a long journey, probably suggest being accommodated for the night,' Arthur said.

'It won't happen, Arthur, as always, we are like the lovers who ever run before the clock,' Charlotte said.

'Let me guess. Shakespeare?' Arthur asked.

'Well done, you learn quickly, Mr Bell Nicholls,' Charlotte said.

'But you say we are "like" the lovers, are we not the lovers?' Arthur asked, placing his index finger against his chin by way of a question.

'I am not a fan of that word, "lovers", Arthur, there is something about it that suggests illicit dalliances,' Charlotte said.

Arthur looked out as the carriage made its way down the quays, as the morning sun sparkled on the Liffey to their right.

'I haven't had much of a chance to parade my knowledge of the city these last few days,' he said, 'between Allen, Joseph ... and dare I say it, Barney, I have been rendered a dumb show of ignorance.'

'Well, now is your chance to shine again, let me see,' Charlotte said as she leaned towards the window, 'ah, a bridge that is not chiselled from stone, enlighten me as to the history of that metal arc.' The arc she referred to was an iron, foot bridge, which would have been a drab affair, were it not for the three decorative arches that spanned it, each holding aloft a gaslight, like a chalice being raised to the Gods.

'That is Wellington Bridge, called after your Duke, or at least it was supposed to be Wellington Bridge, but nobody knows it by anything other than the Ha'penny Bridge, so called because of the rate of the toll; a halfpenny.

'It rather puts me in mind of a wedding cake, it is a pretty affair, a delicate frill amidst all the brickwork,' Charlotte said.

'Speaking of wedding cake, is there likely to be any left when we get back?' Arthur asked.

'Not if Martha has anything to do with it,' Charlotte said, tugging her gloves at the wrist for a snugger fit, 'such an appetite for sweet fare!'

'Poor Martha,' Arthur said, and as he was sitting facing in the direction of travel, he could see that they had arrived, 'here we are, where our coach into the heart of Ireland awaits us.'

The Palladian style building that was King's Bridge Terminus, reminded Charlotte of a grand opera house that you might expect to dominate an Italian Palazzo. Allen, Joseph and Mary Anna stood waiting at the entrance. Mary Anna lost no time and was at the door before Barney had had time to climb down from his driver's perch. As the men dealt with the luggage, she gave Charlotte a step by step account of how she had gone to Cannock and White's with Joseph, perused the drawers of threads for over an hour before deciding which one matched her dress, then how when they arrived back at Allen's, how she had mended the hem; she went into all the detail of threading the needle with an accurately measured length of thread, how she remembered to put a tiny knot at the end to prevent it from pulling through the material, and described the type of stitch she used, and even had Charlotte known nothing about sewing, the entire recounting still would have been of no interest to her. Making and mending was something she did out of need and necessity, something she saw as another tedious task for the less privileged woman in society. As they walked down the platform, Mary Anna once again linking her, Charlotte found herself straining her neck to find Arthur who followed behind with the others; she could not endure a journey of domestic prattle. However, she need not have doubted Arthur's attentiveness to her every need, having reclaimed her from his cousin, he directed her to the window seat, settling himself beside her. The others sat on the opposite side of the aisle.

'I trust you gave Barney a king's ransom by way of a tip?' Charlotte asked, 'I do hope we meet him when we return to Dublin, I want to give him a signed copy of *Jane Eyre* for his wife. I should have done so now were they not packed away in the trunk.'

'I gave what I deemed to be his deserts,' Arthur said, taking off his hat and placing it on the table in front of them.

'Oh, dear, use every man after his deserts and who should scape whipping?' Charlotte said, and before Arthur could answer she added, 'Hamlet, and I promise that is the last quote from me, I am even beginning to bore myself. This constant need to borrow the words of others, it is a disease, Arthur. You must cure me.' What Charlotte did not share with Arthur was how she envied the unpractised, easy exchanges between him and his relatives, natural exchanges that she felt exposed her to be stilted, measured and pretentious in her conversation. No wonder Thackeray made fun of her. She hoped that this informality of her new family might soften some of her starchy ways.

Shortly after leaving the station, the train travelled through open countryside quilted in greens and browns and yellows, the various size dwellings appearing as white and black shapes dotting the patches. Charlotte was charmed by the setting and could already see why it was a popular destination for travellers, there was something magical and primeval about the way the misty rain veiled the fields, giving the sense that you were entering an unearthly realm. As the landscape levelled into sweeping plains of uniform green, she could see what looked to be a hunt taking place, as a cluster of men on horseback moved along a neatly trimmed hedgerow. She tapped Arthur's shoulder and pointed.

'It must be jockeys training, they hardly run races on a Friday. That is the Curragh, Charlotte, famous for racing, and I believe, sheep. All that land you see belongs to the Crown, but nearby farmers can graze their sheep there. Quite the sight, is it not?' Arthur said, as he lifted out of his seat to retrieve a book from his pocket. It was the Forbes book. 'Why don't I read what your man has to say about it?'

'Do, please,' Charlotte said, glad that the train was slowing on the approach to the next station thus reducing, ever so slightly, the noisy, constant rattle and hum of the wheels. She knew that the pressure she was experiencing at her temples would soon be a throbbing headache.

As Arthur flicked through the pages, pausing to quickly scan the text, he looked increasingly bewildered. 'Well, well,

I am afraid our Doctor does not have much by way of praise for this part of Ireland, "The only things of any interest in Kildare are the fine ruins of the Abbey or Cathedral, and the Round Tower in their vicinity". Tell that to the horse racing enthusiasts, the stud farmers, the crown forces, the descendants of the Fitzgerald's – loyal viceroys to former monarchs – and all those who worship Brigid, both the Goddess and the saint. That is what I say to you, Doctor Forbes,' Arthur said, addressing the book as if a Lilliputian Forbes was sitting on the page awaiting this verdict on his conclusions.

'Look, Arthur, there, I can see the round tower. Do you not think that there is something more of the whimsical than the aesthetic about them? When I look upon them, I see medieval damsels waving handkerchiefs from the highest point, their silken veils trailing from conical hats, like wispy smoke signals of distress,' Charlotte leaned forward to look backwards at the scene as the train left the station and the religious edifices behind.

'You mean you can't see the monk with his quill and his white cat heading towards the scriptorium to put some finishing touches on a decorative "m" in "Amen"?' Arthur said, and addressing Joseph in a loud voice, to compensate for the noise of the train, 'Joseph, I am afraid you need to do a better job of narrating the eccentricities of early Christian monks.'

Joseph smiled and nodded, neither gesture demonstrating in any convincing fashion that he had properly heard Arthur. Mary Anna clearly had as she said, 'Pay no heed, Joseph, if Arthur had been giving you his entire attention, he too would be able to see Pangur Bán skulking around headstones, but I am afraid our cousin is easily distracted these days.' Arthur looked pleased and turned to Charlotte, perhaps to share with her the implications of Mary Anna's surmise but was met with the back of her head as she continued to gaze on the passing countryside.

Charlotte had been listening very attentively to all Joseph had said the previous day in Trinity college regarding the genesis of the Book Of Kells, of how monks sometimes used the valuable vellum pages to chronicle their own lives and stories as well as those of the evangelists, and of how the same book had miraculously survived a sea voyage, just like her mother's copy of *The Remains of Henry Kirke White*. Of all the volumes in the Parsonage, this was the most cherished. The book itself was a collection of the poems of White, who had died at the young age of twenty-one. The book was the most read, the most annotated by every member of the family, it was their treasure casket where when children they stowed their own precious manuscripts, fragments of prose and poetry placed between the pages in the hope that the spirit of their Mama would guard them until the young author was ready to complete the piece. Papa loved to tell the story of the book's remarkable survival, of how his young bride to be, realising that her future would be in Yorkshire, had her belongings shipped from her home in Penzance, of how the ship carrying them was stranded on the Devonshire coast and most of the cargo destroyed or lost at sea, and of how, along with copies of The Lady's Magazines, the aptly named book of White's poetry was among the few possessions salvaged. Charlotte wondered what Papa would be doing at that moment; because of the hectic nature of her journey thus far she had forgotten about being homesick, and instantly felt guilty, making a mental note to write to both Martha and he as soon as she had some quiet time in Banagher, although if Mary Anna, Joseph and Allen were accurate representatives of the extended family she very much doubted that such a thing as 'quiet time' would feature in the household, and to a large extent, she would be right.

The train continued to steam through a world of brown and

black and green, so much green, as bog lands became the seats of the Irish gentry, their country demesnes and lavish villas partially visible through towering trees. Whenever Charlotte caught sight of yet another sprawling mansion, she would tap Arthur's forearm, and he, understanding their new code, named the area according to the owner, so that the journey, particularly between Monasterevin and Maryborough became an inventory of Leinster's aristocracy.

'The Marquis of Drogheda.'

'The Earl of Portarlington.'

'Oh, dear, I am afraid that poor castle has seen better days,' Charlotte said, referring to a ruin they could see on a distant hill.

'The Rock of Dunamaise, quite the tourist attraction or so I believe, and why is that I hear you ask,' Arthur said, although Charlotte had not asked, 'apparently those ruins are the result of the first canon fire in Ireland during Cromwellian times. That stony hill could tell the history of Ireland from its days as a Celtic fort, through Norman times when Strongbow occupied it, to the Gaelic chieftains, the O'Moores, and I think is currently the property of Lord Congleton.'

'I am so ignorant of Irish history, and yet the more I hear, especially the names, the more romantic it sounds. The Rock of Dunamaise. Magical,' Charlotte said, closing her eyes as she conjured up images of knights and chieftains.

'Perhaps your next book will be a tale of Irish forts and castles, set back in the mists of time,' Arthur said, his nods affirming the sagacity of his concept.

Charlotte, opening her eyes in time to witness his nods, stared without saying anything, a gesture which obviously disconcerted Arthur who quickly added, 'but, who am I to talk about what you should or should not write about, I who find letter writing a creative challenge, as you, poor thing, are only too aware.'

'Your letters are fine compositions, and all the finer for the honesty therein, and you misinterpret my delay in responding to your suggestion. I was thinking, perhaps, because my work is so often labelled as being autogenous, you would prefer me to write about a distant time that we could not possibly have belonged to?' Charlotte said, and before Arthur got a chance to respond, she continued, 'my critics love to speculate on who my characters are based on and I would not have you, Arthur, become the subject of their guessing games.'

'Your imagination is your only master, Charlotte, when it comes to what you decide to write about.'

The train slowed down allowing Charlotte to watch a worker in a field straighten from a stooped position, flick a lock of dark hair back from his brow as he wiped the same brow with the back of his hand. He reminded her of John Brown back home. She waved at him, knowing it to be a rather bold act, but the fleeting nature of the exchange gave her courage. He returned her wave, and even from the distance of the train she could see that he smiled.

'Where are we now?' she asked.

'Maryborough, just two more stops and then the carriage should be at the station to bring us home,' Allen said, 'did Arthur tell you that I was able to send notice about our changed arrangements?'

'Yes, thank you,' Charlotte said. When Arthur had told her about the carriage being sent for them, she wanted to ask if it belonged to the household but desisted as she was beginning to realise that Arthur's social status was greater than he had ever alluded to, and for her to treat as a novelty what was commonplace to him, risked showing her up in a vulgar light.

A carriage, drawn by two horses, was indeed waiting for them when they disembarked in Ballybrophy, and the greeting

Arthur got from the driver, answered her question as it was clear that he was an employee of the household.

'And this must be the lucky lassie,' Jimmy, for that was his name, said, as he doffed his cap in greeting.

'Oh, I'm not sure about lucky, Jimmy, patient might be nearer the mark,' Arthur said.

'Will ya stop, I'll tell ya one ting for sure, missus, you're after landin' the prize catch, and breakin' many's a heart,' Jimmy said, and taking Charlotte by both hands, he continued, 'but, I know b' the cut o' ya, wit' your lovely big eyes, tha' ya deserve him.'

'And on that note, Jimmy, I think it is time we got underway,' Arthur said, taking Jimmy by the forearm and leading him to the driver's seat.

The party laughed as they settled into the coach and Joseph assured Charlotte that she would soon get used to the ways of everybody.

'I'm afraid nobody stands on ceremony here, Charlotte, not even the queen herself would be treated any differently than Minnie, the chambermaid. You'll be meeting her soon too, along with the rest of the clan.'

Charlotte went to answer Joseph, but a coughing fit overtook her, causing Arthur to lean out the window and ask Jimmy to go as fast as the road and the horses allowed.

Chapter Sixteen

Charlotte could see they were approaching a stone pillared gateway, which had to be the entrance to a substantial estate, and she hoped that the carriage turned in. She was not disappointed. As it made its way up a tree lined avenue, she wanted to lean out the window such was her curiosity to see the house, but a sense of pride and a throbbing headache kept her still. The carriage had no sooner come to a stop when the door was opened and across a gravel yard a large square mansion dwarfed the welcoming party standing at the end of the steps. Charlotte was taken aback at the size of the house; she had expected something much more modest. So, this was where her husband had been reared and educated, she was unsure whether she should be impressed or annoyed, she had taken his origins to be of a much humbler bent. If this house was anything to go by, Arthur had quite the gentrified upbringing and yet he never acted in a way that indicated privilege. Misinterpreting the perplexity in her expression, having let the others disembark, Arthur whispered in her ear.

'Don't be put off by that block of stone we call Cuba Court, its harsh, masculine exterior belies the softness you'll find within,' and then stepping out and extending his hand to help her, he continued aloud, 'welcome, my dear Charlotte, to Banagher, and to what is for now, your home.'

The following moments were a blur of introductions, as

servants curtsied and relatives shook her hand or, in the case of the ladies, squeezed her tight against their bosoms. There were too many names to remember, and when finally, she and Arthur reached Aunt Harriette who was framed in the doorway at the top of the steps, Charlotte was sure she was going to faint.

'Goodness, Arthur, this little lady is not well, thank the Lord I had the presence of mind to have a fire lit in your room, quickly, follow me,' Aunt Harriette said and turned to go towards the ground floor room which she had had prepared as the bridal suite, but noticing that Charlotte was following, she quickly turned back, 'Arthur, come, come, tradition, your wife must be carried over the threshold, besides,' this time addressing Charlotte, 'you have done quite enough walking, my dear, you poor thing, you are in a far more advanced state of ill health than Allen's letter indicated. How pale you look; we need to nurse you back to ruddiness.'

Arthur did as he was bid, and too weak to resist, as he swept her up into his arms Charlotte lay her head on his shoulder, glad to be relieved of its heaviness.

Many hours later, Charlotte woke in a confused state. She was reluctant to open her eyes; the reluctance of the guest waking in an unfamiliar bed. In her sleep she had dreamt of warm fires and soothing drinks, she had heard soft female voices, their soothing sounds calming the pain in her head, there had been a scent of menthol and intermittently she had either imagined a soft, moist, cloth bathing her brow, or some invisible hand had placed it there. As her awareness increased a clicking reached her ears, she recognised it as the sound of knitting. As she listened, sleep was beginning to seductively take hold of her once more and were it not for the sound of a familiar voice, she would have succumbed. Arthur was addressing the unknown knitter.

'Has she woken at all?' he said.

'No, Masther Artur, nothin' but twistin' an' turnin'. I think she has th' fever; she was talkin' to herself, somethin' 'bout Flossy, whoever she is.'

Charlotte could not recall any dream that involved the spaniel back at home. How curious that she would call her name. She opened her eyes to see the owner of the voice, a young girl of maybe sixteen or seventeen, perched in an easy chair, clacking needles as she spoke to Arthur.

'Ya have her nearly kilt already, Mrs Bell said it was all the traipsin' ya did around Dublin, that ya should've come straight here, she said that for all yer learnin', like the rest of the men, ya haven't an ounce o' sense.'

'I think I preferred you, Minnie, when you were a little girl following your mother around the kitchen,' Arthur said to the girl, who folded her knitting into a basket by her side and leaving the chair went to a washstand where Charlotte watched her rinse a cloth in the basin of water and approach the bed. Arthur intercepted her approach, 'I'll take over now, Minnie, thank you, Aunt Harriette has asked me to tell you that there are some errands down the town she needs you for.'

'Christ, but there's always somethin',' Minnie said, giving Arthur the cloth but continuing to the bed.

Charlotte tried to sit up but because of how tightly the bed clothes were tucked beneath the mattress, all she could move was her head, and because of its weight she was unable to hold it off the pillow for long.

'Hello, Missus Nicholls, my name is Minnie and while yer here, I'm goin' to be yer lady-in-waitin'. Anthin' atall ya need, just ax.' As she spoke it seemed to Charlotte that she was pushing the bedclothes further beneath the mattress, imprisoning her even further in a cell of cotton and damask.

'Minnie! Out! Now!' Arthur said, taking her by the arm

and leading her to the door.

'What about the fire, it's goin' low, Mrs Bell said if it twas th' last thing I did, I was to keep it roarin',' Minnie strained away from Arthur towards the fire as she spoke.

'I think I can manage to put some sods on it, Minnie,' Arthur said, closing the door behind her, he turned, and leaning back into the door, sighed loudly.

Despite how sleepy she still felt, Charlotte laughed to see Arthur usher the girl out as she added a further protest against leaving, stating that she was telling the truth, that Mrs Bell had said she could be a lady's maid for the week and that meant being in attendance to the lady at all times.

'My apologies, Charlotte, that was Minnie, who, by the end of our stay, will have you thanking the stars above for Martha Brown, even if she does eat all the wedding cake before we get home. The girl has no sense of boundaries and is a fierce warrant to talk, and if you want to know anything about anybody in this town, Minnie is the one to ask,' Arthur said as he sat on the side of the bed and placed the cooling towel on Charlotte's forehead, 'but now, much more importantly, how are you feeling?'

'Tired. A little overwhelmed. Very trapped.'

'Trapped?' A wave of horror washed over Arthur's face.

'The covers are too tight, I can't move,' Charlotte said.

Arthur laughed and sounded relieved, blaming Minnie, as he tugged the layers of sheet, blankets, and blue damask bedspread out from under the mattress.

Evening sun streamed in from two windows basking the room in an orange glow that competed with the glow from the turf fire burning in a wide old chimney. Through the window facing the bed, Charlotte could see fields of green stretching out across the landscape. Following her gaze, Arthur said that she looked on two counties, King's County and Galway, and that if she were outside the house and turned in the opposite direction, she would see County Tipperary. She repeated the names, Galway, Tipperary.

'How ancient they sound, and utterly Irish, I feel I ought to adopt a brogue in pronouncing them correctly,' she said.

'Aunt is anxious that you eat something but is adamant that you remain in bed, or at least here in this room for now. I think that is wise, but I want you to be happy to do that,' Arthur said, 'I can fetch your meal, although I know that Aunt will want to see how your health progresses.'

'And what about my lady-in-waiting?' Charlotte smiled. She had already warmed to the young girl; besides, she preferred the company of the help in these situations, they were always far more talkative and interesting, unencumbered by societal politeness.

'Oh, don't you worry, Minnie will be back, whether invited or not.'

Charlotte saw that a round table, covered in a fine lacy cloth, was already set for two. The room was spacious and had the feel of a gentleman's study with its easy chairs, scroll couch, writing desk and shelves of books. Apart from the bed, it was very much a larger version of Papa's study, and therefore, the sense of familiarity afforded her a feeling of ease.

'I would very much like to properly meet Aunt Harriette, I am afraid I have little recollection of our first encounter. Was I terribly rude?' Charlotte said.

'Quite the contrary, despite your exhaustion you were the essence of politeness. You even attempted to convince Aunt Harriette that you were not in the least tired, and that was just before you swooned,' Arthur said, 'it is just as well you avoided lunch, some friends had joined us in order to meet you, so it was quite the gathering around the table.'

'Arthur I can't remember who I was introduced to, I am

afraid you will have to do the honours again, perhaps one at a time, that way I can properly take in their features and personality so that I will know who's who,' Charlotte said and just as she finished her sentence there was a knock at the door. Arthur looked to her for guidance. She nodded.

'Come in,' he said.

It was Aunt Harriette. Her physique was so similar to Aunt Branwell as she crossed the room, Charlotte expected to hear her aunt's Cornish cadence admonish her for letting her health deteriorate to such a state. As Aunt Harriette drew nearer and addressed Arthur, her soft features and smiling, kind eyes, and the quiet, neutral tone of her speech reminded Charlotte, not of Aunt Branwell but of her publisher's mother, Mrs Smith, which was not surprising, as according to what Mary Anna had been telling her, Aunt Harriette had been brought up in London.

'And how is our patient?' she said.

Before Arthur got a chance to respond, Charlotte sitting up further in the bed said that she was feeling much better and ready to get up, which Aunt Harriette might have agreed to were it not for the coughing fit that followed.

'Oh, my poor dear, I hate to be a rotten old spoil sport, but I am going to insist that you remain exactly as you are until the morrow. We have such wonderful plans for your time here, so let us make sure that you are hale and hearty enough to enjoy it all. I know it seems wrong that you should be alienated away like this on your first night, but, as the saying goes, to do a great right, we must do a little wrong. Isn't that correct, Arthur, dear boy?' Aunt Harriette, as she spoke, had been checking Charlotte's temperature, like a doctor, by placing a hand to her brow, and shaking her head in apparent dismay at her findings.

Charlotte took note of the use of Portia's expression from *The Merchant of Venice*, about great rights and little wrongs.

She knew that Aunt Harriette was a woman with whom she would be able to converse freely, but there was something else that Charlotte was feeling, she was being mothered and that had her fighting back tears for what was past, and gratitude for the present.

'Don't upset yourself, my dear, why don't we try some mutton stew with a small portion of buttery potatoes. You will need nourishment as well as medicine if you are to regain your strength. I will go and organise that and leave you two to decide if you will take your food in bed or if you would rather sit at the table. I suggest the bed, dear boy.' The last sentence was whispered to Arthur. From the door, Aunt Harriette turned and asked if Charlotte would prefer that she, and not Minnie, would bring the food.

'I know that Minnie can irritate easily but the girl means well. We do not stand on ceremony here in Cuba Court, but she has been insisting that she be your lady-in-waiting for the duration of your stay. The silly girl has been reading too many romance novels,' Aunt Harriette said and left before either Charlotte or Arthur replied.

'Oh, Arthur, you must have had a wonderful childhood, she is the dearest lady. I feel I have known her all my life, such a welcome and such care of me,' Charlotte said, lifting the covers and motioning towards getting out of the bed.

'No, no, you must stay as you are,' Arthur said, replacing the bedclothes over Charlotte, 'yes, I knew you would like Aunt Harriette, she is the kindest of ladies, and the most positive despite the tragedies that have beset her.'

'Tragedies? I only know of her husband's death some years ago,' Charlotte said.

'Yes, Uncle Alan in 1839, a year we will all remember because of his sudden departure, and the devastation caused here by what is now commonly referred to as the Big Wind, a ferocious storm swept across the country on the Feast of the Epiphany, leaving a wilderness of felled trees, roofless dwellings and general havoc in its wake. Many lives were lost. Five years later we had another personal storm when Cousin Susan died. She was twenty-one, Charlotte, with all her life ahead of her. And just four years ago Cousin Frances, sweet, sweet, little Frances, barely fifteen, followed her big sister. And yet, rather than wallow in her loss, Aunt Harriette chooses to revel in her gains and celebrate the achievements of her remaining brood, including Allen's and mine,' Arthur said, 'and I know that our marriage and your presence here is a source of great happiness for her.'

'Arthur, why didn't you tell me before of these personal upsets, you too must have been devastated, I mean effectively these were your sisters. How churlish I feel having burdened you with my grief, when all along you had your own inner turmoil to conquer. For my Anne and Emily, you had your Susan and Frances,' Charlotte leaned forward as she spoke and taking Arthur's hands she drew him closer until their foreheads touched. The moment of intimacy might have advanced were it not for what sounded distinctly like someone kicking the door.

'Well, I am guessing it was decided that Minnie would bring our food,' Arthur said, as he got up to open the door, and indeed, there was Minnie, balancing a tray of covered dishes, and a bottle of wine.

'Quick, move, this thing is heavy,' she said, as she swayed towards the table already set.

'Did you just kick the door, Minnie?' Arthur asked.

'Well I hardly used me hands now, Masther Artur, seein' as the' were otherwise occupied. Men!' Minnie said, addressing the last comment to Charlotte, as she threw her eyes towards the ceiling.

Charlotte lowered her head so that Arthur could not see her smile.

'Now, M'Lady, the Missus says you are t' ate as much as ya can, and not b' fraid to put salt on it. She had to ax Mammy, me mammy's th' cook, not to be puttin' in any salt 'cos she was puttin' in too much, lacin' it in she was, accordin' to Missus, but she sez that you need to be drinkin' plenty of water, and the salt will give ya a thirst to help ya. That's her there, the wan with the one hole in the top,' Minnie arranged the food on the table as she spoke.

'I think, Minnie, that we can tell the pepper from the salt,' Arthur said, looking increasingly agitated.

'Well, 'tis a pity ya can't tell the differ between a fire and a hape of ashes, serve ya better t' throw on some turf 'stead of standin' there like a gawk,' Minnie said, and even Arthur forgetting his agitation, laughed at her audaciousness.

'M'lady, have ya somethin' t' throw over yer shoulders, and I'll help ya t' the table,' Minnie was already bending over Charlotte's trunk as she spoke.

'You must just call me Charlotte, Minnie, I am not used to being addressed as a lady. I hate to put you to more trouble, but I have been given clear instructions that I must remain in bed, so perhaps if you could bring my plate on that tray, I will be able to manage it myself.'

Arthur had finished attending to the fire, and once again, repeating the earlier scene, he took Minnie by the forearm and accompanied her out of the room, 'I can take it from here, Minnie, and we will see you tomorrow.'

'Ya won't, you'll see me sooner, t' collect th' ware, no wan goes to bed in this place until th' kitchen is put right and ready for th' morrow,' Minnie said.

'I will see to it that everything is returned to the kitchen. Good night, Minnie,' Arthur said, closing the door against

Minnie's continued protests.

Charlotte enjoyed the small amount of food she ate, declaring the meat to be the tenderest she had ever tasted. When they had finished, true to his word, Arthur loaded the tray and went to the kitchen. When he returned, he had a hot drink made from whiskey and honey for Charlotte and a cough bottle with instructions that she take two spoons before sleep and two again on waking. There was no label on the bottle, which caused Charlotte some concern because of her previous experiences with medicines.

'You have no need to worry, Charlotte, this concoction is what we were all reared on, it is made up by a local woman, the Widow Conlon, a wise old woman who knows a thing or two about herbs,' Arthur said, shaking the bottle.

'A wise old woman, otherwise known as a witch, you mean,' Charlotte said.

'We have no witches in Ireland, Charlotte, only wise women,' Arthur said as he poured the black liquid on to a spoon and offered it to Charlotte, who opened her mouth to take it in. She grimaced and shook her head from the bitter taste but dutifully took the second spoon offered, swallowing harder this time.

'Ugh, I believe I know how this works, the thoughts of waking up to it will keep me asleep so that nature can work its restorative magic,' Charlotte said, taking the glass of hot whiskey and putting it to her lips.

Arthur drank more wine as Charlotte sipped on her drink.

'Were you awake earlier when Minnie mentioned that you were calling for Flossy in your sleep?' Arthur asked.

'Yes, yes, I knew there was something I wanted to ask you. I think I remember why I was dreaming of her,' Charlotte said.

Flossy, the spaniel, was well known to Arthur, after Anne's death he took over as the dog's walking companion. Every day, the dog would leave the parsonage and wait outside the Sexton's house until Arthur emerged for his daily walk across the moors, and off the pair would set. Arthur was very fond of the dog; in fact, it was this fondness that had caused some anguish for Charlotte that perhaps his feelings for Anne had run deeper than anyone had realised.

'Do you remember last year, in January, when I was in London, if you stopped bringing Flossy with you on your walks?' Charlotte asked.

'Charlotte, I remember so little of that time, coming as it did after my bumbled proposal, and your ... quite justified as I now see it, your refusal. I was not myself, and although I don't remember specifically, it is likely that I preferred not to associate with any aspect of parsonage life,' Arthur said, 'why do you ask?'

'Papa wrote me a letter as if it were from Flossy, which was a jolly thing to do, but alas the contents were not so jolly,' Charlotte said.

'A letter from a dog! The man will never cease to astound me,' Arthur said.

'Oh, don't be so jejune in your thinking, Papa was being creative, as children we loved to imagine what the animals would say and sound like if they could speak, but I digress, I am afraid that this letter from Flossy was not very complimentary towards you,' Charlotte said.

'Why what did she ... no, he, what did he say?' Arthur gulped down his wine and rose to replenish the glass.

'Let me see, I think her exact words were, "my former travelling companion has lost all his apparent kindness, scolds me, and looks black upon me", tut, tut, Arthur, the poor, old dog,' Charlotte smiled with amusement.

'Aha, I see what he was doing, projecting my behaviour towards him onto the dog,' Arthur said.

'Arthur, that is worse!'

'Well, he wasn't exactly my favourite person at that time being the main obstacle to my happiness, but as for Flossy, yes I may have missed bringing her for a walk on one or two occasions, because of the inclement January weather not any vengeance I wished to take out on a dumb animal,' Arthur said.

'Not so dumb if she can write.'

They both laughed. Charlotte held out her empty glass for Arthur to take.

'Would you like me to sleep in my old room tonight, to give you some peace and quiet,' Arthur asked, his preference being clear from the lack of conviction in his tone.

'No, no, besides not wanting to be alone in this strange room, I fear I have been neglecting you, how many nights now have you slept on chairs?' Charlotte said.

Arthur smiled and proceeded to settle the room for the night by closing the curtains, heavy affairs of blue damask to match the bedspread; he stoked the fire before placing a brass screen in front of it, and then one by one, extinguished the many candles, leaving the bedside one to last. Charlotte had watched him as he moved, so purposeful, so masterful, and now listening to his movements as he undressed in the dark, she longed to feel his closeness. Her husband. Her dear Arthur.

Chapter Seventeen

Charlotte awoke to the sound of a poker being rattled in the grate. Without opening her eyes, she slid her hand across to Arthur's side, but he was not there, so logic suggested that it was he who attended to the fire. Still without opening her eyes, as a heaviness made the effort too much, mulling over, in that half wake, the night that had passed, she addressed him:

'I think your Widow Conlon dabbles in more than cough syrup, I fear we may have been bewitched by whatever mysterious ingredients flows through her black, viscous potion,' Charlotte said.

'Oh, you may be sure she threw somethin' to do with hanky-panky in there, up to her auld shenanigans, wise woman me eye, that wan's a witch, make no mistake 'bout it. Shure th' hooked nose on her is enough t' give th' game away.'

It was Minnie who had spoken. Charlotte shot up in the bed, mortified to see the young maid, her face besmirched with black ashes, waving the poker in the air.

'I'd say she's down there now, wavin' some class of a wand like this, makin' sure it works, she's a great one for the babbies, women are always goin' to her when nothins' happenin', and lo and behold, nine months later, they're back agin to her, their bellies like th' full sails goin' up th' river, to get her to pull out th' child,' Minnie said and turned back to her work at the grate.

Charlotte was unsure whether to laugh or cry, Arthur was

correct, the girl knew no boundaries, no sense of decorum, and yet there was a freshness to her honesty that allowed you to forget her audacity.

'Minnie, is Arthur about?' was all that Charlotte could manage in response.

'Oh, ya know him now, a fierce wan for th' walkin', he's off on his rambles, probably gone off down th' Crank road to that auld fort. Only thin' of interest there is th' soldier on sentry duty, wouldn't mind givin' him the glad eye now but he's fierce serious and stiff like, wouldn't ever pretend t' notice ya. Maybe I should be goin' up t' th' auld Conlon wan for a concoction. Ha ha,' Minnie said, and this time, wiping her face with the ends of her apron, she approached the bed and gave, possibly the most awkward curtsy Charlotte had ever seen.

'I'm forgettin' me manners. Mornin' m'lady, and what would ya be likin' for the breakfast?' Minnie said.

'I think I might just sleep some more and wait until Arthur returns,' Charlotte said, and anticipating Minnie's reply, added, 'There is no need for you to stay, I will be quite fine by myself.'

'Well, if you're sure, tell ya th' God's honest truth, I'm delighted to be attendin' on ya, but I still have all me other work to be doin', the hins won't brang in the eggs themselves, and Mammy gets fierce cross if she don't have them early for the bakin'. I'll leave ya to it so, and shure when himself is back I can come and take yer order for the breakfast,' Minnie said, and tucking the covers tightly under the mattress, she gave her lopsided curtsy again and left.

'You're too kind,' Charlotte said, as the covers tightened around her.

'Oh, an' I nearly forgot, there's a hape of letters for ya, that come durin' the week, so I left them there on the table for ya, an' if you're lookin' for writin' stuff, there's plenty over in that desk by th' wall,' Minnie went to the desk she had indicated and rattled the drawers, 'ah, good, just checkin' that they weren't locked.' And with that she left Charlotte, who after some wrestling with the bedclothes managed to free herself to retrieve the letters.

There were six letters, and from the handwriting on the envelopes Charlotte could discern all but two of the senders. How quickly they all had embraced her new title, as all were addressed to Mrs Arthur Bell Nicholls, although the addition in parenthesis of 'nee Bronteé' on one of the envelopes suggested a lack of complete confidence in the newness of the title finding its rightful bearer. Charlotte knew that that letter was from Mrs Elizabeth Smith, her publisher's mother, as she had similarly misspelt her surname in previous correspondence. The other known letters were from Ellen, Mrs Gaskell and Papa. She decided to open the mystery ones first but before doing so, seeing that Arthur had left the Widow Conlon's bottle, along with a spoon, beside the letters, she dutifully took it as had been recommended by Aunt Harriette, wincing and shaking her head as she swallowed hard.

The first of the letters was from Francis Bennoch, a short letter congratulating she and Arthur on their nuptials and once again inviting them to come stay with him and his wife in Blackheath, London. Charlotte had first met Mr Bennoch the previous autumn when he visited the parsonage. He was a London businessman and self-styled patron of authors and literature, who also dabbled in poetry, with no great measure of success. He was interested in being a patron to Charlotte. His visit to the parsonage, briefly overlapped with that of Elizabeth Gaskell, a cause of utter consternation to Charlotte as she was afraid that Bennoch, would also pester her regarding patronage. He was on the steps taking his time about leaving when Mrs Gaskell arrived by cab. Charlotte hastily said her goodbyes to Bennoch and leaving him in the company of the Reverend, she went to meet the new arrival, ushering her back up the steps, past the two men and straight into the house. Later, when she had explained the matter to Gaskell, they both agreed that these would-be patrons were a terrible nuisance. While this opinion coloured Charlotte's already prejudiced regard for the man, because of her Papa's great respect and liking for him, she politely answered all the letters he subsequently sent, each one extending an invite to London. And here was the latest one. Perhaps someday she and Arthur would get around to accepting, it was good to have places, other than hotels, to stay in the capital, and Bennoch had assured her that he would not be treating a visit as an opportunity for him to show off to his friends how he was acquainted with celebrated authors. If there was one thing Charlotte felt an insurmountable repugnance to, it was being lionised. She saw it as a vulgarising process and as she could not 'roar' when bid to do so, she knew she was a great disappointment to those who wished to put her on display.

The second envelope with the mysterious handwriting contained a brief note of congratulations from one of the churchwardens back in Haworth, George Taylor of the Manor House in Stanbury, a few miles from Haworth. At her father's insistence he had been placed on her wedding card list, although she herself was indifferent as to whether he was or was not informed, and yet, there was a certain gratification in receiving the good wishes of such an eminent member of the community.

In her letter, Ellen recounted how she and Miss Wooler had enjoyed the rest of the wedding day in the parsonage, and because the day turned out to be so fine they even managed a walk on the moors with Mr Sowden and Mr Grant. She assured Charlotte that they did not go far, despite Miss

Wooler's persistence that she was capable of walking any length that suited the party. Mr Sowden was mentioned on a few occasions which made Charlotte smile as she fully intended to play the matchmaker when she returned feeling certain that if Ellen were ever to marry, who would be more suited than Arthur's best friend. What better way to ensure that their friendship would survive beyond their spinster days? The latter part of the letter irked Charlotte, as Ellen expressed her concern for Revd Brontë, as to how he would adapt to the new circumstances in the parsonage, and how change was never easy for those of advanced years, and most irksome of all, was how she had written to Papa stating similar sentiments and congratulating him on his great magnanimity in so readily agreeing to the new arrangements the marriage occasioned. Charlotte knew that the last thing Papa needed was sympathy or an ally to champion his martyred cause as the put-upon father. Her diplomatic skills had been exhausted in convincing him of the benefits her marriage would bestow on him, in fact, at times it sounded as if her only reason for marrying Arthur was to bring a healthy male into the parsonage to do what the Reverend no longer could without much effort and risk to his health. This liberty of Ellen's was the result of their intimate correspondence since their school days, but Ellen would need to learn that a married woman could not enter into such confidential communication, her marriage to Arthur and how it did or did not affect Papa could not be the subject matter of future exchanges between them.

Mrs Elizabeth Smith's letter amused Charlotte, the profusion of delight expressed and rather overstated good wishes for the future happiness of the Bell Nicholls, suggested a sense of relief that Charlotte was finally spoken for. Charlotte was aware of a time when Mrs Smith worried about an attachment between her and Mrs Smith's son, George. Ever since his acceptance and publication of *Jane Eyre*, when he was just twenty-four, he and Charlotte enjoyed an intellectual relationship, both professionally and personally, based on common literary interests and a mutual respect. The tone of their correspondence was more akin to what you would expect between siblings, where one can speak one's mind without fear or favour. When she was in London, he played the role of host, bringing her to the theatre and the opera, introducing her to other literary figures, like Thackeray. There were times when others conjectured more romantic notions into this partnership, including his mother who was dismayed when he invited Charlotte to accompany him on a trip to Edinburgh, and again on a family trip down the Rhine. Charlotte accepted the first invitation but declined the continental trip as she saw it as one step too far in terms of how it would fuel already existing rumours. And, yes, there had been times when Charlotte questioned George's intentions, sending her gifts such as the portrait of Wellington, and boxes of books, and the genuine affection evident in his letters, but his engagement and marriage to another gave her the answer she always knew, theirs was a platonic affair.

Mrs Gaskell's letter brought as much joy as any of their previous interactions had, Charlotte loved more than anything to see her large, masculine handwriting scrawled across an envelope for she knew that the contents would be a mixture of gossip, intellectual musings, updates on family members, and advice on Charlotte's future projects or appraisal of what was completed. Apart from the congratulations on the wedding and the hope that she would see them soon in Plymouth Grove, Charlotte was thrilled to hear about Julia, Mrs Gaskell's youngest daughter and a great favourite of Charlotte's. Now, eight years old, Charlotte had first met her when she was five, and had after declared that the child had stolen a piece of her heart. When Mrs Gaskell had visited Charlotte the previous year, Charlotte had given her a book, *New Friends or a Fortnight at the Rectory*, to bring home to Julia and was now delighted to hear that the child had loved it and said that she would treasure it forever. As Charlotte thought about Julia, a warm feeling filled her heart, a rather strange one as it contradicted previous held convictions, and that was that someday she too could have a little Julia of her own.

She had deliberately left her papa's letter to the end, antici-pating his usual medical report on his health, and, selfishly, she felt that she had enough to be doing to concentrate and focus on restoring her own. Besides, other than worry, there was not much she could do from this remove if he had fallen ill since they had left. She had only read, 'Dearest Daughter,' when there was a slight tapping at the door followed by Arthur's en-trance. He looked so healthy, his cheeks flushed from the brisk morning air, and he looked hearty, the gaunt, drawn look from earlier in the year had been replaced by a robust physique.

'Arthur, I do believe you have gained some weight since our wedding day,' Charlotte said, and seeing that Arthur was un-sure as to whether that was a good or bad thing, she quickly added, 'which I am glad about, you need those extra pounds, a man of your stature.'

'And how is my Charlotte this morning?'

'You know, I feel quite well, perhaps not so well as to be able to tread your childhood paths just yet, but I do believe that another day of rest, and you will be able to resume your role of tour guide. Now, let me tell you what our friends have been saying in their correspondence, these letters are as much yours now as mine.'

Arthur listened attentively to her news, every now and then raising his eyebrows and nodding in agreement with Charlotte's understanding of what had been written, but when it came to her relaying the contents of Ellen's letter a frown flashed across his brow.

'Something is amiss, Arthur, why do you scowl?' Charlotte asked.

'Oh, it is just that she seems to be very liberal in her correspondence, I mean is it really her place to write to the Reverend, surely his welfare and his acceptance of the changed arrangements at the parsonage is our affair, our concern,' Arthur said.

'Ellen means well,' Charlotte said, surprised that her spontaneous reaction was to defend her friend, when Arthur's opinion completely concurred with her own.

'I am not sure that she would be a suitable match for Sutcliff,' Arthur said.

'Hmm, I wonder how many have said that of us? These matters are often beyond human understanding or indeed human interference. What will be, will be,' Charlotte said, immediately changing the subject to breakfast.

At a glance, Charlotte could see that the dining room table was set for ten people. On a sideboard, silver domes sheltered the food, tasselled circles of lace covered jam pots, and a basket made of woven reeds contained farls of soda bread and scones. Arthur insisted that she take her seat at the table while he served the food. Soon they were joined by Aunt Harriette, Cousin Harriette and James, another of Arthur's cousins, who, since his father's death, had assumed the role of the man of the house, as well as succeeding his father as the headmaster of the adjoining Cuba Royal school. Charlotte had pushed her chair back to rise and greet them, but Aunt Harriette insisted that she remain seated.

'Like I have already intonated to you, we do not stand on ceremony here, my dear. Gosh, I believe I have expressed a witticism,' she said, as James tutted but clearly enjoyed the pun.

'We have not met, Charlotte, I am James, the boring member of the family, unless you find Latin and Greek grammar interesting. I am afraid I spend too much time in the schoolrooms out back to know anything other than academia,' he said.

'Oh, pay no attention to him, Charlotte, it is a ploy to avoid having to be sociable. Our James prefers the company of books to people, even now, when there are no boys to be taught as school has finished for the summer,' Cousin Harriette said, seating herself beside Charlotte, 'we met briefly yesterday but I do not expect you to remember, you poor thing, you were a frightful colour, but I am glad to say that I see some pink in your cheeks now. Did you rest well? Do you like the room? Mama had it specially adapted to act as a bridal suite. Did you not, Mama?'

'I am afraid, Charlotte, that my name sake is the loquacious daughter, and you must feel free to bid her be quiet, whenever the prattle gets too much for you,' Aunt Harriette said, speaking from the sideboard where she was helping Arthur prepare plates of bacon, eggs, and black pudding.

Harriette was even prettier than her sister, Mary Anna, and possibly younger. Charlotte, looking at her side profile marvelled at her hairstyle. It was swept back from her face at the top and sides, and at the back, plaited hair had been twisted into a neat chignon. Charlotte wondered if she had achieved this style herself or if a maid had done it. When they would be better acquainted Charlotte intended asking as she would like to be more inventive with her own hair. She had tried hairpieces before with disastrous consequences. She still winced whenever she recalled posing for the artist George Richmond for her portrait when he mistook her hairpiece for a piece of brown merino wool that had detached from her hat and asked her to remove it. In recollecting the moment Charlotte could never decide which she found more mortifying, his comment or the fact that she burst into tears.

Throughout the meal, there was constant chatter back and forth regarding the latest news in the local paper, *The King's County Chronicle*, gossip about tenants, upcoming social gatherings with their, apparently, very wide network of friends, and questions to Arthur about their honeymoon thus far. Charlotte noted that there were many earls and lords mentioned and it pleased her greatly that the family she had married into were genteel people. The plated food that Arthur had placed in front of her was too much, she merely picked at the bacon, but the soda farl, still warm from the oven, with a scraping of butter melted into it was as delicious as any bread Emily used to make, perhaps more homely, though she knew it was heresy to even think that. Aunt Harriette who had been observing her must have read her thoughts.

'I think you are enjoying Brigid's bread. You will meet her anon when the morning busyness has subsided. Brigid is our cook, Minnie's mama, and the hardest working woman you will ever meet. I have to encourage her to sit down and take breaks, otherwise I fear the woman would keep going until she dropped from fatigue. Thankfully, these summer weeks give her more opportunities for rest periods as there are not thirty plus students as well as the family to cater for,' Aunt Harriette said.

'We are not slave drivers, Charlotte, Brigid has plenty of help during term time, although admittedly the turnover of local girls is quite high as they seldom measure up to her standards,' James said, and Arthur added, 'Oh, Charlotte knows all about the fussiness of servants and how they like to monopolise control of their kitchen, isn't that so, my dear?'

Charlotte was pleased that Arthur alluded to the fact that she too had servants, although she suspected that the little kitchen back at the parsonage would be no match for the kitchen in Cuba House, and she would be right. As there was no sign of Joseph, Allen or Mary Anna, Charlotte enquired as to their whereabouts.

'Sleeping late, Charlotte, the pace of life flows slowly here and, on a Saturday, it is a mere trickle,' Cousin Harriette said, and placing her hand on Charlotte's arm invited her to retire to the drawing room where they could become better acquainted over more cups of tea.

'Now, now, Harriette dear, you must let Charlotte and Arthur decide what they would like to do, besides, Charlotte may prefer to rest again. Am I right?' Aunt Harriette directed the question to Charlotte who replied that she would enjoy some more tea in the drawing room and, of course, Cousin Harriette's company.

'Well, Arthur, I think we are being dismissed, perhaps you would accompany me on some visits I must make to certain tenants. There is, yet again, a dispute brewing between the Dalys and Whelans over turf plots on the boglands,' James said as he rose, dropped his napkin onto his empty plate and pushed his chair back.

Arthur who was sitting opposite to Charlotte looked to her for approval, which her smile, albeit it a rather watery one, seem to bestow.

As the diners left the room, Minnie came bustling in declaring that she thought they would never get up, 'some of us have work t' do, even of a Saturday.'

'Pay no attention, Charlotte, one would think we were asking her to work for nothing,' Cousin Harriette said.

Charlotte gave Minnie a little wave, which she returned with her unique take on the curtsy.

The rest of the morning was pleasant enough in the company of Harriette, and Mary Anna who joined them.

Charlotte enjoyed hearing about their summer pursuits, which consisted of walks down country roads, flower and berry picking, visits to the poor of the parish, drawings they liked to do, lace making, entertaining their friends or visits to the friends' houses. Their lives were not that dissimilar to hers, apart from the gentry they entertained and visited: other than clergymen, and a few of her female friends, the parsonage was not frequented by many guests. Perhaps it would be different with Arthur there, he was so much more outgoing than she was, and it was beginning to be obvious where that social propensity had been nurtured.

Charlotte had hoped to respond to the letters in the afternoon but instead she curled up on the scroll couch in front of the fire in their bedroom and slept. On waking, Minnie, who was standing over her, declared that it was time for dinner. How Charlotte longed to remain exactly as she was, where was Arthur when she needed him.

Chapter Eighteen

Sunday morning was warm and sunny so it was decided that the family would walk to service. What a novelty it was for Charlotte to stroll down a country road, with the tolls of the church bell competing with buzzing and chirping from the hedgerows, as opposed to negotiating her way alongside the headstones between the parsonage and chapel at home. If alone the journey was ideal for reflection suitable for Sunday prayer and worship, alas sandwiched between Cousin Harriette and Mary Anna and their constant chatter Charlotte could barely hear herself think. How different life with Anne and Emily had been, the former's sweet, gentle tones often barely audible, and the latter, for the most part, silent. Perhaps it was the cousins' youth that Charlotte found tiring, it seemed such a long time since she herself was in her twenties, the time that she remembers as her Heger days.

Monsieur Heger was her teacher in Brussels, and embarrassing though it was for her mature self to admit, he was her first love, her first obsession, and her first, indeed, her only heartbreak, her passion being unrequited. Charlotte could now understand that what she mistook for affection was in fact admiration for his star pupil, his expressed excitement at her achievements was the mark of a great teacher eager to be the one to nurture a talent. Those two years spent in Brussels were the most formative years of her life. Apart from her educational advancement these years inspired two of her most memorable fictional characters, Mr Rochester in *Jane Eyre*, and Paul Emmanuel in *Villette*, both versions of this teacher Constantin Heger. She knew she had made a fool of herself in her letters to him following her return to England, all of them written in French, which she also regretted, as writing in a foreign language added a greater liberty to her sentiments, a greater passion, not unlike the act of creative writing where the more imaginative, daring self, moves the pen. It was her hope that he had destroyed them, lest they fall into the hands of his wife, or worse, what if they were ever to be brought to Arthur's attention. Charlotte knew they would read as one long whine about how miserable she was when Monsieur Heger did not write back, or when he restricted her correspondence to two letters in a year. Why could she not tell that he had no interest in her, and not only because he was a married man, but because there was nothing about her to attract the passions of a black swan, the sobriquet she ascribed to him. At least she had had the good sense to destroy all his letters, hoping at the time that the flames would also consume her passion. For the most part, the fire obliged.

Watching Arthur stride ahead with his cousins and brother, his broad shoulders and back held erect, his coat tail flapping from the vigour of his gait, how he contrasted with the squat, dark little figure of Heger, here was the hero of her juvenilia, her Zamorna, or the nearest she could hope to come to such a fiction. How grateful she was for the unanswered prayers of her youth, perhaps she should share this wisdom over the days with Cousin Harriette and Mary Anna, encourage them to refrain from making life changing decisions until they are more advanced in years and experience.

Standing at the gates of the church Charlotte got her first proper view of the town of Banagher as it stretched down the hill before them towards the River Shannon. And such a hill it was! Charlotte had thought the one in Haworth to be the steepest imaginable, but this long road surpassed the gradient of the Cobbles. The party of seven waited in the yard for Aunt Harriette and the youngest Bell, William, who were arriving by carriage.

Inside the church was radiant with red velvet cushions brightening the wooden pews, and vases of flowers perfumed the air. The Bells' pew was to the right of the altar, and as their guest, Charlotte was seated in the front row, next to Arthur, Aunt Harriette and William. As the other parishioners came in, Aunt Harriette whispered their names: Armstrongs, Molloys, Purefoys, and many others, who waved hellos to Charlotte, or approached to shake her hand, congratulate her and welcome her to Banagher. It was clear to her from their interactions with Arthur and the Bells that she had married into a well-respected, important family. So many of them informed her that she had married one of the best gentlemen in the country and broken many an Irish heart. This pleased Charlotte. When everyone was seated, Revd Turner, the parish rector, coming from the rear of the church approached the lectern which was near enough to Charlotte for him to be able to reach over and offer her his hand. She could feel her cheeks redden to be singled out in this way. Arthur later apologised for not preparing her enough for the affable ways of the people of Banagher. For Charlotte, the strangest part of the Eucharistic service was how she felt like she was experiencing something for the first time despite the familiarity of the prayers and hymns. Was it the unfamiliarity of the people, except for Arthur? Did the voices sound more joyous? Or was it because for the first time since the passing of Branwell, Emily and Anne, she sat in church surrounded by family, surrounded by ... dare she think it ... love.

Aunt Harriette insisted that Charlotte return to Cuba Court in the carriage, which Charlotte welcomed as it gave her an opportunity to become acquainted with William, with whom she had had little interaction. For a boy of fifteen, he was rather grave, but from the short conversation with him, Charlotte could tell that he was intelligent beyond his years. In answer to her question as to whether he hoped to follow in his relatives' footsteps and attend Trinity, he said that he was torn between medicine and joining the navy.

'His older brother, Arthur, another Arthur, is a doctor in the army, and my eldest son, Alan, yes, another Allen, is a captain in the army, as is my brother, who is currently in the Crimea. So, as you can imagine, Charlotte, the last thing I need is for my pet robin here to join up. I am afraid that Heaven will tire of my countless petitions for all of their safety,' Aunt Harriette said.

'Was it not rather confusing for you, Aunt Harriette, with so many Alans and Arthurs to distinguish between them?' Charlotte asked.

'Not in the slightest, my dear, their unique personalities voided the sameness of name,' Aunt Harriette said as the carriage came to a stop, 'ah, we are home, you must be hungry, let us see what Brigid has prepared for lunch.'

Lunch was a noisy affair now that all nine were present. Charlotte had never experienced such ebullience at a dining table, even when the parsonage table had been full, meals had been consumed in a quiet fashion. She wondered at the tenth place setting that remained empty. Mary Anna, who seemed to be on constant watch followed her gaze.

'We mustn't talk of the empty chair, Charlotte, or I am afraid we will have to deal with a scene from Harriette,' Mary Anna said.

'Hush, hush, don't be so obtuse, Mary Anna,' Aunt

Harriette said, and placing her hand over Cousin Harriette's, who was seated next to her, she continued, 'I am sure John has a particularly good reason for his absence.'

'Thank you, Mama. Mary Anna, sometimes you can be so tiresome. Charlotte, my sister is referring to our cousin, John Evans, who was due to arrive on the same day as you and Arthur, but as you can see, has failed to show,' Cousin Harriette said.

'He is not just any cousin, Charlotte, he is to marry Harriette, or at least was to marry her,' Mary Anna said.

'That is quite enough, Mary Anna, now you are being impertinent. Let us discuss our plans for this afternoon, I believe it has been proposed to bring Charlotte to the river to cross our splendid new bridge and to see our Martello tower,' Aunt Harriette said.

At the mention of a Martello tower, Charlotte looked to Arthur.

'Yes, we have a tower, one of the few inland ones. We are full of surprises here in Ireland,' Arthur said.

'Of course, this excursion depends on how you are feeling, Charlotte. Do you continue to take Widow Conlon's cough bottle?' Aunt Harriette asked.

'Yes, is that the correct thing to do?' Charlotte asked.

'Of course, my dear, it will do you no harm, only good … only good,' Aunt Harriette said, and leaning back to address Jimmy, the cab driver, who was now, it would seem, doubling as the butler, she asked that he make sure that the carriage was ready to take Arthur and Charlotte.

'Oh please, I think I would rather walk, Aunt Harriette, the day is so fine, and I wish to take in the sights more leisurely,' Charlotte said.

'If I must go, I will take the carriage,' William interrupted.

'William, my dear, you do not have to do anything that is not your preference,' Aunt Harriette said.

James gave his young brother a stern stare.

'What? You are not master of me in the house. We are not in school. Mama, can you see how he glares at me,' William said.

'Boys,' Aunt Harriette said.

'You are too soft on him, Mama,' James said.

'Welcome to the real Bells, Charlotte, where no meal would be complete without inappropriate banter and backchat,' Joseph said, and rather than anyone take offence there was general laughter, including William. Charlotte laughed even more to see Minnie's expression of derision as she stood with her back against the sideboard, her arms folded, tapping her foot, clearly impatient at how long the lunch was taking.

Later that afternoon, Charlotte was pleased to be able to walk arm in arm with Arthur; since arriving in Banagher there had been little opportunity to enjoy each other's company without the constant presence of family. Cousin Harriette wished to remain behind in the hope that John Evans would arrive in the afternoon; James declared that he had administrative work to prepare in readiness for the new school term; and Arthur's brother, Allen, was preparing to return to Dublin, so there was only Mary Anna and Joseph to accompany the couple on their walk to the river: Aunt Harriette and young William were visiting their friends, the Armstrongs in Garrycastle, but hoped to meet up with the walking party in the evening. Aunt Harriette felt that Charlotte should return to Cuba Court by carriage, as over exertion would surely occasion a relapse.

'You must tell me about this elusive John Evans, Arthur. Did I hear correctly that he is a cousin? And engaged to his cousin! Apart from Queen Victoria, I thought this practice was rather frowned upon these days?' Charlotte asked.

'Ah, yes, but strictly speaking they are not first cousins, John's father and Aunt Harriette were half brother and sister, they shared a father but had different mothers. By all accounts, John Evans is a law unto himself. He lives in the wilds of Connemara and if she marries him, it is there that Harriette will have to go. Aunt is not pleased but will not stand in the way of her daughter's happiness. Evans is a man of the world; he has been to the Americas and back on more than one occasion. Decent fellow, but flighty, always looking to the next adventure, I hope Harriette knows what she is doing,' Arthur said.

'Does the course of love ever follow a reasoned trajectory?' Charlotte asked.

'Hmm, you speak out of ignorance of my cousin, she is a home bird, I cannot see her ever being happy in any place other than Banagher, it is a worry,' Arthur said.

'Your concern for your cousin is great, if her happiness is of such importance to you perhaps you should have married her yourself and remained here,' Charlotte said, and although she said it in jest, Arthur did not react accordingly, 'oh dear, your face, my thane, is a book where men may read strange matters, is there something I should know?'

'Yes, you should know that my family see in you what I see, they are charmed by you and so honoured to have a celebrity in their midst, and now, I am forgetting my role as guide, I should tell you a little about this hotel and it's most famous guest to date, non-other than Anthony Trollope,' Arthur said, avoiding the question asked, as they stopped outside a building bearing the name, The Harp Hotel.

Charlotte had no interest in hearing about Trollope, Arthur's avoidance of her question had not gone unnoticed. What was to know? Had Arthur and Harriette been more than cousins to each other? Well, if Arthur wanted to shy away from his personal history, she knew someone who would be only too willing to spill the beans. Minnie!

'Oh, Arthur, I am not sure I want to know anything about Trollope, the little I know is already too much. You know that Emily and Anne's trickster publisher, Newby, also published Trollope's debut novel that same year, but from what we have been able to discern, despite the absolute obscurity of his novel, we believe he had a more lucrative arrangement with the scoundrel, Newby. I can't even remember the name of the failed thing,' Charlotte said, indicating with a slight tug on Arthur's arm that she wished to continue down the street towards the river.

'*The MacDermots of Ballycloran*,' Arthur said.

'Who? Where?' Charlotte asked, looking around, expecting to see a family group.

'Trollope's book, it was called *The MacDermots of Ballycloran*, and I am afraid, you might not like this, but it was, and probably still is, a great favourite in these parts. The town continue to follow his achievements with great pride as he is seen somewhat as a son of Banagher,' Arthur said, and perhaps realising how this might sound to a literary rival, he quickly changed the subject to point out the local distillery and Crank Road, which he declared to be his favourite country walk, one which they must do before leaving.

Mary Anna and Joseph had stopped to allow Arthur and Charlotte to catch up, and Charlotte, feeling rather stung by the celebrity status Trollope held in the town where she had believed she was the most celebrated author, asked the siblings for their opinion of her rival.

'Oh, I have no interest in ever reading anything by him. Once I met him on horseback on a country lane down by the river. I was walking and quite taken aback by the gruff manner in which he yelled at me to get the devil out of his way. Quite an unpleasant man if you ask me,' Mary Anna said, 'clearly I am no Jane Eyre and Mister Trollope was no Rochester.'

'Exactly what I was thinking,' Charlotte said, knowing the reference Mary Anna was making to her heroine's first encounter with her future husband in *Jane Eyre*, 'Arthur tells me he is a great favourite in the town.'

'Arthur is misinformed, he was popular in certain circles, mostly horsey ones associated with fox-hunting, and I believe was a great dancer at social gatherings, but he fell out of favour when he chose an English lady as a wife and had the audacity to bring her back to Banagher and parade her among the locals,' Joseph said, and perhaps seeing the shocked expressions on everyone's faces he added, 'well … you know … it was expected that he would marry a local girl … especially after waltzing so many of them around the dancehalls.'

'You are absolutely clueless, Joseph,' Mary Anna said, prodding her brother's arm.

'What have I done?' Joseph asked.

'Fell out of favour for marrying an English girl? What do you think Charlotte is? Pay no heed, Charlotte, both these two are misinformed, Trollope was never liked by the ordinary people of the town and district, and his wife less so, and not because she was English, but because she was a prissy snob who looked down her pointy nose on all of us,' Mary Anna said, and taking hold of Charlotte, led her down the street towards the bridge, leaving the two men looking at each other.

'Sorry, old boy,' Joseph said.

'I am the one who is sorry for bringing him up in the first place,' Arthur said, as they followed behind the ladies.

Standing in the centre of the bridge, Charlotte was reminded of how they had stood on Carlisle Bridge, but this view could not have been more different to that of the metropolis. Here the expanse of the Shannon glistered like glass in the July sunshine mirroring the clouds as they slowly drifted across its surface; on either side fields dotted with the yellow and whites of summer flowers stretched horizontally until the many shades of green met the azure of the sky. Sheep and cattle grazed in indolent fashion along the banks, a goat and its kid sat majestically on a wooden jetty: queen and successor to this ancient land of theirs. Charlotte had never seen such beauty, she breathed in deeply and held her breath as if to capture the essence of the scene, imbibe it into her very being. Joseph had begun to talk about the construction of the bridge, and the great day it was for the town when it opened, just over ten years previously, and Charlotte, perhaps momentarily forgetting her position as guest, asked him to stop.

'You are not feeling well, my dear?' Arthur asked, 'I knew this walk was not a good idea, come we will find somewhere on the bank for you to sit down.'

'Au contraire, Arthur, this is the most well, the most alive I have felt since leaving home. Pardon me, Joseph, I did not mean to be so abrupt, but listen, what can you hear?' Charlotte said.

They all raised an ear in unison.

'Nothing.' It was Joseph who spoke.

'Precisely. Silence. Even the birds and bees are stilled by this magnificence,' Charlotte said, and for the following moments the group stood, until a clanging sound from the nearby mill broke the stillness. Arthur suggested that they walk to Connaught. Charlotte frowned, but Mary Anna understanding his meaning, took a step forward and declared to be there already.

'You see, Charlotte, the middle of the bridge is the border between King's County and Galway, Leinster and Connaught. You do know about our four provinces?' Mary Anna asked.

Charlotte was aware, but rather than enter into a conversation about it, having absolutely no interest in the geography of Ireland, she declared that perhaps they should find a spot to sit and admire the scene. Her mood had suddenly shifted as it was often wont to do. She would have liked to be left alone, as for the first time on her honeymoon a strange sense of loneliness was creeping in, maybe it was the reference to Trollope's English wife, or more likely it was the idea that there was something more than familial affection between Arthur and Cousin Harriette, Charlotte was feeling her otherness, a feeling that not even a band of gold had the power to alleviate. She thought about her Papa, saw him sitting alone at his desk, and wished that she could either magic him here to witness his homeland in all its verdant splendour or failing that, spirit herself, momentarily, back to the parsonage and ask him if he would like some tea. This was not new to her, whenever her heart soared with joy or plummeted with despair, it was always family she sought with whom to share the transport.

They continued across the bridge and found a spot on the bank. Joseph, undeterred by the earlier request to stop talking, gave a detailed history of the Martello tower behind where they sat, Cromwell's castle to their right, and the barracks and mills that they could see across the river. Charlotte allowed the sound of his voice to follow the clouds gliding along under the bridge as she focused on the languid movements of the cattle who were drinking from the river, down in front of them. She had never been this close to cows; every so often one would raise its large head and fix her with its bulbous eyes, giving her the sense that she was being judged, not by a dumb animal but by some Celtic God who was appraising her worthiness to be a part of their pastoral scape. Arthur had positioned himself in such a way as to allow her to lean against his left shoulder. When she took off her bonnet, he kissed the top of her head and that sensation of loneliness began to lift, she felt accepted again, included in her new family: but she resolved that she would, notwithstanding this sense of acceptance, make inquiries from Minnie.

Chapter Nineteen

Charlotte and Mary Anna, as had been arranged, returned to Cuba Court, with Aunt Harriette and William in the family gig. Aunt Harriette was in a heightened state of animation, declaring that she had a stupendous surprise to share later with Charlotte and Arthur. Charlotte did not like surprises and strained to express excited anticipation. Mary Anna compensated for her dearth of enthusiasm with clapping and whoops of delight.

'Oh, knowing where you have been, Mama, I am guessing this surprise will involve fiddlers and quadrilles,' Mary Anna said.

'It may, my dear, it may, but you must desist from further speculation, lest you steal my thunder,' Aunt Harriette said, and addressing Charlotte explained that Mary Anna was referring to how the Armstrongs, whom she had been visiting, were well known for their social gatherings that always involved music and dancing.

Charlotte hoped the surprise involved nothing of the sort.

Afternoon tea with sandwiches and lemon cake was being served in the dining room. There was still no sign of John Evans which Charlotte assumed accounted for the sense of dejection she detected in Cousin Harriette's demeanour, and fearing this might elicit sympathy from Arthur and perhaps rekindle old desires, she felt a greater imperative to know their emotional history. She excused herself from the table, and asked Minnie, who once again was hovering by the sideboard looking decidedly impatient, if she would accompany her to the bedroom. Minnie brightened up and ran to the door to open it, clearly delighted to have a reason to leave her serving duties.

'Charlotte, dear, you must join me in the drawing room, we have yet to have a tête-a- tête, there is so much I wish to discuss with you, including that matter I hinted at in the carriage,' Aunt Harriette said, and seeing that Arthur was about to speak, she added, 'you may join us later for the announcement, but you cannot monopolise all of her time, my dear boy, we of the fairer sex need time exclusively to ourselves.'

As soon as Minnie closed the bedroom door Charlotte asked if she could be so bold as to inquire about Arthur's life before she knew him.

'It is a curious thing that everyone here seems to be more knowledgeable, more intimate with my husband than I, even though I have known the man for almost ten years. Tell me all the secrets a wife ought to know,' Charlotte said, endeavouring to sound flippant and gay, qualities that did not come naturally to her.

'Secrets! Jaypers, there are no such things in this place, shure, ya see wha' they're like, never stop yappin', everyone knows everyone's business, and if wan o' them had a secret itself, they wouldn't be able to howld it in, as me mammy sez, couldn't howld ther' piss. Oh, cripes, sorry Miss, m'lady, that's shockin' talk,' Minnie said, giving her now customary curtsy, 'but ya know wha' I mean.'

'Indeed, I do, Minnie. Tell me then, I am told that I may have broken some hearts by snatching Mr Nicholls away, do you know who these grieving females might be,' Charlotte said, deciding that a more forthright approach was called for.

Minnie narrowed her eyes and a rather wicked grin stretched in a line across her face; the look of one who has had an interesting epiphany.

'Ah, now, I'm getting' th' drift. Someone's bin talkin', haven't the'?' Minnie said, 'well, wha' I'm goin' to say to ya now, Miss, is from wha' I know, th' only woman Masther Artur ever wanted was a certain English writer of books, and I'm lookin' at her right now. And if anyone tells ya differ, don't you b' mindin' them.'

Charlotte was not happy with this answer, but she could not bring herself to mention Cousin Harriette's name, not to Minnie, it wasn't fair to interrogate her in this underhand fashion, besides it was also a terrible breach of trust in Arthur, and Minnie was a clever girl and would see it for what it was, the roaring twin tigers of jealousy and insecurity. If anyone were to be asked outright, it was Arthur, but she would wait until they had left Banagher, and she had him once again all to herself.

The evening sun had retreated to the window end of the drawing room when Charlotte joined Aunt Harriette, who sat in front of the fire, and were it not for the glow from the fire, the lamps being unlit, Charlotte would not have noticed her presence upon entering. There was something decidedly regal about Aunt Harriette, who sat forward on the two-seater, brocaded couch, there was a likeness to images Charlotte had seen of Queen Victoria, although this queen of Cuba Court was older. She indicated the chair opposite for Charlotte. Normally, this would be an occasion of great anxiety for Charlotte, to be alone with someone she barely knew, but such was the charming, easy mannerisms of the older lady, Charlotte was relaxed. A circular ornate table at Charlotte's elbow held a glass of sherry and a decanter; Aunt Harriette who was holding a similar glass, motioned for Charlotte to pick hers up.

'Let us raise a toast to continued female companionship throughout your married life. It is one thing, my dear, to have the support of your husband, but it is an altogether greater necessity to have the support of your female family and friends, and alas, my poor child, in your case, I am aware that along with your good papa, we must now be considered your family. Here's to our daughter and sister,' Aunt Harriette said, raising her glass. The crystal sparkled in a ray of sunlight giving the impression that the old lady was a sorceress casting a spell.

Aunt Harriette wanted to hear all about Haworth, the parsonage and the Revd Brontë, and how married life would be for them on their return. Was the town vastly different to Banagher? How had life been since the tragic losses that so recently befell the family? How was her Papa's health? Had she heard from him since the wedding? Would Charlotte continue to write? How onerous would Arthur's duties be as curate? Would there be an expectation that she would assist? Charlotte was, at first, conservative with her answers, especially regarding the more personal matters of her family and her writing, but the interest and empathy that Aunt Harriette expressed in everything she said, loosened her reserve, and before the first glass was emptied, Charlotte felt as comfortable as she would have felt with Ellen Nussey.

'Here I am seeking your sympathy for my grief when you too have had such tragedies. It is a terrible thing to lose a sibling but what must the torture be to lose a child, and Arthur tells me that two of your daughters were prematurely called to their heavenly home,' Charlotte said.

'It is sweet of you to say that: Susan and Frances,' Aunt Harriette said, looking into her glass as she swirled the contents, 'I cannot think of them lying in the cold ground of the churchyard, I prefer to see them as little girls skipping around the garden, playing hide and seek around the lime trees. They were not so little when God brought them home, but I prefer to remember their boisterous days of fun and laughter.'

'I understand completely, when I think of Anne and Emily, we are forever climbing to Top Withins or stepping gingerly on the stones that cross the brook by the waterfall,' Charlotte said. Top Withins was a farmhouse on the moors that was a particular favourite with Emily, and according to her the inspiration for Wuthering Heights farm. The waterfall was a spot on the moors where the sisters went on sunny days to sit on large boulders on the bank of a brook, read to each other from their latest instalments, sometimes write a little, but mostly bask in the sunshine, their eyes closed, listening to the babble of flowing water from the stream compete with the rumbling, cascading sounds of the waterfall.

'It is important to remember, Charlotte; I think of my girls and my Alan every day. Alas, life is for the living, and we must not dwell on the past, we must embrace the present and plan for the future. My boys and girls and their welfares keep me occupied, and no doubt some day you will be equally employed with children of your own,' Aunt Harriette said, picking up a bell from the table beside her chair and ringing it, 'I will get Minnie to refill our glasses.'

Charlotte, feeling courageous from the effects of the sherry, decided that Aunt Harriette might be the more appropriate person to ask about the relationship between Arthur and Cousin Harriette.

'Harriette, can I be so bold as to ask you something rather delicate, something that has been playing on my senses, and I fear if I do not address it, my thoughts will become as daggers of my mind?' Charlotte asked, hoping Minnie would not be too punctual as her opportunity would be lost.

'Of course, my dear, what concerns you?' Aunt

Harriette said.

'You are no doubt conscious of Arthur's handsome stature, his education, his kind ways, in fact, every aspect of his character that is superior to my plainness,' Charlotte said, and seeing that Aunt Harriette was about to protest, she continued, 'no, a moment, there is a reason for this preface. Seeing how much more suitable your daughters would have been, I am left wondering why a marriage between Arthur and Harriette or Arthur and Mary Anna was never considered. Or perhaps it was, and one or other of the party rejected the notion?'

'Oh dear, someone has been talking and filling your head with falsehoods,' Aunt Harriette said, as Minnie appeared, panting.

'Well, th' blessin's o' God on me good ears, I keep tellin' ya to use the bigger school bell, just as well I was nearby,' Minnie said.

'As nearby, no doubt, as outside the door listening, Minnie. Never mind, would you be so kind as to replenish our glasses and then ask your mother to come and say hello to Charlotte,' Aunt Harriette said.

'Right,' Minnie said, tutted, for no reason that was apparent to Charlotte, refilled the glasses from the decanter, tutted again, and left.

'Minnie is herself. Now, let me put your mind at ease regarding my daughters and your Arthur. Firstly, there is something you need to know; since he first laid eyes on you, Arthur has longed for this day, a longing that had many interludes of despair, as it would seem that you were rather niggardly in your early responses to his advances. I might add advances that you, no doubt, were completely unaware of; the courtship of men is a clumsy affair of starts and stutters,' Aunt Harriette said.

Charlotte smiled and agreed.

'Well, a few summers ago, Arthur arrived home for his annual holidays, a rejected, lonely soul. He declared that all hope of ever having the courage to propose to you had deserted him, that before leaving Haworth he had taken tea with you in the parsonage, that he was in top spirits and had resolved that he would ask if you would be interested in accompanying him to Ireland, but before he got a chance you dismissed him, stating how inconsiderate and inconvenient it was for him to invite himself to tea, that he seemed to think you had nothing to do but entertain Irish curates, and that perhaps he needed to reread *Shirley* to be reminded of your opinion of the same breed,' Aunt Harriette said.

Charlotte remembered the evening well, she remembered how she had anticipated an advance of sorts, from how he comported himself, and as she was unsure of her own mind at that time, she deliberately wrapped herself in the mantle of the scold to dampen his ardour. She hung her head in shame at the memory.

'And as you know the lonely heart will do anything to ease the ache, so, Arthur, the dear boy, decided to propose to Harriette, who was only nineteen at the time. You see what he was doing, seeking comfort in the known. He did not have to fight for Harriette's affections, they were already his, but they were those of a sister, not a sweetheart. It was I who pointed this out to him, besides, I told him, he and Harriette would never last as a married couple, they are both too headstrong, if either daughter was suitable, and I might add, I do not believe they are, it would be Mary Anna. It was never serious, Charlotte, a whimsical moment in the life of Cuba House, which we subsequently laughed about,' Aunt Harriette said, her smile morphing to a frown as she added, 'but, who has been speaking about this of late?'

'Only my inner demons of doubt in the happiness I am

experiencing, a happiness I never expected. Your daughters are beauties, Harriette, they will step lithely down the primrose path towards matrimony. When I looked in the mirror, I saw only the wide brow of a spinster,' Charlotte said.

'You need to change your mirror, my child. Have you any idea of the happiness you have bestowed on Arthur? I knew from the moment he helped you out of the carriage that yours was a marriage of souls. The magnetism between you both is palpable,' Aunt Harriette paused as Minnie and her mother, Brigid, entered, 'welcome, welcome, Brigid, come, come and meet our very special guest, Charlotte.'

Charlotte could tell that Brigid had none of the swagger of her daughter, as she vigorously rubbed her hands against her sides before taking Charlotte's extended hand, keeping her head bowed, avoiding any eye contact.

'It is lovely to meet you, Brigid, and compliment you in person on your wonderful food, I am going to have to steal some of your recipes or I will never satisfy Arthur. Indeed, if I thought I could, it is you I would steal, as one of our cooks is very advanced in age,' Charlotte said, instantly regretting the comment, as it sounded more bumptious than she had intended.

'Will there be anythin' else, Mam,' Brigid said, looking rather like a frightened animal, as she addressed Aunt Harriette,

'I would invite you to share a sherry with us, Brigid, but I know the consternation that would cause you, I am sure you just want to get back to your loom,' Aunt Harriette said, 'Charlotte, not only is Brigid an extraordinary cook, she is one of the town's top weavers, and that is saying something, the women of Banagher are known the length and breadth of the country for their skills at the loom,' and turning her attention back to Brigid, 'I am sure you are busy getting ready for the September fair, it won't be long coming around now, will it?'

Brigid smiled, and jerking her shoulders slightly forward in what could have been an attempt at a bow, she turned and scurried out the door. Minnie, who was all this time standing with folded arms, rolled her eyes in obvious dismay at her mother's obsequiousness.

'You may go too, Minnie, and perhaps, seek out the others and ask them to join us,' Aunt Harriette said, and waited until the door was closed before taking up the conversation from where they had left it.

'So, my dear Charlotte, I hope I have reassured you against your earlier concerns. Arthur Bell Nicholls has only ever wanted one woman for his wife and that woman sits before me now.'

Charlotte was very reassured, and she said so. While they waited, the conversation turned to literature. Harriette was curious as to what Charlotte's next project would be. Charlotte said there was nothing much to say, as she was unsure yet of the plot, which prompted Harriette to ask about the plots of her previous books and where they had come from.

'I start with a character and an idea, and then I write, and often what appears on the page before me is akin to the surprise the alchemist witnesses in his phial after he has mixed his matter, unclear of what the outcome will be. My base metals are my imagination, my experiences, my knowledge of literature, and as I write they all merge so that when the tale is told, I can seldom account for what was fact or what was fancy,' Charlotte said, 'but as you no doubt are aware, it would seem that those who declare themselves as experts at analysing fiction have concluded that all that I write must be autobiographical, and other than I allow the next of my heroines to commit a dastardly crime of murder, I fear I will never dissuade them of their mythology.'

'Oh, do, I declare I am rather partial to gruesome tales, it is why Sheridan le Fanu is a great favourite in this house,' Aunt Harriette said, and motioning towards a cabinet sandwiched between bookshelves, 'we keep all of our magazines, journals, periodicals in there. If you get some spare time, I am sure you will find plenty to interest you among the contents. Le Fanu's stories are in the Dublin University Magazine: a wonderful publication.'

'Yes, I am familiar with it, I was given a very pleasant review in it,' Charlotte said.

'How silly of me to forget, you know, sitting together over the fire like this, I quite forget I am talking to the celebrated authoress!' Aunt Harriette said as the door opened and in came Arthur, Mary Anna, and William.

'I cannot wait any longer, Mama, to hear about this surprise, and no amount of bribery can extract detail from William,' Mary Anna said, rustling her way across the floor and joining her mother on the couch. Arthur stood by the fireplace, while William sat at the table near the window, on which lay a round wooden board with marbles, Charlotte marvelled at it as she associated the game of Solitaire with chic parlours in London.

'Charlotte, are you familiar with Mary Rosse, actually, I should say the Countess of Rosse, but we are on first names terms, as she is with half the county, or so it seems?' Aunt Harriette asked.

Charlotte knew of the Countess because she came from a very well-to-do family in Yorkshire, the Fields of Bradford, her father, an extremely wealthy landlord owned extensive tracts of land in that area. At one stage it was popular knowledge that Mary and her sister were the most eligible heiresses in possibly all of England, and therefore no surprise that she attracted the attention of an Earl.

'Other than her being from Yorkshire, I am afraid that I am ignorant of the lady,' Charlotte said, hoping against hope that this question was not leading to a possible introduction.

'Well, my dear, Mary is quite a force to be reckoned it, I do not know where she gets her energy, she is renowned for her lavish luncheons, always splendid affairs with large gatherings in the most extensive dining room you will ever witness,' Aunt Harriette said, and Mary-Anne added, 'Oh, I knew it, please say we have been invited, Mama, I knew it, I knew it, and Charlotte, there will be fiddlers and quadrilles.'

Charlotte looked to Arthur to gauge his reaction, knowing that he would understand how loathsome these occasions were to her, but he was grinning, as she saw it, like an idiot.

'Mary, even though she has recently had another child, has taken up a new hobby, photography. I should explain, the family are obsessed with the latest advancement in scientific matters, such a clever family really, and, obviously, financially secure enough to indulge their interests, no doubt you have heard of Lord Rosse's telescope, the Leviathan?' Aunt Harriette asked.

'Oh, Mama, Charlotte is not interested in science stuff, are you Charlotte?' Mary Anna said, 'have we been invited to the castle?'

'Yes, indeed, we have. Mary heard that the author, Currer Bell, was here and she is insisting that we attend tomorrow, not just for lunch, but to enable her to take a photograph of, as she put, the most famous Yorkshire lady of them all,' Aunt Harriette said, beaming at Charlotte.

It was too much for Charlotte, there was no way she could control her abhorrence at the prospects of not just a large gathering where it was likely that she would be the focus of all stares, but also having to have her photograph taken. From what she understood, these photographs, unlike the kind-ly brush strokes of the artist, would present her image as it was when she looked in the mirror, with all her imperfections on display. And as to the mention of a castle, she was only just coming to terms with the size of Cuba Court, she did not like the sound of that at all. Again, she looked to Arthur, desperation beading its way down her brow, and trickling into her neck.

'My dear, I can see you are flushed with excitement,' Aunt Harriette said, misinterpreting the sweat on Charlotte's brow, 'we are expected at noon tomorrow, so I suggest we have a light breakfast, as the food will be as sumptuous as the surroundings.'

'I'm not going.'

It was William who spoke, as he hopped one marble over the other on his board game. 'I will be stuck again with Laurence and his brothers who will have me running all around the castle and grounds, talking non-stop about telescopes and mirrors and stars. It is exhausting, Mama.'

'It is a house of great energy, there is no doubt about that. Please yourself, William,' Aunt Harriette said, and turning her attention again to Charlotte suggested that it was time for bed, that an early night would ensure enough energy for the excursion to Birr Castle on the morrow.

When they were back in the room Charlotte gave vent to her horror and vehemently chastised Arthur for remaining dumb, knowing how she would feel about the invitation.

'If I must feign a relapse I will, I had thought that our days here would be spent leisurely strolling down country roads. Lunch in a castle! Half the county in attendance! I might be a known Yorkshire woman, Arthur, but I am not in the same league as the Fields of Heaton Hall. Posing to have my image taken! I am just about recovered from my experience with Richmond. You must get me out of this predicament, Arthur, you must. I would as lief spend the day knitting with Minnie … in the kitchen!'

'Charlotte, I think you will like the Countess, she is a kind lady, and I have no doubt will immediately put you at your ease. This is a wonderful opportunity, and to be able to say that you saw the greatest telescope in the world. You told me how much you enjoyed the Great Exhibition, well, the home of the Countess and the Earl, is like one enormous display,' Arthur said, as he fed sods of turf on to the fire.

Charlotte continued to pace the room, wringing her hands in evident distress, a state of affairs that previously would have seen Arthur acquiesce to her wishes, but he remained calm and seemingly nonplussed as he suggested that she should do as Aunt Harriette suggested and prepare for bed.

'Just because you want to go and hobnob. Really, Arthur, I was unaware of this shallow aspect of your personality,' Charlotte said.

'Now you are being silly, Charlotte, I am trying to save you from yourself, sometimes you are too headstrong for your own good. Trust me, you will enjoy the visit,' Arthur said, and advancing towards her, he stretched his arms inviting her in, 'come, come, lest we have our first wedded altercation, I want to hear all about your 'tête-à-tête' with Aunt Harriette.'

Charlotte allowed herself to be held but remained rigid, until Arthur's stroke of her back eased her tenseness, and, although, still resolved to refuse to attend the lunch, she found herself melting into his embrace, before they were interrupted by a loud knock on the door. Without moving, they both said, 'Minnie!'

Clearly Minnie heard them and took it as an invitation to enter.

'Missus Charlotte, please please, pretty please, take me wit' ya t'morrow'. I only was the wanst in Parsonstown, ain't that righ' Masther Artur, but never, ever in th' castle. I promise I'll keep me mouth shu', I'll keep to th' shadda, please bring me wit' ya. This is a wanst in a lifetime,' Minnie was holding her hands in prayer, shaking them up and down as she spoke,

'Masther Artur, ax her to say yes.'

'Well, Missus Charlotte, does the maid beg in vain,' Arthur said, his mouth turned down in feigned anguish.

How could she refuse the wide expectant eyes that fixed her to the spot?

'Okay, Minnie, I am—,' was as far as she got before Minnie flung her arms about her neck, and then ran out the door as she shouted back a profusion of thanks, declaring that Charlotte would have to get herself ready for bed as she had a 'hape' of work to do to be able to get away.

'And so that was all it took! I declare I might have to kidnap Minnie and bring her home with us. Imagine what Martha and Tabby would make of her,' Arthur said, closing the door after the maid and coming back to where Charlotte stood, taking her once again in his arms, and asking, 'now, where were we?'

Chapter Twenty

Once again, Charlotte awoke to find Arthur was already up and gone. She was rather pleased as it avoided any awkwardness regarding their night's intimacies which seemed to shy away under the watchful glare of daylight. Neither was there any sign of Minnie, who perhaps was continuing to deal with her 'hape' of duties to be ready for the trip to Birr Castle. Charlotte was feeling resigned about the excursion, as she did trust that Arthur would not place her in the line of fire, and, yes, she was curious to meet a Countess who had begun life, albeit a very privileged one, as a Yorkshire lass, only a few miles from Haworth.

Having decided on her paisley dress as the one to allow her to blend in, it being of a neutral tone with a subtle print, rather than breakfast without Arthur, she used the interim to catch up on some letter writing.

In response to the congratulatory letters, she wrote perfunctory notes of gratitude. Likewise, her reply to the Revd Brontë was rather expeditious, outlining their itinerary thus far and informing him of their onward journey. She avoided any mention of her cough, knowing how he would fret. As her annoyance with Ellen Nussey endured, concerning the latter's letter to the Reverend, she decided that she would write instead to Miss Wooler and ask her to forward the letter to Ellen. It was always easier to write to Miss Wooler, as the nature of their relationship did not draw so much on the emotions, theirs was a friendship of practical, factual affairs, leaving no space for dramas of the heart or mind.

My dear Miss Wooler

I know that in your kindness you will have thought of me some-times since we parted at Haworth, and I feel that it is time to give some account of myself

We remained in Wales till Tuesday. If I had more leisure I would tell you of my impressions of what I saw there, but I have at this moment six letters to answer and my friends are waiting for me to take a drive. I snatch a moment to devote to you and Ellen Nussey to whom you must kindly forward this note, as I long to let her know how I am getting on, and cannot write to her to-day or indeed this week.

Last Tuesday we crossed from Holyhead to Dublin, the weather was calm, the passage good. We spent two days in Dublin, drove over a great part of the city, saw the college library, Museum, Chapel &c. and should have seen much more had not my bad cold been a restraint upon us.

~~Two~~ 'Three' of Mr. Nicholls' relatives met us in Dublin, his brother and 2 cousins. The 1st is manager of the Grand Canal from Dublin to Banagher, a sagacious well-informed and courteous man, his cousin is a student of the University and has just gained 3 premiums. The other cousin was a pretty lady-like girl with gentle English manners. They accompanied us last Friday down to Banagher, to his Aunt, Mrs. Bell's residence, where we are now.

I cannot help feeling singularly interested in all about the place. In this house, Mr. Nicholls was brought up by his uncle Dr. Bell. It is very large and looks externally like a gentleman's country-seat, within most of the rooms are lofty and spacious and some, the drawing-room, dining-room &c. handsomely and commodiously furnished. The passages look desolate and bare, our bed-room, a great room on the ground-floor would have looked gloomy when we were shewn into it but for the turf-fire that was burning in the wide old chimney. The male members of the family, such as I have seen, seem thoroughly educated gentlemen. Mrs. Bell is like an English or Scotch Matron quiet, kind and well-bred. It seems she was brought up in London.

Both her daughters are strikingly pretty in appearance, and their manners are very amiable and pleasing. I must say I like my new relations. My dear husband too appears in a new light here in his own country. More than once I have had deep pleasure in hearing his praises on all sides. Some of the old servants and followers of the family tell me I am a most fortunate person for that I got one of the best gentlemen in the country. His Aunt too speaks of him with a mixture of affection and respect most gratifying to hear. I was not well when I came here, fatigue and excitement had nearly knocked me up, and my cough was become very bad, but Mrs. Bell has nursed me both with kindness and skill, and I am greatly better now.

I trust I feel thankful to God for having enabled me to make what seems a right choice, and I pray to be enabled to repay as I ought the affectionate devotion of a truthful, honourable, unboastful man. Remember me kindly to all Mr. Carter's family. When you write, tell me how you got home and how you are.

I received Ellen Nussey's last welcome letter, when she reads this she must write to me again. We go in a few days to Kilkee, a watering-place on the South-West Coast. The letters may be addressed, Mrs. Arthur Nicholls, Post Office, Kilkee, County Clare, Ireland.

Believe me my dear Miss Wooler
Always yours with affection & respect
C. B. Nicholls.

Reading back over what she wrote, she sat back and gazing out on the ephemeral, morning mist wisp its way into oblivion, she felt the truth of her words and remembered the name for that feeling: happiness.

Arthur returned as she was addressing the last of the envelopes. Once again, he had been for his morning walk and had a glow of rude health about him.

'Another splendid dress, that I don't believe I have seen before, you will be the belle of the ball,' he said.

'In that case, I ought to change it, I had thought its muted colour would allow me to slip into this castle and stand where I can see but not be seen. There remains a muscular resistance in my very being to this trip,' Charlotte said, dabbing a stamp against the cylinder of the stamp licker, and pressing it on to the envelope with perhaps more vigour than was necessary.

'Have you had breakfast?' Arthur asked, and once again Charlotte noted how adept he was at changing the subject when he disliked the content.

'No, I was waiting for you,' Charlotte said, tying her bunch of letters with black ribbon, 'and afterwards, can we get these to the post office, before crossing the bog to this Camelot of yours!'

Aunt Harriette was unhappy to include Minnie in the party heading to Birr Castle, and had voiced her opinion over breakfast, but when she saw the efforts the young maid had made with her dress and hair, she relented, declaring that as young Harriette was otherwise occupied, John Evans having finally arrived from the West, it would be a shame to leave an empty space in the carriage. It had earlier been decided that Arthur and Joseph would travel there separately on horseback, which had made Charlotte unhappy, but Arthur assured her that he would wait by the entrance so that they could enter together.

Minnie was surprisingly quiet on the journey but Mary Anna filled the vacuum with endless speculations as to who would be there, what they would be wearing, what fare would be served, what music, and on and on. Aunt Harriette said that you could be guaranteed to meet the most interesting folk from Artic explorers to famous authors.

'Of course, I am referring to you, dear,' she said to Charlotte, 'Mary, the Countess, I am to understand, is beside herself with excitement at the prospects of meeting you. I know she has read all your works. Do you know that here in Ireland we do not get the three decker volumes, and so we made many journeys to Parsonstown to collect the single volumes as they were published? With eager anticipation I might add. And on each occasion the bookseller let me know that Mary had also ordered the volume.'

'How interesting,' Charlotte said.

'Jaypers, we're here, me heart is racin'' Minnie announced as the carriage joined a cavalcade making its way down a long avenue, through a stone keep gate, before coming to a halt in front of the castle.

'Minnie, curb your enthusiasm, and refrain from vulgar expressions, and try to be mindful of your place while you are here,' Aunt Harriette said.

'Sorry, Mam, yes, Mam,' Minnie said, as she lowered her head and tittered into her neck.

As they alighted from their carriage, Charlotte saw that Arthur, true to his word was waiting by the door, the perfect husband or obedient dog, neither analogy sitting well with her just at that moment, social anxiety tended to heighten and unleash all of Charlotte's habitual doubts and insecurities. The castle was exactly how a medieval fortress should be, a vast, solid, stone edifice, austere and commanding, it was rather intimidating, and yet familiar, this was Thornfield Hall in *Jane Eyre*. Charlotte's gaze was drawn towards the battlements and she wondered if a governess had ever paced there, inwardly raging against her lot, remonstrating with her inner demons as to why women should be content to be still, to knit and sew, and accept a life of stagnation, why the world that stretched out below could not also be theirs to explore and conquer. And what about Bertha Mason, rebellious, deranged Bertha, trapped in a female sensuality that was denied expression in 'civilised society', did such a soul stalk those battlements, contemplating a leap into eternal freedom. As she watched Arthur striding manfully across the stones to take possession of her arm and escort her into the gaiety, Charlotte tried to channel that other female from *Jane Eyre*, Blanche Ingram, only Blanche could get her through the falsity and foppery that lay ahead.

As carriage doors opened and steps were lowered pouring forth lords and ladies, maids and valets, the front yard became a riot of colour and noise. Charlotte had worried needlessly about exposure, here, she and Arthur's family were mere flies in the Countess of Rosse's societal web. Parasols were being raised, although the day was not particularly sunny, nor the door any distance to walk, dresses were being plumped out, while gentlemen's shoulders were being brushed to remove invisible particles of dust. The entire scene, with all its ruffling superficiality was like nothing Charlotte had ever witnessed other than between the covers of a Jane Austen novel, and it was no secret as to what she thought about them: feasts for the senses but alas, famine for the heart and soul.

Their party of six moved with the general mass through the house and into a great hall that was the dining room. The drawing room, where guests would normally be brought before being called for lunch, had been rearranged for the entertainment to follow. As they walked through the halls, Aunt Harriette exchanged pleasantries with some of the other female guests, and Charlotte was grateful that she refrained from making any introductions, there was not one among the flock of exotic birds, with their satin robes, feathers, scarves, pearl ornaments and lofty statures, that Charlotte had the least inclination of becoming acquainted with. The dining room was as vast as a great ballroom. Everything was on a grand scale, the grandest of all being an oak panelled sideboard; how it was brought into the room – despite the door being a gargantuan, gothic concern – defied logic; Charlotte would later discover that it was built where it stood and according to the Countess, would thus stand in all its armorial splendour until the end of time. The windows looking out on the extensive grounds were draped in rich brocade. Window seats were cushioned in matching fabric, some already occupied by the larger of the ladies. Throughout the room, along the walls were round tables of walnut and mahogany containing glasses and decanters filled with wines and spirits. The main table, almost the length of the room, was set with delicate china, decorated with the most exquisite green leaf pattern, and the centre piece was a life size silver swan. Vases of flowers, some containing flowers Charlotte had never seen before, completed the festive setting. Everywhere Charlotte looked she saw wealth and a world that she knew she had no inclination to ever be part of, and as for the high-pitched babble that deafened, she was beginning to regret agreeing to come to this Tower of Babel.

'Arthur, I really think I ought to ...' Charlotte was about to suggest that they leave, when she was interrupted by the bustling entrance of a lady, who, by the easy, bon vivant manner in which she greeted all and sundry, was clearly the Countess herself. Her ordinariness in style surprised Charlotte, here was a woman who was like any other ordinary, Yorkshire, woman Charlotte knew. Her dress was not dissimilar to her own, except instead of a paisley pattern it was tartan, and she wore her hair in an identical fashion to Charlotte. As she made her way through the room, it was as if she fed on the energy, her voice grew louder, her gestures more exaggerated, every female was a doll or a pet or a dear, every man her dearest old chap. By the time she stood in front of Charlotte and Arthur, such was the magnetic force of her presence, Charlotte felt faint and would have been happy to slip into unconsciousness.

'You made it, welcome my dears, and you must be Currer Bell, what a little doll you are, I see we have similar taste in hair styles, so practical, isn't it my dear, and I do believe, or so my William tells me, so fetching for our plainer visages. Ha ha ha, but what of that, my pet, why bother fussing over strands of dead cells when there is so much life to be arranged, books to be written, food to be enjoyed, and on that note ...' And with that the Countess continued her navigation of the room with the force of one of the nebulae her husband had discovered with his telescope.

Under different circumstances the 'little doll' reference and the intonation that she was plain would have stung Charlotte, but because, essentially, they were facts, and she could see that the Countess of Rosse clearly only dealt in facts, what was there to carp about?

'Don't worry, dear, she will be back to us once everyone has settled into the gay occasion, she is the most vivacious, wonderful hostess, is she not? Where does she get her energy, you know she has recently given birth to another son, poor dear, I am sure she wished for a little girl,' Aunt Harriette said, and in the doleful expression that accompanied, 'little girl', Charlotte conjectured some tragedy.

'She has no daughters?' Charlotte asked.

'Alas, my dear, not since rheumatic fever took her little Alice away. Only eight years old, little angel,' Aunt Harriette said, immediately brightening as she took Charlotte's lace mittened hands and added, 'but, today is not about loss, it is about joy and celebration, what do you say, we take a turn about the room and introduce you?'

Arthur was quick to suggest that as there seemed to be little formality about the place settings, perhaps it would be better to get seated, and avoid having to eat their lunch standing at one of the side tables. Charlotte whispered her gratitude to him as they made their way to the table. She was still thinking about the Countess Mary's recent birth and wondering how old she was, she definitely looked as old if not older than she and that gave Charlotte hope, it had been a concern of hers, marrying so late.

When everybody had located a seat, the great doors swung open and a procession of waiters with trays held aloft entered and proceeded to serve bowls of soup. Even as the guests ate the noise level did not drop, one of the ladies sitting opposite to the Bell party attempted to engage in conversation with Charlotte, but it was impossible to hear what she was saying.

Joseph who was beside her attempted to be an interpreter but even he gave up when the next course of Fricassee chicken arrived.

'That lady is Mary King, her mother is a Lloyd of Gloster House, Charlotte, quite the cleverest child you will ever meet, she is a cousin to Lord Rosse, and if you believe the rumours she is his superior when it comes to matters of science,' Aunt Harriette said, and leaning a little closer to Charlotte, whispered, 'she always looks so pensive, mournful one might say, don't you think?'

'What was she saying to me?' Charlotte asked.

'She was asking how you are finding married life, as she too is to be married later this year, she was wondering if you intend to continue with your career as a novelist,' Aunt Harriette said.

Charlotte looked across the table and catching Mary's eye she mouthed, 'yes'. Mary smiled knowingly.

Three further courses of salads and pickles and jellied desserts were brought out, one more sumptuous than the next.

'So much food, Arthur, surely there is enough here to feed the entire town, do you not find it all a rather decadent display of wealth?' Charlotte asked.

Arthur, who was seated next to her, looked around in horror before answering, 'Hush, Charlotte, you will be overheard, it is unkind to suggest that there is anything decadent about the overstated generosity of the Parsons. And as regards feeding the town, that is exactly what they did in the terrible years of '47 and '48, and not only that, they, to preserve the dignity of the menfolk in the town, instead of just dealing out alms, gave them employment building walls and keeps. I wish you could accept this occasion for what it is, a friendly reaching out; the Parsons have nothing to prove to anybody, this is not a show to win anyone's approval, this, my dear, is Irish hospitality at its most beautiful. Pray, accept it for what it is, without feeling the need to be so judgemental.'

Charlotte could feel tears well in her eyes, she wished she had not used the word, 'decadent', it wasn't really what she meant, she was feeling uncomfortable because she did not belong among the fine lords and ladies present, but then neither did Arthur or Aunt Harriette and her children, for all their genteel ways, and Arthur was right, she would probably never witness anything like this again, so she should enjoy it while it lasted, embrace it for what it was: a kind welcome to a stranger. If only she could have that suggested photograph over and done with, her mood might be more open to embrace the occasion.

As if reading her mind, Arthur, placing his napkin on his empty plate, pushed back his chair, and offering her his hand, suggested that they take a walk to aid digestion.

'Arthur, where are you going, we have not been invited to the drawing room yet?' Aunt Harriette asked.

'You know well, Aunt, that nobody stands on ceremony here, Charlotte and I are taking some air before the music commences, I am rather warm, especially after that feast,' Arthur said, and seeing Mary Anna also push back her chair he added, 'I wonder Mary Anna if we could have some time alone, there is some detail regarding our trip to Kilkee that I need to discuss with Charlotte.' Mary Anna smiled and resumed her seat.

Getting to the door felt like running the gauntlet as so many gentlemen tipped back their chairs to greet Arthur and inquire as to who the little lady was. Arthur told them, so that as they left Charlotte could hear her name echoing through the room amidst 'oohs' and 'ahhs'.

'I am sorry, Arthur, that comment was mean-spirited, and emanates from my own insecurities among the aristocracy, and furthermore you know how ill at ease I am in large gatherings,'

Charlotte said. She pointed to where the stables were, 'I would rather jump on one of those animals and gallop back to Banagher than have to face back in there.'

'But you don't ride!' Arthur said.

'Precisely, and there you have it,' Charlotte said.

'That would be quite the sight,' Arthur said, and laughed, 'you can be ridiculous at times, my dear, but in a humorous way.'

'The only reason I came was so that Minnie could come, and since we arrived, I declare, I have not laid eyes on her,' Charlotte said.

'No doubt entertaining the servants in their quarters,' Arthur said, and taking Charlotte by the hand, suggested that they walk down the field to view the famous telescope.

The telescope and the scaffolding around it had earned its popular name, the Leviathan. While its enormity impressed Charlotte, she would have preferred an opportunity to observe the heavens through its lenses. Before returning to the house, they walked by the lake, listened to the birds, and remarked that this was the first time since arriving in Banagher that they had been alone with nature.

'I am looking forward to whisking you off to the wild west, Charlotte, where once again, I can have you all to myself. I apologise if I seemed cross with you earlier, perhaps I too am never quite at ease amongst these grand folks, one always feels rather inadequate and always just one misplaced comment or one misinterpreted gesture away from being exposed as an imposter,' Arthur said as he drew her closer, kissing her deeply, causing her to arch her back in order to press further into him.

By the time they returned to the castle the dancing was in full swing. The room was taken up with lines arranged for quadrilles, as everyone hopped, skipped and circled their partners, some more gracefully than others. Mary Anna and

Joseph had taken to the floor and what they lacked in skill they were making up for with youthful enthusiasm. Aunt Harriette, seated by the wall, was waving at them to come and join her. Charlotte could sense a slowing in Arthur's gait as they moved along.

'Absolutely not, Arthur, you will need another partner if you wish to dance, perhaps Aunt Harriette will oblige, I would rather saddle up that horse and take my chances across the swampy, spongy terrain of the bog,' Charlotte said, taking her place beside the aunt. Arthur stood, tapping his toe, and clapping at the relevant intervals in the dance. Charlotte noted that there was no sign of the Countess or her husband in the room, which was in keeping with what Arthur had suggested, they did not host these gatherings to entertain themselves but to provide an opportunity for others to be happy. She did notice the miniature army of kilted boys, all sons belonging to the castle, boisterously racing in and out between the dancers. She could see Mary King, the young lady who had tried to engage her in conversation at the table, holding what must have been the youngest Parson. A strange feeling came over Charlotte as she took in the image, like a presentiment of sorts and she wondered if, seeing that Mary would also be married soon, she witnessed Mary's future or her own.

When it was time to go, Lord Rosse and the Countess stood by the door to wave their guests off. It was Charlotte's first time to see the Lord, and she could tell by his physiognomy that he was a pure intellect, and the best sort at that, as his kind eyes and coy smile suggested his lack of awareness of it. As Charlotte passed them, the Countess took her aside to apologise for not being able to arrange a photograph due to the poor light but insisted that she come back again.

'Perhaps, next year, my dearest, and who knows instead of a photograph of a married couple I will be taking a family portrait,' the Countess said as she kissed Charlotte on both cheeks, 'give my regards to Yorkshire when you get home.'

Charlotte envied the countess her confident manner, it must be so liberating to be that uninhibited, even when one has failed to honour a promise.

The carriage was silent for the return journey. Charlotte reckoned, judging by her constant smile, that the person who had had the most fun was Minnie.

Chapter Twenty-One

For their final day in Banagher it was decided that a trip to Clonmacnoise was in order, and Arthur agreed with Charlotte that it would be an appropriate balm for the soul following the epicurean extremes of the previous day. As Charlotte was feeling much better, she rose at dawn with Arthur and accompanied him on his morning walk. They walked to the river, where a fog hovered just above the water creating an eerie stillness, which to Charlotte, felt like they were the last humans on earth, it was an uneasy feeling, and for some reason it focused her thoughts on the Reverend back in Haworth.

'This is how I imagine death, Arthur, a mist that you walk into, never to be seen again, such a mist Papa will no doubt encounter ere long. Longevity, as you will have observed is not a family trait,' she said.

'Well, there's a cheery thought for a July morning, easy telling you did not grow up beside these banks or you would know that this very scene is the harbinger of a glorious, sunny day,' Arthur said, 'why such morose thoughts, did he say he was unwell in his letter?'

'No, nothing more than his usual doomsday report on his ailments, it is just that he is aged, and well … I suppose, I associate fog and mist with oblivion, give me the energy of wind and rain any day,' Charlotte said.

Rather than dwell by the river, Arthur brought her down

Crank Road towards Eliza Fort, chatting all the way about his childhood days with his brother and cousins, how they picked berries from the hedgerows along the way, always hoping to turn them into something remarkable, like jam or dyes, but alas, only ever managing to create grey, fungal messes from their forgotten caches.

'We were not very thoughtful children, the challenge was always to see who could pick the most, and once that challenge was won or lost, we moved on to the next sport, forgetting about our glut of berries until someone nosed them ... usually in one of the barns,' Arthur said.

'Tut, tut, that would never have happened in the parsonage, we, on the other hand were careful children, we only took from nature what we needed, it is probably why I hate to see flowers dying in vases, what good are they there to the birds and bees,' Charlotte said.

'Gosh, we are in high spirits this day, perhaps you are tired, I can cancel the proposed trip to the monastery,' Arthur said.

'You are being satirical, and tiresome, and patronising, and yet I can't think of anyone else I would like to be jesting with, or any other road I would like to be travelling down, on this July morning,' Charlotte said, stopped and turned back the road they had come, 'but as there is still no sight of this fort that I have zero interest in seeing, I suggest we return to breakfast.'

As they walked in silence, Charlotte noticed one or two ripened blackberries among the clusters of tight green knots and thought how she would like some time in the future to be back here in the autumn, sometime when perhaps they would have little Arthurs or Charlottes with whom she could pick berries and show their father how to make jam. Maybe Minnie would still be around to help, she hoped so as she had taken an uncommon liking to the girl.

'You know Minnie has asked to come to Clonmacnoise

with us?' Charlotte said.

'Well, I am guessing it is not for any religious experience, as Minnie, you can bet, will always have an ulterior motive for doing anything she has not been instructed to do,' Arthur said.

'Oh, Arthur, you are funny, you know her well. She confided in me that she met a certain young man at the castle yesterday, one of the other guest's valets, and she told him about our planned excursion, and has arranged to meet him there if we allow her to come,' Charlotte said, and before Arthur could speak she continued, 'and you need not bother objecting, I have already said yes, I am sure we can travel as we did yesterday if carriage space is an issue.'

'Stand in the way of courtship? You forget, Charlotte, I am the sentimental, hopeless romantic in this relationship,' Arthur said.

'I have looked in both our guide books and there is no mention of Clonmacnoise, will Joseph be coming, I remember from the Book of Kells his vast knowledge of Ireland's, ancient, ecclesiastical history?' Charlotte asked, 'otherwise I am afraid the site will be nothing more than a mess of ruins to me. Minnie tells me it is a great place to go asking for things, I presume she means as a pilgrim, but I can't see how Irish saints would be interested in my Protestant petitions, so it would be of more value to know about the history of the place.'

'I am not sure if Joseph is coming but I am sure there are books at home we can consult. Aunt will know,' Arthur said.

At breakfast Charlotte met John Evans. He was possibly the most loquacious man she had ever encountered. He regaled everyone at the table with stories involving his neighbours in Connemara, his successes in farming, the repair work he had done on his 'dream home' – his expression – called Kill Cottage, the latest pursuits of his family, the state of the nation, and how he missed the theatre scene in Dublin now that he lived in the wilds. He interjected his outpourings with questions to specific individuals around the table but seldom waited for an answer.

'Am I to understand that you are a Shakespeare enthusiast?' he directed this to Charlotte as she was about to bite into some toast, 'the fellow was my saviour on my first trip to the Americas. Nobody who has not ventured to sea understands the monotony of those voyages, I believe I read the entire works on that occasion', and then turning his attention back to the table in general added, 'I am sure I have told you before of those terrible journeys, of the poor folk who died on board and how they were shrouded in a piece of canvas and tipped overboard? Dreadful sight.'

Aunt Harriette, who looked exhausted, jumped in, 'Yes, you have indeed, besides, it is not the jolliest of topics for so early in the morning. Now, dear boy, you must reveal your little surprise for our excursion today.'

'Ah, yes, almost forgot, because of my background in shipping, I still have a few contacts here and there, and so I have been able to secure a boat to bring us up the river to Clonmacnoise. It is the only way to travel to the spot. What do you say to that? Harriette, dear, don't look so worried, I have also secured a skipper so you will not be putting your life in my hands,' John Evans said. Mary Anna whispered, 'not yet', which Aunt Harriette heard, and nodded as if to agree. She really was most concerned for her Harriette's welfare having to live in such a remote spot after her marriage to John Evans.

Charlotte liked him, she liked how opinionated he was, and she sensed that he was a man of extreme common sense, she could tell from what he had to say about some of the Members of Parliament that he did not suffer fools gladly, and she greatly admired that trait of character. This was the type of discourse that she enjoyed the most. She was interested in what he had to say about Irish nationalism as it had often been discussed at home, especially when Daniel O'Connell was at the height of his career. The Revd Brontë had been in favour of Catholic emancipation but very much opposed to the Repeal movement, Charlotte recalled how he would rail against the idea of repealing the Act of Union as he feared for the Protestants of Ireland, even going so far as to write a letter to the newspaper, The Leeds Intelligencer, outlining his philosophical views as to how the repeal of the union would surely herald a revolution with devasting effects for members of the established church. She shared some of these ideas with the table.

'Could you speak some more about the Repeal movement, where does it all stand these days?' she asked of John Evans.

'As dead as O'Connell I am afraid to say, it is all about tenant rights these days, and as a landlord I wish to God they would introduce reform before the more revolutionary factions of Irish Nationalism take hold. I had hoped we had seen the last of the Ribbonmen,' he said.

'Ribbonmen?' Charlotte asked.

'Yes, dastardly secret societies who like to take agitation for reform into their own hands, many landlords have suffered fiercely at their hands, they are fond of burning and maiming—', Aunt Harriette interrupted, 'Right, well, we have heard quite enough of that for one meal—', 'But, Mrs Bell, I was led to believe that you yourself have a history of involvement in agitation, was I mistaken?' John Evans asked.

'Mama, I believe John is referring to the meeting,' James suggested.

Charlotte looked from one to the other questioningly.

'I see you are confused, dear, James and Mr Evans are referring to a time when I allowed a meeting to take place in the grounds here, there was more in attendance than they had anticipated and so I obliged, it hardly qualifies me as a Repealer,' Aunt Harriette said.

Undeterred, John Evans said that he would like to speak again to Charlotte about her views on Irish nationalism, considering her Irish roots. Charlotte was unsure as to what he had been told regarding her Irish roots or indeed her views on Irish nationalism, her 'Irishness' was not something she had ever considered too much before this honeymoon. She was discovering that there was a lot more to Ireland and the Irish than what she had gleaned from literary references, newspaper articles and anecdotes her Papa had shared.

'Did you hear me, Charlotte?' It was Arthur who interrupted her thoughts.

'I am sorry, what did you say?' she asked.

'Are you excited to travel by boat to Clonmacnoise? At least it means that Minnie tagging along will not be a problem,' Arthur said.

Minnie who had been standing right behind them, on hearing her name, asked if she was being addressed.

'No, I was just saying that there would be room for you on the boat,' Arthur said.

'Tanks, now will wan of ya, for the love of Christ make a move or I'll have no time t' ge' ready, tha' fella over ther' doesn't know when t' shu' up. Jaypurs he's a fierce dose, isn't he, poor Harriette has her work cu' out for herself, no wunder Missus is in a hape 'bout her marryin' him,' Minnie whispered, leaning in between Arthur and Charlotte, referring to John Evans who sat opposite them.

It was Aunt Harriette who moved first, declaring that she might need to rest a while before the journey. Charlotte rose at the same time, asking Minnie to pass her compliments on the marmalade on to her mother.

'Brigid did not make it,' Mary Anna said on hearing

Charlotte's request, 'it is bought. Fruitfield is the brand, quite new to the market. It is rather scrumptious, is it not?'

'Fruitfield! The Lambs of Waterford! More Quakers taking over the markets. If I had known that was what I was spreading on my bread …' Charlotte heard no more of what John Evans had to say as she left the room, followed by Minnie.

Back in her room, Minnie was asking her about how she knew that Arthur was the one for her.

'It's just tha' I like Kevin, that's his name, but I also like th' look o' th' soldier down a' th' fort, and there's a butcher up th' town that looks dacent enough too, but now, shure I can't have them all, well, I could if I was wan of them yokes ya see knockin' around here durin' the fair week, but I am a good child of Mary and the wan husbint will be just grand,' Minnie said, all the time cleaning out the ashes and setting the fire.

'I am not much of an expert on affairs of the heart, Minnie, but this I can say, if his regard for you is great; if you know that he respects you; and he will allow you to continue being your unique self after the wedding day, then you have the foundations for a strong partnership,' Charlotte said.

'A partnership! I don't want ta go into business wit' him, I want ta love him and have him love me, but I don't know what love feels like, is it like a pain, or a longin'?'

'Neither, it is a comfort, a constant feeling of security that no matter what, there is somebody in this vast world that will always be there for you,' Charlotte said.

'So, it's like replacing your ma or da when you outgrow them, or God takes them away from ya?' Minnie asked.

'Hmmm, not quite, although perhaps the emotional dependency is similar,' Charlotte said.

'Put it t' ya this way, if ther' was wan thin' about himself that tauld you he were th' man for you, wha' would it be?' Minnie asked, standing with her hands on her hips.

Charlotte did not have to think for long. 'His kindness, especially to my Papa, even though the same Papa was not always kind to him.' What she did not share with Minnie was how her feelings for Arthur were changing every day, how her admiration had grown, how much prouder of him she had become, and how, as each day drew to a close, she looked forward to their physical intimacies.

'Right, that's enough blather outta me, the fire's set, time now to do the same to meself, or I won't have to worry wha' Kevin thinks of me, one look a' th' scarecrow state o' me and he'll jump inta th' Shannon and swim for th' hills,' Minnie said, as she did her trademark curtsy and left.

Charlotte sat between Arthur and Minnie on the deck of the boat. Aunt Harriette declared that Minnie was going too far with her liberties, monopolising their guest's time, that perhaps Charlotte would prefer to have Mary Anna or Harriette beside her, that she was certain Charlotte would have wise words regarding matrimony to disclose to the latter. Charlotte assured her that Minnie was no inconvenience, and it was she who had suggested the proximity when Minnie expressed a fear that she might 'topple' into the river.

'Oh, the child is ridiculous, as if we were on a rowing boat—' Aunt Harriette said, as the sound of the engine starting drowned out her words.

'I am fearful, Charlotte, that I will open your trunk when we get home, and find Minnie looking up at me,' Arthur whispered into her ear.

'How absurd … as if she would fit,' Charlotte said, and they both smiled, enjoying the humour, 'besides, if destiny is smiling on our Minnie today, she will have a different journey to embark upon.'

'I say, but you two have become quite the confidantes, am

I to understand that Minnie has confessed all her intentions to you?' Arthur asked.

'What you are to understand, Arthur, is I am straining to hear you and would prefer to enjoy this magnificent prospect of the countryside,' Charlotte said, patting Arthur's knee before placing her hands in her lap, straightening her back and jutting her chin to extend her gaze over the heads of the others who sat on the opposite side of the deck, in the interests of ballast, according to John Evans.

As the boat made its way up the river, the plains stretched in varying strata of green on either side. Cows grazed near the water line, indolently lifting their heads in momentary curiosity as the boat steamed by, here and there, the chimneys of mansions could be seen above clusters of trees, and at regular intervals, atop navigation poles strategically positioned in the channel, black coots perched and watched the intruders from the world of men disturb their tranquillity. At one point the river narrowed and John Evans, shouting above the engine noise pointed out a sign that read 'Grand Canal, Shannon Harbour' and explained, still shouting, that it was from there the boats from Dublin entered the Shannon waterways. Further on, Minnie prodded Charlotte's arm and pointed to a herd of wild horses galloping away from the banks. Charlotte nodded her appreciation of the sight. The stone fort visible on the left bank as they passed through Shannonbridge put Charlotte in mind of the mills back home and she breathed deeply, thinking how different life would be on their return, how far from cruises to ancient, holy sites her daily tasks would take her, but rather than allow the thought to alter her mood, she wriggled in her seat, lifted her torso and expanded her chest to take in the sweet air of adventure.

Because of the meandering nature of the river, Clonmacnoise came into view long before they were near enough to disembark. Rather than just one or two ruins, Charlotte could see many structures of what looked to be former churches and at least two round towers were visible on the risen site. On the approach, the river, now being at its widest since they left Banagher, was like a sheet of blue glass mottled with puffs of white, and it appeared that if you stepped out of the boat you could walk across it. How appropriate, Charlotte thought, that this approach should put her in mind of a biblical miracle, as, according to Minnie thousands came here to plead for just that, a miracle.

As soon as Charlotte stepped from the boat on to the grounds of the monastic site, she knew she was in a special place, she felt it rise from her feet to the crown of her head, there was no logical explanation but she was aware that she trod on sancti-fied ground. It was a short climb up an embankment to reach the first of the ruins, from where Joseph, who had come along, wasted no time in beginning his history lesson.

'So, although, it is hard to imagine today, this was once a monastic city, where the monks came to be close to God, to hear his voice carry on the wind, to see his majesty in the lofty mountains, to worship his creation in the glory of the summer woods. I am paraphrasing here from one of the great books of late that gives us an insight into the magnificence of where we are,' Joseph said, 'founded in turbulent times by our Irish carpenter's son, Ciaran Mac In Tsair: St Ciaran, and to keep with the similarity to Jesus, Ciaran died shortly after its foundation, his work being done, at the age of thirty-three!'

Charlotte made a mental note to ask Joseph about the book he quoted from as she would also like to read it, but for now, rather than tune in to Joseph's lecture she wanted to listen to the sounds of the curlew and the plover, she wanted to imagine holy men knelt in prayer, or hunched over desks, their quills slowly and deliberately swirling and spiralling across the parchment, she wanted to see them raising chalices to corbelled roofs, or simply standing in meditation to the sounds of the Shannon waters burbling beneath them.

'Such a shame you will not be here then.' It was Aunt Harriette who was addressing Charlotte.

'Not here for what, Harriette, I am sorry my mind was miles away?' Charlotte asked.

'The pattern day, September 9th, when pilgrims come from all over Ireland to pray for their needs, while it is a holy day, there is often a festive air around the vicinity,' Aunt Harriette said.

Charlotte would not like to visit it at such a busy time, but she did not share this with Aunt Harriette. Joseph listed out the ways in which Ciaran lived an extremely ascetic life, when he mentioned how he never told a lie, John Evans interrupted.

'A man after my own heart, if there are two things I abhor in men it is lying and cursing.'

'Here, here,' Arthur said.

All the church ruins were called after important men, high kings and princes of Ireland, many of whom were buried beneath high crosses engraved with Celtic designs and scenes from the scriptures. Joseph said that these wealthy men chose Clonmacnoise as their final resting place as they believed it was a direct gateway to heaven, that it had the reputation of being the most sacred site in all of Europe. Charlotte, once more, was relishing the names. She heard the word 'Teampall' mentioned a lot, which to her ear sounded like champal, and asked what it meant.

'Of course, it means church, how silly of me not to intuit that,' she replied to Arthur.

'How are you enjoying being in the epicentre of this land of saints and scholars, Charlotte?' Arthur asked.

'It is a special place, I feel a strong connection with the past, listen, it's as if these ancient men and women are whispering down the wind, reminding us of our shared heritage,' Charlotte answered.

Joseph had moved on to the darker history of the site and how it was plundered and burned on at least ten occasions down through the ages by the Danes, and possibly more than double that number by the native Irish and, following the plantations, the English from Athlone. Charlotte moved away as he was describing slaughtering, to explore on her own, and go closer to the stones to decipher the inscriptions: her short-sightedness, occasioning her to bring her gaze remarkably close to the object being looked at was often a source of embarrassment to her as she was aware how unsightly it looked. As she made her way to the larger of the round towers, she noticed a peasant woman with a baby in her arms. The forlorn expression on the woman's face as she stared towards the Heavens attracted Charlotte's attention. She was barefoot and dressed in rags, and yet a more beautiful Madonna figure, Charlotte had never seen, she had to know what caused her anguish and suspirations.

'Hello, my apologies for intruding upon your prayers, are you distressed, can I be of assistance?' Charlotte asked.

The woman held her baby closer as she rose from her knees and spoke in a tongue Charlotte did not comprehend.

'I am sorry, I do not understand you, I have no knowledge of your native language,' Charlotte said.

'Beggin' your pardon, Mam, stay well back, the babby isn't well, I'm afeared it's the speckled monster, I'm here axing Mael Mhuire the virgin herself to aid me,' the woman said, and turned to leave.

Charlotte knew that she referred to smallpox and was surprised that it continued to afflict children when vaccinations were available, she inquired from the woman why the child had not been inoculated against the disease. Perhaps not understanding Charlotte's meaning, the woman bowed her head, brushing her lips against the blanketed mound in her arms. Charlotte wished she had some money to offer, suspecting the want of it to be the cause of the child's affliction, but apart from her wedding ring the only item of value she wore was a brooch. Taking it off she offered it to the young woman.

'It is not highly valuable, but it should fetch enough to secure the medicines you need.'

The woman seemed reluctant to move forward, so Charlotte placed the piece on the ground and moved back. Understanding what to do, the woman bent and picked it up and speaking once more in her native language, Charlotte smiled as she knew that the words were ones of gratitude.

'There you are.' It was Arthur who spoke as he came up behind her.

'Oh, Arthur, this poor woman,' Charlotte said.

'Where?' Arthur asked.

And turning back Charlotte could see no sign of her Madonna figure. 'Never mind,' she said, linking him as they made their way to where the others were sitting on blankets enjoying the picnic that Brigid had packed for them. Charlotte noticed Minnie over by a high cross speaking with a rather handsome looking young man. She beckoned to her to join them which they duly did.

As they ate and drank, John Evans regaled them with his knowledge of George Petrie's account of Clonmacnoise, describing in detail a painting from Petrie that commemorated a pilgrimage there. Charlotte had heard of Petrie but was unfamiliar with his work, in fact her only knowledge of him was a reference in some article she had read describing him as the Irish Turner. She asked where she could view the painting, but John Evans was unaware of where it currently exhibited.

'I think we have heard enough from the academics for one day. Minnie, I believe it is time for a song. Come, come, we know you are not shy,' Aunt Harriette said.

'Ah, Missus, yer puttin' me on th' spot now, especially in front of himself,' Minnie said, cocking her thumb in her friend's direction. And before anyone could press her further, she stood up and began in a sweet, melodic voice that sounded nothing like her speaking voice. It had a plaintive air that echoed around the space and closing her eyes, Charlotte felt more spirituality connected to the world than she had ever felt before, as she allowed the words of the song to enter her heart.

'tis the Last Rose of Summer left blooming alone
all her lovely companions are faded and gone
No no flower of her kindred no rose bud is neigh
to reflect back her blushes or give sigh for sigh

I'll leave thee thou lone one to pine on the stem
Since the lovely are sleeping go sleep now with them
Thus kindly I scatter thy leaves o're the bed
where thy mates of the garden lie scentless and dead

So soon may I follow when friendships decay
and from love's shining circle the gems drop away
when tru hearts lie withered and fond one's are flown
Oh who would inhabit this bleak world alone?

As Minnie sang the final line, Charlotte opened her eyes and saw, making her way along the top of the hill, her peasant Madonna and baby.

Chapter Twenty-Two

It was the day of departure from Banagher. Arthur was off on his last early morning walk while Charlotte finished her packing with a rather heavier heart than she had anticipated. The previous night, reflecting on their time amidst his family, Arthur asks what her highlight was, she told him, that it was the haunting sound of Minnie's song. From the reactions when Minnie had finished, of applause and whoops and even a whistle followed by a shout of 'Erin go Bragh' from John Evans, Charlotte concluded that what was an interlude of entertainment, perhaps a common occurrence, for the gathering, had been a moment in time for her, something rarefied and special in a spiritual way, something she knew she would never experience again, and maybe it was that feeling, more so than the leave-taking that weighed heavily on her mood. She loathed the fuss of departures, the kisses, the hugs, the often empty promises of return visits, and if she had had her way they would have secreted themselves away at dawn before the cock crew. Would she return to Banagher? She certainly planned on it, possibly the following year, she even contemplated bringing her papa, besides, how could she deny Arthur his annual visit home. As she placed the last of her garments into the trunk, Minnie, unceremoniously, stuck her head in the door.

'Mammy wants to know would you take a few soda farls wit' ya for th' road?' she said.

'Good morning, Minnie, your mother is most kind, but there is no need for her to go to any trouble on our behalf,' Charlotte said.

'She knows tha', but she wants ta, so yes or no?' Minnie asked again.

'Why, yes, that would be most welcome,' Charlotte said.

'And she said she'd wrap a bit a butther for you too, nothin' as bad as dry bread, a gallon of wather wouldn't wash it down. Sorry I wasn't here earlier, I had somethin' to do. Did ya need a hand wit' th' packin'?' Minnie said.

'I will miss you, Minnie,' Charlotte said, which was not what she had intended to say, it just came out when she stood up and saw this funny, Irish maid, still leaning half in, half out of the door. Charlotte had never encountered anyone like her before, and even if she did return the following year there was no doubt in her mind that Minnie would not be part of the household: she had seen how the young valet had looked at her in Clonmacnoise.

'Ah, now, don't ge' me started or you'll have me blatherin' like a babby, and believe me, Missus Charlotte, no wan wants to see tha' first thin' in th' mornin'', Minnie said, and closing the door said that she would go and sort out the bread.

As Arthur helped her into the carriage, the last of the good-byes having been exchanged, Charlotte struggled to fight back tears, such a display of emotion would be undignified and misleading, as she knew her tears were not necessarily for any person she was leaving, they were for who she had been whilst among them, and the fear that she was also saying goodbye to that Charlotte. The women remained on the steps, most of the men having re-entered the house, and Minnie and her mother, Brigid, stood by the gable end of the house waving, as James closed the carriage door.

'Goodbye old chap, and goodbye to you, Charlotte, please don't be strangers, you know as long as we are here, Cuba Court is also your home. Give our regards to the Revd Brontë and know that he too is always most welcome. Safe onward journey … enjoy the Shannon, and the sea, and yes … indeed … goodbye for now. All set, Jimmy!' James said, immediately turning back towards the house.

And so, the honeymoon couple were alone again as the horses trotted up the avenue leaving the hustle and bustle of the Banagher sojourn in their wake.

'I do believe our James was beginning to choke up there, Charlotte, you have made quite the impression on my family, everyone is so sad to see you leave,' Arthur said.

'It is extremely sweet of you to say so, but I think the sadness relates to you. You are much cherished here, Arthur, I hope we can replicate that regard for you back in Haworth,' Charlotte said, and now that there was a greater ease between the two, she reached for him and they embraced, and laughed when the horses increased their pace causing her to fall forward into his lap.

The paddle steamer was waiting at the pier in Banagher, and as there were always fewer passengers to embark going down the river, they were safely boarded in no time with Jimmy helping to load their luggage.

'Jimmy, my good man, what can I say, ever the gentleman, give our regards to your family, I am sorry I did not get to call down to see them on this occasion. Next year, God willing.'

'I will Masther Artur, God speed to ya both,' Jimmy said, heading back across the pier to where he had parked the carriage.

Members of the crew gave them a warm welcome, and they were shown to superior seats on deck where they could enjoy the trip if the weather held. They were aware that Allen,

Arthur's brother, in his role as manager of the company who operated the boats, had arranged this leg of their journey, and had also, obviously, put in special requests for their comfort.

The weather did hold so that they were able to enjoy the motion and the meanderings of the tranquil river, and slowly sink into an easy togetherness. They passed the time by sharing episodes from Banagher not experienced together and speculating on what this famous watering place of Kilkee would bring.

'Minnie was such a character, Arthur, I will write about her someday. You know I gave her the copy of *Jane Eyre* I had brought for Aunt Harriette. It was when she presented me with a page on which she had written the words of the song she sang. Such a lovely thing to do, she was up early this morning working on it, and I was so taken with the gesture I wanted to give something in return, so I thought of the book. We can forward another copy to your aunt,' Charlotte said.

'"The Last Rose of Summer"! Can I expect a rendition?' Arthur asked.

'And blight both the song and the memory of her singing it. No, Arthur, I will leave singing to those who have voices, I will keep to my writing,' Charlotte said.

They smiled and a comfortable silence swathed them in private reflections on the honeymoon thus far. Charlotte was happy to have Arthur once more to herself, his family had been wonderfully entertaining but exhausting: perhaps when she got to know them better, it would be less of a strain on her nerves. She had been relieved to find their manners, and their speech, so similar to what you would expect from a genteel, English family, and yet, they were decidedly Irish, and she could not discern what precisely it was that made them so, other than maybe their outgoing natures and rather more cavalier, relaxed approach to life.

'Aunt Harriette was everything I had expected, such a dear lady. You know she wanted to have Jimmy bring us by coach all the way to Limerick as she felt that the boat would be too lengthy a journey for me,' Charlotte said.

'Perhaps you would have preferred that? It was just that Allen was so eager to arrange everything for us, especially seeing as he did not get to organise our passage from Dublin to Banagher with his company, and I thought that—' Arthur said, before Charlotte interrupted, stating that there was no need for any justifications, she was more than happy to take the scenic route.

'Aunt Harriette was also quite adamant that we stay at The West End Hotel, where she once stayed with James. Did she give you that letter of recommendation for the hostess there?' Charlotte asked, referring to how Aunt Harriette had sung the praises of one, Mrs Shannon, the proprietor of the Kilkee hotel, with whom she had struck up a great rapport, and she insisted that a letter of introduction would guarantee a wonderful stay for the couple. Charlotte was not sure it was what she wanted; anonymity might make for a more comfortable, relaxing holiday.

After Portumna, the river opened into Lough Derg and with the expanse of the waters Charlotte felt her spirit expand. Arthur pointed out castles, ruined monasteries and islands with round towers and Irish names that sounded as mystical as the world of stilly waters and silent hills they were passing through. Not even the hiss of the engine or the peaty, sometimes choking smell of the turf fuelling it, could detract from her mood as she repeated some of the placenames, Tirdaglas, Agnish, Inis Cealtra.

At Killaloe they transferred onto a coach that took them to Limerick from where they would get a steamboat to Kilrush. Limerick quay was a lively spot. There were jaunting cars galloping down it, the eager faces of the occupants relaxing as they saw that they had not missed the sailing; passengers, men, women and children from all walks of life jostled to secure a better position in the queue to board; pigs squealed as they were crane lifted on; and a fiddler played and sang to ears deafened by the hissing and belching of the steam engine as it was being fired up for the journey. Their boat was called *Erin go Bragh*.

'Is that the expression that John Evans was so fond of using?' Charlotte asked.

'Yes, indeed it is, well remembered, Charlotte. Evans likes to remind us all that he is a true Irishman, likes to give voice to his patriotism. Don't quote me, but if you ask for my opinion, most of us who are Irish do not feel the need to be so constantly demonstrative of the fact,' Arthur said.

'So that is what it means, "I am Irish"?' Charlotte asked.

'Well, more, "long live Ireland", it is declaration of allegiance, not unlike your "long live the King or Queen",' Arthur said, as he reached down and took hold of a carpet bag.

As the day was fine, they were able to sit on deck for the most part of the five hours voyage up the Shannon Estuary. The countryside they passed through was rather uniformly flat and featureless, and so the couple passed the time, eating the picnic Brigid had packed for them, reminiscing over their days in Banagher or sitting, silently contemplating their future.

'Arthur, if the Lord decides to call Papa home before either of us, which is more likely than probable, would you see yourself as taking over from him so that we would continue to live in the parsonage?' Charlotte asked.

'That would depend entirely on what your preference would be, you might find it difficult to move too far from your family's final resting places,' Arthur said.

'Quite the opposite, Arthur, I should like to move far, my

closeness to them does not depend on the proximity of their remains, I don't see them as shrouded figures in the earth,' Charlotte said.

'Far away. I see, and would you consider here?' Arthur asked.

'Ireland! Never! If this were our habitual where could we escape to for pleasure? Yorkshire is in my bones, Arthur!' Charlotte said.

'Yorkshire it is then, but for now, I like the idea that here is our escape, and such it has been for me, Charlotte, I must be the luckiest man in Ireland,' Arthur said, taking her hand in a determined manner, and placing it against his breast, repeated, 'the luckiest man in Ireland.'

Approaching the pier at Kilrush, Charlotte was surprised to find it thronged with jaunting cars, drivers, porters, workmen and perhaps relatives of some of the people on board. They were expecting to be collected by a jaunting car from the hotel and were not disappointed. As soon as the luggage was loaded, the car took off in the direction of the town of Kilrush. As the road inclined, the mouth of the Shannon yawning out into the Atlantic came into view and in the distance the mountains of Kerry rose out of the ocean. Charlotte gasped as she took in her first sight of the great ocean. Arthur too, seeing it for the first time, shook his head in disbelief. The road turned inwards, and the view disappeared behind stretches of bogland dotted with small pyramids of turf and gnarly stumps of enormous trees erupting here and there through the swampy surface. Already Charlotte was feeling the ancient wildness of the place possess her. And wild it was, the only signs of life were the cabins they passed, which to Charlotte's horror were mere hovels with black holes for windows and smoke billowing out the door because of the non-existence of chimneys. Ragged, barefoot, children stared hollow-eyed at the passing car, and some more robust looking ones ran after them, their arms stretched in search of alms.

'We should stop and give them something, Arthur, there is plenty of Brigid's bread left,' Charlotte said.

The driver was not happy, stating that unless they could work another miracle of loaves and fishes, they were at nothing, and besides, there was a grand workhouse in Kilrush that they could go to, but he obliged. Arthur gave the entire picnic basket to one of the children, who was immediately surrounded by others who appeared as if from thin air. Charlotte watched in dismay as more and more people came through the ditches, the scene was becoming apocalyptical, as the driver urged Arthur to remount to continue towards the seaside resort. They talked about the plight of the poor people and how the famine clearly remained in these parts and how terribly guilty it made them feel to be as privileged as they were. The only consolation they could offer themselves was how their contribution to the local economy as tourists gave businesses more money to donate to charitable institutions, and the influx of holidaymakers would mean increased attendance at church services and therefore an increase in offerings on the church collection plate. As the Atlantic came back into view, their holiday mood returned as it was impossible to look down on the sparkling, white ruffled vastness of blue and not feel uplifted.

The proprietor of the West End Hotel, where they were staying, had not stopped talking since they arrived at the reception desk and because of her distinct Irish accent and expressions, Charlotte was having difficulty in understanding her. She suspected that Arthur was also struggling but was too considerate to make it obvious.

'Thank you indeed, Mrs Shannon, that is most helpful,' Arthur said with respect to the litany of activities she had suggested they do during their stay.

'Oh, and I must be warning you, if you'll pardon me, my good lady, if you, Sir, have an inkling to go splashing in your all together, you best be up early, 'tis banned after nine,' Mrs Shannon said, and as Charlotte and Arthur looked at each other in confusion, she continued, 'ahem, begging your lady's delicacy, I do be meaning, naked. Oh, yes, well you might look shocked, nothing will do some men folk but frolicking in the foam without a screed. You wouldn't be th' better of what you might lay eyes on. Now enough about that, why don't I escort you to your chamber.'

Mrs Shannon reached behind and unhooked a large bundle of keys from where they hung on a wooden frame. 'Leave your luggage, that shall be carried up for you be our porter,' Mrs Shannon said , and then shrilly addressing a young man, wearing a suit that clearly was not tailored for his slight frame, she railed at him, 'Danny O'Brien, look sharp or they'll be more docked from your wages this week.'

As they followed her up the stairs, she continued talking, asking about Aunt Harriette and James who she claimed had the most wonderful 'sodjourn' in her establishment. The stairs creaked as they climbed, and perhaps it was because of the day's journey, but Charlotte found the smell of cooked vegetables nauseating. The room was sparsely furnished with nothing matching, and Charlotte could not see how Arthur was going to fit in the bed such was its length. Showing them a piece of wood and demonstrating how they should place it in the hasp on the door in order to secure it, Mrs Shannon spoke as if it was the latest advancement in locksmithing when it was clear that it was the makeshift answer to a broken bolt system. There seemed to be no end to her discourse even though many sentences were interjected with how she was run off her feet, how the hired summer staff were next to useless, and how it was a wonder that everything ran as it did considering she did it all herself. Charlotte had heard enough.

'Mrs Shannon, would you be so good as to check if there is mail for me, I had asked my correspondents to direct their letters here,' Charlotte said.

'I don't need to check, I know, for I am also the proprietress of our local Post and Stamp Office, and that same office is right here in my dwelling. You have a right bundle, I'll go and fetch them this very minute,' Mrs Shannon said and was gone out the door before Charlotte got a chance to say she would come and get them to save Mrs Shannon having to come back.

'Well of course she is the local post mistress, such a busy body, and what a warrant of speech,' Charlotte said, 'I can tell you right now, Mr Nicholls, we will be spending as much time outdoors as the weather allows, keeping far away from our hostess and her humble abode. To hear her praise for the place you would think it was the Shelbourne of the West, I am rather surprised at Aunt Harriette's recommendation. Did you take good note of those intricate instructions on how to secure the door?' At the last comment they both started laughing, as Arthur enacted a pantomime of placing the stick in the hasp, in the same exaggerated fashion as Mrs Shannon had done, and they laughed even more as there was a knock on the door just as he had finished wedging it in.

The ill-suited Danny could not be seen behind the luggage as he carried it into the room, and the illusion of a trunk with legs caused further amusement for the couple.

'Apologies, my good fella, we are being rude, you are not the source of our amusement, we are sharing a private joke,' Arthur said to the boy.

'Ní thuigim,' Danny said, and shrugged, 'ní thuigim béarla.'

'Ah, I see, you are a native speaker,' Arthur said, and addressing Charlotte said, 'he doesn't speak English.'

'I am surprised he can speak at all, as I am sure he never gets an opportunity with our genial hostess, he is Lorenzo to her Gratiano,' Charlotte said, to which Arthur replied, '*The Merchant of Venice*, I know that one.'

As Danny left, Mrs Shannon re-entered wielding a bundle of letters above her head, 'Here we are, Mrs Nicholls, enough reading for a clatter of scholars, speaking of which, did I tell you there is a reading room down the town where you can peruse newspapers from Dublin and London, and not that you will be interested in local matters, there's the provincial papers. I declare t' God I could stay and chat with you all day but·as I said, this fine place won't run itself, so if that will be all for now, I'll love you and leave you.' And with that she left.

'A week of this, Arthur!' They laughed once more.

Chapter Twenty-Three

Comical and at times irritating as Mrs Shannon was to the Nicholls, her recommendations regarding activities proved to be helpful, and welcome as most of them took the couple away from the hotel. On their first morning, as soon as they had finished breakfast, they headed off on a cliff walk, which according to fellow diners, was the reason for coming to Kilkee.

Although the sun shone, the wind on the cliffs was strong as the couple climbed higher and higher to a more advantageous viewing point. The roar of the water, which had been thunderous around the rocks closer to the bay faded with altitude, allowing the skylarks to be heard in all their melodious magnificence. Charlotte was able to identify the different species, like the shags and the fulmars, much to Arthur's delight.

'It is so annoying when all one can recount is the number of birds one sees as opposed to the names of them, I am so appreciative of your superior ornithological knowledge,' Arthur said.

'That would be the result of a misspent youth copying drawings from Bewick's *History of British Birds*. How I loved that book, Arthur, I wonder where it got to, I have not seen it in some time. I was obsessed with the work, I even wrote a poem about Bewick,' Charlotte said, pausing for a rest as she breathed deeply, her balled fists pressed into her waist.

'Do you remember it, you must recite it, I am sure the birds would enjoy your tribute,' Arthur said.

'It is too long, besides, I have hardly the breath to propel me up this incline, never mind recite poetry. Phew! The air really does get thinner at this height, I believe I will have to rest soon,' Charlotte said.

'Whenever you wish to stop, we shall,' Arthur said.

'Just indulge me for a moment or two and then I will be fit for further walking. Look at that scene, Arthur, see the breaking waves bejewelling those islands of rocks,' Charlotte said referring to how the white foam glistened on mounds of rock scattered about the bay far below them.

'It is a marvellous sight, indeed, how blessed are we to behold it,' Arthur said.

Having recovered her breath, they climbed further and reaching a grassy plateau that jutted out towards the ocean, Charlotte hinted that it was an ideal spot if one wanted to sit with one's private thoughts, something she always found to be so satisfying.

'I know, here's an idea, why don't you sit here a while, and do just that. I shall not be far, and that way, we both get to privately ponder on these waters boiling and foaming beneath us,' Arthur said, as he placed the rug he had been carrying over Charlotte's lap.

Charlotte felt as insignificant as an ant sitting on the cliff top, the Atlantic Ocean stretched out as if to infinity as its blueness merged with that of the sky, and the tiered, antediluvian strata in the rock faces to her left and right reminded her of how miniscule man's impact was compared to that of nature. And yet without the eyes of man to witness and marvel at God's creation, without his words to lyricise in aesthetic tones, what was it but nameless, natural phenomena. The wind blew bracingly against her face as she closed her eyes and lifted her chin breathing in the exhilaration. How alive she felt at that moment. How blessed were locals who could witness this magnificence on a regular basis. As she had this thought, she remembered the poor peasants they had come across on the road from Kilrush and wondered if they ever came and witnessed this sight and if they did, what would they make of it. Would it lift their spirits, or would they, like the cattle that grazed nearby, their heads bowed to the ground, ignore that which could not satisfy their physical hunger? She thought that she would like to offer the wretched of the world more than her pity and resolved that when she returned home, she would investigate ways of assisting more than just the few families she had visited in her role as the clergyman's daughter.

A chough, with its red legs and red bill landed nearby. Charlotte edged closer to it to take in the detail. Arthur's voice, carrying across the wind, warned that she was going too near the edge. 'Do you hear him, Mr Crow, my Poor Tom, ever watchful of the dangers that might befall me,' Charlotte whispered to the bird, who cawed loudly before lifting back into the air.

The trek back down was easier and the views equally as engaging. The water's colours were constantly changing from bright blue to dark green and the soundscape became a thunder rumble as the breaking waves rolled stones towards the shore, the ebb bringing them back out to sea. Fishermen were gutting their catch on the rocks as seagulls waited patiently for the discarded heads and entrails. A solitary log floated in the bay and Charlotte wondered if it belonged to the ship that Mrs Shannon had told them about: she might ask her later.

The afternoon was spent leisurely walking around the town, reading the newspapers in the local Reading Room, and sitting by the beach eating Indian rock bought from the noisiest vendor on the promenade, which was saying something as the resort was far from quiet. From late afternoon throngs of men wearing coloured caps had descended on the strand to play hurling. Arthur declared it to be the most skilful game in the world, which baffled Charlotte as to her eyes it was gangs of youths running from one end of the shore to the other, chasing some invisible fiend, with murderous intent. Occasionally they descended on said fiend in a tangled mass of arms, legs and sticks, forming a human onion which then shed its layers with explosive force and the racing continued. Despite Arthur's efforts the glare prohibited her from seeing the ball. Children ran in and out of the water, unattended, and Charlotte found herself anxiously counting heads each time the waters washed back from the shore. Canoes dotted the bays, most of them ferrying tourists around the calm waters to get a closer view of the cliff faces and the caverns, and nearer to the shoreline, ladies emerged from horse drawn bathing boxes, and descending some steps immersed themselves in the water up to their waist. Some were attended to by bathing women. Charlotte had seen them before in Scarborough, and then, as now, she thought the sight of these huts on wheels to be the most ludicrous spectacle ever. Following her gaze, Arthur asked if that were something she would like to do.

'I think you know me well enough by now to know the answer to that question, Arthur,' Charlotte said, 'but if you wish to bathe at any time, do not let my reticence prevent you.'

'What about this fellow, Hogan, and his baths, and all the claims he makes?' Arthur asked in reference to a local spa centre where, according to his guidebook, the proprietor, Hugh Hogan, made remarkable claims as to the restorative powers of his seaweed baths, his saline vegetable baths, hot and cold treatments, usage of sulphur, iodine, chlorine, steam, and much more, 'I read that his seaweed bath cured a certain Baron James De Basterot from the tic doloreaux he was a martyr to, and I thought perhaps, considering how you have often suffered from the same condition, that seeing as we are here, why not give it a try.'

As any form of bathing would involve some state of undress, Charlotte knew that while it was something she was curious about and obviously, as a treatment and possible cure for her ailments, something desirous, there was no scenario in which she could envisage herself, in a state of half dress, in either a bathing box or in one of Hugh Hogan's treatment rooms, 'I will place my faith in this Indian rock and the vendor's claims for its cure of the colic and the cold and the rheumatics, if you're old,' Charlotte said, imitating the noisy sales pitch of the vendor as she licked the gnarled stick.

'Well, if I cannot tempt you towards bathing, perhaps, if the weather remains this calm, we might hire a canoe,' Arthur said, 'it appears to be jolly good fun.'

'Perhaps,' Charlotte said, although she had no intentions of sitting into what she considered to be rather makeshift looking vessels. While strolling through the town earlier she had noticed an advertisement for a lecture on phrenology taking place that evening in one of the other hotels, and that was something she would like to do, but she was not sure how Arthur stood in relation to the science. She had been waiting for an opportune moment to broach the subject and now seemed as good as any.

'Arthur, can I ask where your opinions stand in relation to the science of phrenology?' she said, continuing to gaze out to sea, effecting nonchalance.

'Truthfully, I know little about the craze, other than the lack of acceptance for it amongst serious scientists. The department of science in Trinity would have nothing to do with it. It is rather bogus, don't you think, that one's personality and behaviour can be determined by the shape of one's head,' Arthur said, as he bit off a piece of rock and crunched it noisily.

'It is rather more cerebral and scientific than that, Arthur,' Charlotte said, unable to mute the defensive tone in her voice, 'you know, I have been examined by a phrenologist.'

Arthur laughed. Charlotte's expression remained earnest.

'You are serious!' Arthur said, swallowing hard the shards of rock in his mouth.

'I believe truthful is the more appropriate word, but yes, I have been to the clinic of a Dr Browne in London,' Charlotte said, and proceeded to tell him about how she and her publisher, George Smith, using the pseudonyms of Mr and Miss Fraser, were examined by Dr Browne, and issued with a report of his findings.

'I can hardly believe it of you. Yes, I can understand how Smith would do such a thing, but you are so reasonable, Charlotte, and this whole business of phrenology and its sister, physiognomy, why, it is a load of quackery,' Arthur said, and yet added, more sheepishly, 'what were his findings?'

'Very accurate as it happens, I made a copy of the report, which if you can suppress your cynicism, I might show you one day. You will be pleased, for instance it says I am very circumspect in my choice of friends and ascertains that it is just as well I am so inclined as I will have nothing to do with those whose dispositions do not approach the standard of excellence with which I can sympathise. What do you say to that, Mr Bell Nicholls?' Charlotte said.

'I say it needs no scrutiny of your head or measurements of the distance between your eyes to reach that conclusion; one's actions, words, and the changing expressions of the facial features reveal one's character. The idea that the permanent fixtures of the face dictate the character are quite absurd, I have encountered too many rogues with cherubic visages and likewise good men with unfortunate hardened faces, to subscribe to that theory,' Arthur said.

'You will not dissuade me, Arthur, besides, I have put my knowledge to great use in my fiction, providing the reader with a better understanding of my characters. Remember how I describe Rochester?' Charlotte asked, 'that is if you have indeed read it, you say so little of my writing, I begin to think your disinterest is based on ignorance.'

'Now you are becoming petulant. We do not have to adhere to the same opinions, my dear, after all, is it not the case that science informs us of the attraction of opposing forces,' Arthur said, as he bit another piece from his Indian rock, and titled his head back to face the sun.

'Surely you believe the eyes to be agents of one's character?' Charlotte asked.

'Ah but that is an entirely different phenomenon. The eyes as windows to the soul is something more spiritual than physiological,' Arthur said, without opening his, as he reclined onto his elbows, continuing to bask in the sunlight, 'what a day!'

'I take it then we will not be attending the lecture. It probably would be a terrible shame to miss out on the latest instalment of Mrs Shannon's boasts and blarney,' Charlotte said, and even though she wanted to recline as Arthur had done and enjoy the sunshine, she felt it would be interpreted as an act of surrender to his will, so she sat up even straighter and licked her stick of rock.

'We can do whatever you wish, Charlotte, I am happy to hear what this phrenologist fellow has to say, just do not expect it to sway me,' Arthur said.

They did not go to the talk, the entertainment on the strand as the evening slipped into night proved to be more interesting. Apart from the ongoing game of hurling, a band struck up from a nearby platform; young girls danced jigs and reels in what appeared to be a competition of sorts, their lithe, unearthly movements reminding Charlotte of the fairy tale of the

Twelve Dancing Princesses; canoeists raced each other across the bay, as donkey races nearer to the east end attracted by far the noisiest, most boisterous spectators. Instead of returning to the hotel for dinner the couple dined on shellfish and breads sold by local women from baskets they carried on the jutted hips. The soporific sinking of the setting sun into the horizon and the more muted sounds of twilight lulled Charlotte into a mood of acquiescence, she felt she was exactly where she was meant to be: on this shore with a man she was becoming more familiar with each passing day, more respectful of, more contented to call husband, and she did not need phrenology, physiognomy or any science to tell her so.

The following morning, Mrs Shannon was all questions as to their failure to show for dinner. She had imagined all sorts of horrors that could have befallen them.

'At one stage, I had you on the seabed along with the rest of the Esmond and the wretches who were never recovered,' she said, referring to an emigrant ship that had wrecked off the rocks a few years previously.

Charlotte and Arthur exchanged knowing glances, both straining not to smile, as they had earlier betted on how long it would take Mrs Shannon to bring up the shipwreck. It was her favourite boast, as a relative had been involved in the rescue of over one hundred passengers on the fateful night and had received a medal of honour for his efforts. To change the subject, Charlotte enquired about the post.

'Yes, I was coming to that, another letter and a parcel for you Mr Nicholls. So, what are the plans for today? I left Mary Knotts' book on Kilkee in your room to give you more ideas,' Mrs Shannon said, turning to a shelf where she had placed the post.

The book reminded Charlotte of the willy nilly way Mrs

Shannon entered their room when they weren't there, some letters and a shawl had been moved about, and she wanted to say something about it but Arthur had asked her not to in the spirit of 'least said ...'

'Good morning, Mrs Shannon,' Charlotte said, taking the letter and walking away. Arthur retrieved the parcel and followed, leaving a bewildered looking Mrs Shannon, who seeing Danny O'Brien leaning against the wall, snapped, that if there was money to be made from gawking, he would be richer than Colonel Vandeleur.

Arthur's parcel contained art materials for Charlotte which he had ordered when they were still in Dublin.

'Here we go, as promised, pencils, some cakes of paint, two brushes and a sketch pad,' he said.

'Thank you, Arthur, you are most considerate, and a man of your word. These might decide us to take a day trip after all to the Bridges of Ross as recommended by Knott's *Two Months at Kilkee*. I should like to try an illustration of the phenomenon like the one in her book,' Charlotte said. The phenomenon she referred to were natural bridges of rock over an inlet of the Atlantic, considered by many as the greatest curiosity of the coastline, but as the sight was twenty-four miles away, near Loop Head, it would be a full day's excursion.

'Hmm, I remain unconvinced as to the judiciousness of such a trip, Charlotte, now that your health has recovered, I wish to keep it that way,' Arthur said, 'the point of this sojourn in this remarkable watering place is for rest and recuperation. Besides, have you read Mary Knott's account, apart from the Bridges, the area is remote and desolate, wouldn't you prefer to watch a game of hurling on the strand now that you have become a fan.' Arthur laughed at his own joke; Charlotte had dubbed the game to be nothing more than an organised brawl.

Charlotte's smile faded on opening her letter. It was from

Martha Brown, always a cause of alarm as Martha did not like to write and only did so when there was great cause. The Reverend was not well, and asked night and day as to when he could expect to see his daughter again. Charlotte's initial reaction was anger tinged with disbelief.

'He has put Martha up to this, thinking that it will have greater import coming from her, as if he did not have the strength to hold a pen and write himself. You had better get accustomed to this, Arthur, he is like a child fretting for its mother, I wondered how long it would take him to commence his usual shenanigans,' Charlotte said, lowering her head close to the letter to reread it, 'and yet, it is a worry, what if there is a real wolf this time. What do you think, Arthur, is it time to think about our return?'

'As long as you continue to enjoy this holiday, I suggest we remain, but as soon as any concerns begin to distract and detract from the beneficial nature of our stay, we will return,' Arthur said, 'Let us walk up the cliffs, it will clear our thoughts.'

'First I must respond to this letter and some of the other dozen I received on our arrival, they already nag my thoughts, and will not be silenced until I have corresponded,' Charlotte said, settling herself at the only desk in the room as Arthur reclined on the bed with Mary Knott's book.

Most of the letters were notes of congratulations from those who had been notified about the marriage and therefore, other than an acknowledgement and thanks, they required little attention. Regarding Martha's letter, Charlotte decided that she would not respond just yet, as she knew as soon as she addressed the matter of her Papa's health, regardless of whether his sickness was real or imagined, the seeds of worry and guilt would be planted and begin to grow. She decided, instead, to respond to Catherine Wooler, Margaret Wooler's sister, who had taught her French at Roe Head. Charlotte considered her to be a sour spinster, and there was a rather wicked delight in writing to fill her in on the success, thus far, of her honeymoon.

> *My Dear Miss Catherine*
>
> *Your kind letter reached me in a wild and remote Spot, a little watering-place on the South West Coast of Ireland.*
>
> *Thank you for your kind wishes. I believe my dear husband to be a good man, and trust I have done right in marrying him. I hope too I shall be enabled always to feel grateful for the kindness and affection he shows me.*
>
> *On the day of our marriage we went to Wales. The weather was not very favourable there, yet by making the most of opportunity we contrived to see some splendid Scenery. One drive indeed from Llanberis to Beddgelert surpassed anything I remember of the English Lakes.*
>
> *We afterwards took the packet from Holyhead to Dublin. If I had time I would tell you what I saw in Dublin, but your kind letter reached me in a parcel with about a dozen more, and they are all to be answered, and my husband is just now sitting before me kindly stretching his patience to the utmost, but wishing me very much to have done writing, and put on my bonnet for a walk.*
>
> *From Dublin we went to Banagher where Mr. Nicholls relations live, and spent a week amongst them. I was very much pleased with all I saw but I was also greatly surprised to find so much of English order and repose in the family habits and arrangements. I had heard a great deal about Irish negligence &c. I own that till I came to Kilkee, I saw little of it. Here at our Inn, splendidly designated 'the West-End Hotel', there is a good deal to carp at if one were in a carping humor, but we laugh instead of grumbling, for out of doors there is so much indeed to compensate for any indoor short-comings; so magnificent an ocean, so bold and grand a coast, I never yet saw. My husband calls me.*
>
> *Give my love to all who care to have it and believe me dear Miss Catherine, Your old pupil*
>
> *C. B. Nicholls.*

'Finally, Charlotte, you are a slave to the pen,' Arthur said, fetching her bonnet from the coat stand.

'Well of course I am, you do remember you married a writer. Besides, you would not be so impatient for me to finish if you knew how I sing your praises in these epistles of mine,' Charlotte said, tying a bow beneath her chin, 'and so, I am ready.'

Chapter Twenty-Four

The days in Kilkee took on a familiar routine of walks on the cliffs, strolls through the town and afternoon and evenings – except for one when it rained – spent relaxing on the beach, taking it all in. They did not go to the Bridges of Ross for the reason Arthur had outlined: the arduous nature of the journey there and back, but also because another guest in the hotel advised against it, declaring it to only be of interest if you were a geologist. On the rainy day, their time was spent between the town's Reading Room and in front of a fire in the hotel's drawing room; it was in the latter place that they chatted to the other guest, a gentleman from France, on a short vacation to escape the constant news of the war with Russia. Charlotte was disappointed to find him so reluctant to speak about the war as she was up to date with the latest happenings from the London papers, and she longed to discuss Napoleon's strategies against the Russians with an interested party: Arthur had as little inclination to debate politics as the French tourist.

On the morning of their final day, Charlotte insisted that they call to the grocer, the baker, and the victuallers to make up a food hamper for the inhabitants of the mud hovels they had passed on the road from Kilrush. Mrs Shannon thought it was the most ludicrous idea and if they were so inclined, they would have been better off putting some money into the collection box in the church, that way you could be sure that the neediest got it. Arthur, fearful of a repeat of the scene when they gave out the bread brought from Banagher, suggested it would be more judicious to leave the hamper of food with the local curate. On their journey away from Kilkee, their gesture seemed so slight an effort given the multitude of mud hovels they passed, and the groups of ragged, spectral individuals trudging towards the workhouse in Kilrush. However, by the time they were crossing the Shannon estuary, headed towards Tarbert, their mood had lifted. Surrounded by the gay clamour of tourists, either going home from their holiday, or, like the Nicholls, destined for Kerry, it was difficult to be anything other than gay. They swapped accounts of what they had read about Kerry in Forbes' and Thackeray's books, and planned the rest of their honeymoon.

'My suggestion is we travel as far as Listowel today and stay in this "Jeremy Diddler" of a hotel that Thackeray mentions, as it appears that neither he nor Forbes are particularly enthusiastic about Tralee, and it is too far to continue to Killarney,' Arthur said, his finger pointing to the hotel's reference, as he extended the book to show Charlotte.

'I would still like to see this Tralee with its singsong name,' Charlotte said.

'And so you shall, it is on route to Killarney, possibly where the horses will need to be rested and watered,' Arthur said.

'Aha, and here is another gem from Mr William Makepeace, "… make sure to take your seat on the Bianconi car as quickly as you can or you will end up sitting on the roof on top of bandboxes, where you can expect to be fairly jostled about on a particularly, rough road."'

As it happened there were at least four Bianconi cars waiting on the pier at Tarbert so there was no need to rush for a seat. Charlotte was dismayed at how exposed it was and as the day was not particularly sunny, the thin blankets the coachman distributed appeared to be wholly inadequate. Thackeray was correct about the road, Charlotte could feel a headache coming on as the horses galloped at a lively trot over a stony terrain jolting every bone in her body without any relief to be gained from a picturesque countryside, as once they left the neat town of Tarbert, the landscape, except for the odd gentleman's country seat, proved to be featureless.

Entering the town of Listowel, the couple turned to each other and nodded, evidently pleased with what they saw, and their decision to sojourn there for the night. The hotel, the Listowel Arms, was in the corner of a square and from its front door could be seen the ruins of a castle, a neat church in the centre of the plaza, shop fronts displaying colourful dresses and bonnets, and buildings of exceptionally fine architectural design. Apart from a few peasant-like characters, the people milling about their daily pursuits appeared pleasant and jovial, as many hats were tipped, and heads bowed in greeting to the tourists disembarking. As the coach was stopping for a while to rest the horses before continuing to Tralee, the driver offered to help the Nicholls find a place to stay if they had no luck at the hotel.

'Before we unload your bags, let me check for ya wit' herself, 'tis always fairly busy this time 'a year,' he said, as he headed into the lobby. He arrived back with a young woman who was clearly a frequenter of the shop with the dress and bonnets. Charlotte thought she would have fitted in well with the London socialites who swarmed like honeybees around the likes of Thackeray. She spoke with a hint of a local accent, but her speech was pronounced and sharp, the tone of a seasoned businesswoman, even though she could not have been more than twenty-five.

'Hallo, so, you are looking to stay the night with us?' she asked.

'Yes,' Arthur said.

'Normally now, I would insist on at least a two-night stay, but seeing as it is not yet the weekend, I will make an exception. Elizabeth Adams at your service,' she said, extending her hand.

Momentarily forgetting her changed status, Charlotte answered, 'Charlotte Brontë.' She could see Miss Adams' nose wrinkle as suspicion crinkled her forehead, she must recognise the name.

'Hmm, Jimmy here said a couple by the name of Nicholls wished to stay. I have only the one spare room and if you are not man and wife, I am afraid there will be no room at this inn, I am not in the habit of encouraging that sort of thing,' Elizabeth Adams said, looking to Arthur for an answer.

'We are on our honeymoon, my wife is still getting used to her new name, although, because of the celebrity nature of that maiden name I suspect it will always be more known than the one I gave her,' Arthur said, 'you do recognise it, of course, you have the appearance of a well-read lady.'

Charlotte knew what Arthur was doing and it amused her, especially when she witnessed the pantomime of pretence that followed. It was clear that Miss Adams had no idea who they were, but she did not allow her ignorance to stand in the way of her obsequious praise for all the books Charlotte had ever written. By the time she was turning the key in their door, having linked Charlotte up the stairs, she was joking about how she would need to have a cup of tea later with Charlotte to get some tips on marriage as she herself was soon to be wed.

Alone in the room, the couple laughed heartily at the antics, then when Arthur tripped a little because of the unevenness in the floor, they laughed even more, and yet more still when they looked out the window – the same one according to Elizabeth Adams from where the great Daniel O'Connell once addressed a crowd – and saw their hostess railing at the coachman, as she orchestrated their luggage from the coach, her arms flailing like a demented spider.

As it turned out, Elizabeth proved to be a much more genial host than this introduction suggested. Following their evening meal, she, along with her intended husband, a Gerald McElligott, brought the couple on a tour of the town, introducing them along the way to many of the locals, to whom Elizabeth was always quick to add that Charlotte was none other than Currer Bell. Charlotte had visions that some local scholar had been nabbed in the interval between their arrival and dinner, and grilled on all things literary, as it was evident that Elizabeth Adams possessed knowledge she did not have earlier. Charlotte asked about Thackeray staying at the hotel, Elizabeth was disappointed that her father was not around to tell them the story of his stay as she was only a child at the time. Her father, John Adams, was the owner of the hotel, but as she and Gerald would be taking over the running of it after their marriage, he was inclined to leave them to it, spending as much time as he could walking the cliffs at the nearby seaside resort of Ballybunion, frequenting race meetings or relaxing on the hotel veranda overlooking the river Feale. It was the second pursuit that occupied him on that occasion.

By the time they had returned to the hotel, Arthur declared that Charlotte had enough material to write a library of novels, as every person they had been introduced to had had a story to tell, or as they said, 'one for yer next buck.'

'Such a town of talkers, I declare someone does need to write down these stories, but I am afraid my taciturn, Protestant nature would not do justice to their wit,' Charlotte said, as she undid the bow of her bonnet and flopped into the easy chair in their bedroom, 'these tall tales need the witticisms of a native bard.'

Leaving Listowel early next morning, with a stop in Tralee

for light refreshments, the couple arrived at the Railway hotel in Killarney the following evening. They had not intended staying there, it was Elizabeth and Gerald who had convinced them that it was the only place to book as it had just opened and everything was of the highest standard, with all the latest innovations, including gaslight. Arthur questioned availability considering its novelty, but Gerald reassured that there would be plenty of room, it had been a slow season for the region due to the inclemency of the weather. Arthur, ahead of unloading the luggage, went to check if Gerald was correct in his assumption. He was.

The drive over from Tralee, in a private, closed carriage instead of public transport, had been pleasant if a little bumpy at times. As they neared Killarney, the view from the window presented a towering screen of mountains looming higher and higher. Charlotte understood why the natives referred to the county as The Kingdom, for such it appeared to her now, this was the equivalent of the land of her childhood imagination, this was her Kingdom of Angria, and as the buildings began to appear, singularly at first, but then clustering to form her Glass Town, her Verdopolis, rising up in the shadow of the surrounding ranges of rock, it felt like a homecoming, but alas, a sad one, as there would be no Brani, Emi or Anni among the hosts and hostesses to welcome Chief Talli. These characters that she and Branwell created in their childhood stories of Angria were thinly disguised versions of the four siblings. As she sat and waited for Arthur to return, old demons of defeat and despair began to bat about her heart, she thought of Martha's letter; what if Papa was terminally ill and lay now, as all his family had lain before him, pale, gaunt and feverish, praying for acceptance into the kingdom of Heaven while simultaneously wishing to be granted more time on earth. And here she was hoping to be admitted to the most magnificent of

Glass Town's mansions. Perhaps it was time to put down their twinkling glass of honeymoon mead and take up their chalice of reality.

'We are in,' Arthur said, extending both hands to help her from the carriage. She went as if to take his hands in hers, but instead he took her by the waist and lifted her through the air as one would do with a young child as he swung her to the ground.

'Stop it, Arthur, I am not your Mary Anna,' Charlotte said, remembering how they had greeted each other back in Dublin, slapping at her skirt as if to rearrange it, although nothing had been disturbed.

'My dear, what is the matter, why this sudden alteration in your mood, not five minutes ago we were giddy with anticipation for this latest adventure?' Arthur asked, bewilderment raising his eyebrows, 'is it a headache, the drive was rather jolting?'

'Oh, Arthur, what if Papa is fatally ill. I will never forgive myself if he dies alone, I am no Cordelia, but neither am I a Regan or Goneril to willingly abandon him on the blasted heath of sickness,' Charlotte said as she removed a handkerchief from her pocket.

'Let's get settled in here and we can talk more and decide on what is practicable and fair to everyone,' Arthur said, bending and kissing the top of her bonnet, 'and no you are not Cordelia, thank the Lord, for then I would have lost out to the King of France. See, the illiterate curate knows his Lear.' This comment made Charlotte smile, but it would take more than jest to allay her fears and lift her spirits.

The hotel was everything their Listowel hostess had said it would be, the pungent newness reminding Charlotte of the renovations she made at the parsonage, with smells of wet paint and plaster, polished wood, and newly spun carpet. Before having a chance to dwell on home again, an official looking gentleman approached, and bowing before her declared, in an accent that sounded more continental than Irish, how delighted they were to welcome such a celebrated authoress to their hotel. Charlotte looked to Arthur, who smiled sheepishly and shrugged.

'Mrs MacGillycuddy might have had her Thackeray, but we now can boast of our Currer Bell,' the gentleman said, taking Charlotte's hand, bringing his head down and kissing the air above it. Charlotte, who had read Thackeray's account of Killarney in *The Irish Sketch-Book*, knew that was who he had stayed with. As the manager escorted the couple across the marbled floor to the reception desk, he rattled off, in what was clearly a rehearsed patter; mealtimes in the hotel; the facilities, such as Turkish baths, at their disposal in the interims; the 'must-see' local attractions, such as the Gap of Dunloe, Torc waterfall, and of course, the lakes. He advised a healthy, cautionary suspicion of the guides, carmen, and boatmen who were not recommended by the hotel; an avoidance of beggars, who were seasonal imposters to the area, the native needy being adequately supported by the local charitable institutions; and most importantly, smiling, he expressed a great hope that they brought better weather with them.

'And before I leave you to begin your wonderful stay, I can advise that one of our most sought-after tour guides is available for the next two days, and I recommend him highly, he will enrich your vacation with information, of course, but also with story and song, a true Irish welcome,' Mr Schill, for such was this manager's name, said, as he bowed low and took his leave of the couple.

The bedroom had the same whiff of newness as the rest of the hotel but was sparsely furnished, which was in keeping with Mr Schill's apologies for the fact that they were waiting on furniture deliveries. Arthur sat Charlotte down on the only chair and he sat on the window ledge, his raised position giving her the appearance of a little girl about to be addressed by one in a position of authority or guardianship.

'Charlotte, I hope you know by now, that your welfare, dare I say, your happiness is not just my selfish hope for our marriage, seeing as how I benefit from it, it is my duty as your husband. I know we are less than a month married and I would not be so bold as to claim to know you any more than I did before we exchanged our vows, but I do know this, since that day I have seen you smile and laugh more than I have ever witnessed in all the years of our acquaintance, as I watch you walk I imagine there is a lightness in your step that I had not noticed before. Please do not be insulted if I say that there is a greater softness about you. Now, I am not so deluded as to believe that I am the cause of this change, although I would like to think I have some part to play in it, but my conclusion is, this happy alteration is because, my dear, you are relaxed, freed from domestic cares and concerns, of always having to be the one making decisions, you are allowing yourself, possibly for the first time since childhood, you are allowing yourself to be minded. We both know that once we return home familiar patterns of behaviour will re-establish themselves, I will again be the dutiful curate to the Reverend and you the bidding daughter. Allow me, for a little while more, to have you all to myself, allow me to continue organising this honeymoon as I had envisaged, allow me, dear, dear Charlotte, to mind you,' Arthur said, and rather than sound pleading, there was an assertiveness in his voice, the assured tone of one who knows that reason and wisdom is on their side.

Charlotte could not dispute anything he said, other than his diminishing of his part in her changed demeanour. She looked up, and in his eyes could see the love and protection he was offering. She knew that what she was feeling contradicted ideas and principles she had held regarding the status of women, but there and then in that moment of silent understanding between them, what a wonderful, liberating thing it was to accept another's will, another's decision. If this was what the Harriet Martineaus of the world meant when they referred to the subordinate role of women within the institution of marriage, Charlotte imagined that she would be a contented inmate.

'You believe we should carry on as intended?' she finally said.

'And if the continuation has a counter effect on your mood, if that rather futile emotion of worry, pertaining to something that might never happen, or its twin sister, guilt, pertaining to events we cannot change, if these continue to hold you in an unhappy grip, I promise, we will immediately make arrangements to return to Haworth,' Arthur said, alighting from his window seat and crouching in front of her, 'I am aware of the regard the Reverend has for this place, and I might be wrong, but I suspect that perhaps a sense of guilt at being here without him, has been the source of this dip in your mood.'

Up to that moment, it had not been a conscious thought but now that Arthur alluded to a novel, *The Maid of Killarney*, written by her father, Charlotte remembered and wondered if that had been, in a subliminal way, the root of her sudden despondency. Growing up, they had often heard him refer to the glory of the lakes of Killarney, how they were a symbol of everything that was good about Ireland, how he hoped someday to walk the shores of what he believed to be his spiritual earthly home. She thought it was a terrible novel, not a conclusion she had ever shared with anyone else, how what could have been a beautiful love story was marred by evangelical didacticism. Papa was not a romantic, and when it came to matters of the heart, the puritanical ideals of Calvin's

Presbyterianism were his guide.

'Are you referring to Papa's novel, *The Maid of Killarney*? How on earth do you know about that, seeing as he published it anonymously?' Charlotte asked, hoping that Arthur had not read it.

'Know of it! I have read it!' Arthur said.

'How unfortunate,' Charlotte said.

'Why unfortunate, I believe it helped me see the Reverend in a different light. He gave it me to read shortly after we had announced our engagement, declaring how the story of Albion and Flora was like a reverse of our situation, he being the English party and she the Irish maid,' Arthur said, straightening up and rubbing his knees quite vigorously, 'I had not thought the Reverend capable of such lyrical passages of description, especially of a place he had never seen. Remarkable really, easy to see where your literary talent comes from.'

'Oh, please, do not align my skill with Papa's, I would like to think that there is more style than sermon about my writing. There is much merit in his writing to be sure, but I do not think it belongs on today's fiction shelves. I will say one thing though, the very fact of having a father who had published poetry and prose, albeit self-published, was a great encouragement for Emily, Anne and myself when we decided to publish our collected poems,' Charlotte said, already beginning to feel her mood lift.

'He asked me to pay particular attention to the practical advice Captain Loughlean gave his daughter, Flora, and her intended, regarding how to guarantee a successful marriage,' Arthur said.

'And no doubt you have it off by heart,' Charlotte said in a sardonic manner.

'Funny you should say that … ha ha, I am joking. Your face just then,' Arthur said, 'I recall it was rather didactic, although there was sage guidance there too.'

'Remind me,' Charlotte said.

'Let not the sun go down on your wrath?'

'We have been obedient children so far,' Charlotte said, retrieving a pen and paper from her bag.

'Don't tell me you have some more letters to write, we haven't even——' Arthur was interrupted by Charlotte kissing him.

'No, Mister Hibernia, we are going to make a list of what we intend doing for the rest of the month,' Charlotte said, and kissed him again.

Chapter Twenty-Five

Even though a soft rain drizzled their days in Killarney, it did not stop them from touring the lakes, walking through the grounds of Muckross and trekking through the Gap of Dunloe. And they might have extended their stay were it not for the dreadful incident that took place at the Gap, convincing Charlotte that it was akin to a ghostly voice carried on the wind, beckoning her home.

On the first morning they met the recommended tour guide, one Stephen Spillane, who had more the air of a man of business than the folksy storyteller Charlotte had expected. The previous evening in the drawing room, they had enjoyed the drama of a local seanchaí with his impossible tales, as well as the music of an aged, blind musician by the name of Gandsey. Both Charlotte and Arthur were enchanted by the whole setting and perhaps drank a dram more of whiskey than intended in celebration of the spectacle. On their way to bed they were stopped by Mr Schill who was delighted to inform them that he had secured the services of Spillane so that they could expect a lot more of what they had enjoyed from the evening's entertainment. The man now sitting opposite her in the coffee room, with his tailored suit and polished shoes, and his meticulously written itinerary was a far cry from the rough, rustic garb and spontaneous, chaotic bursting forth of story, song, and music from the blind uilleann piper and garrulous storyteller. So many places with, to Charlotte's ear, unpronounceable names were being suggested, she particularly liked the sound of Torc waterfall, possibly because it reminded her of Anne and Emily and their waterfall on the Moors, and so it was decided that the first day would concentrate on the picturesque estate of Muckross Demesne, belonging to the local MP, Henry Herbert, Torc Waterfall and the upper lakes.

'Micky Sullivan is going to be our driver, but ya know, I'm t'inkin' here now, if ye were considerin' travellin' on to Kenmare by road, when yer done here, you will be seein' th' upper lakes, well if you schtop to look that is, so, I'm t'inkin', twould be a complete waisht of yer time goin' ther' now. What does me good lady t'ink, haw?' Spillane asked, closing the copybook he had been writing in and replacing a stub of a pencil into the breast pocket of his frieze suit.

Charlotte was not sure she entirely understood his meaning, so she left the reply to Arthur.

'Ah, yes, I see what you mean, why travel the road twice when our time here is so limited. Now, we have not yet decided, but we may be travelling onwards by train, but as Mrs Nicholls has expressed a keenness for the demesne and the waterfall, I propose that we confine our tour to these sites. How does that sound?' Arthur said.

'The fineisht altogether, a man wit' his head on his shoulders,' Stephen said.

Charlotte wondered how she would ever understand the logic of the Irish, or their Hiberno-English, and as for Micky, their driver, well, he may as well have been speaking Gaelic. She was amazed at Arthur's comprehension of the brogue.

For the duration of the drive to Torc waterfall, for it was decided to go there first and make their way back towards Killarney via Muckross, Spillane regaled them with the history, the geography, and the mythologies of the area, often interrupted by Micky, keen to make corrections. And when Spillane was not speaking, he was singing snippets of old Irish songs or sounding a bugle. Charlotte felt a contrivance in his delivery, it was a practiced performance for the tourist, and so she was happier to focus instead on the beauty of the landscape that distracted at every turn in the road. Majestic yews and ashes, and hollies interwoven with the briary magnificence of the arbutus watched closely as the jaunting car made its way under their arched branches, Charlotte heard their whispers and wondered if they were deciding her worthiness to their enchanted land, the heavy heads of fully bloomed rhododendrons swayed and bobbed in the wind seeming to nod an approval of sorts, as the mountains looming up ahead, mythological creatures of stony splendour, expanded their chests at every turn, spread their craggy arms in, what was hopefully, a welcome to the dwarfed visitors from the world of men.

The jaunting car could not make it up the last part of the track to the waterfall, but Charlotte was glad, as it allowed her to distance herself from Spillanes' constant patter. Arthur kept him company as she trekked in their wake. The unseen waterfall roared increasingly louder until the last turn and there it was right before your eyes. In a deafening volume from many feet above, a frothy, cascade curtained the rocky face of the mountain before spilling its foam into a ravine of boulders. Spillane was explaining something about the recent heavy rain, as Arthur leaned towards him and nodded, while Charlotte found a rock to sit on and watch their dumb show play out against nature's superior theatrical display. In the patterns of the spray, that disappeared as soon as they had formed, she thought she saw Emily and Anne, and could that have been Keeper leaping over mossy stones. This place was beautiful, of that there was no doubt, but it was not her place, this was a cataract compared to her waterfall. How she longed to behold the ribbons of water gently flow over the tiers of her Yorkshire hill, ripple into the stream on whose bank they would have sat, hear their laughter mingle with her own: be together again.

Arthur remarked on how quiet she had become as the horses turned in to the gates of Muckross.

'Loathe though I am to say it, as I am sure I must be the only person on earth to feel this way, this place, rather than lift my spirits is drowning them in excess. I am trying to fathom it out for myself and I can only conclude that the immensity of everything here makes me feel insignificant, a buzzing fly whose noise has been silenced by the louder thunder,' Charlotte said, 'I think maybe, Arthur, I am becoming restless for home and the comfort of familiarity.'

'Remember what I said, as soon as this trip has lost its function we are back on that packet on the Irish Sea,' Arthur said, as he tightened the tartan blanket draped over their knees.

'We will give it another day, perhaps it was the whiskey last night, maybe my constitution is too English or too female for it, a hot toddy is one thing but neat measures I suspect is a step too far. And now we are being rude, chatting while he sings, but other than some mochree, whatever that is, I have no idea what this is about,' Charlotte said, referring to the latest song that Spillane was regaling them with.

Muckross with its woodlands, streams, stone bridges, ruins, manicured gardens, quaint cottages, chapels, and big house felt like being driven through a gallery of watercolours. According to Spillane it was not just the Eden of Ireland, it was the Eden of the world. Charlotte wondered if a humbler attitude would have instilled a greater appreciation in her, as it was, she felt that this constant reference to being in God's own country diminished everywhere else, her Moors included.

The evening was spent walking through the town, enjoying the animation of the streets; musicians, young girls selling toys made from the wood of the arbutus tree from baskets resting on their hips, gentlemen who light-heartedly flirted as they bartered with pretty peasants touting their mountain goats milk and poteen, fellow tourists who bowed their hellos as they passed, bare footed children who chased each other down arched lanes, the gay revelry of the diners and drinkers, and the bandbox splendour of groups of red coated Dragoons stationed in the area. Charlotte was disappointed to discover that there was no bookshop in the town, but they stumbled across a reading room with a sign that greatly amused them, 'None but members, or strangers, are admitted'. Charlotte caught up on the latest war news in the papers, while Arthur read from a tour guidebook by a Mr and Mrs Hall.

Back in the hotel, the scene was being set for a repeat of the previous night as guests gathered in the drawing room and musicians and dancers arrived. Arthur suggested an early night, which delighted Charlotte, she welcomed the quiet of the bedroom in the hope that it would silence the clamour of the day and arrest a throb that was beginning to niggle at her temples.

The rain had returned the following day, but Spillane was undeterred regarding their plans to visit the Gap of Dunloe.

'Shure now, 'tis only a drop o' rain, 'tis good for the land, besides, mar a déarfadh m'athair, "Tagann An Ghrian I Ndiaidh Na Fearthainne", there be always sunshine after th' rain, so my guess is by the time we reach th' viewin' point, 'twill be July once more,' Spillane said, pointing towards a covered car.

Arthur kept Charlotte close, holding a large umbrella aloft as they made their way to the vehicle. As they drove along a tree-lined road, Arthur remarked on how similar to Wales the countryside was. Charlotte disagreed, she said the mountain girls with their goats' milk and poteen and extended chipped cups and tin cans towards the passing carriages told her that they remained in Ireland. She had never seen anything like this before and she wanted to be able to admire their enterprising spirit but instead she felt there was something craftily exploitative in all the business ventures they had encountered in Killarney. It was as if every native was performing and she imagined that when the season was over, there was a mass sighing of relief as everyone doffed the mantle of showy pretence, shut fast their doors, and became their ordinary selves again. Spillane had not once ceased as he told them the legend of how the Gap of Dunloe was formed.

'And so wit' one almighty schwing of his sword, th' giant cleft th' great mountain in two, and isn't it glad we are t'day to have this fantastic Gap. Have you ever seen th' likes, God's own counthry. Now, we are runnin' outa road, so shortly, we'll b' meetin' me man wit' th' ponies, and th' brute beasts will take us th' resht a' th' way,' Spillane said, and immediately burst into song about Kate Kearney and her potent mountain dew. Just before they had entered the Gap, he had pointed out the cottage where the Kerry beauty used to live and from where she distilled her poteen. To Charlotte she sounded more like a fairy tale witch, attempting to lure the weary traveller into her 'she-bean', which was how she had heard the name Spillane gave to her cottage.

Charlotte was initially nervous to be mounted on the pony, but the creature, a mare, was so slow and deliberate in her movement, Charlotte soon relaxed and began to enjoy the wild sounds of the Magillycuddy Reeks to her west and the Purple mountains to her east, with their lapping waters, screeching birds, skittish, laughing sounds of goats, and what could have been the throaty roar of a mountain stag. The plants that grew impossibly from rock fascinated her, especially the fern-like one that she wished she could stop and sketch. Perhaps

that was what she disliked about this Killarney visit – the
guide's presence. If only she and Arthur were alone. Spillane,
who had dismounted from his pony, advised everyone to do
likewise, as the path was broken and slippery from the rain.
Charlotte, trusting her steed, declined, but when the pony
became agitated and seemed to lose her grip, the earlier nervousness returned. At one point, as if something had lunged
at her, the pony started and backed away from the invisible
fiend, Charlotte shaken but still seated, looked to Arthur who
was behind. Calling to Spillane up ahead, Arthur gingerly navigated past Charlotte and handed Spillane his pony's rein, so
that he could lead Charlotte's pony. The caravan continued,
Spillane recounting the legend of O'Donoghue Mór, once
Chieftain of the lakes, and how his ghost rises each May Day
from beneath the lake waters where he drowned. Perhaps it
was the talk of phantoms, but Charlotte felt a change in the
air, the purple mountains darkened, a cold breeze made her
shiver. She could tell that her mare also sensed some grimness
descend. A dark shadow was making its way down the steep
slope ahead, the mare raised its head high and stopped dead,
there was something up ahead that this pony did not want to
encounter, and with that it reared up, throwing Charlotte on to
the stones. Instinctively, Charlotte curled into a foetal position,
her arms protectively cradling her head from the trampling
hoofs. The mare kicked and plunged. Was this the end? What
would Papa do? What would Arthur do? Had not Spillane said
that seeing the ghostly shape was a good omen?

'Help, Help!' she screamed, but her voice was surely too
faint.

'What the …' Arthur shouted, the mare's antics causing
him to turn. Realising, Charlotte was no longer mounted, he
immediately let go, the mare sprung over the crouching shape
and bolted back in the direction they had come, revealing

Charlotte's form on the stones. Arthur fell to his knees and gathered her into his arms, summoning Spillane, who had not seen what was playing out behind him as he was busy playing his bugle.

'Oh, darling, darling, Charlotte, speak to me, speak to me, Oh Lord, not this, not this, it is all my fault, speak to me, say something, Charlotte—'

'Shh, Arthur, calm yourself, I am unhurt, her hoofs did not touch me, and I think this blanket broke my fall,' Charlotte said, attempting to sit up as she untwisted the blanket that had been draped over her knees. Arthur lifted her up, as Spillane, finally noticing the drama, came alongside them and leaping from his pony, went to Arthur's aid. He was as distraught as Arthur, but Charlotte convinced them that other than her bruised pride she was unharmed. Arthur placed her on his pony but rather than continue to the highest viewing point they made their way back to the jaunting car and returned to the hotel. Arthur had not let go of Charlotte's hand once and every time he squeezed it, as if to reassure himself of her continued presence, Charlotte felt waves of gratitude wash over her, gratitude for her life, her marriage, and the home she would see again. And see sooner than expected as that evening, they decided it was time to start making their way back to Dublin and thence back to Haworth.

Chapter Twenty-Six

The journey from Killarney to Glengarriff took them over, and in some places through, the Kerry and Cork mountains. Although they decided to opt for a closed coach, they were still able to marvel from the carriage windows at the vertiginous magnificence of the landscape. This was the view that had Thackeray speculating as to why the tourist seeking the picturesque bothered with the Rhine or Saxon Switzerland, when they could be travelling to this part of Ireland, where, in his words, the astonishing beauty was beyond the power of the pen. As the road ascended, spiralling its way around hard rock, Charlotte felt the altitude in her ears. At one point, they were so high up, Glengarrif Bay below them, had the appearance of a series of rain puddles. Charlotte again felt her human inadequacy like some dizzying light-headedness, knowing that when she and Arthur were returned to dust, the rocky, stoic majesty of these mountains would prevail. She thought of Shakespeare's strutting and fretting brief candle and how near she had come in the Gap of Dunloe to the final extinction of hers. But that day did not end in tragedy, the dark force sent to possess the pony and cause a fatality had been defeated by some kindly spirit, someone, somewhere wanted her to be happy, and she was happy, happier than she would ever have imagined. Yes, she was anxious about Papa, but she would trust in that same kindly spirit to keep him safe until they returned.

'Arthur, I sense that your preference is to complete our planned itinerary. I know you to be most practical, but also compassionate, if you believed there was peril in not returning immediately you would voice that concern, would you not? I have decided to concur with you; we will stay a while longer and see this honeymoon out,' she said in a resolute manner, pressing down on his hand as if to seal the decision.

'Charlotte, you are correct, and it is that pragmatism, that informs me of how different your life will be when we return. Apart from the constant care you give to your father, I am aware how busier life as the curate's wife will be. Haworth is a demanding parish. So, it were good that we use this time to relax and be as idle as we wish. To store our energy for what lies ahead. Yes, let us, as you say, see this out,' Arthur said, as the coach was suddenly plunged into the darkness of another mountain tunnel, causing Charlotte to gasp.

'Well, thankfully I am not of a superstitious disposition or I might be inclined to take this sudden darkness as a warning of some sort,' Charlotte said, 'that's decided then, we stay a while longer and pray more fervently that Papa's health will recover.'

As the day was fine, having booked into the Glengarriff Inn, the couple walked back into the village to get some lunch. For a time, as they walked along, with the bay to their left and the mountains rising up to their right, Charlotte felt dwarfed by the magnitude of it all, even Arthur striding beside her seemed to have grown in stature. The road meandered inland and the gentle swish swash of the bay was replaced by a distant roar of rills racing down the slopes. Water and rock were replaced by the heavy scented foliage of the woodlands that swept down to the road and arched their pathway. The scent of woodbine suggested a fairy land of witching charms, the air was cooler in this shaded spot of road, causing Charlotte to shiver. Arthur noticed and drew her nearer, which made walking rather difficult such was the height difference, but it was of short duration as the road opened again into bright sunshine revealing the village. Village was possibly too lofty a term for the few cottages and public houses that were scattered along this stretch, and yet the amount of people milling about the place suggested otherwise. Judging by their dress and leisurely promenading, most were tourists, there to experience what most of the tour guides described as Ireland's hidden Garden of Eden. They passed a sign advertising a trip to Garnish Island to view its Martello Tower, but both were too hungry to consider it.

'Perhaps we could avail of it tomorrow,' Arthur said.

'It seems you are determined, Arthur, to introduce me to Ireland's entire battery of these fortifications,' Charlotte said, 'if the weather remains this fine, perhaps we shall go.'

They had reached a public house with tables and chairs positioned in front of its windows for outdoor dining. No sooner had they paused to consider whether this was where they would like to dine, when a rather squat, barrel shaped man appeared before them.

'Well, aren't you the handsome couple, don't tell me, you have a French, regal look about ya, are we talkin' from somewhere like said country, bein' France, or would I be right in sayin' Belgium. C'mere and sit yourselves down here, and tell me, anythin' you want, anythin' at all, I have it, stew wit' th' flouriest spuds you'll ever taste, or would ya be fancyin' a bit o' fish, caught this morning b' th' son and heir, ya have th' look o' a man that knows his whiskey, I have it b' th' gallon for ya, and yourself, missus, has th' look o' a discerner o' fine teas, I can give you India in a Chiner cup, if ya plaise. Sit down, sit down,' the proprietor, for such he was, said, as he swiped a cat from a table, and ushered Charlotte to a seat with his hand pressed firmly into her lower back. A couple at a nearby table who had probably been press-ganged in a similar fashion smiled sympathetically. 'I'll bring you th' menus for your perryusal and a drink on th' house to quench th' thirst o' th' day, don't go anywhere now, I'll be back in two ticks, anythin' you want, anythin' atall, I'm yer man.'

Charlotte and Arthur were too surprised to do anything other than laugh.

'So that's decided then, we are having lunch here,' Arthur said, and they laughed some more.

'I wonder if Dickens' has ever been here, for I believe we have met the original Mr Fezziwig. And French, he thinks we are French, if only you spoke the language, Arthur, we could continue the ruse, what a jolly old laugh that would be, I dare say he would probably pretend to an understanding,' Charlotte said.

Arthur, who may have been stung by the reference to his linguistic shortcomings, or maybe it was the idea of making fun of a fellow Irishman, said that he was glad he did not speak the language, as he felt the fellow, despite his brash, persuasive manner, would yet prove to be an entertaining, interesting character. And so he did.

Reappearing from the dark interior of the public house, the Irish Fezziwig placed menus and two glasses of Guinness on the table before them, as he continued in a rather singsong manner, listing out his entire bill of fare, 'an' I'll give you a chance to make up your mind and sip on your stout and be back to you in two ticks.'

'A talking menu no less.' Charlotte said, completely unphased by Arthur's earlier defence of the fellow.

'You are wicked yet, Mrs Nicholls, the poor man should not be scorned for his commercial patter,' Arthur said, restoring the gay mood from when they first sat down.

Over the fish dish that they had both chosen, enticed by the idea that it was fresh from the bay, Charlotte talked about her time in Belgium.

'So, you see, Arthur, while it sounds romantic, it was an awfully lonely time for me, especially that summer spent in the school. Unlike the pupils who went home, or the other teachers who had the means to travel in Europe, my impecunious status confined me to solitary walks through the streets of Brussels and the surrounding country roads,' Charlotte said.

'Ah, so what you wrote in *Villette* was autobiographical? I am discovering all of Currer Bell's secrets,' Arthur said, pursing his lips to remove a sliver of bone.

Arthur was referring to the chapter in *Villette* when the heroine, Lucy Snowe spends a summer rambling around Brussels, her spirits sinking lower and lower until depression was followed by physical fever that confined her to bed for nine days and nights. The episode referred to as 'The Long Vacation', ends with Lucy, who was Protestant, going into a Catholic church and going to confession. This was exactly what Charlotte herself had done at that time, an act that she had never been able to rationalise for herself as she was wholly opposed to every aspect of the Roman Church and fearing now that Arthur was about to allude to it and speculate on the autogenous nature of the visit, she quickly changed the subject.

'What do you say we walk as far as this Cromwell's Bridge, it will help us walk off the apple pie our host is determined we have,' Charlotte said, referring to the dessert their host had gone to fetch from the kitchen. Mick Shea, the said host, had filled them in on the history of the area and had highlighted Cromwell's bridge as a fine spot for, in his own words, 'the panorammy.'

Although Cromwell's Bridge was their destination, Charlotte found the musty, aromatic scents emanating from the hedge-rows and woodland they passed much too difficult to resist, she had to find a pathway into the enchanted wonderland. And so they did. It felt like they had stepped into another country, the air was balmy and heady and reminded the couple of their visit to the Botanic Gardens in Dublin, except here there were no glasshouses, no labels, nothing was contrived, they had entered Ireland's tropical rain forest. Charlotte felt like they had found a portal to a magical kingdom. She recognised the gnarly branches of the Oak, the tall slender birches, the white flowered rowans, the foxgloves and the rhododendrons in their finest regal attire of reds and purple, and fuchsias everywhere lanterning their trail in fiery red, but there were varieties of ferns, heathers, trees she had never encountered before.

'Arthur, where are we, this is some trick by Mother Nature, surely this is a fairyland, see those white flowers weaving their way around that tree, if we go closer, I am sure we will find Puck, or Titania or Oberon fast asleep in their petal beds,' Charlotte said, taking Arthur's hand and leading him to the plant she referred to.

'Aha, *Midsummer Night's Dream*, at last a reference I know. I am sure we will not see any fairy folk, Charlotte. I also happen to know that the plant you refer to is called enchanter's night-shade, but the only real source of enchantment for me here, or anywhere, is you,' Arthur replied, and bent down as if to kiss her.

There was a part of Charlotte that wanted to succumb, intoxicated by woodland fragrance, charmed out of her conservative human form, she was a sprite, a lusty Peaseblossom or Mustardseed, who wanted to lay down on the ferny floor, reach for her husband, welcome his advances and allow their lovemaking to entwine them like the delicate flower gyring round the sturdy bark. But what of the time following their passion, what of that walk back into their stuffy, middle-class reality? There was the rub. So instead of meeting his lips, she kissed his knuckles.

The moment had passed but the magic remained. They strolled through the forest that every so often opened into meadows of myrtle, rainbowed with wildflowers, the only sounds were of rivulets and waterfalls and the crunch of twigs. Charlotte wished that she could stay there forever, she felt so alive, so in love, so at one with the world.

As they passed Mick Shea's place, once more he tried his best to inveigle them in with the offer of a couple of drinks on the house, he said the rain was coming and they would be glad of the shelter.

The rain did come and continued the following day, and so they decided to leave Glengarrrif for Cork. Charlotte suspected that Arthur would have been more than happy to go hiking, even in the inclement weather, but that type of activity was for a different holiday, or so he assured her. However, he did ask to be indulged in a prolonged stop in the town of Bandon, as it was where he had once taught.

'You are full of surprises, why am I only now hearing that your pedagogical career was of a peripatetic nature?' Charlotte asked as she had only known of Arthur's teaching in the Royal school in Banagher.

'Hmm, perhaps for the same reason I have never told you about the interruption in my education at Trinity,' Arthur said.

'I am intrigued, please do continue,' Charlotte said, moving away from the trunk she was packing and settling in a chair.

'After spending one year in Trinity, let me see, this would have been from '36 to '37, Uncle decided that he needed me more as a teacher in Cuba school and so my education was brought to an end and instead Uncle paid me a small salary as his Master of Classics, which I continued to do until '39,' Arthur said, and paused, seemingly examining his hands.

'You were not happy with this situation?' Charlotte asked,

sensing the memory brought discomfort.

'Oh, no, I was happy to be of use. Times were not good, pupil numbers had been dwindling and money was tight, so I was only too aware that it made more fiscal sense to employ me as a teacher—' Charlotte interrupted him with, 'than educate you as a son. He takes you on as a charity and then, as is often the case with charitable institutions, you are treated with a hard-hearted kindness that benevolence deems to be a necessary cruelty. God forbid that you forget your place,' Charlotte said, as thoughts of Cowan Bridge raced through her mind.

'I am ashamed to admit it, Charlotte, but I did feel aggrieved as the others would continue in Trinity. I mean, I enjoyed the teaching, it was tough, especially trying to discipline boys, some-thing that just wasn't in my nature to do, but by all accounts I was not half bad at it,' Arthur said, smiling sheepishly.

'And then in '39 your Uncle died,' Charlotte said, her tone that of the prompter coaxing Arthur to continue.

'Uncle died, and a replacement school master was sought. The first candidate, horrified at the task ahead, did not last long. I am afraid, Charlotte, Uncle Alan, was not the most efficient manager and as a result the school needed a lot of work to rebuild it both physically and reputationally. The second candidate was the Revd John Brown, who was then the master of Bandon Endowed school, and he did not stay much longer such was the enormity of the work involved. He asked me to return with him as his Classics teacher, and so I did,' Arthur said, shrugging.

'Abandoning, no pun intended, your grieving Aunt Harriette as her fortunes collapsed around her,' Charlotte offered.

'No, no, that was not how I saw it, it broke my heart to leave her, but I deemed it better for me to go as it would be one less burden on her. She was adamant that I return to Trinity and finish my studies, but I knew that was a financial impossibility for her, so I left, prepared to make my own way in the world, and allow experience to compensate for lack of education,' Arthur said.

'But that was not how the narrative ended,' Charlotte said, 'how did it come about that you returned to college?' Charlotte asked, although she knew what he would answer.

'Aunt Harriette. To her I was a son, and she would not rest until I was back in Trinity. Now you understand my feelings towards her, she is more than a mother, for she has such love even without the biological mother's instinctual, unquestioning nature,' Arthur said, as tears welled his eyes.

'A remarkable woman. We must never underestimate the value of Aunts,' Charlotte said, thinking of her Aunt Branwell.

'Bandon was a successful time for me, albeit a lonely time. I believe I improved as a Classics Master and the experience certainly stood to me when I returned to my studies, it gave me a discipline one does not normally associate with the giddy undergraduate,' Arthur said, clapping his hands against his knees and rising from the side of the bed where he had been sitting, 'and now, let us finish packing and get this show on the road once more. I do hope some of my former colleagues are still at the school, they were good people, good friends.'

Chapter Twenty-Seven

Their driver, organised by the hotel, suggested that they detour after Bantry to Skibbereen, and take the more coastal road through Rosscarbery and Clonakilty to Bandon. Charlotte wondered if he were mainly interested in increasing the journey time and thus his fare, but Arthur, who was the more astute observer of the crafty Irish cab man, declared it to be a capital idea as he would like to visit Skibbereen. According to him, it was the most famine afflicted town in Ireland, a fact, the driver, Taddy Rigney, agreed with.

'You would not believe the devastation until you see it first-hand, boy, craturs crawling along be the roadside, thryin' to reach the Poorhouse, and shure, never knowin' they were at notin', for even if they survived itself, there would be, as you might say, no room at th' inn,' Taddy said, loading the last of the bags onto the top of the coach.

'And is that still the case?' Charlotte asked, remembering the spectral line of wretches in Kilrush.

'Well, tanks be t' God, th' crawling be no more, but th' workhouse is burstin' at th' hinges, arra, 'tis a desperate situation. I believe the Quaen sent a few shackles to help, but shure, wha' would she know, girly, 'bout the full extent of their plight. I can't see her takin' a trip down here again any time soon, can you?' Taddy said, and stood, his hands on his hips, apparently waiting for an answer. When none was forthcoming, he continued, 'speakin' the truth to ya, I wouldn't be rushin' to shtop in Skibbereen. I'm only suggestin' tha' route as 'tis as you might say, th' more scenic one. If ya pardon me saying but you are afther makin' a hames of your journey, you put th' cart before th' horse, 'tis from Cork to Glengarriff you should have come, not Glengarriff to Cork. Th' best view 'tis all behind you goin' this way but at least if we take th' coastal road, you have a chance of seein' th' sea, and that, boy, is always a sight worth travellin' for. Am I correct?'

'I suppose so,' Charlotte said, understanding most of what Taddy had said, as she took Arthur's hand and stepped up into the carriage.

'Would you rather we bypass Skibbereen, my dear?' Arthur whispered.

'Quite the contrary, we must go, and we must dine there or buy something, contribute to the local economy, how else can a town recover?' Charlotte said.

'Kind, compassionate, and a shrewd economist! How blessed am I?' Arthur said, reaching out and tapping the side of the carriage to indicate to Taddy that they were settled in and ready to proceed.

Skibbereen proved to be as dreary and desolate as Taddy had suggested, and indeed as Forbes had described it according to Arthur, who had been reading his memorandums on the way. The only inhabitants visible along the road into the town were as pitiful as the peasants witnessed on the road to Kilkee, and as you neared the town their numbers increased. Charlotte thought that there was something apocalyptic about the scene.

The town was busy and judging by the singular cows and pigs being led around on frayed ropes it appeared to be a market day. Those leading the animals, supposedly the farmers, did not look any healthier than the more ragged inhabitants, distinguishable only by the additions of caps on the men and extra shawls wrapped around the females. And yet, despite what the eye observed, laughter and good-natured chattering, squeals of children's delighted play, and the strains of Irish music assailed the ears. It humbled Charlotte to see such good humour and celebration of life amidst dire impoverishment, there was a lot to be learned from these peasant Irish and how they dealt with adversity.

Taddy stopped the coach in front of the local hotel, and rather than open the door for the couple to alight he spoke through the opened window.

'Beggin' your pardon, I do have a head like a sieve, I clear forgot 'twas market day, you will hardly want to be taking your chances ramblin' around t'day of all days. Will I keep her goin' 'til we get to Rosscarbery. The horses are good for another few miles?' Taddy asked.

'You fear drunkenness? An influx of beggars? Or as you might say yourself, no room at any inn?' Arthur asked.

'Drunkeness! Nar a' tall, shure this town is livin' proof of th' successes of our beloved Father Mathew. You won't know of him, but him and his abstinence society has us all turned to th' teetotallin' side, meself included. A drop of the hard shtuff has not whet my whistle since I took th' pledge from th' holy man himself and received benediction from him. But that now 'tis neither here nor there. No, what I'm thinkin' is, like you said yourself, 'twill be a lot be way of beggin' and blackguardin' that might offend you or put you in harm's way. Once they see you to be moneyed folk, they will be on you like th' plague of locusts,' Taddy said.

'Ah ha, I am inclined to agree with you, Taddy, so if you are of a similar mind, Charlotte, perhaps we could post a donation back here on our return,' Arthur said, and before Charlotte had a chance to reply, Taddy was back in the driver's seat and the carriage was moving again.

'Well, that seems to have settled that!' she said, 'It does feel a little churlish of us not to want to walk among these people, but you are right, we should source a more efficient and convenient way of contributing to this cause. And what a cause, Arthur, did you notice the enormous structure on the road in, I take it that was the workhouse, judging by the high walls and the forbidding iron-gated entrance. Misery and want on this scale baffles me, surely this green country we have traversed can produce enough food for everyone?' Charlotte asked rhetorically.

'The tyranny of commerce will make beggars of us all yet,' Arthur said, taking up his book, 'Let me see what, if anything Dr Forbes has to say about Bandon.'

Along the way the scenery reminded Charlotte of the journey to Scarborough, and those images would ordinarily plunge her into a slough of despond as she yearned for Anne and Emily to be back by her side, but on this occasion she was consumed with the haunting images witnessed in Clare and now Cork, giving evidence to the grave fact that the spectre of famine continued to ghost the Irish countryside; a countryside presided over by the same men who governed her Yorkshire and all of the British Isles. How had they let it go this far? Was it a callous disregard for human life? Or had cold, economic practicalities prevailed, demonstrating the male affinity to rule with the head instead of that superior organ of feeling, of compassion. Would female governance have done any better? She thought of the woman and child she met in Clonmacnoise, she thought of Minnie, she thought of the poor wretch she spoke with in Bedlam, how different their lives were to the Countesses of Ross, the Lady Kay-Shuttleworths, the Mrs Gaskells, and the Currer Bells and yet, despite the privileges of birth right and education enjoyed by the latter group, they all had something in common: powerlessness. Surely what government lacked was the feminine rule of the heart to support the hard logic of the male perspective. Although she could but claim scant experience being less than a month married, she understood the wisdom in counterbalancing opposites, marrying differences to create wholeness. Fairy tale instructed how order rose out of chaos with the 'happy ever after' ending of the union between the Prince and the Princess, and while not one to succumb to such a romantic notion of her union with Arthur, they were happy, she was happy and confident that all future vicissitudes were surmountable when faced as one. So, why was it taking society so long to recognise the need to empower woman, to accept that mankind will always remain outside the walls of the Garden of Eden, always be floundering in an earthly pandemonium, until Eve's equality to Adam is recognised? She would have shared these thoughts with Arthur, but he was engrossed in his book. Another time, perhaps.

Bandon was a disappointment for Arthur, Revd Brown, who had brought him from Banagher had moved on and was now Master of a school in Kilkenny, and none of the remaining teachers remembered him, so rather than stay the night they got a late train to Cork city and, following the parting advice from their driver, they were able to get an Omnibus to the Imperial hotel where they booked in for two nights. Following the day's travelling, they decided to have a quiet night, reading and writing in their rather commodious and elegantly furnished suite. Arthur, having seen on a wall plaque that the hotel opened for business in 1816, the year of Charlotte's birth, said that he would have expected nothing other than the best considering its vintage.

Charlotte used the evening's leisure to address some final correspondence from Ireland, while Author who was flicking between Thackeray's book and Forbes, interrupted often with what he considered, 'interesting facts'.

'Aha, I read here that our man, William Makepeace, had tea in this very hotel with none other than Father Mathew, the fellow who brought about national sobriety, listen to how he describes him—', Arthur said, but did not get to share the description as Charlotte, focused on the letter she was composing, indicated with a finger to her lip that she did not want to be disturbed. Arthur frowned but acquiesced.

Charlotte was writing to Katie Winkworth and it was of the utmost importance to her that the tone and content of the epistle conveyed a true reflection of her feelings towards Arthur since their marriage. Katie, a pupil of Elizabeth Gaskell's husband, had been introduced to Charlotte a year previously when Charlotte was visiting the Gaskells. She made an immediate impression on Charlotte with her easy, forthright manner one is accustomed to see in youthful, uncomplicated creatures, that and her knowledge and enthusiastic praise of Charlotte's novels was hard to resist. Katie's inquisitive mind manifested itself in the copious number of questions she persuasively urged answers to. Perhaps it was Charlotte's sheltered existence that engendered in her a naiveite that failed to see the gossip in Katie at the time but ever since she had begun to feel uneasy about their last conversation in the presence of Mrs Gaskell less than a month before the wedding. Charlotte was feeling extremely apprehensive at the time and was ashamed that she had voiced concerns about the differences in intellect between her and Arthur, how hurt he would be to hear that, and how sad it would make her to witness that hurt. She intended to put the record straight in this letter; give Miss Winkworth something positive to relate to Mrs Gaskell, for Charlotte had no doubt but the two women were intimate confidantes.

Dear Katie,

It was at a little wild spot on the South-West coast of Ireland that your letter reached me; of course I did not first recognise the handwriting and when I saw the signature and afterwards read the full and interesting communication, I was touched, you are very good, Katie, very thoughtful for others.

Yes, I am married, a month ago this very day I changed my name, the same day we went to Conway, stayed a few days in Wales, then crossed from Holyhead to Dublin. After a short sojourn in the capital, we went to the coast; such a wild, iron-bound coast, and such an ocean-view as I had not yet seen, and such battling of waves with rocks I had never imagined.

My husband is not a poet or a poetical man, and one of my grand doubts before marriage was about 'congenial tastes' and so on. The first morning we went out on to the cliffs and saw the Atlantic coming in all white foam, I did not know whether I should get leave or time to take the matter in my own way. I did not want to talk but I did want to look and be silent. Having hinted a petition, licence was not refused, covered with a rug to keep off the spray I was allowed to sit where I chose and he only interrupted me when he thought I crept too near the edge of the cliff. So far he is always good in this way, and this protection which does not interfere or pretend is I believe a thousand times better than any half sort of pseudo sympathy. I will try with God's help to be as indulgent to him whenever indulgence is needed.

We have been to Killarney, I will not describe it a bit. We saw and went through the Gap of Dunloe. A sudden glimpse of a very grim phantom came on us in the Gap. The guide had warned me to alight from my horse as the path was now very broken and dangerous. I did not feel afraid and declined, we passed the dangerous part, the horse trembled in every limb and slipped once but did not fall. Soon after she (it was a mare) started and was unruly for a minute, however I kept my seat, and my husband went to her head and led her, suddenly without any apparent cause, she seemed to go mad, reared, plunged and I was thrown on the stones right under her. My husband did not see that I had fallen, he still held her. I saw and felt her kick, plunge, trample all round me. I had my thoughts about the moment, its consequences, my husband, my father. When my plight was seen, the struggling creature was let loose, she sprung over me. I was lifted off the stones neither bruised by the fall not touched by the mare's hoofs. Of course the only feeling left was gratitude for more sakes and my own.

I can write no more at present. Only this, under the circumstances, I can't see that Mrs. Gaskell is one whit in error. Mr Dickens, I think, may have been somewhat too exacting, but if she found or thought her honour pledged, she does well to redeem it to the best of her ability, as she will, and I have no doubt it will be worthily done. I go home soon; goodbye, dear Katie. I direct

this to Plymouth Grove, not being sure of your address.
C. B. Nicholls.

'What is it you write that brings such a high colour to your cheeks?' Arthur asked, looking over the rim of his book for the umpteenth time.

'I am telling Miss Katie Winkworth about my mishap at the Gap of Dunloe, and no doubt I am flushed as the memory has excavated the dread I felt at the time. How different that ending might have been, and what would my dear boy have done then?' Charlotte asked, folding the letter, and tucking it into a blue edged, white envelope.

'Perish the thought, Charlotte, now that you are mine, not the devil himself, even if he cometh in the form of a dumb animal, will take you from me,' Arthur said, laying the book to one side, crossing the room and sweeping her up into his arms.

'If you squeeze me any tighter, I will begin to think that same devil has now taken possession of your arms,' Charlotte said, holding Arthur away, 'come, let us see about dinner.

'Not before this,' Arthur said, bending down, cupping her face, and bringing his parted lips to hers.

Chapter Twenty-Eight

Charlotte and Arthur were relatively quiet on the journey back to Dublin, both lost in thoughts for the future and memories of the recent past, and perhaps feeling a little downhearted now that the end of their honeymoon loomed. Charlotte was anxious over the matter of the marriage settlement she had made which she would like to discuss with Arthur with a view to altering it. If an opportunity arose, she would broach the subject with him. It was not unusual for women to draw up legally binding settlements to protect wealth they brought to a marriage, otherwise, according to marriage law, all their assets belonged to their husband. What was unusual vis-á-vis her marriage settlement was the clause that in the event of her dying childless, the wealth from her writing, which at £1,678 9s, 9d was a substantial sum, went to Revd Brontë, and not to Arthur. When drawing it up with her solicitor Charlotte's logic was, in the event of her predeceasing him, Arthur would be able to continue to earn a living, but without her income, poor Papa would be left destitute. She felt repentant for ever doubting Arthur's nature and his concern for Papa's wellbeing, he was as kind and considerate a man as any you were likely to meet this side of Heaven, she saw how it might be interpreted as a chink in her trust of him if she were to leave that clause in the agreement.

Dublin was bathed in late July sunshine as the cab made

its way up the quays, the light danced in iridescent bubbles on the Liffey in compensation for the stench from the same waters that hung heavy in the air. The malty smells from Guinness's brewery were not helping and for the first time in quite a while Charlotte felt nauseous, but she knew better than to say anything, lest she raise false hopes in Arthur as to its cause: she often felt thus from travelling. Once again, they had decided to book into the Shelbourne, at Charlotte's insistence.

'Charlotte, are you sure about the Shelbourne, Allen is more than willing to accommodate us. The only reason I had not prearranged a hotel was because of the uncertainty around when we would be back here,' Arthur said as the carriage made its way over Carlisle Bridge.

Charlotte suspected that Arthur's real reason was a cost-saving one, and she was careful not to embarrass him, 'Oh, I know, but please indulge me, you have been so generous throughout this honeymoon, I would like to treat you. See it as a forward gift for how you are going to aid Papa, I am very aware that the bulk of his duties is going to fall on your shoulders,' she said.

'Well, if you insist, I will graciously allow it,' Arthur said.

The hotel was as splendid as they had experienced before, their room even more so, as they were in a larger suite having asked not to be given the room, they previously occupied; although Charlotte had since put her ghostly encounter down to the fever she obviously had at the time, she did not want to test her theory. Arthur had gone to meet his brother to explain the changed plans, while Charlotte wrote to Martha Brown and Ellen.

Charlotte was in the middle of writing to Ellen when Arthur returned, and seeing what she was doing he went to reception to enquire as to the last time for posting, rushing back to inform her that she ought to write sprightly or she would miss the collection. It suited Charlotte, as she was experiencing a degree of labour in her letter to Ellen, something which was singularly alien, she found herself guarded and deliberate in every word and wondered who she was protecting and from what.

Dear Martha,

I write a line to tell you that if all be well, we shall come home on Tuesday, August 1st at about seven o'clock in the evening. I feel very anxious about Papa, the idea of his illness has followed me all through my journey and made me miserable sometimes when otherwise I should have been happy enough.

I longed to come home a fortnight since, though perhaps it would not have done much good and I am sure that you would have done your best for him.

Have things ready for tea on Tuesday Evening and you had better have a little cold meat or ham as well as we shall probably get no dinner and Mr Nicholls will want something.

I hope you and Tabby have been and are well, and I do earnestly hope to find Papa better.

I am in haste and can only bid you good bye for the present.

Yours faithfully, C.B.N.

Dear Ellen,

I really cannot rest any longer without writing you a line, which I have literally not had time to do during the last fortnight. We have been traveling about, with only just such cessation as enabled me to answer a few of the many notes of congratulations forwarded, and which I dared not suffer to accumulate till my return, when I know I shall be busy enough. We have been to Killarney, Glen Garriffe, Tarbert, Tralee, Cork and are now once more in Dublin again, on our way home, where we hope to arrive next week. I shall make no effort to describe the scenery through which we have passed. Some parts have exceeded all I ever imagined. Of course, much pleasure has sprung from all this, and more, perhaps from the kind and ceaseless protection which has ever surrounded me, and made traveling a different matter to me from what it has heretofore been.

Still, Nell, it is written that there shall be no unmixed happiness in this world, Papa has not been well, and I have been longing, longing intensely sometimes, to be at home. Indeed, I could enjoy and rest no more, and so home we are going.

I can't write another line, the post is going out,

Yours, C.B.N.

Having dropped off the post they decided to take a stroll

around St Stephen's Green. The evening was balmy and indolent in that late July fashion, as Mother Nature languidly relaxed in her oasis of calm away from the bustle of the city. Arthur filled Charlotte in on his afternoon excursion, his brother perfectly understood their desire to end their honeymoon in style and he passed on his best wishes, hoping that he would see them again soon. The hotel concierge had tracked down Barney and hired him to take them to Kingstown harbour. Charlotte liked the symmetry of Barney bookending their Irish stay and she would be able to gift him her book for his wife. Walking along the structured pathways, greeting the other fashionable strollers, breathing in the aromas of the manicured gardens, the dichotomy between this Ireland and the Ireland of Kilrush and Skibbereen struck Charlotte in a sombre manner. She could not long more endure this life of luxury they had been living since June 29th, and she looked forward to getting back to a daily routine of domesticity, service to the community and, of course, her writing, or perhaps more sketching: Arthur's gift of the pencils, cakes of paint, sketch pad and brushes had yet to be put to work. He seemed quite enthusiastic about her painting skills, making her wonder if his enthusiasm came from a conservatism that saw less threat in brush strokes than the perilous potential of the pen.

'Charlotte, is there anything in particular you would like to do for our final night?' Arthur asked, 'the concierge tells me there is some sort of extravaganza on at the Portabello Gardens, music, fireworks and all that, or a drama about Brian Boroimhe at the Royal Theatre?'

'Oh, dear me, no, Arthur, the very thought of all those people and all that noise exhausts me. I should be more than content to take a few more turns around the Green, perhaps seek out a coffee house for some late evening refreshments and finish the night with a meander by gaslight. How does all that sound to the great walker?' Charlotte said and smiled.

'Were we to stand still and gaze at the sunset and the moon rise, with you by my side, I would be forever content to just be,' Arthur said, leading her to a park bench.

As they sat there, watching the world go by, a robin came and perched beside them, its cocked head listening attentively.

'Hello, little bird, and who might you be today?' Arthur addressed the robin referring to the Irish superstition that robins were souls of the dead returning to reassure of their continued existence albeit in a different realm.

'Perhaps it is Charlotte Brontë,' Charlotte said.

'What! You mustn't say such things,' Arthur said.

'But she does not exist anymore, Arthur. Besides, I prefer my married name,' Charlotte said, taking Arthur's hand in hers, 'can I tell you a secret?'

'Oh, my, I am not sure, you look so serious,' Arthur said, twisting to face her.

'I thought your love for me would be enough to make this marriage work. I was wrong, I know that now.'

'What are you saying, Charlotte?'

'Arthur Bell Nicholls, my dear boy, I am saying, I now believe that the recipe for matrimonial success is our reciprocated regard for each other.'

With that the robin flitted into the air. They followed its erratic flight path until it landed and disappeared in the foliage of a weeping ash. They sat in silence for a little while more, both momentarily lost in thought, perhaps both thinking the same thought, that this was not an end but a beginning, the beginning of Charlotte and Arthur.

Epilogue

Writing to her friend, Ellen, a week after their return home, Charlotte describes her changed status thus, *'Since I came home I have not had an unemployed moment; my life is changed indeed— to be wanted continually—to be constantly called for and occupied seems so strange: yet it is a marvellously good thing.'* Papa's health improved and the amiable relationship between him and Arthur exceeded Charlotte's expectations. But the Reverend was never strong enough again to carry out parish duties and so the bulk of the workload fell to Arthur, assisted by Charlotte. And perhaps it was the extent of this new domestic life and occupation that prevented Charlotte from continuing her writing career, but other than fragments of a novel called, Emma, we have nothing more from the pen of Currer Bell following the marriage.

Later that August the couple were so delighted with the *'hearty welcome'*, received from the Haworth parishioners, they hosted a tea and supper party for five hundred of them in the schoolroom. In a toast at the event, one of the parishioners described Arthur as, *'a consistent Christian and a kind Gentleman'*, words that moved Charlotte enough to write to her friend, Margaret Wooler, *'I own the words touched me— and I thought—(as I know you would have thought—had you been present)—that to merit and win such a character was better than to earn either Wealth or Fame or Power. I am disposed to echo that high but simple eulogium now. If I can do so with sincerity and conviction seven years—or even a year hence—I shall esteem myself a happy woman.'* Alas, Charlotte did not survive *'even a year'*: writing the following January to Ellen she informs of a continual faint sickness and decrease in appetite. It is clear she suspects she is pregnant but cautions Ellen, *'Don't conjecture—dear Nell—for it is too soon yet—though I certainly never before felt as I have done lately.'*

Throughout January and into February it was Arthur who wrote to Ellen informing of Charlotte's increasing ill health and wasting, as Charlotte was too weak to do so. His concern and great love for her are evident in these letters, a fact she confirms when she eventually writes to Ellen in late February describing him as, *'...the tenderest nurse, the kindest support—the best earthly comfort that ever woman had.'*

Charlotte never recovered from what is now believed to have been hyperemesis gravidarum, excessive sickness during pregnancy, which of course was fatal to one of her delicate constitution. Nine months, almost to the day, since the happy occasion of their wedding on June 29th the previous year, Charlotte died on March 31st, 1855, with her devoted Arthur by her bedside. Arthur, dutifully wrote to Ellen the following morning, *'Our dear Charlotte is no more ...'*

And the words of that parishioner's toast were realised yet again as Arthur remained on in the parsonage to look after Papa, until the latter's death in 1861. Although united in their grief, it cannot have been easy for Arthur to remain in the place that was the heartbeat of his tragedy. Following the Reverend's death and bitterly disappointed that he was not, despite his huge popularity with the locals, appointed as the perpetual curate of Haworth, Arthur returned to Banagher. He moved in with Aunt Harriette and his cousin Mary Anna, who were at this stage living in Hill House in Banagher, and